OROMAY

BAALU GIRMA

OROMAY

Translated from the Amharic by
David DeGusta and Mesfin Felleke Yirgu

MACLEHOSE PRESS
QUERCUS · LONDON

First published in Amharic as አኖሌይ by Kuraz Publishing Agency
in Addis Ababa, Ethiopia, in 1983
First published in Great Britain in 2025 by

MacLehose Press
An imprint of Quercus Editions Limited
Carmelite House
50 Victoria Embankment
London EC4Y 0DZ

An Hachette UK company

The authorised representative in the EEA is Hachette Ireland,
8 Castlecourt Centre, Dublin 15, D15 XTP3, Ireland
(email: info@hbgi.ie)

A CIP catalogue record for this book is available
from the British Library.

ISBN (HB) 978 1 52942 838 4
TPB (TPB) 978 1 52942 839 1
ISBN (Ebook) 978 1 52942 840 7

10 9 8 7 6 5 4 3 2

Designed and typeset in Palatino by CC Book Production
Printed and bound in Great Britain by Clays Ltd, Elcograf S.p.A.

MIX
Paper | Supporting
responsible forestry
FSC
www.fsc.org   FSC® C104740

Papers used by Quercus Books are from well-managed forests
and other responsible sources.

Translators' Note

Baalu Girma (1939-?) is widely considered to be Ethiopia's greatest novelist and *Oromay* is his best-known novel. Girma started his career as a journalist in the 1960s and gained a reputation for reporting the facts, regardless of how they would be received by Emperor Haile-Selassie and his administration. A revolution overthrew the Emperor in 1974, and Ethiopia fell under the rule of the Derg, a socialist military junta. The Derg was strategic in appointing experienced professionals to handle the day-to-day operations of the government, and so Girma – despite never being a part of any political group – became a top official in the Ministry of Information.

The revolution soon took a dark turn, and the Derg began a brutal campaign of terror against suspected dissidents. Armed resistance grew, especially in Eritrea, then the northern province of Ethiopia. In 1982 the Derg launched an audacious effort to put down the Eritrean insurgency. All the top Ethiopian officials, including Girma, were ordered to Eritrea to carry out the Red Star Campaign – three months of economic, propaganda and military initiatives intended to crush the insurgency and impose socialism on Eritrea. It was a catastrophe, and Girma used the Red Star Campaign as the basis of his sixth novel, *Oromay*.

Oromay was published in Ethiopia in the summer of 1983, became an instant sensation, and is today considered the most famous Ethiopian novel. While its romantic and thriller elements drew a large readership, its unflinching portrayal of the regime and its missteps was unprecedented among the highly censored literature published under the Derg.

Within days of *Oromay*'s publication, the regime fired Girma, banned *Oromay*, and sent soldiers into bookshops and markets to confiscate copies. Six months later, on February 14, 1984, Girma vanished. The consensus is that he was kidnapped and murdered by the regime in retaliation for *Oromay*, but no definitive evidence has ever emerged. Girma certainly knew that he was risking his life by publishing *Oromay*, and it is partly for his courage in renouncing the hated Derg that he and the novel hold such an honoured place in Ethiopian cultural history.

This translation, one of the first of an Amharic novel, was prepared with the full support and close cooperation of the Girma family.

— David DeGusta and Mesfin Felleke Yirgu

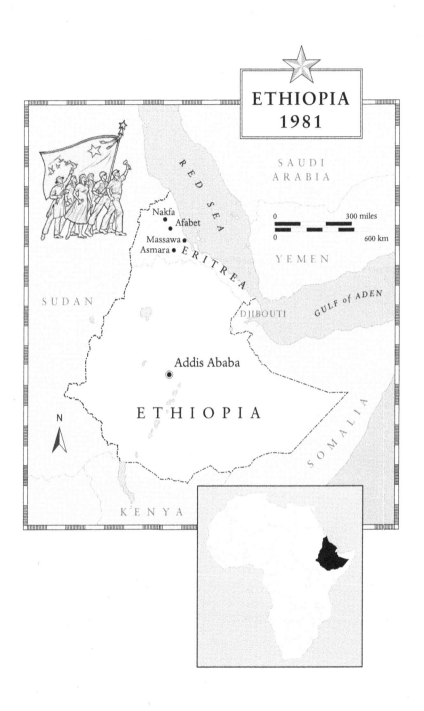

ETHIOPIA
1981

SAUDI
ARABIA

RED SEA

Nakfa
Afabet
Massawa
Asmara

ERITREA

YEMEN

0   300 miles
0   600 km

SUDAN

DJIBOUTI

GULF of ADEN

Addis Ababa

ETHIOPIA

SOMALIA

N

KENYA

CONTENTS

PART III

PART IV

PART V

PREFACE

This is a story from the life of Tsegaye Hailemaryam.

Who is Tsegaye Hailemaryam? Be patient – life is too short to rush. You will get Tsegaye's story in due time. He will tell it himself through his words and thoughts, his feelings and visions, his actions and silences.

Who am I to say this? Really, it doesn't matter. I don't have a name or a face, a time or a place. Suffice it to say, I exist. I was, I am, I will be. Tsegaye cannot be everywhere because he is an ordinary mortal. So I appear now and then, in times and places where he is not. Who am I? Don't concern yourself with my identity, it's not important. But you are worried about it, I can tell. And I hate to see people suffer, so I will answer: I am the author.

I know Tsegaye better than he knows himself. He is a lamb of God. He loves life, but sometimes it is too much for him. He suffers because he does not have room enough in his heart for all the beauty he finds in the world. He is only human, only mortal. You will see that Tsegaye is also a little foolish – though aren't we all? He loves everything he sees, but it's more than he can keep hold of.

Best if we let Tsegaye speak for himself. But where to start? Who knows exactly when the story of a life begins or ends? You might start anywhere. Here is Tsegaye.

PART ONE

1

GALLANTS AT DAWN

Monday, December 28, 1981

A cold and foggy morning. I oversleep, like usual. I'm supposed to be at Bole Airport by six, which leaves me twenty minutes. I dropped my luggage at the airport yesterday, so all I need is my briefcase. But what I really need is a magic potion to get me started in the morning. Roman is different – she's an early bird.

"Please eat, even just a little," says Roman.

"Wa! Do you even know me?" I'm never hungry in the morning. I check my watch. "Better if we go now."

"You slept like you were dead," she says. She puckers her lips like she is about to give herself a kiss. Sometimes she does take out her breasts and kiss them. Such a strange woman, and maybe a little too in love with herself. She is beautiful though.

This morning she's sulking, which only makes her more attractive. I'm going to Asmara for three months, and I failed to give her the loving goodbye she deserves. I'm lazy in the mornings, but still, it's a bad omen. Better I had started my journey with sweetness. I kiss her on the cheek and she smiles, her teeth like white corn.

"Tsegaye, you didn't even shower," she says. "What are we going to do with you?"

"I smell like you, like Chanel No. 5."

It's true, I smell like Roman. We'd spent the weekend the way we usually do, lounging in bed.

"I forbid you from bathing for the next three months," she says. "Swear in the name of Saint Gabriel that you won't! Ah, what's the use? Soon you'll smell like another woman. You make yourself at home wherever you go."

I make sure Roman has all the keys to the apartment and then we leave. For once my car decides to start without being pushed, a good beginning. I want to drive fast but the streets are clogged with people, mostly women. Everyone is headed to the Church of Saint Gabriel this morning to celebrate his feast day. Overloaded taxis shove their way through the crowds, swerving and braking to pick up still more passengers. Even the private cars are packed full. An accident jams traffic. Time slips away. I almost swerve into a taxi and add my insults to the cacophony. The more I hurry, the more obstacles I encounter.

"For God's sake, slow down, Tsegaye," says Roman, her body stiff with fear.

Roman Hiletework is always cautious, no surprise there. I'm cautious with her too – she's a beauty. Every man who sees her, wants her. They undress her with their eyes, head to toe, stripping off her clothes like layers of an onion. Women envy her. "Other women don't like me," she always complains, "it's my curse." In truth, other women scare her. They are the enemy, and she is convinced one will poison her someday. But her beauty is timeless, her body a divine inspiration. I

6

look over at Roman now, her black sweater stretched tight across her chest, and it's like I'm seeing her for the first time.

"They won't hold the flight just for me," I say. I spot a gap in the traffic and hit the gas.

"Be sure it's not just your corpse that gets there – brakes!"

"With a gorgeous fiancée like you to weep over my grave, why should I worry about dying? Your tears will revive my body."

"Can't you stay here for the holidays, then go?"

"And postpone the resurrection of Eritrea?"

"Do you remember how you spent last Christmas?" she says.

"In bed?"

"Drunk. We were at the Ras Hotel. And you were really drunk, Tsegaye."

"I was intoxicated by your beauty," I say and swerve around a few more taxis.

"All this is ridiculous, completely ridiculous," she says. "Why are we all in such a hurry? Every day another campaign of some sort. Campaign for Development, Campaign for Military Effectiveness, Campaign for Economic Growth, Campaign to Eradicate Illiteracy. Now the Red Star Campaign to fix the Eritrean problem. We are addicted to campaigns, but I can't wait until we can be done with them." She is quite the orator when the mood strikes her.

"Our journey is long, our hopes distant, our problems many," I say, mimicking her tone. "What can we do?"

"Nonsense. You're just making fun of me. Do you really believe that campaigns and proclamations will solve Ethiopia's problems? Things aren't that easy, Tsegaye. Our fundamental problem is poverty of the mind, backwardness, but we're bombarded with proclamations, campaigns, missions . . . one confusion followed by another. How does that help?"

"Our country is in a race," I say. "For better or worse, we choose action. This is a generation of action. We're running out of time. We have no time. We're an impulsive generation, an irrational generation. Seriously, I think we're all a little crazy. We're caught between the end of the old era and the beginning of the new. That drives us, forces us to speed."

"So where will we end up?" she asks, then falls silent. Roman prefers romance to politics. Tears pool in her bright morning-star eyes.

Past Revolution Square the traffic thins out. I manage to speed up to sixty on Bole Road.

"It'll be okay, Romi," I say and pat her shoulder. "In three months I'll be back, victorious, and we'll get married. You'll welcome me home, singing 'Here comes the brave warrior, my brave warrior comes home.' And remember, request a song for me every Sunday on *Listeners' Choice*. Dedicate it to your brave comrade, Tsegaye Hailemaryam." I'm joking about the songs, but she doesn't laugh at my dry humour. Instead, tears dot her cheeks like morning dew.

"This campaign will ruin me," she says. "If only it weren't . . ." She takes a handkerchief out of her purse and wipes at her tears. Her long black hair falls across her face, a shadow on the moon, and she brushes it aside. The perfume coming from her bag smells like paradise. I breathe in as much of it as I can.

We were supposed to get married next month, in January. We had been planning the wedding and looking forward to it after two years together. I never thought I would get married, had never even considered it. Then Roman Hiletework happened, and suddenly I was afflicted with the idea of marriage.

Roman and I had known each other for years before we fell in love. Her brother was a friend of mine, but he was killed in a car accident in Mojo. He was a crazy driver who loved speed. When people saw his car approaching, they'd call out to each other, "The lunatic is coming! Grab the children!" He scattered dirt and clucking chickens in his wake. He was the only driver the Addis cabbies feared, and Roman refused to get in his car. Her brother believed life was best lived fast, and it was his passion for speed that killed him.

The night we started dating, Roman was at the Ras Hotel bar with her brother and a friend of hers, listening to the house band. As usual, I arrived there alone. I felt like an adventurer, exploring the Addis nightlife. It was like gambling: some nights I won and got to be with a beautiful woman, other nights I returned home alone and broke. That's life – meeting and parting, winning and losing.

Roman's brother invited me to join them at the bar. Her friend wasn't happy to see me. So, a little tipsy, I asked Roman to dance. On the dance floor she drew close to me. I felt her breasts press against me, but I backed away. Her perfume beckoned me closer. She swayed as if she were part of the music, as if both had been created as one. That was when I saw her beauty. Somehow I had missed it before.

Before that night in the Ras, I hadn't paid much attention to her. I don't know why, maybe it was because she was always holding a Bible. I'm no heathen, but religion has never appealed to me. Life is my religion. I like reading the Bible, but only as literature – Ecclesiastes and the Song of Solomon are beautiful. I had told Roman, "Love comes through acts, not prayer. How can you abandon what is right in front of you for some distant fantasy? We can create heaven here on earth with shovels and ploughs. Don't waste your precious time." So we avoided each other. She probably thought I was the devil, just without the horns.

That night the music in the Ras was pulsing and I danced close to Roman. She moved easily with the rhythm of the song.

"What happened to your Bible?" I asked.

"It's in my bra," she said.

"Isn't the human heart the best bible there is? Is any religion better than life itself?"

"Wow, Tsegaye, what a revelation you've had!" she teased me.

"I did have an epiphany just now."

"How so?"

"I saw it in your beautiful face."

"You've only just realized I'm beautiful?" she said.

"Honestly, yes. I must have been blind not to see it before." The song was coming to an end. "Let's go somewhere else," I said.

"Is that an order or an offer?"

"An offer."

"That's all, just a polite invitation?"

"I'll beg," I said, "if that's what you want."

We disappeared into the Addis Ababa night, leaving her brother and friend behind.

That was two years ago. After that night I gave up my solo expeditions to Addis watering holes. I got used to being with Roman, needed her by my side, got addicted to her. If it were up to me, we would already be married, but it's not that simple. Roman wants us to have our own small house first, complete with furniture and appliances. A little sanctuary for just the two of us. Unfortunately, even a modest place is a challenge to afford on my government salary. But after months of saving we were almost there, and then the Red Star Campaign was announced. We had to postpone our wedding for three months, until I'm back. Who knows, it could even be longer. Not everything goes according to plan. That's life.

I park by the hangar. The airport is swarming with people, both civilians and military, and the army band is playing in the distance. I'm five minutes late.

"Three months is nothing," I tell Roman. "It's like I'll be back tomorrow. Please, send me off with a smile so I can be happy." I lift her chin and look at her, but her sorrow settles into my heart. She smiles for a moment, but it isn't real. I need more, so I tickle her – she'll do anything for me when I tickle her.

"Oh, Tsegaye, please," she says, smiling and giggling. Her laughter is my favourite music.

I look around to make sure nobody is watching – I hate to be impolite – and then I kiss her. I hand her the car keys and move to get out, but she grabs my arm.

"Tsegaye, I'm scared. I don't know why. But I'm scared."

"You're the patriotic fiancée of a Red Star campaigner. We'll be fine. Just smile."

"No, no, that's not what I mean," she says.

"Then what?"

"Everywhere you go, you make yourself at home. Any new place, you get used to it right away. I'm afraid you're going to give my love to someone else. Those Asmara women with their braids – they move fast, like eagles."

"If there's a woman more beautiful than you, then I suppose you could be outdone, but I doubt she exists. So don't worry about it. Oh, and could you please drop the car at the mechanic? I'll call you when I get to Asmara. Ciao!" I jump out of the car to avoid seeing her cry.

I'm about to cry as well. When two people are in love, even a brief separation is a heavy burden. Are time and space the enemies of love? I don't know.

I run to the plane and I'm almost there when the guards grab me – I forgot about the security check. Thankfully it's just a quick inspection. A soldier frisks me, then lets me board.

Everyone else is already in their seat, waiting for the Chairman to arrive. The chief of protocol, Tedla Regassa, looks at me with disdain. If people aren't in their assigned seats on time, he gets nervous, bemoans his bad luck, and curses everyone. He's checking names off a list clutched in his hand. I'm the last to arrive, and he's relieved.

"What happened, Comrade Tsegaye?" he asks.

"I've been here the whole time," I lie, with a smile.

"You Ministry of Information people, what are we going to do with you? Can you ever turn up in the right place at the right time? It gives me a stomachache, heartburn."

"We're only late because we're weighed down by our equipment."

"You're late because you're weighed down by your hangovers." His face hints at a smile. "We should install a special telephone line in the Jimma Bar for you journalists. And maybe one at the July 19 Bar as well."

Now that everyone is in their assigned place, he relaxes and can joke around. The Chief of Protocol can seem stern, but he's a good guy. When he laughs, his mouth, eyes and big rolling belly all laugh along with him. He lacks good looks but makes up for it with his humour and open personality. A major in the army, he traded his military fatigues for stylish three-piece suits the minute he was appointed Chief of Protocol.

The aeroplane is full, front to back. All the important people in Addis are heading to Asmara for the Red Star Campaign. There are journalists and poets, historians and speechwriters, artists and musicians, photographers and filmmakers. Along with them are agricultural experts, engineers, leaders of industry and commerce. Nobody is left in Addis. We better not crash.

Here on the plane are some who are happy and glowing, some melancholy from too much smoking and booze, some rested and some sleepless, some with beards and some clean-shaven. There is hardly anyone I don't recognize. We all know each other; we are all connected somehow, tightly or loosely. We are all from the same generation. Young, in a hurry, ambitious. We are destined to bring about the renaissance of Ethiopia. To bring pride, unity, prosperity and peace to the Revolutionary Motherland. This is a special gathering, maybe the first time our new generation holds the future of Ethiopia in our hands. It is a revolution, the energy and ambitions of the young, fighting for our dreams for this land, this country, this Ethiopia, the land of our ancestors, of patriots. We are a revolution, come to replace our elders, singing songs of triumph:

I shall return victorious,
After vanquishing the enemy,
As my forefathers did.

I move up the plane to find my seat. It looks as if Asmara is going to be the new capital of Ethiopia, at least for the next three months. Maybe the sun is setting on Addis, like the song says.

A writer calls out to me, "Mr TV!"

"Over here, over here," interrupts the Chief of Protocol, waving at me to follow. I don't hesitate. With the Chairman about to arrive, everyone is all business. The Chief of Protocol takes me to the front of the plane and points at the last empty seat in first class. The rest of the section is filled with members of the Derg – the top leadership of the country – along with ministers and party officials.

"Comrade, are you sure this is my seat?" I ask the Chief of Protocol.

"Just sit down, darling." That's how he talks to people he likes.

"This is protocol?"

"Yes, Tsegaye, this is your seat."

The Chief of Protocol is not the kind of man who makes mistakes. He takes his job very seriously, and thinks carefully about who should sit where. He knows where everyone stands politically. Some Derg officials call him "Comrade Hierarchy" and it's no joke – his seating charts reflect who is gaining or losing power.

I'm quite impressed with myself, sitting here rubbing shoulders with the country's leaders. It feels good when the big guys greet me. They know me from being on Ethiopian TV, but their greetings aren't really a gesture of friendship. I can tell by their expressions that they're wondering what the hell I'm doing, sitting up here with them.

There are other professionals like me seated in first class. To my left is Director Betru Tessema, his big round face reflecting his usual serenity. Trained by both the CIA and the KGB, he's an expert at breaking up anti-government movements. To look at him you'd think he's a rich businessman, not a spy. He always greets people with a smile, speaks with a smile, and says goodbye with a smile. Mr Happy. Betru doesn't say much, but he knows the organization and strategy of every opposition group and splinter faction. He smiles at me, and I smile back.

Seated to my right is Metshafe Daniel, our chief economist. He has a small face and a bald patch on his head that makes him look like a squash. His limbs are thin, but his belly is large and protruding, as if he has a kebero drum under his shirt. To make up for his awkward appearance, he wears fancy clothes. That said, he's an expert economist, well-versed in the theory and practice of both capitalist and socialist systems. During the Somalia conflict I travelled with him all over Harrarge, the eastern province, as he documented the economic impact of the war. I know him well. Right now Metshafe looks like he's forgotten something and is worried about it. Sometimes he will insist on talking to you at length. Other times you can say something to him and he will ignore you, scratch his belly and check himself for signs of disease. A hypochondriac, he's convinced that he has every illness known to medicine, and maybe some new ones too. He's scratching his stomach and I silently wish him a speedy recovery.

In front of me is the man we call the Ethiopian Suslov, the chief ideologue of the party. His real name is Yeshitla Masresha and he comes from a long line of priests. He has light skin and a handsome, angular face, all sharp edges. His personality is sharp as well, his words strong and cutting. Even his Afro, though thinning, has sharp edges. He can come across as egotistical, but if you get to know him, he is kind and considerate. I enjoy talking with Yeshitla, but he can be hard to understand.

Behind me is Colonel Wolday Tariku. He seems dejected – longing, I imagine, for whiskey and war. Thin, almost emaciated, he looks like a famine victim. He is tall with long arms, like he was designed to retrieve items from high shelves. His unruly black hair gives him the appearance of a bandit just back from the bush. I went to elementary school with Wolday. Even as a child, his favourite pastime was playing war games with the other boys in our neighbourhood. His family is from Eritrea, and his father, Grazmatch Tariku Bahita, was a celebrated fighter in the war against the Italian invaders. Grazmatch Tariku walked almost seven hundred miles from Asmara to Addis Ababa to fight alongside other patriots and free his beloved Ethiopia from the fascists. Wolday turned out to be a great soldier like his father, and is famous for his battles against the insurgents. When they hear him coming, they take off and don't stop running for days. Give Wolday a drink and a rifle and he is a happy man.

A familiar voice calls my name and I turn around. Standing in the aisle is my friend Firew Zerihun, a photojournalist I often work with. "I saved a seat for you, next to mine," he says, his big voice booming out of his small body. Even sitting down, I'm almost as tall as him.

"Well, it seems my seat is here," I say. "They've put us in different sections."

"So this is a class difference between us?" Firew asks with a smirk.

"From each according to his ability, to each according to his need, comrade."

"Ah, such a democratic revolution." He hurries back to his seat. Firew walks fast and talks fast. He works the same way, swift and daring. People love him, especially women.

The Chief of Protocol gets our attention and announces in a loud voice, "Comrade Chairman."

All the noise and chatter in the aeroplane stops. It is silent. You could hear a tear fall.

"Good morning, comrades."

The Chairman's voice is strong, and his friendly smile projects an earthy humility. He's wearing his military uniform, impeccable as always. His arrival gives me an overwhelming feeling of confidence and courage.

The leaders of a country are human, just like the rest of us, so I don't understand why their presence fills me with patriotism and devotion, as if they were larger than life. Maybe it's because they are the protectors of the people, responsible for our dignity and well-being. Nevertheless, for whatever reason, I do respect authority. My colleagues notice this and behind my back will say, "There goes Tsegaye, wagging his tail for the big bosses." But I'm not that kind of person at all. There are many things I don't know about myself, but I know I don't wag my tail. Where would that get me? My goal is not to have a powerful high-profile position. I want to be admired and respected for being good at my job. That much I do know about myself. My work drives me, and that is a fact. If you don't tackle life's challenges, then what is the point of being alive? To live is to strive. Being a passive observer is not for me. You swim through the waves of life, you float on top of them, or you drown, that's it. The true meaning of life is to work for a cause. As long as I can do that, I am at peace.

"Come here quickly," says the Chief of Protocol and waves at me to follow him. He's always in rush.

"Where to?" I ask and get up from my seat.

"The Chairman is asking for you. Hurry!"

I follow the Chief of Protocol up the aisle to the front of the plane. Everyone follows me with their eyes.

The Chairman has a hearty smile, and an unassuming manner and modesty that brings out the humility in others. His eyes continually shift from side to side, never fixing on any one spot. He is usually reserved, like a panther, though sometimes he can be an angry wounded panther. The anger comes, I suppose, when he is given bad information by some expert or another. I know him, to a certain extent. During the past eight years I have travelled with his entourage in Ethiopia, and abroad to East Germany, Czechoslovakia, Hungary, Moscow and Yemen. In that time I have watched him grow from a curious man to a wise one, from an eager patriot to a seasoned revolutionary, from an upright military officer to a shrewd leader. Is there any better way to learn than being in the driver's seat? Compared to him, the rest of us haven't done much during the eight years of the Revolution, other than grow our hair grey and our fingernails long. Someone once said that engaging in class struggle in the streets, factories or farms will teach you more than any university education. I don't remember who said that, but they were right.

"Comrade Tsegaye, the cameras and the film ordered by your Ministry of Information for the campaign, have they arrived?"

"Comrade Chairman, the photo film is here," I say. "We're still waiting for the movie cameras and their film."

"And why is that? It's been twenty days since the money was allocated – 800,000 Birr. Is the importance of this campaign and its urgency not clearly understood? Orders were given to import these items without delay or unnecessary bureaucracy. What happened?"

"Comrade Chairman, the movie cameras we ordered are professional grade, the kind that are not kept on hand but assembled at the factory only after the purchase order is made. We are making every effort to—"

"Comrade Tsegaye, we do not have the luxury of time. We are men of action fighting to cement the survival of a proud and respected Socialist Ethiopia. Our revolutionary mission is critical and momentous, and, as such, every aspect of our operation must be recorded and documented because what we do today will be tomorrow's legacy. We might not be capable of manufacturing the cameras ourselves, but why are we incapable of buying them?"

"We are constantly in touch with the manufacturer via telex and telegram, Comrade Chairman. They should arrive—"

"They have to arrive in Asmara by January 18th. I repeat, January 18th."

"Yes, Comrade Chairman," I say. I calculate in my head how much time we have. Three weeks. God help me.

"We will be making a major speech in Asmara, at our high-level policy conference with representatives from worker collectives, the Church and every ethnic group. All the necessary arrangements must be made so that everyone in Ethiopia will be able to listen to the conference on the radio, watch it on television, and read about it in the newspapers. The Eritrean problem requires the efforts of every patriotic Ethiopian. Popular opinion is critical, now and for the future, so propaganda and activism will play a major role in this campaign. You will be given a detailed set of instructions before the conference."

I bow my head and start to leave, but he isn't done with me yet.

"There is more. The two Asmara newspapers, *Hibiret* and *Ethiopia Today*, need to be changed to align with the objectives of our Red Star Campaign and we must also find ways to increase their distribution and readership. Don't worry about money or manpower, do what it takes. The programmes on Radio Asmara should also be reviewed to make them reflect the purpose, objective and progress of the campaign. Another critical task is jamming the signal of the insurgency's radio station, Dimtsi Hafash, to stop the lies they are broadcasting. We're not going to Asmara for a holiday – we'll be working day and night, and everyone must contribute their energy and intellect to make this national campaign a success. Am I clear, Comrade Tsegaye?"

"Yes, Comrade Chairman."

I silently pray to Gabriel, Saint of Kulubi, and ask him to get me out of this fix. Then I curse whoever nominated me for this job and go back to my seat. As soon as I sit down I fasten my seat belt tight, before the flight attendant even tells me.

Next it is Metshafe Daniel, the chief economist, who is summoned for a discussion with the Chairman. He isn't wasting any time getting the Red Star Campaign started. His words, "We are men of action," echo in my ears. Nothing goes over the Chairman's head and he does not forget. He remembers names, dates, figures. He keeps track of everything. When I think about it, I'm not just impressed, I am astounded. How would I manage if I were in his place? Good thing I'm not. It's lonely up there.

Word comes that the plane is about to take off, or else the Chairman would have kept giving us instructions. With this kind of start, I know it will be even busier once we arrive in

Asmara. The Chairman never has enough time, so he won't allow us any rest either, unless Saint Gabriel intervenes with a miracle.

A voice on the loudspeaker announces, "On behalf of Comrade Chairman, welcome to Special Flight 709. We will be flying at an altitude of 29,000 feet and our total flight time will be 55 minutes. Please fasten your seat belts."

We all need to buckle up for this historic mission, and I pull my seat belt even tighter. The plane taxis down the runway and gains speed. A special flight, its mission the Red Star Campaign. I cross myself as we rise into the sky and head north.

2

PALMS OF PEACE

Asmara, our northern beauty, is the jewel of the Red Sea. Her streets are lined with stately palms, their fronds shading elegant women with elaborate braids. Together they inspire poetry. What could be more delightful than to sit under a palm with a beautiful woman on a clear night, the north star lighting the moon? Yet amid this beauty, I crave peace. More than anything, I despise the destruction and desolation war brings. When will people learn to settle their differences peacefully? Life is too short, even without war.

We land in Asmara and I don't have a moment to catch my breath. There is no time to spare. Our patriotic campaign has two prongs: one hand will wage war against the Eritrean insurgents, the other will rebuild the local economy. My role is critical. I am to design and lead the propaganda effort to build popular support for the Red Star Campaign. This will be no easy task. No matter how sincere and honest the mission, it takes time and effort to win people's hearts and minds. If it were easy to control public opinion, then there would be no need for war. Our battlefield is the human psyche, and victory depends on winning over people's souls, one at a time. This is true wherever there is fighting and conflict. A rallying cry comes to me: "Journalists of the world unite! Stand together and guard the welfare of mankind. You have nothing to lose but your role as instruments of deceit!" I laugh at my new slogan.

I get off the plane and am quickly issued a car and directed to where I will be staying for the next three months. It's a room in a large house that used to belong to Dr Yohannes, on Revolution Avenue behind Asmara Palace. I drive straight there and drop my luggage on the bed before leaving again. I'm eager to start work on a new TV programme, *Palms of Peace*. On the flight, the idea came to me to film a segment showing the beauty of Asmara, in order to reduce tensions in Eritrea. The palm trees here always make me feel calm for some reason, even romantic, so . . . *Palms of Peace*.

I meet up with my camera crew and we start filming on the western edge of the city at the Forto, a massive beige building on a low hill overlooking the Tsetserat neighbourhood. From there we go to the Hazhaz district in the north, past the women's prison and the television station in Biet Gheorgis. We film in Arbate Asmara, where the city was founded when, legend has it, four women convinced their rival clans to unite against an invading force. We film all over Asmara, from the humble homes in Geza Birhanu to the mansions of Ras Alula, from the hills of Geza Banda to the wide avenues of Combishtato. Asmara, Asmarity, Asmarina – a shining jewel on a high plain with palm-lined streets, ivy-covered buildings and perfumed flowers. She is decorated like a bride, a beautiful city, a work of art. Asmarina, *mia bellezza*, I love this city.

And I love being a journalist. It keeps me on the move, shows me new things, and has brought me to Asmara several times. Asmara is beautiful, but it has limitations. It's a small city and it can smother you. Unlike Addis, you can't just turn a corner and disappear into yet another neighbourhood. The only escape is to get out of town, maybe drive down to Massawa and the Red Sea. The sea is life, and the life of Ethiopia is bound to the Red Sea. That's where we can breathe freely.

Dusk settles on Asmara. The sun, like a shy Eritrean bride in all her braided glory, goes to hide under the horizon, setting it aglow with twilight rays. The air grows cold with a gust of northern chill. The palm fronds sway in the wind, their sound a dirge:

> *Children of the same womb*
> *Discordant dreams*
> *Driving them apart*
> *The peaceful defeated*
> *The madmen reign*

The next morning I again go with my camera crew and film all over Asmara: Sembel, Godaif, Big and Little Gejeret, Tiravolo, Mai Chihot, Edaga Arbi, Edaga Hamus, Geza Aba Shawl, Mai Temenai.

The streets and buildings are decorated with Ethiopian flags, coloured lights and red banners with revolutionary slogans. Palm trees are decked with garlands, ready for a big celebration. The city looks like it's dressed up for a wedding.

Along the way we spot people we know from Addis – artists and historians, engineers and economists – all here as if invading Asmara. Brand-new Ladas and Land Cruisers ferry officials and their guards all over town. The locals stand outside their houses, cafés and shops, watching the turmoil with dour expressions, probably wondering, "What is all this commotion? Why are you heartlanders here? To force us to bow down to you?"

The city is buzzing, as if all of us new arrivals are singing, "Selam, selam, peace be with you, we travelled from Addis to be with you, selam, selam, peace for Eritrea."

But I suspect the locals are thinking instead of the song from the Italian Occupation, the one in Tigrigna that ends, "Forbidden from walking in Combishtato, could Mussolini hurt me any worse?"

"Now let's go to the market," I tell my camera crew. Worn out from filming, all they can picture is a cold beer in their hands.

"Please, Comrade Tsegaye," pleads one of them. "We have enough footage."

"What? We're just getting started!"

We drive to the market square. Shoppers swarm the stands, talking in Tigrigna or accented Amharic, buying grain without any regard for the price, as if a famine is coming. I approach an elderly lady with my microphone. A scarf covers her plaited hair and she's wearing gold earrings and a gold necklace – Eritrean women always wear their jewellery.

"What are you buying, emmama?" I ask her.

"Wa! Grain."

"How is the price?"

"Wa! Expensive, very expensive."

"Why is that?"

"It is expensive," she says.

"Why? Is grain getting scarce?"

"Because everybody is buying it."

"Yes, but why? What happened?"

The old woman does not care for my questions. She just

looks at me with her wise eyes as if to tell me, *I know what you want me to say, and you know why I will not say it.* The Eritrean is trained to smell war, to expect starvation and annihilation. Their eyes are alert for signs of doomsday, their ears anticipate gunfire and funeral dirges.

Could the grain shortage be a false rumour spread by the insurgents? Right in the middle of the market, I realize that the insurgents are running their own psychological warfare campaign. This is going to be a problem, and I feel sorry for the people. I can see the confusion in their faces, the looming fear and anxiety. They are under the shadow of death, and that angers me.

We are surrounded by onlookers now, young and old, women with headscarves wrapped tight around their braids, teens in T-shirts. Some of the younger ones seem to recognize me from television. They're probably wondering if it's really me. Television presenters can be made to seem attractive on screen, but in real life might turn out to be short, bald and badly dressed. It confuses people.

"Is that him, do you think?"

"I bet it is him."

"It's funny how TV gives people good looks they don't really have."

"Hey, Tsegaye!" a rude one among them shouts.

Only a fool answers every call, but I turn around anyway. I think he lost his bet.

The purpose of filming at the market is to show that everything is stable and calm. Buyer and seller do not bargain – the merchant states a price and the customer pays what is asked. Grains, cereals, coal, firewood, oil and kerosene, we will show that they are all available in abundance. People buy in abundance, load up in abundance . . . and everyone is in a flurry of abundant panic. Of course they learned from the last war, and so they're trying to ward off the approaching evil by hoarding as many resources as they can. They are spending everything they have on the supplies they will need to survive. People hand over their hard-earned money to buy necessities without a second thought, and they should not be blamed for it. What else should people do when they think war is on its way? Hard days came to Eritrea during the fighting in 1977 and 1978. There was nothing to eat and people smashed their furniture and burned it for fuel. But it's not like that now, those days are long past. Though if fighting breaks out again, who knows who will live and who will die? Humans are absurd: none of us think it's our time to die, but it's always someone's turn.

More people have gathered around us, so I decide to tell them the purpose of our campaign. I grab a microphone and address the crowd:

"People of the Eritrean province, for the last twenty years you have suffered from hunger, from thirst. Yet through all this you have held out hope for harmony, for peace. Like everyone else, you want to live in peace. That is the need and the wish of every human being. You seek peace, and those who deny it to you are the stooges of crony imperialism. They want to brand you with an identity that is not yours. They want to give you a history that does not belong to you. They offer you a future that you did not ask for. They make revisionist history that you neither believe nor accept. These are the insurgents agitating in your good name.

"Now the insurgents are up to their same old tricks. They tell you that there will be war and annihilation. None of us are here for war. We came here for peace. Do not fall for the bogus rumour of war spread by the secessionist insurgents, and by the greedy merchants who are no less criminal. Remember, chaos in the market benefits only the thief, so do not fall victim to their treachery. Do not waste your hard-earned money. There is no war, no destruction aimed at you. But those who seek war and destruction will certainly find it on the battlefield.

"The peaceful life you seek is coming. It is almost here. Like you, we desire a life of peace and tranquility, and we are here with you now. Our mission is peace. Peace upon the Eritrean people. We extend the palm of peace."

Back at my new office, I edit the footage into a forty-minute programme. I box up the film and head to the Army Aviation airbase in Sembel, just outside town. The red Lada I was given yesterday is brand new and runs perfectly. It drives so fast it swallows the road as I speed along.

I reach Sembel and find Major Koricho Tadesse. Whenever you go to the Army Aviation base, you can bet he'll be there. Over the years he has become an institution. Everyone knows him, from the janitors to top government officials, even members of the Derg. He is the Chief of Army Aviation Traffic and Scheduling, a critical position. No-one can transport cargo on any military aircraft without his approval. He is always in control, down to the smallest detail, and he knows the location and mission of every aircraft.

"How are you, Tsegaye?" Major Koricho asks as he greets me. He is a tall, muscular and demanding officer.

"Are you busy?" I joke – good humour makes for goodwill – but he doesn't smile. "I need to send this film to Addis Ababa, and it has to get there today."

"You arrived just in time. There's a de Havilland Dash 7

taking off for Addis in thirty-five minutes." He takes the package of film.

I check my watch – it's eleven in the morning. The film will get to Addis in time for the team to broadcast *Palms of Peace* across the nation tonight. It's not easy, but we can accomplish amazing things when we cooperate. Even so, I don't have time to congratulate myself.

"Thank you, Major," I say.

"Of course. The Red Star Campaign is a collective effort."

"I'm hopeful you will continue to assist me."

"Anyone with initiative like yours should be supported. But we seem to prefer knocking each other down."

Major Koricho adjusts the holstered pistol hanging from his belt. He has grown a belly since I last saw him. And there's something else different about him, a hint of bitterness.

"By the way, how long have you been serving at this airfield?" I ask.

"Seven years, Comrade Tsegaye," he says. "Being here is second nature to me now, even with the cold winters and hot summers. As long as I can hear the roar of aeroplanes, I'm happy."

"I should film a story about you sometime." I'm serious. He has witnessed it all – life and death, victory and defeat.

"You'll need to do it before I retire," he says. His voice is sad.

"So you're close to retirement?"

"Almost. I work so hard, I forget that my retirement date is coming up. But I don't own any property or have any other business. Everything I have is here. I'll miss my planes. Watching them take off and land brings joy to my heart. We get used to things, and it's hard to let them go."

29

It is moving to hear him talk that way about his work. People like him, in key positions with so much experience, still healthy and capable – why get rid of them with a mandatory retirement age? They benefit the country, and who says age is a measure of revolutionary ability? Even those of us who are so proud of being young, one day we will be old. No-one stays young for ever. Wouldn't it be nice if we did? Maybe our children will rebel against us, accuse us of being too conservative. What happens if the children of revolutionaries revolt? The idea makes me laugh. One generation confronting another is an inevitable part of history.

Two MiG-23 fighter jets take off one after the other. They shoot through the blue sky like arrows and head towards Nakfa. Major Koricho watches them, transfixed.

"I'll phone my colleagues in Addis and have them meet the plane when it lands," I tell him. Then I hop into my Lada and speed away.

3

ASMARA ON THAT DAY

I need to get back to my office for an 11.30 a.m. meeting. Not too many cars are on the road and, maybe because of that, the local pedestrians forget to stay on the sidewalks. Even so, I make it back to my office in plenty of time. A new gold-plated nameplate on my door reads COMRADE TSEGAYE HAILEMARYAM, HEAD OF THE RED STAR CAMPAIGN POLITICAL AND PROPAGANDA INITIATIVES SECTION.

"Rezan," I call to my secretary. "Connect me first with Ethiopian TV in Addis, phone number 12 39 74. Then connect me to the Regional Telecommunications Chief, okay?"

"Right away, yes, consider it done."

Rezan Mihreteab is my secretary. She has delicate features and beautiful hair, long and silky. For most Asmara women, their face is their best feature. Few are blessed with good legs.

"Addis," says Rezan.

I pick up the phone. "Hello, this is Tsegaye. Yes, we arrived safe in Asmara. We've already started working and that is the purpose of this call. I've sent you a film on a Dash flight due to arrive in two hours. Please send a courier to Bole Airport to pick it up. It has to be broadcast tonight. Ciao."

Then the call from the Eritrean Telecommunications Office comes through.

"To whom am I speaking? . . . Yes, comrade, my name is Tsegaye Hailemaryam. I'm calling from the new Political Initiatives office . . . Yes, we arrived safe . . . That's nice. It's very important that we meet right away . . . Yes, now. In what used to be the Public Security building. It's behind the Palace and in front of the Government Employees' Club. Ask for the Political and Propaganda Initiatives office. We don't have much time so yes, now."

I'm surprised by my own attitude, which has suddenly assumed an air of authority. But it has to be that way. It's remarkable how people respond to power, to an important official with the Red Star Campaign.

The sudden and forceful opening of my office door startles me. It's Solomon Betregiorgis, a government official who's been based in Asmara for several years and is now the head of operations for the Red Star Campaign. His earnest smile brightens his dark face, as it always does. He's short with a stout frame and an energetic personality.

"I want to give you this," he says and hands me a stack of folders. He's in a hurry as usual. He's everywhere and, at the same time, also nowhere – a riddle.

"What's this?" I ask.

"The plans and organizational structure for the Red Star Campaign. It should go without saying, but to be clear, all of this is top secret. Our job is to translate it into results, put it into action right away."

The folders have labels like "Military Campaign Strategy and Roadmap", "Political Policy", "Economic Prosperity

Roadmap", "Homeland Security and Civic Safety Strategy" and "Collective Farming and Development Strategy".

"When were all these plans done?" I ask.

"We've been working on them since the last Central Committee conference. It's taken us more than a year."

"Good job."

"Yes, the campaign is well planned. But what's the point? When it comes to translating plans into action, we fall apart. We don't know how to work from a script. We do better when we improvise. I'm just being honest with you. Look at how we do our weddings, our funerals, our birthdays. How we live and how we eat. All of it is based on spontaneity. When it comes to acting on impulse, we're the best in the world." He smiles again, then continues. "I'm looking forward to the day we divorce ourselves from impulse. The foundation of socialism is strategic planning, organization, and centralized execution. Without those aspects of socialist strategy, I don't know how we can advance to the next phase."

"We will learn," I say. "Eight years of revolution is not very long. And if we fail, our children will pick up where we left off and get it done right."

"If we can even have children," he says and laughs.

"Why not?"

"Who has time for their spouse nowadays? By the time we get home we're dead tired. What's even worse is the badgering from our wives. They think we're leading a carefree life, with time on our hands to chase other women. In the morning I pray I won't have the kind of day my mother worries I'm having, but instead will have the kind of day my wife thinks I'm having. We have so many meetings – meetings in the morning, more meetings in the evening – then when you get home exhausted at midnight, another meeting with the wife. Our life has turned into one long meeting. That's why I doubt we'll have any time to procreate." He enjoys making fun of our situation.

He's about to leave my office when he stops and asks, "Is there anything else you need, Comrade Tsegaye?"

"Not really, everything seems good. The organization, the planning – all excellent."

I'm not exaggerating, my gratitude is sincere. Providing everyone who has descended on Asmara for the campaign with lodging, a fully equipped office, a car and everything else they expect – that is no easy task. But Solomon is the man. He gets things done not by being harsh, but by being entertaining and delegating the work. His philosophy is, "Give people a reasonable goal and limit the time they have to accomplish it, and you'll get the results you need."

"I haven't slept much lately," he says.

"You don't look tired," I say.

"Every official from Addis is here now. And every one of them is demanding their own car, their own house, their own office. Where am I going to find all that for every little functionary who's come here to meddle in things? I tell you, it's almost driving me crazy."

"It'll be okay," I say.

"Do you have any idea how many people have been invited here for the conference and the festival?"

He is not only responsible for managing the general operations of the Red Star Campaign, he's also in charge of preparing for the Asmara Conference of the Supreme Council and coordinating the Massawa Festival. He's running himself ragged, the poor guy.

"How many?"

"More than two thousand. From all over Ethiopia. It's just

four hundred here now, so can you imagine what it's going to be like to deal with two thousand?"

"Oh boy!" I like saying "Oh boy!" when something overwhelms me.

"For the conference, delegates from seventy organizations will be addressing workers' councils and religious leaders from all over the Eritrean province, along with representatives from all the major ethnic groups. All of them will be delivering speeches. Do you get it? Every one of them is our responsibility. On top of that, the festival songs have to be inspected and censored in advance. We have to make things like posters, flyers, brochures, slogans. It's hell, I'm not kidding." He finishes with one long sigh.

"It'll get done," I say.

"That's what I like to hear. Right now, I can't handle dealing with complaints. I'm up to my neck in my own problems. When people go on about their personal issues, I could throw up. Better to leave that at home. Anyway, you handle everything to do with propaganda for the campaign, the conference and the festival, that's it."

There's so much going on in his mind. He doesn't like to carry a notebook but instead writes things down on whatever scrap of paper is handy. It's a good thing he is blessed with an excellent memory.

"I'll do my best," I say.

"Great. I like the positive thinking, it's what keeps me going. I'm not sure what's happened to everyone, but people seem to be doing the right thing so far. Maybe people are learning a few things from this campaign. By the way, don't forget about jamming the insurgent broadcasts, and finding a way to set up our own radio transmission from here. Comrade Chairman says those are important tasks."

35

"I have a meeting later to discuss just that."

"Well, no need to cut up meat for a lion then, you can handle it yourself," he says.

Solomon leaves and I realize that I've been had by the man. Now I have propaganda responsibilities for the conference and festival, in addition to the campaign itself.

Even so, I'm not angry. I like working with Solomon. He's always clear and straightforward. He makes decisions fast and doesn't know the meaning of fear. Some say he's reckless and will do anything for more power. But he says you can't run a revolution by putting things off until tomorrow – make quick decisions, take calculated risks, and leave the judgement to history. I like people who take action. Man is not a rock. We make decisions, those decisions define our character, and our character is our destiny.

People file into my office for the 11.30 meeting, and all the women are wearing headscarves. I guess here they don't take them off even indoors – weird. The meeting is to bring together everyone who will be involved in the propaganda efforts for the Red Star Campaign, the journalists and officials who came here with me from Addis and those from the Eritrean branch of the Ministry of Information.

I welcome everyone and address the group: "Greetings, comrades. The purpose of our being here in Eritrea must be clear. There is no ulterior motive, we do not have any secrets. There is nothing to hide from the public. We must explain the campaign to them in clear, understandable terms. It's called the Eritrean Province Red Star Multi-Faceted Revolutionary Campaign, or the MFRC for short. Its purpose is to remove the insurgents from the province, the leeches who for the last twenty years have been sucking the blood of the Eritrean working people and denying them peace. We want to remove them once and for all and rebuild the economy their reckless adventurism has destroyed.

"Comrades, our top priority starting from this very moment is to make the Red Star Campaign's re-building mission clear to the people. As you have probably seen, the insurgents are already causing disruptions by claiming that we're here to unleash war and destruction. Because of this, there's panic buying, the market is emptying of goods, and greedy merchants are taking advantage of the situation to exploit the public.

"The immediate goal of the insurgents, both the Shabia and the Jebha factions, is to mislead people and create mass confusion by making the innocent public think the Revolution is destroying their life. When people feel that way, they turn bitter, and that's what the insurgents want. When people are angry and bitter, they reach a point when they can't take it any longer. As a final act of desperation they flee to the bush to join the insurgents. And by doing this the honest proletariat of Eritrea unwittingly helps the secessionist bandits accomplish their goal.

"I want you all to understand that the sad history of the Eritrean war in 1977 and 1978 will not be repeated this time around. Starting right now, we must fight back and destroy the false propaganda of the insurgency in order to calm the public and allow them to resume their normal life. Editorials and newspaper articles, radio and television programmes – all these media have to be revamped to promote the true nature and character of the Red Star Campaign. I'll need a report on all these efforts within two days. Regarding the campaign's military aspects, we'll cross that bridge when we get there. When the time comes, we'll discuss that in detail, in the open. As I said, we will hide nothing from the public.

"So fix your bayonets and charge! I am referring, of course, to the tools of our trade, our pens and pencils. I should be more careful. We need to refrain from using violent words like *kill, stab, beat, charge.* As you know, the situation here in Eritrea is complex. Every family in Asmara has someone – a husband or wife, a brother or sister, an aunt or uncle – who fled into the bush to escape the violence. Our propaganda should not lump everyone together. We can't forget the class struggle aspects of the campaign."

My explanation took longer than I had intended. When you're at the front of the room, it is tempting to say a lot, throw your weight around, talk down to people. Eventually you can become self-important and arrogant. I worry that I'm heading in that direction.

Someone raises his hand and asks, "Comrade Tsegaye, many of the songs we play on the radio have violent lyrics, like 'chase him, whip him, kill him'. What should we do about that?"

"If the songs are too harsh, we should find more light-hearted music."

"Well, there are pop songs we could use," he says.

"So what's the problem?"

"The problem is most of them are by Tsehaytu Beraki." She's a beautiful singer, but Eritrean and melancholy.

"Starting today, her songs are approved. If they make people sad, that's their problem, not ours." I give the order: "Play those songs."

There are no other questions. I take a list of twenty campaign slogans from one of the folders Solomon gave me and pass it around.

"Okay, comrades, we'll use these slogans in all the things we do. Work them into our articles and broadcasts. We'll make posters with them. Our slogans reflect our clear and honest approach, and we will act on each and every one of them. Going forward, we all need to be upright and right-eous. A socialist public is upright and pure, and demands its writers be the same. From now on, Revolutionary Ethiopia has no place for cynical journalists!"

I laugh at myself for getting so carried away in the moment. I'm a great example of how Ethiopians are spontaneous.

"That's all, comrades," I say. "This historic campaign will require all our creativity and ingenuity. But we must avoid being individualistic, emotional or impulsive. We need to be deliberate, open, and respect the principles of our centralized process. Thank you and ciao."

Everyone seems excited about what is ahead of us. Straightforward people engaging in straightforward action. I'm hopeful, optimistic even, but I could be wrong. Most revolutionaries make the mistake of assuming humans are by nature good, upright and honest. That assumption might be right, but it might be wrong. I don't know. I haven't figured that one out yet.

I dismiss everyone, but ask three officials to stay behind – the head of the Asmara Radio Station and the regional branch managers of the Ministry of Information and the Telecommunications Office.

"Alright. comrades, the three of you have very specific and urgent tasks, starting this very minute."

The gentleman from telecommunications doesn't seem to fully comprehend why he is here. He is tall and heavy. In contrast, the radio man is short, with light skin and eyes so big they are bulging out of their sockets. The Ministry of

Information manager, bald with chubby cheeks, is giggling like an idiot. I don't understand why he's laughing. Maybe the rest of us look funny to him.

"Comrade," I say to the radio man, "starting today, this afternoon, or if not today then definitely by tomorrow morning, the news broadcast of the Shabia insurgency radio station must be shut down. Jam it using any means necessary." I hand him a sheet from the top-secret files with Shabia's Dimtsi Hafash broadcast hours, and the wavelength and frequency used for each transmission.

He examines the paper with his bulging eyes and asks, "How?"

"What do you mean, how?" I understand the way technical people think. Their initial reaction is always negative. They tend to focus on the obstacles.

"Comrade Tsegaye, we don't have enough technicians," he says.

"Everybody should help."

"Our jamming transmitter will blow up if it gets overloaded."

"Find ways so it doesn't get overloaded," I say.

"Besides, we don't have enough vehicles to get everyone from Combishtato here to the Tract B transmitter at Kagnew Station that we use for jamming."

"Comrade, regarding transportation, you need to take that up with your team. They can spend the night at Kagnew Station if there's no other choice. The lies of the Shabia insurgency must be silenced. How you accomplish this is up to you, but it must be done. Okay, comrade?"

This makes his bulging eyes protrude even more. Like I said, I understand technical people. In their view, everybody else is crazy or stupid. Maybe they're right.

Next I turn to the telecommunications manager. "Comrade, please accept my apology for taking you away from your busy schedule. I do so because the task ahead of us is an urgent one."

"That's alright. What is this about?" He has his notebook ready. I take him for a real bureaucrat, part of a large and uncaring organization. I can tell he's wondering who the hell I am, but he doesn't want to ask me directly.

"We're going to hold a big conference here to kick off the Red Star Campaign and it needs to be broadcast to all of Ethiopia."

"And?" he asks, moving his eyebrows up and down.

"It is imperative that the necessary cables be run between Tinsae Hall in the Palace and our studio here."

"By when?" he asks.

"We have five days. And we'll need the same thing between Revolution Square and Saba Stadium." Again his eyebrows wiggle, and he has a phoney smile on his long dark face.

"Comrade Tsegaye, it would be better if the order is in writing," he says.

"We don't have time for bureaucracy." I'm getting angry. "We're busy running a campaign."

He realizes he doesn't have a good argument on those grounds, so he changes tactics. "I'm not even sure that the job can be done," he says.

"It has to be done. Anything else is not acceptable. Do what you have to do." That's all I can say to him.

"How do you mean?" asks the Ministry of Information guy, still giggling with his mouth wide open. "Is the plan for the main radio station in Addis Ababa to receive the broadcast from here and then relay it?"

"Yes, comrade, the Addis station will receive everything

from here and re-broadcast it to the rest of the country. All day long, for three or four days. Asmara is effectively our capital city for the next few months. It's the command centre for the Red Star Campaign. Do we understand each other? And, by the way, it's your responsibility to follow up and make sure the jamming and relay tasks are accomplished. The jamming should be done by tomorrow, and the relay set up within five days. That is all, comrades."

I say that loudly. My tone carries authority, and the way I'm getting my point across is definitely assertive. It seems like delegating responsibilities is becoming quite popular. Maybe I'm getting used to this?

A telephone starts ringing. I have three different phones lined up on my desk and I'm not sure which one it is. The inter-office phone turns out to be the correct answer.

"Hello?" I say.

"This is Solomon."

"Yes, comrade."

"You haven't left for lunch yet?" he asks.

"No." I look at my watch and it's after 1 p.m. I never eat at any set time anyway. I can't claim it's because I'm a journalist, as some of us are real gluttons.

"You need to slow down." He gives me advice that he doesn't follow himself. "I'm calling to tell you there's a general meeting at two o'clock."

"Where?"

"In the assembly hall at the Palace, at exactly two, okay? Ciao."

I hang up.

"Comrade Tsegaye, one thing is not clear to me." This is coming from the Ministry of Information man, the giggler.

"What?"

"I need to understand the working relationship between my office and the Red Star Campaign Propaganda Initiative," he says.

In other words, he's questioning my authority. To him, I am a nobody. He's the Senior Director of the regional branch office for the Ministry of Information, and I'm the Director of the Ethiopian Television Administration in Addis Ababa. Why would he consider me his superior? It's fine, I shouldn't take it personally.

"Yes, comrade, that's a good question. We have a number of journalists and photographers here along with representatives from the Central Committee, the military, the Ministry of Information and a host of other organizations. The Red Star Campaign has its own organization, and under the Political division is a Propaganda Initiatives section. And the Red Star Campaign's Propaganda Initiative section will have under it news, talk shows, radio, and television subsections. The organizational setup, the process directives along with a timeline as well as task priorities, strategy and tactics, all of that is ready and will be provided to you in the next two or three days. Any propaganda initiatives undertaken as part of the Red Star Campaign will come from this office. Do we have an understanding, comrade?"

"That's fine."

"Is there anything you're unhappy with?"

"Not at all."

"Good. Look, those of us from Addis, we're here to help and support you, not to replace you or take your jobs. I want to be clear about that. Our efforts will be compromised if we don't have mutual understanding and goodwill." I speak slowly with the intent of sending a strong message, and I have more to say. "Those of us from the heartland are not under any illusion that we know more than you about the problems of the Eritrean province, or that we have all the answers, or that we care more about the Revolution, or that we work harder than anybody else for the success of the Red Star Campaign. If anyone believes that, they're wrong and need to be straightened out right away. It's that kind of attitude and thinking that will derail our progress. We need to be very careful that, in our attempt to resolve issues in Eritrea, we don't end up creating more trouble. Like the foreigners say, we're here to be part of the solution and not part of the problem. There are enough problems already, we don't need to create any new ones.

"By the way, before I forget – the circulation numbers for the newspapers *Hibiret* and *Ethiopia Today* must be increased. Don't worry about the cost. And we need to start a daily radio programme, 45 minutes in both Amharic and Tigrigna, broadcasting in the early morning, between 6.30 a.m. and 8.00 a.m. Please get it going within the next five days. It is best if the structure and format of the show are standardized, not changing around every day. And this is your responsibility, within five days, and I wish you success."

Five days – they're not too happy about that. Neither am I. I'm not a ruthless person, but the job has to be done. Is there any choice? Life is a chain of obligations. The three men file out of my office.

I did talk a lot, one speech after another, a sign of our time. Some people associate socialism with speeches, with lots of discussions but nothing to show for it. Others link socialism with meetings, one meeting after another, one assessment after another, leading to many agendas but few results. Some connect socialism with slogans – we do come up with a lot of them. And everything we do is urgent, everyone rushing to take action. No time to rest and no time to love, hardly enough time to die. Didn't someone say a revolution devours its own children? I'm beginning to worry about the cameras and film we ordered from abroad and I say a silent prayer for their delivery.

It's almost two o'clock. I get up and run to the assembly hall.

4

A PROMISING START

The assembly hall fills with officials for the first meeting of the Red Star Campaign. There are long tables with nametags arranged according to the usual hierarchy. I look for my name and find it on the far end of the front table. At each place is a special notebook adorned with the Red Star Campaign logo. Nobody is yelling and everyone is wearing a tie. The change is obvious: the mark of a revolutionary used to be a big Afro and a long beard, shirt wide open and pistol dangling from the waist, a jacket with the sleeves cut off. Those days are gone and now decorum rules. Will anyone object that the Revolution has been turned inside out? Some of us prefer the old ways.

A large organizational chart for the Red Star Campaign is positioned at the front of the hall between timelines and maps. Preparing everything for this meeting must have taken days – no detail has been overlooked. That bodes well for our success. The main doors to the assembly hall open and the Chairman strides in. A commotion ensues as we all stand up to welcome him.

"How has your day been, comrades? Sit down. Sit down."

He sits down quickly, so we all do the same. He is wearing a black striped suit with a blue shirt and a white tie with black hexagons. There's a bright smile on his face and he seems to be in a good mood. I remember the old saying, let your boss's expression be your guide. Everyone is smiling and I do the same.

The Chairman has the eyes of a raptor, tracking everyone around him. He is both fire and water, a lamb but also a lion. To see him is to believe in him.

"Comrade Chairman, we are ready to begin," says the First Secretary of the Red Star Campaign. "I declare the meeting open." The First Secretary has a round face, big eyes and a bald head – he looks like a kind soul, and he is. Even as he talks, he smiles. When he speaks, he has an odd accent, emphasizing some letters but not others. He likes to complain that he has a hard time understanding Amharic ever since the new character was added to the alphabet. His favourite expression is "nuts". To him, everyone is nuts, totally nuts. He never misses a chance to say something funny.

I remember a joke he told me. "Once there was an old man who had to register his house with the local government board. When he went to the kebele chairman to register it in 1968, he gave his age as sixty years old. When he returned in 1974 to register it again, he again gave his age as sixty years old. The kebele chairman noticed this and asked the old man, 'Haven't you been alive the past six years?' The old man replied, 'Ha – you call that living?'"

Things got really bad in those years before the Revolution, but the First Secretary can find humour anywhere, even at his own expense. Of his bald head, he likes to say, "A well-traveled path grows no grass." Being able to laugh at yourself is healthy, but it's a rare gift.

47

The agenda is distributed and the Chairman starts the meeting.

"Comrades, the purpose of our meeting today is to thoroughly review the scope and charter of the Eritrean Province Red Star Multi-Faceted Revolutionary Campaign and then immediately start work on the historic task that confronts us. This Red Star Campaign is part and parcel of our class struggle, so it is collective in nature, encompassing cultural, economic, political and military efforts, but the key attribute of this national revolutionary campaign is that it comes from the people.

"From the operations guide and organizational chart – you should each have your own copy – it should be clear that the purpose of this campaign is to defeat the insurgency operating here in our northern province of Eritrea and free the people, the workers, from imperialism. With our bayonets pointed forward, we will stand side by side with the proletariat to build collective cultural, political and economic institutions that will not only benefit from the fruits of our Revolution but also contribute to its forward progress.

"Our Red Star Campaign has three main phases. The first phase was to conduct all the necessary research and preparations, and we are here today because that has been completed. The next step is for us to introduce the campaign, and so in the coming days there will be a major conference here in Asmara and a grand festival in Massawa. The second phase will be to get the military operations underway, as well as our efforts to rebuild the local economy. The third phase is intended to organize and arm the farmers living in the areas that will be liberated from the insurgents, as well as in the rest of the province, and to raise the awareness of the proletariat. The key factor is organization, because our ultimate goal is not just to defeat the secessionist insurgency, but to build a socialist society here.

"Comrades, the commitment we are making here today is a serious one. The people of Ethiopia will judge us, history will judge us, and we must succeed, if not by totally eradicating the insurgents who have terrorized this province for twenty years, then by breaking their back.

"Today, our armed forces – the guardians of our Revolution, our shield and our sword – are the strongest they have ever been in our long and magnificent history. Without concern for comfort or wealth, they are ready to live in a foxhole and fight with purpose, ready to kill the enemy in hand-to-hand combat, ready to die. This army, built from Ethiopia's cherished youth, wants nothing more than the success of the Revolution and national unity. You might not always be comfortable while you are here in Asmara, but remember that our Revolutionary Army is living in foxholes."

I am so moved by his speech that I am shaking, and my eyes fill with tears. I don't know about everyone else, but I was so caught up in his words that I forgot to write anything down. The Chairman spoke without any notes. When he does that, I'm always amazed by how easily his words flow, how coherent his thoughts are. I wish he would always give his speeches that way. That's when you realize his real conviction, his authority and his ability to inspire people. Such a remarkable skill.

Back in 1976, I remember a certain minister asking me, "Tsegaye, what if you convinced him to give his speeches without any written notes? When he speaks from the heart, he gets right to the core of the issue in a way that inspires everyone, giving us pearls of wisdom." That minister later fled the country, but he was right.

I have watched the Chairman run numerous meetings. He listens to everyone with serenity and patience. I believe that is how he has been able to learn so much in such a short time. He has an innate ability to understand the character of a meeting, to know just when to provide his thoughts. He moves things towards a solution, peels through an issue layer by layer to get to the heart of it. The Chairman's thinking is always clear and direct, and he doesn't hesitate to question the experts about the economy or any other topic. He delivers the truth without fear.

I have seen the Chairman's many talents. The idea of being tired never occurs to him. I don't know if work relaxes him, but I know he works hard. He devotes the same intense effort to all tasks, big and small. At times I worry that he might get lost in the details. During the Somali War, I actually saw him making an inventory of our supplies and counting bullets. If only the rest of us worked as hard as the Chairman, we could bring prosperity to this beautiful but sad country of ours. However, most of us avoid hard work. Instead, we plot and scheme to make sure someone else will take the blame for anything that goes wrong. The well-being of a country should not depend entirely on the work of one man, or even of a small group. It is everyone's responsibility.

The Chairman continued: "We have the misfortune of having to use one hand to fight the insurgents while the other hand tries to rebuild the economy. This was not our choice, it was forced on us, but we are determined to build a socialist society in Eritrea and are ready to make any sacrifice that is asked of us. It took us over a year to prepare this campaign, and we took into account our experience with previous campaigns. We will learn from this one as well, because revolution is a school that never closes."

One of the habitual clappers begins to applaud and now we all have to clap. Some people will start applauding as soon as they hear the word "comrades". Personally, I think it takes wisdom and experience to know the right time to clap. Applause should be given only when the moment calls for it.

The Chairman smiles, his toughness cloaked as usual by modesty, and continues speaking. "The planning for the Red Star Campaign was initiated at the second Central Committee Congress based on the three resolutions adopted there regarding the Eritrean insurgents:

1. We resolve to eradicate the anti-unity and anti-revolutionary insurgents who are actively engaging in attempts to disrupt the economic progress and development resulting from the Revolution within the Eritrean province. By eradicating them, we will deny imperialism a foothold in Ethiopia and ensure peace and security.

2. To those individuals who knowingly or unknowingly joined or collaborated with the insurgents opposing their country, but now realizing their transgression, have apologized and wish to return to join the Revolution, they will be integrated back into the community and be fully engaged in the struggle to build the new society.

3. During the Somali invasion, the proletariat of eastern and southern Ethiopia stood alongside our Revolutionary Army, confronted the enemy, gave what was required, and were soon victorious. Now they are engaged in the battle to rebuild the country. We call on the people of Eritrea to do the same and collaborate with our Revolutionary Army to exterminate the insurgents that have taken up residence in that province, reducing it to indignities and tarnishing its good name.

"Those are the resolutions from the second Central

Committee Congress, and the main purpose and function of this historic Red Star Campaign is to turn these noble goals into reality. All our actions must be revolutionary in nature, free of bureaucracy and in service of the people. We will need to communicate within the campaign, both horizontally and vertically, as our organizational structure is based on equality and consensus. Before we proceed with further details, if there are any questions or statements, we are ready to conduct an open and democratic dialogue."

Everyone is silent and we all look at each other. We are reluctant to speak up with any direct objections or criticisms, regardless of what we might really think. To me, this veiled aspect of our character is the enemy of the democratic principles we are supposed to follow. This weakness endangers democracy and strengthens centralized dominance by concentrating power in the hands of one person. It's hard to keep the Revolution going when we leave one man to carry such a heavy load.

My stomach rumbles. I haven't had anything to eat since this morning. Time marches forward. Someone raises a hand.

"Yes, comrade," says the Chairman. "It's alright, you don't need to stand up."

The man who raised his hand is thin, like a burned-out matchstick. His body, his hands, his lips are all shaking. He is sitting near me and even his chin is shaking.

"Comrade Chairman, this campaign, hmm, revolutionary campaign, hmm, I mean the Eritrean Province Red Star, hmm, this effort, why now? Why at this particular time?"

The Chairman is not just an accomplished speaker, he is also a good listener. He is in the habit of listening to everyone with measured care and patience.

"Yes, comrade, that is a good question," says the Chairman.

It is a good question indeed, and I get ready to jot down his answer. My stomach has stopped making noises.

"As you know, due to the hard work of the Ethiopian public, especially the continued sacrifice by our Revolutionary Army, and with assistance from friendly socialist countries, we have successfully transformed our Revolution from defensive to offensive. By adapting our tactics and strategies to the demands of each situation, we demolished the counter-revolutionaries and the external aggressors who rose against us in the central, eastern and southern regions. Now what stands in the way of national unity and the well-being of our people, harming our economy and denying our Revolutionary Army even a moment of relief, is this secessionist and reactionary insurgency nesting here in Eritrea.

"As one of the many problems we inherited from the previous administration, this mercenary and reactionary insurgency spent years working to carry out its destructive mission, and with the start of our Revolution it found the perfect opportunity to strengthen its organization and expand its capacity to launch terrorist attacks. Assisted by opponents of the Revolution, along with our internal enemies whose greed has been impacted by the class struggle, and with substantial support from our external enemies, this reactionary secessionist insurgency has grown strong enough to carry out destructive raids.

"In particular, during the time when our resources were stretched to the limit by too many challenges elsewhere, this insurgency gained a high level of material and moral support from reactionary factions as well as imperialist countries. They were almost able to achieve their goal of dominating Eritrea three years ago, when our Revolutionary Army pushed back the insurgency, driving them out of the seven cities they had taken over and forcing them to seek shelter along our border with Sudan in the Sahel Region.

"When Ethiopia was being pulled apart by internal and external conflicts, when our unity and the success of the Revolution were being tested, we needed a quick resolution to the Eritrean insurgency. Our haste resulted in a Revolutionary Army with limited training and limited readiness, so we paid a very high cost to drive the insurgents out of Eritrea. With that in mind, we have limited our combat operations over the last two years in order to rebuild our army, address our shortcomings and prepare a fighting machine that will completely demolish the insurgency once and for all. Towards that end we have also been coordinating with the liberated areas of Eritrea, providing them with needed training and organization.

"A peaceful resolution of the Eritrean problem is unacceptable to the insurgents, and we have undeniable proof of this: they have repeatedly ignored the many invitations we have sent them to discuss the issues and negotiate. We must realize that for terrorists who do not understand the language of peace, we have no choice other than to strike them with overwhelming force. We are compelled to carry out military action that will bring us the desired results once and for all, so we are not fighting because we desire war, but because we are forced to. What we desire is peace, our goal is prosperity.

"Let me get back to your question. Why now? The working people of Ethiopia cannot be at peace when one part of their country is occupied by enemy insurgents, just as when one part of the body is suffering from a painful disease, the person cannot be healthy. Removing the cancer that has been in this region for far too many years is now our top priority.

As you know, we have some breathing room on our other borders, so now is the perfect time to concentrate on the northern front, on Eritrea.

"Today, Siad Barre of Somalia faces growing opposition, our neighbour Sudan is wrestling with serious and persistent internal conflicts, the Arab nations are locked in political disputes because of the Camp David accords, and Iran and Iraq are at war. As a result, the secessionist insurgents can no longer obtain material and moral support from our external enemies. The insurgents are breaking up into factions due to internal conflicts, leaving them disorganized and vulnerable. By contrast, our Revolution has blossomed, growing stronger than ever before, and Socialist groups and progressive organizations all over the world stand in solidarity with our Revolution, while the Eritrean insurgents have been chewed up and spat out by their imperialist collaborators. Now is the perfect time, the perfect opportunity, for us to bury them, to crush them into dust for ever. Am I clear?"

The room is silent.

"Are there any other questions or suggestions?" asks the Chairman.

I have a nagging question that I picked up from a thin book on military tactics by Paret and Shy. I raise my hand and the Chairman points at me.

"Comrade Chairman, guerilla fighting is effective when implemented using hit-and-run tactics carried out by a small mobile force. So when confronted with our large, well-organized army, will the insurgents really all retreat to their mountain stronghold in Nakfa and wait to fight us there? Wouldn't that spell their end?"

"Yes, Comrade Tsegaye, that is a good question," says the Chairman. "What you describe is the first stage of a guerilla insurgency, but it cannot stay in that stage for ever. If they grow beyond a certain size, they are forced to switch to conventional warfare and adopt conventional tactics and strategy, and in broad terms, this is the stage the Eritrean insurgency is at now. It will take great effort and political skill on our part to keep them from sliding back to the guerilla stage. But a fish dies if taken out of water, so we need to strengthen the revolutionary, political and organizational capacity in Asmara to prevent the insurgents from using it as their sanctuary. Does that answer your question?"

His answer is sufficient and I nod.

Another person raises his hand. It is Colonel Wolday Tariku, the well-known counter-insurgency fighter. The Chairman is smiling at Wolday – he respects men of valour.

Wolday gives a military salute. He is even taller when he straightens up to salute, growing upward like a bamboo shoot.

"Comrade Chairman, I have one idea I would like to add." His voice has depth to it.

"Yes, comrade."

Wolday salutes again, which isn't necessary. "As accurately described by Comrade Chairman, every guerilla insurgency has its own dialectical processes and developmental stages. A guerilla force is made up of small groups of combatants that employ surprise tactics like ambushes and small-scale raids. Once its strength and the number of its combatants increases, it will be forced to form a bigger group and fight a conventional war. Unless it does that, it has no hope of victory, and may even begin to fall apart.

"The disputes between the Shabia and Jebha factions of the Eritrean insurgency are not only because of their religious and ethnic differences. It is also a struggle for power.

The Shabia faction of the insurgents pushed the rival Jebha group out of the region because Shabia wants sole control of Eritrea. They want political and military supremacy.

"We also see those rivalries play out in districts and villages over ethnic and clan conflicts. The highlander thinks of himself not as an Eritrean, but as a Hamassien, a Serae or an Akeleguzai. The lowlander thinks of himself as a Semhar, a Barka, an Afar. This drives factionalism within the insurgency. In point of fact, none of the insurgent groups have clear political aims or policies. They are fundamentally ethnic-based organizations.

"Let me go back to what I was saying. The Shabia insurgents have switched to conventional combat tactics and strategy. In fact, because of their internal weakness they must gather their forces together and fight in traditional combat. Most of their fighters are untrained conscripts, young farmers snatched from their fields. The only way to make them fight is at gunpoint. Those who joined the insurgency back in 1975 with the dream of returning to their villages after liberation, they have lost all hope. They are tired of the rough life in the bush and want to go home. If we can allow them that opportunity, Shabia will cease to exist.

"Overall, the morale of the insurgency is in ruins. Their political indoctrination is ineffective. The insurgency does not have the support of the public and so it survives by enforcing its will through the barrel of a gun. At this point, the Eritrean proletariat wants peace.

"The insurgents are also not getting any formal military training these days. Of course there is no better training than combat itself. But peasants are being herded like sheep onto the battlefield, only to end up as food for the vultures. The leaders are spoiled and tyrannical. They are terrorists. As far as sanctuaries go, Shabia is now out of favour with Sudan. Their rival faction, Jebha, is lurking in the background and preparing to retaliate. Nevertheless, Shabia has done well in obtaining equipment, and its logistics and organization are quite efficient.

"Their main strength is the location they've chosen to make their stand. Nakfa is a natural fortress, a mountain stronghold. Once outside their fortifications, they lack the courage to fight and will retreat. We must keep in mind that a deciding factor in combat will be the terrain. Thank you."

With that Wolday gives one more salute and sits down. It is not a bad analysis; he is an expert in his field. I don't envy the seven years he spent fighting the separatist insurgents and earning his fierce reputation.

The Chairman listened carefully and took notes, as usual. Like I said, he is a good listener. He does not automatically dismiss or discard other people's ideas. I think of him as a perpetual student. Yes, a revolution is the best school – it demands that the student stay focused at all times.

"We thank you, comrade," says the Chairman. "With sacrifice and struggle, we can conquer even the obstacles of nature. Any other questions or comments? Yes, Comrade Yeshitla."

Yeshitla Masresha is our version of Suslov, the famous Soviet ideologue. His pointed face looks even more pointed this afternoon. He takes his time when he speaks, making sure his words and sentences are precise and to the point.

"The issue I want to raise," he says, "is regarding propaganda. As accurately stated earlier, a fish will die of natural causes when taken out of water. In other words, we must separate the insurgents from the general public. That is not an easy task. Our propaganda campaign should avoid adventurism and impulsiveness. It must be well planned and well executed.

"While political and organizational activities are necessary, the solution to the Eritrean problem depends primarily on propaganda, and we have the Marxist-Leninist tools to carry that out. But to what end do we apply these modern scientific tools? It should be for the benefit of the working class, the proletariat. We are here for equality, peace, prosperity, justice and democracy. Our propaganda campaign should communicate exactly that, in very clear language. It should also expose the true motives of the insurgency and their anti-people mission, and be used to improve the morale of our own Revolutionary Army.

"We must clearly identify what we want to communicate with our propaganda initiatives, here in Eritrea, throughout Ethiopia, and around the world. Our revolutionary campaign is both national and global. This requires careful planning.

"So far the propaganda we have been making reflects a narrow-minded nationalism. We should replace such emotional appeals with a more analytical approach. Teach class warfare, not class reconciliation. We did not come here to cover up the problem, but to fix it with a lasting solution.

"A previous speaker said we are here to bring peace to the people. Yes, but what kind of peace? We need class peace, not a class truce. We can only achieve that if the proletariat understands and recognizes the true enemies of the working class. I believe our propaganda and our struggle should focus on this. Thank you."

His speech stings me like a nettle. Is he faulting the Ministry of Information? I think Yeshitla is right, in theory. But things can appear simple in theory and yet be difficult to put into practice.

Nobody else has a question or comment.

Before we move to the discussion of the organizational structure, the First Secretary calls up the Security Chief of the Red Star Campaign, Director Betru Tessema, to give us a briefing about personal security.

Everyone seems interested in this topic. I've heard that some Red Star officials are upset because they aren't among those who have been provided with security guards. Are we really at risk? Should we worry about who might be a threat to us? I don't know, I don't think about death. It's a debt each of us owes, and it will come without warning like a thief in the night. *Vaffanculo*, why worry about it? Anyway, the real reason people want armed guards is for the status. It's less about personal security, more about personal importance.

"Comrades, for every action there is an equal and opposite reaction." That is how Betru begins his security briefing. "There are agents in this city, maybe even here among us, who do not want the Red Star Campaign to achieve its goals. That is the heart of our security problem. Since we are all the same people, all Ethiopians, it is hard to tell friend from foe. We spend time together, we eat and drink together, we live together. The situation is complex. Nevertheless, each one of you is here because you were carefully selected for this historic mission. So you must stay alert and aware of your surroundings at all times. Being suspicious is a useful skill here, and part of your job. Remember, the unsuspecting end up the conquered.

"We stand for what is right, but just because we stand for good does not mean we can avoid darkness. Our enemies are watching us, and so we need to watch them. For the Red Star Campaign to succeed, we all need to be spies for the Revolution.

"A few other points on security. At this very moment, our enemies are creating confusion and agitating the public, trying to create chaos in the markets and the economy. The insurgents want to cause a panic so people will join them. Of course, not every Eritrean is an insurgent or a sympathizer, and we must distinguish friend from foe.

"On that point, I have some news. An influential insurgent named Silay Berahi has surrendered. He was the head of internal security for Shabia, a member of their central committee and the commander of one of their brigades. There is much that he knows, and our propaganda unit should exploit him to the maximum."

Betru pauses for a moment, then continues. "But just as we try to turn insurgents to our side, our enemies are trying to infiltrate us. The insurgents will figure out your vulnerability and then exploit it. They believe men from Addis have two weaknesses: women and kitfo." People laugh at this. "Yes comrades, be very selective about the kitfo you eat and the women you eat with." Now people are laughing harder.

"I'm serious," says Betru. "Those are the vulnerabilities: women, sex, drinking, money. People with financial problems, or the disenchanted, they become targets. And if they can't find a vulnerability, they can create one by framing you for some crime or misdeed. Or they will manipulate you in a very subtle way. That's how it is, comrades. So keep what is yours tied down tight, especially your dirty laundry."

Our laughter fades and everyone eyes each other. I'm sure we're all wondering what the other guy's weakness is. Who knows how they will approach me. We take pride in our strengths but give little thought to our weaknesses. It's hard to be that honest with yourself. Is there any sin I wouldn't commit? Is there any sin I haven't committed? I love all the temptations that this short beautiful life offers. Who doesn't? What is the purpose of life, if not happiness?

Back to business. I write the name Silay Berahi in my notebook and circle it. It is a very big name in the Shabia insurgency. Our Revolutionary Army fought him in Eritrea in the late 1970s and knows him well. He's a dedicated fighter and a smart strategist. A man like that deserves respect, even if he's the enemy. I think his defection will demoralize the insurgents, help break their will and speed their downfall. Our good fortune. I start thinking about how to use him in our propaganda.

Next comes a presentation of the campaign's organizational structure, but I'm not giving it my full attention. I'm tired more than bored. That's the problem with long meetings – the mind wanders. I'm also hungry and my mouth is dry.

Thankfully the meeting is almost over, I think, and I try to take some notes. People are discussing the procedural phase of the economic development programme. On it goes. The Production Services group will handle taxes, government-owned farms, industry, commerce, and hydroelectric power. Under the Support Services group will be workers and community affairs, public health, construction, transportation, city administration and the rebuilding of infrastructure. Twelve task forces for twelve disciples. I glance over at the Economic Development chief, Metshafe Daniel. He is worried and rubbing his tummy, undoubtedly cursing the day he was born. This time I share his unhappiness.

5

EVENING IN ASMARA

It is dark out when we leave the meeting hall. Yawning and stretching, everyone hurries off in different directions. My head throbs like an old engine. All I want is to go back to my room, take a cold shower, and fall into bed. Sweat coats my skin and the sensation is not a pleasant one. The cold breathy wind gives me a little bit of energy. It is a moonless night and the North Star is a bright jewel in the dark sky, silhouetting the palms. I'm almost at my car when Solomon Betregiorgis calls to me.

"Tsegaye, where are you going?" he asks.

"Where do you think I'm going after such a marathon meeting? I'm tired and I'm heading back to my shelter station."

Solomon laughs. "You journalists, calling your room a 'shelter station'! What are you going to call your dinner?"

"Performance fuel?"

He laughs again, deep from his belly. "Well now, let's go to my place."

"Some other time. I'm really tired."

"No, no, I want you to meet Silay Berahi, the insurgent

who just surrendered to us. I can't wait to talk to him, he's going to be very valuable to us. Plus I have good whiskey. Two things all journalists love – news and booze."

"You're right, we do like that." My throat is a desert, and I do want to meet Silay. "What else do we like?"

"Women!" Solomon laughs. "But not food. No journalist knows how to eat right. And I'm not a fan of how you present the news either. I'll tell you on the way."

"What do we need to change?"

"The news is too dry. Socialism is not about statistics, it's about people. This many acres of land has been tilled, this many tons of grain has been produced, this many people are literate . . . it's just numbers. Of course you have to report the facts, but there are real flesh-and-blood human beings behind those facts. You're too cold-blooded. The news you broadcast should always have people in it. The inspirational stories you trot out are too vague and generic. They bore me. They should be about real achievements. Come on, get in the car, let's go."

"If the news we present has to be focused on people," I say as I get in his car, "then we need to find some journalists who actually believe in the goodness of mankind."

A couple of aggressive-looking armed guards are in the backseat, with more behind us in another car. Solomon steps on the gas and we accelerate instantly with enough speed to leave my breath behind. Combishtato blurs by, the lights on the buildings streaks of green and yellow. Solomon doesn't stop for red lights. As long as we don't crash, we will be safe – enemy bullets can't catch up with us.

"Look," I continue, "if our propaganda initiatives are to be based on real achievements, then we'll need good communication from everyone. We don't have a crystal ball – we need regular reports from our intelligence agencies, the army, foreign affairs and so on. That's what we need, not more critics."

"Regular reports, that's a great idea, Tsegaye," says Solomon. "I'll get someone on it right away."

"Aren't you tired?" I ask him. He looks relaxed at the wheel, like it was his day off. I want to know the source of his endless energy.

"What else is there to do? The Eritrean problem has taken over my life. Seven years as the Chief of Operations here before the Revolution, and now for another three years under the Derg." He swerves around a corner. "But I'm tired of trying to solve the Eritrean problem. I'm drowning in it."

We cross National Avenue and drive north past Revolution Square and the Mai Jah Jah Fountain to Geza Banda, past the Nyala Hotel and then out towards the airport. The trees, the houses, the streets – they are fleeting shadows as we speed by in the dark.

"Cheer up," I say. "The solution is near."

"It would be nice if the solution gets here before the problem kills me. I'm forty-two. I don't know if my heart can handle the stress of this fast-moving revolution, this race, this marathon." Solomon laughs, but this time his laughter sounds caustic.

"I'm getting to that age too."

"Are you married?"

"I have a fiancée."

"Good for you," he says. "You'll invite us to your wedding then."

"If not for this campaign, I would already be married."

"No worries, the campaign will be over soon. If we do it smart. But . . ."

"But what?" I ask as we speed past the Croce Rossa Cinema.

"We have to be patient, and careful. There are people who would prefer to see Eritrea remain in chaos. For four hundred years, there's always been some kind of war going on here. People are sceptical of peace. Some are opportunists, looking to take advantage of the campaign. That's why I say we need to slow down some, because the problems are very complex."

He makes a U-turn and the tyres squeal. It looks like we're heading back into town, back the way we came.

"People from the heartland," he continues, "they come here and think they have answers for everything, but they only end up making things worse. We have to be careful not to cause more problems than we solve. We're fighting history here."

Solomon makes a few more turns and we arrive at a big house with a large gate.

"We're home now," he announces.

Two soldiers open the gate for us and stand to attention. Solomon drives in at the same high speed and parks next to a large well-lit courtyard.

"I brought you the long way," he says.

"Yes, we took the scenic route."

"I wanted to get some fresh air."

The night air is fragrant. The grounds are planted everywhere with flowers and the landscaping is immaculate.

"So you like to garden?" I ask.

"It's one of my hobbies. I enjoy taking care of the plants if I have a few minutes. And I like to cook. When I get home from work, I put on my apron and head to the kitchen. It relaxes me. Maybe I'll have you over for some wot one night."

"I hope so," I say. "All you can get here is pasta."

"I know, they're the best at pasta. And they do okay with shiro wot too. But their doro wot is lousy. They wait until the end to add the tomato paste, and they use oil instead of butter. Doro wot in oil, can you believe it? I beat them when it comes to stews. You'll see."

We walk into his house together. It looks like a small palace, with red Persian carpets, elegant blue curtains and crystal chandeliers. Solomon points me to a bathroom where I splash some water on my face and wash my hands.

When I come back, Metshafe Daniel, Colonel Wolday Tariku, Director Betru Tessema, and three men I don't know are in the living room. Metshafe is making everyone laugh. He's probably telling funny stories about his time at the United Nations – he loves entertaining people with his tales of the UN. Everyone is drinking whiskey and I'm thirsty too.

I find the drinks trolley and pour myself half a glass of Seko whiskey on ice, then head over to Solomon.

"Which one is the guest you promised would be here?" I ask him. "Which one is Silay?" Other than Colonel Wolday, none of the men look like fighters.

"He said he would be coming with a friend and might be late."

"Man or woman?" I ask.

"Woman."

"Ah, he's already enjoying the dividends of peace and settling down."

"Silay? No, he's a hell-raiser," says Solomon. "Courageous, but a hell-raiser. Quick-tempered."

"So you're saying he's Eritrean."

"Not all Eritreans are quick to anger, Tsegaye. I know we think they'll tell us everything to our face, but that's not really how they are. Especially these days, it's hard to know what is in their hearts. People here are wary."

I look again at the three men I don't know and realize I do know them. I interviewed them on TV after they defected from the insurgency. Was that one year ago? Or two? I can't remember when I did that interview. Memory lapses are a bad sign for a journalist. I hope I remember the important things.

But I do remember these guys. Fitwi Berhe, a tall, handsome young man, had been an important member of Jebha and part of their internal security team. Zeray Haleka had run their political indoctrination programme. He's a young man too, thin with light-brown skin, and he's looking down at the floor, as if he's shy. Mesfin Tsirui was a big shot in the Shabia insurgency, definitely one of the wild ones, and cunning. All three look educated and very polished, not at all like former insurgents. Then again, why should they look different to everyone else? Insurgents are not aliens.

I go over to greet them and they remember me – we shake hands and hug like old friends.

"You know each other?" Solomon asks.

"I interviewed them on TV after they defected to us." I turn to them. "I think I gave you a hard time."

"It was worth it," says Fitwi with a smile. He speaks Amharic with only a slight Tigrinya accent.

"You three had a lot to say, but it made for a good show," I tell them.

"It made us famous," says Zeray.

"The whole country appreciated what you did," I say.

"Old news! We're old news," says Mesfin. "Silay Berahi, he's the big star now." Mesfin is drunk, and maybe Fitwi too. Probably all three were out drinking before they got here.

Colonel Wolday joins us and begins talking with the three defectors.

"Hey, Mr TV!" I turn around and it's Metshafe. I'd rather keep listening to Wolday and the three defectors sharing war stories, but I don't want to be rude.

"Hi, Mr Economy," I say.

"What's the news?" he asks. The lights in the room reflect off his bald head and glasses. His little eyes dart around.

"We were both in the meeting today, so you know as much as I do," I tell him.

"The average person in the street knows more than you journalists." He laughs, but it seems forced.

"How so?" I ask.

"You journalists, all you do is shove a microphone in someone's face and ask, 'What do you think?' You broadcast other people's ideas like you came up with them. If you could just accurately report the facts, that would be so much better. Instead, you twist people's words. If that's journalism, then forget it."

This is the usual attack on journalism. It's not worth a response. Everyone wants media attention, but then they get angry if you say one word they don't like. People treat us like wedding singers, like our only job is to sing the songs the audience wants to hear. It's infuriating.

"I'm sorry that journalism is not an exact science like economics," I say and gulp down more whiskey.

"Have I upset you?"

"Not at all."

"Nobody wants a feud with the media," he says. "You people fight ugly."

"If only we did fight."

"The media is a powerful weapon, you just don't how to

use it right." Classic Metshafe: flattering and annoying at the same time.

I take another sip of my whiskey.

"What did you think of today's meeting?" he asks.

I don't hesitate. "It was educational. Now I understand the challenges we face."

"Really? I wish it were that clear to me. I guess I'm just not that smart."

In diplomatic lingo he's suggesting that I'm the idiot. Metshafe spent years stationed at different embassies and at the United Nations. He knows how to look at ease standing with a glass in his hand, knows how to greet people. Everything is smooth. His wardrobe is chosen to fit the occasion and the weather. If there's a hint of rain, he'll have an overcoat and an umbrella, rain boots and a scarf. I've never visited his home in Addis, but they say he takes off his shoes twice before he goes inside, just to be sure. I've been to Metshafe's office and it's cleaner than an operating room. If he spots a spilled drop of coffee or a cigarette butt, he gets so angry that the few strands of hair he has left all stand up straight. When his co-workers want to get back at him, they go to his office and sprinkle cigarette ash on the carpet. He's skilled at finding fault in other people's work. When he has to review or approve something, he'll complain about how he's wasting valuable time fixing other people's mistakes. Nevertheless, he is an expert, and he does actually know what he's doing.

"I appreciate all the praise you heap on me," I say. "How about you? What's your take on the meeting?"

"Well, comrade, I love my country, but if I said anything they'd call me a reactionary, a counter-revolutionary."

"What are you talking about?"

"Well, comrade – and I hope you are my comrade – one campaign will not resolve a twenty-year problem. And the Eritrean problem is not simply an internal Ethiopian issue. It's the kind of thing that demands real diplomatic engagement with other countries in the region, sound economic development here at home, astute political messaging, and cooperation across the board. There's no easy solution. Sure, we can launch a big campaign and everyone will scramble around for a while, but that creates its own problems."

I refill my glass with whiskey while Metshafe keeps talking. "When you move almost a thousand trucks from the heartland to Eritrea for the campaign, what does that do to the economy back in Addis? Remember, it's harvest time there. I wouldn't be surprised if there were shortages of bread and grain. And what do you think happens when we focus all our attention and assets here on Eritrea? Development elsewhere stops. That means unemployment. And then what? I don't know how you build a socialist society with an army of the unemployed."

Now I really am angry with him. "What kept you quiet during the meeting?" I ask. "The stage was open to everyone. Why weren't you honest?"

"You're joking, right?" Metshafe says.

"No, I'm not. I'm serious. We need openness and honesty from experts like you. The Chairman always says that he wants people to be frank and truthful with him." Metshafe just stares at me, so I continue. "The Revolution isn't only about the leaders and the Derg. Everyone who makes it his Revolution has equal ownership. Any Ethiopian who claims his Revolution, claims his country, is equal to every other Ethiopian."

Metshafe looks like he has something to say, but I keep

talking. "No, no, listen to me, Metshafe, you can't walk away from the fire after starting it. What will happen if experts and intellectuals fail to participate, refuse to contribute? You can't stand around debating responsibility, like the United Nations, you have to get in and participate, not wash your hands of it like Pontius Pilate. And, comrade, the Eritrean problem is not what you think it is. We are not rushing in. It's been strangling the country for eight years, and we can't keep on waiting until we all run out of air and die. Payment is due, a solution must be found. And the only language the separatist insurgents understand is violence. You can't talk to them in any dialect other than war. So it's blood for peace. The young people of this nation are willing to pay that price, and we should be grateful for that."

Solomon walks up to us. "What are you two arguing about?" he asks.

"Nothing," Metshafe and I answer at the same time, as if we had rehearsed it.

"Aren't you surprised?" Solomon asks and points over to Colonel Wolday and the three former insurgents. They're having a lively conversation, the three men looking up at the taller Wolday, who stands straight as a pillar. I'm not sure what is surprising though.

"Aren't you surprised?" Solomon asks again. "Not that long ago they were shooting at each other, and now here they are drinking together. Fitwi led the cell that controlled the road from Mendefera to Asmara, captured and killed a lot of our men. He made us bleed. Zeray, when he ran their political arm, recruited kids to join the insurgents in the bush and become fighters. And Mesfin planned attacks here in Asmara. Colonel Wolday fought all three of them, but now they stand around talking like it's nothing."

Solomon keeps talking too. "Do you know that in Asmara people call Wolday 'Colonel Glass'? You see, if it wasn't for him, there wouldn't be any glass bottles. We'd be drinking everything from tin cans, even areke. Because when the insurgents captured Dekemhare, the trucks carrying sand couldn't get out to the glass factory, so production stopped. Then Wolday started riding on top of the trucks with an AK-47 in each hand, so the sand made it to the factory and we had bottles again!"

I start to say something but Solomon continues, gesturing again to Wolday and the others. "It's true that we've made some mistakes, but even so, I don't think any other revolution has been as compassionate as the Ethiopian Revolution." He turns to me. "Tsegaye, why don't you do a show on the former insurgents and Wolday?"

"Good idea," I say. "It could counter Shabia's propaganda that any insurgent who surrenders to us is tortured and murdered." I can already picture the title sequence: "The Merciful Revolution".

Metshafe wipes his bald head with his handkerchief. "Do you really think these people have stopped hating us?" he asks quietly. "I don't buy it. Yesterday they were hunting and killing us, and today they believe in our Revolution? No, they're just waiting for the right opportunity to strike again."

"What choice do we have, other than to believe them?" Solomon says. "The greater mistake is to assume they can't be trusted. We have to be patient. Building trust takes time, but it is our responsibility to make it so that the next generation can live together without questioning each other's motives. It is outside forces that have created such distrust among us. The Eritrean problem had a historical beginning, and it will have a historical end."

I don't understand what Solomon is referring to, so I ask him what he means.

"Eritrea was under Italian occupation for sixty years," he says, "until Italy lost World War II. Then the British took over, which started the next wave of conflict. And then when the British gave up Eritrea, they left behind some political time bombs that would eventually explode, one by one."

Solomon loves talking about Eritrea. If you let him, he'll lecture you for hours about its history. So he tells us about Britain's plan to hold on to parts of Eritrea, or to at least maintain influence, by claiming that Ethiopia wasn't up to the task of managing it and playing up ethnic and religious differences. Then the Arab countries got involved, trying to secure their grip on the Red Sea and its valuable shipping lanes for their oil. But all those efforts failed to overcome the long history of a people who share a common past, and Eritrea once again became a province of Ethiopia.

I take a drink of my whiskey as Solomon continues to hold forth about how the Arab nations supported the separatists even after Eritrea was reunited with Ethiopia. Egypt especially wanted to gain access to the source of the Nile. The Ethiopian monarchy's handling of the situation in Eritrea only made matters worse, and soon several armed opposition groups sprouted there. From these, Jebha emerged as the most powerful and took over in parts of Eritrea. It was really just its tail that was in Eritrea, though – its head was in Arab countries. Then one of Britain's political time bombs exploded as conflicts broke out between the different ethnic groups in Jebha, along with tensions between the Christians and Muslims, and personality clashes between Jebha's leaders. One of those leaders, Salah Sabeh, got driven out of Jebha and founded a rival militia, Shabia.

The conflict between Jebha and Shabia played out in the Eritrean bush until the Ethiopian Revolution in 1974. The insurgents took advantage of the chaos of that year to seize control of most of Eritrea. Jebha and Shabia appeared to be anti-feudal and anti-imperialist, so the revolutionary government initially took a conciliatory approach towards them, but the insurgents saw this as a sign of weakness. Could Ethiopia have both the Revolution and Eritrea? We got no help from the outside: the United States announced an arms embargo, the Soviet Union was waiting to see what kind of ideology the Revolution would embrace, and our neighbouring countries – long jealous of Ethiopia and her resources – were like hyenas circling a wounded antelope. By 1975, the only places in Eritrea still under government control were Asmara and parts of Massawa – Jebha and Shabia were in charge everywhere else.

Everyone is gathered around Solomon now. He is not the kind of person who talks just to make noise. When he speaks, it is from the heart, and people naturally gravitate to him.

"And by 1978 it looked like only a matter of time before Asmara and Massawa would fall too," he says. "The insurgents were within seven miles of Asmara and had us surrounded. They were suffocating us, not letting anything in. No food, no water, no fuel. We were running out of bread, almost out of grain. People were breaking up their furniture to use it as firewood. Asmara was silent at night, except for gunshots on the outskirts. When those stopped, the city was like a graveyard. Everyone could hear the angel of death fluttering her wings and whispering to us. You could smell the death, the destruction. No smoke came from the factories, nobody was working in the fields. The marketplace was open, but nobody had anything worth buying, just empty cans and cactus. Children cried, mothers wailed. The old men sat on their steps and wondered what they could do, but there was nothing they could do."

Yet Asmara did not fall. We all know this, of course, but Solomon was there, so we listen to him tell it again. He tells us how some people in Asmara were rooting for the insurgents while others were ready to fight to the death. Some said it was wiser to welcome in the victors, whichever group that might be. After centuries of war in Eritrea, suspicion and opportunism are a natural response. But Asmara was saved by the Revolutionary Army, marching under the banner of "Revolutionary Ethiopia or Death". The insurgents who were about to enter Asmara as conquerors were instead forced to flee into the bush when the army arrived. Since then, both the Jebha and Shabia factions of the insurgency have continued to bedevil the people of Eritrea.

Solomon finishes his lecture on the history of Eritrea, but he's not quite done holding court. "So in the end, what do we learn from all this? It is a fact that much of the trouble in this region comes from outside influences, and the Eritrean people must know that. How long are we going to endure fighting in our own country that is instigated by outside forces? We must defuse the sectarian time bombs the colonialists planted. We can only accomplish that goal when there is trust between us, when we open our hearts to each other."

A man and a woman walk into the room holding hands, and I stop paying any attention to Solomon.

6

FIAMMETTA UNDER THE NORTH STAR

The man walking into the room must be the defector, Silay
Berahi, but my eyes are drawn to the woman, an Eritrean
beauty who could break King David's heart. She's wearing
a long dress with a shawl draped loosely over her shoulders.
Around her neck is a black velvet choker with a gold star
of Solomon. Her dark hair tumbles down and rests on her
shoulders, dancing with her as she moves.

She looks across the room and I follow her gaze to Colonel
Wolday Tariku. The two of them glare at each other, a little
wildcat facing off against a big leopard. They aren't clawing
at each other, but their eyes tell me they are locked in
combat just the same. I don't know what's going on there,
but it's not my business. She is lovely to look at, a real
northern beauty.

Solomon Betregiorgis hugs Silay and takes him around
for introductions. I end up standing with Wolday, but I eye
the northern beauty and edge away from him. I'm not that
short, but next to him I look tiny.

When Silay hears Wolday's name, his ears perk up like a
surprised rabbit. He eyes Wolday carefully, then greets him

in Tigrigna. "How do you do, Colonel?" And with that he gives Wolday a big hug.

Silay doesn't look like a famous warrior. But what is a fighter supposed to look like? I'm not sure I know. Some I've met have been short, others fat, and a few too shy at parties to look you in the eye. Silay is tall and lean, and there is something arrogant in the way he holds himself. His eyes are small, his hair thin and on its way out, but he knows how to dress with his three-piece suit.

My gaze returns to the northern beauty. I keep catching her looking at me with her seductive eyes. She's probably wondering where she's seen me before – on television, no doubt. People think they know me from seeing me on the news all the time. Then we talk and they realize I'm a stranger to them. It can be amusing, but usually it puts me in a bad mood. People recognize me, but they don't have any idea who the real Tsegaye is. Fame is slippery that way.

Silay is still admiring Colonel Wolday. "Well, you're some kind of devil, aren't you," he says.

"You're a devil too," says Wolday.

"We tried everything to get rid of you. You must have nine lives. Remember when we had you surrounded in Dekemhare? Somehow you escaped. It's like bullets can't hit you."

"Maybe it's because I'm skinny," says Wolday.

"You're certainly brave. An AK-47 in each hand, firing at us as you drove right through our ambushes? I hated you, but I also admired you." Silay talks fast and makes quick little gestures with his hands. "It's good that's all over, and that we're here tonight, alive and well."

"Agreed," says Wolday. He really does tower over everyone. "I respected you as much as I hated you. I thought we had you cornered in A'la, but somehow you broke through our lines. And when I saw how you destroyed Dekemhare, my hometown, I swore I would punish you."

I can feel some tension in the room now, and Silay is frowning.

"I'm ready to make amends," he says. "The past is the past. What matters now is the future."

Solomon quickly ushers Silay over to me and introduces us. Silay studies me like he's a photographer. Then he sighs. "Why do you say on TV that insurgents who defect are like stray dogs crawling back home? We are not dogs. We are human beings. Defectors have it hard enough already. Separatist sympathizers spit on us in the street, in bars. The insurgency's radio station calls us traitors and selfish cowards. The government says they welcome us back, but I doubt they will ever really trust us. And then you journalists compare us to stray dogs. What does that even mean? Once a traitor, always a traitor?"

"We should probably use a different term," I say.

"Find one now."

"Well, we used to call you 'desert foxes' but, as you point out, you're not animals. Maybe 'peaceful returnees'? Or should it be 'infiltrators'?"

Silay looks like I just slapped him in the face. "What did you say?"

"Ah, you know I'm just kidding."

He stares at me with his sharp little eyes, like he's trying to get into my head. Then he goes over and joins the three other stray-dog defectors.

Director Betru touches my back. "What did you say to make him so upset?"

Betru has a steady smile. It makes him seem detached

from what's going on around him. That's no accident – it gives him a chance to observe how others are behaving, to study them.

"I asked if it was better to call him a returnee or an infiltrator."

"Now why would you ask him that?"

"I was trying to be funny. But why do you care?"

"No reason. But that woman he came with has her eye on you. Go and talk to her."

"Didn't you tell us in the security briefing to not approach women here?" I say.

He leans close to me. "You don't want to miss your chance, do you?"

I go over to the northern beauty. I'm bored with fighting men and their tough talk, so it's a nice change of scenery.

"Why are you standing by yourself?" I ask her. "And what can I get you to drink?"

"Beer with Sprite."

I raise my eyebrows. "Beer with Sprite? I've never heard of that."

"It's a beautiful drink, really." Or I think that's what she said – she used Tigrigna.

"And you're a beautiful woman," I say in Tigrigna.

"You know Tigrigna?" Her hair moves along with her words, like it's talking too.

"Yes, a little."

"Let me hear you say 'ka'."

"Ha."

"Say 'ah'."

"Uh."

"No," she says, switching to Amharic. "You definitely

cannot speak Tigrigna, I'll swear to that." She laughs and her teeth are like Red Sea pearls.

"It's a hard language, you know, a real throat-scratcher," I say.

"We made it that way on purpose. We don't want you to like it."

"Okay, but can you say 'meto'?"

"Moto," she says.

"Now 'ante'."

"Antay."

"Nope, you can't speak Amharic." I laugh and go to get her drink.

On my way back Solomon stops me. He looks upset.

"What's going on?" I ask.

"My phone is ringing every minute." He never shows fatigue, only annoyance. "And the Massawa Festival committee is giving me a hard time," he says. "They want me to call them at ten tonight."

"That's late. I hope your heart doesn't fall asleep."

"We need to build two tukuls on the beach there for the festival, but they can't find enough wood for the walls or straw for the roofing. They claim they're working around the clock on it."

"So why not give up on tukuls? Use canvas tents instead."

"We'll find the materials somewhere, even if we have to airfreight them to Massawa."

"Good luck with that," I say. "I need to go and deliver this drink to that woman."

"So kind of you to take charge of public relations. You're such a professional. Go on then, keep her entertained."

"I think your phone is ringing. Oh, and can we turn on the television in a few minutes?" I ask.

"What programme is on?"

"Mine. It's about Asmara."

"Wow, you work fast. Yes, let's have people watch it."

With that Solomon runs to answer the phone. He runs even inside his own house.

I return to the northern beauty.

"Hey there, Tigrigna," I say. "Will you teach me some more? My name is Tsegaye Hailemaryam."

I take a sip of her drink before I hand it to her. It actually does taste good.

"I know you from TV," she says. "Maybe you can help me with my Amharic." Her Amharic is fine, in fact, just a little accented.

"What's my student's name?" I ask.

"Fiammetta Gilay." She can tell from my expression that I'm surprised. "What?"

"Fiammetta sounds foreign."

"It's Italian."

"What does it mean?"

"Little fire."

"Really? I'd better keep my distance then."

"Why?" she asks.

"They say angels pick our names, and yours is dangerous. Burning is the worst way to die. I hope you're not like your name."

"Oh, I am, I swear," she says with a smile. "I was like a fire when I was a child. Crying, breaking things. I gave my parents a hard time. I refused to sleep on my own and I'd cry all night long. If they put me in their bed, I'd cry if I heard them talking to each other. Right away, they knew Fiammetta was the right name for me."

"And now?"

"I'm different – I'm a big fire now. But not with people I love. For someone I love, I am nothing but milk and honey."

"And the someone you love, what kind of person is he?"

"Hard as rock, hot as lava, sweet as sugar." She laughs again.

"Really?"

"No, I'm just kidding. I can't tell you my secrets yet."

"Why not?" I ask.

"Because they're secrets, moron."

"Well, maybe someday." We each take a sip of our drinks. "You know, I think you should try a different name."

"Why?" she asks.

"Fiammetta is a foreign name. In Asmara everything has a foreign name, leftovers from the Italians. It can give people a foreign perspective, and that's a problem."

"If you don't like Fiammetta, call me Fana."

We stand in silence with our drinks. I can tell she has lost interest in the conversation. No surprise – people here avoid politics. They're tired of it or are scared to talk about it. But I don't think they can escape it. Sooner or later they will have to decide where they stand. With the Red Star Campaign starting, there won't be any more middle ground.

But I don't want to push her. Strange beauty, strange name, strange drink. A rare opportunity, so I ask for her number. She gives me her home and office phone numbers, no hesitation.

"You move fast," she says.

"Life is short."

"Are you part of all this confusion?" she asks.

What an odd question. I guess she means the campaign. "You call it confusion?"

"What else is it? Asmara is in total disarray. Seriously."

She's about to ask me another question when Silay announces in a loud voice, "Let me show everyone what Fitwi Berhe did to me!"

Silay takes off his jacket, then his tie and waistcoat. Everyone stares at him, wondering what he's doing. Fitwi is standing next to him and they both look angry. Silay unbuttons his shirt, pulls it up, then turns around. His back looks like a farm ploughed by a madman, crisscrossed with ragged scars, the evidence of lashes that tore through skin into bone. He pulls his shirt back down and starts to button it.

"The scars on my back are the marks of how progressive Jebha is, how humane! Isn't that right, Fitwi? He was the one who ordered my whipping, and did some of it himself. Why? Because I was accused of infiltrating Jebha and tortured for being a government spy or a CIA agent. Did I cry when they poured boiling water on me? Did I scream? No, but I wished for death. I prayed for it, but it didn't happen. And since then, I'm not afraid of death. Jebha taught me that."

Fitwi smiles. "If not for me, you would have been killed."

"I'm so grateful for your humanitarian act," says Silay. His tone is acid.

Fitwi flicks the air with his hand. "Look, we had to confirm your loyalty somehow, and force is one way to do that. The survival of Jebha was no small thing, it needed to be protected from infiltrators. And we had good reason to be suspicious of you."

"Me? Silay Berahi?"

"Yes, you, Silay Berahi." Fitwi is resolute. "You were a district administrator for the Haile Selassie regime. You were a close friend of the Shabia commander Isayas Afeworki. And that is not all. You introduced Isayas to Richard Copeland, the CIA spy in Kagnew Station. Given all that, did you expect us to welcome you with open hearts and open arms?" Fitwi pauses, but Silay is silent. "Look, back then, we believed in our cause. That's over now. We both left the insurgency, left it to the reactionaries. Now we need to cooperate and work together. The scars on your back are history, and we need to forget history." Fitwi takes a gulp of his whiskey. He's still angry. "I fought against the Revolution and shed the blood of the Ethiopian people. That's what I regret. But whipping you? My conscience is clear on that, Silay Berahi Dejazmatch."

Everyone starts talking at once, mostly about family history – Silay and the three other former insurgents are all descendants of the Dejazmatch family. I learn from their conversation that all four of their fathers were members of the Unionist Party, not separatists at all. In fact, Silay claims his father invented the slogan, "Ethiopia or death!" These guys are a monumental insult to their heritage. The sadness of our mother country, bearing children who bite the breast that nursed them. A mother's womb is many colours, and no two siblings are alike.

Now Silay turns to Mesfin. "After escaping Jebha, I joined Shabia. Who do you think welcomed me there? It was Mesfin. I showed him the scars on my back, but still he didn't trust me. There's no honour among insurgents. They held me for a month, investigated me. Then one day Mesfin called me into his office and made me empty my pockets. He went through my belongings and picked out a photo, asked me who it was. I said it was my mother. He said, 'From now on, Shabia is your mother,' and ripped the photo into pieces. He held up another photo and asked, 'Who is she?' I told him it was my girlfriend. 'From now on, Shabia is your only lover.' He tore up the photo. Then he took my necklace and my gold ring.

'The medals of Shabia are your jewellery now.' He took my clothing and gave me a burlap wrap. They had me split wood and bake bread. They wouldn't let me bathe, and I itched from lice. It was like dying while still being alive, you don't feel like you are anything anymore.

"Then after a month the military training started. Mesfin followed me every day, my shadow. We marched for a day, a week, two weeks. Never enough food, never enough water. Marching marching. Hot days, rainy days, night or day, just marching, marching. Have you ever fallen asleep while walking? I marched that way for miles. You watch your friends stagger, watch them fall. You can't pick them up, you can barely carry yourself, so you leave them for the hyenas. You march on. You wish you were in their place, dead. Death is all you think about, but life refuses to leave you. It fights you for its own survival.

"Then one day they take you to where they execute prisoners. You dig a ditch and you tie a prisoner to a tree, bind him tight. You can't avoid looking in his eyes, you have to. You tell yourself death will be a relief for him, that he won't suffer anymore if he's dead. You tell yourself that because you want the same thing for yourself. You want to die but you do not die. You are ordered to bayonet the prisoner. Your commanders are looking into your eyes, you know that they're testing your strength and courage. You stab him, kill him, bury him. You are no longer fully human. You have killed one of your own to survive."

Silay has captivated everyone, like an actor on the stage.

"Mesfin, isn't that exactly how it happened?" asks Silay.

Oh damn, I forgot about Fiammetta, the same way I hope death forgets about me.

"Can I get you another drink?" I ask her.

"No, no," she says, shaking her head. The happy look she had before is gone, and she seems lost in thought.

In one corner Director Betru is laughing with some others. He pretends he's not listening to the rest of the room, but I know he is. Colonel Wolday is sitting on the couch, looking lost in his own thoughts. Solomon is already back from his phone call. He probably cut it short because he hates missing out on conversations at a party.

"Why did you defect?" Metshafe Daniel is quizzing Silay.

"Wow," says Silay. "You shouldn't question why I'm here. You should welcome me as a brother, don't you think?"

"Welcome, then," says Metshafe. "But still, why are you here?"

"Why am I here? I don't think I understand your question."

"What I mean" says Metshafe, "is that you were a member of Shabia's Central Committee, in charge of their internal security. You ran the city of Dekemhare for them, and were the head of their southern command. You had a powerful and influential position. So, why did you come back to us?"

"You're right," says Silay. "I loved Shabia like my own mother, and I served her in good faith. I bled for her. But eventually I realized something. We didn't really have a legitimate reason for fighting and dying. It was for power, really, for personal profit. We Eritreans are no different than the rest of the Ethiopian people. The sixty years we spent under Italian colonialism isn't anything we should be proud of. It didn't make us any more civilized. If we go to the Eritrean countryside, our farmers are illiterate and backward, the same as any Ethiopian farmer. You cannot write a true history that proves Eritrea is different from Ethiopia. We can claim Ethiopia colonized Eritrea, but it's just not the case. And if it's not, then there's no reason to fight."

I take a sip of my whiskey and Silay continues with his analysis. "The arguments about which is the true progressive movement, Shabia or Jebha – forget all that. It's just a racket to raise money from outsiders, a tin cup to go begging with. The conflict between Shabia and Jebha is not ideological, and it never has been ideological. I know because I lived it and I traded on it myself. The origin of the conflict is religion, ethnicity, highlander versus lowlander. And what did those conflicts cause? The atrocities of the 1973 war between Shabia and Jebha. All you heartlanders had to do was wait over the border in Gondar and watch us tear each other apart. We had our slogans, our cries for self-determination, but they didn't mean anything. Or they didn't mean the same thing for the Woreyu, for the Akeleguzay, for Hamassein, for the Barka, for the Sahel, for the Afar. It was pointless."

My whiskey is almost gone, but Silay still has more to say to Metshafe. "Now, my friend, once you realize that, you can no longer survive in the insurgency, in Shabia or Jebha. Once your heart isn't in it anymore, you get the hell out of there fast. Or you die."

Silay turns to me. "But for the love of God, please don't call us stray dogs who've come crawling back home." He's still angry about that.

"When can I interview you?" I ask him.

"Are you sure you want to interview an 'infiltrator'?" His voice is thick with sarcasm.

"How about tomorrow?"

"I'll be there."

Metshafe Daniel continues with his probing. "You say there's no real purpose to the insurgency other than power and profit. But there is: the Arab countries want to make the Red Sea their private lake. That's the real source of the Eritrean problem. That and you thinking the rest of us Ethiopians are a bunch of ignorant donkeys. Donkeys that you, as cosmopolitan Eritreans, should be able to herd. Now, you told us why you came back to us. But why did you join the insurgency in the first place?"

"Stop trying to do my job," I tell Metshafe.

"I want to hear it directly from him before you screw it up tomorrow."

"I joined the insurgency to save my life," says Silay. "It wasn't the call of the Eritrean motherland, or thinking liberation was at hand, or the corruption of the monarchy. None of that nonsense. Terror made me flee into the bush. There were massacres then, the government forces would kill anyone. They thought every Eritrean kid was a separatist, an insurgent, so they wanted to eliminate us. Why should I die hiding under a table? Better to join the insurgents and die fighting. You people are your own worst enemy."

"True," says Solomon. "Some people want to keep the country in chaos, because it serves their interests. It covers up their theft, their corruption, even their adultery. They are among us, and we're going to have to deal with them. We have to get people to believe there is justice, there are laws, and equality. If we can do that, then we can solve all the other issues. I'm telling you the truth: our biggest problem is a people problem."

"Let me tell you a story," continues Solomon. "There was a couple in a town here. The husband was a rich businessman and the wife very attractive. A government official, whose name I won't mention, approached the wife, but she wasn't interested in him. So he had her husband arrested. Still the woman would not budge. Realizing his failure, the official freed the businessman from jail, though of course only after extracting a large bribe from him. Shortly after that, he began to fear that the businessman would expose his corruption, so he had the poor man put back in prison for a second time."

Solomon's stories are never short. "Within a few days the businessman was nowhere to be found. The wife looked everywhere for him, visited every prison in the region. Some officials took advantage of her by asking for money in exchange for telling her where her husband was being held. Some told her that he had been sent to the Ogaden Front to fight against Somalia, others said he had joined the insurgents in the bush, and still others said he was in Alem Bekagn Prison in Addis Ababa. She travelled to all those places but her husband wasn't there. She spent so much money searching for him that she went broke. She was despondent. Finally she came to me and explained her unfortunate situation and pleaded with me to help her. I investigated and then told her what I found: her husband had died in prison. I apologized to her and told her how sorry I was. She started crying, not with sadness or happiness, but with relief because she finally knew the truth. She asked if I thought she could still observe the mourning period, still perform the arba, and I told her she could do whatever she thought was right. And I tell you that hers is not an isolated case. There are others that are similar, or even worse. But is it right to disparage the Revolution because of such miscarriages of justice? I don't think so. It's not fair to blame the Revolution for mistakes made by a few traitors, a few selfish officials. And that time has passed. These days no-one gets sent to jail without proper evidence."

"So we all hope," says Metshafe.

We stand there holding our drinks. Metshafe turns to me and whispers, "I do not trust that man."

"Which one?" I ask.

"The stray dog." He means Silay.

"Why not?"

"I don't know. I just don't trust him."

"That's your suspicious nature," I say. "Never mind other people, you don't even trust your own body. By the way, how's your blood pressure?"

"Today at lunch I went and got a reading. You know my hypertension . . ."

"And?"

"Sky high," says Metshafe.

"Really?"

"Leave me alone, man. Some military types, when you tell them the task they want done in three days will take at least three weeks, they take out a massive revolver and put it on the table and growl at you. What happens then? You get stressed out and your blood pressure goes through the roof. Don't you think this campaign will probably kill me? I don't have enough to retire yet."

It is time for my *Palms of Peace* programme so I go over to the television and turn it on. The nightly news covers a flood, a small plane crash and several government meetings. Next is my programme. There are a few ill-timed cuts, but it's not too bad. The first to congratulate me is Fiammetta Gilay.

"So you liked it?" I say.

"Yes, it's very well done, for sure." When she says "yes" it's almost like a cat purring. Silay is looking at us from across the room. He is giving us the evil eye and I don't care for it.

Solomon comes over. "*Palms of Peace*, that was good. It helps us see the Eritrean problem in a new light, a new spirit that—" Before Solomon can finish, Fitwi Berhe crashes to the floor with a loud thud. Everyone rushes over to him. His glass is in pieces and his drink is all over him. He isn't dead, just drunk to the core.

Metshafe leans into me and whispers, "The penalty for his guilty conscience." Metshafe isn't exactly sober himself.

"Please, friend, don't say things like that."

"Why not?" asks Metshafe.

"You have no idea how these guys suffered, how they were tortured. We can't comprehend it, so we shouldn't judge it. What would you have done if you grew up here in Eritrea? If all your friends went off into the bush to fight like men? Would you have stayed behind in the kitchen with your mother, hiding underneath her apron?"

"Give me a break," says Metshafe. "Yesterday they were terrorists, so why should we trust them today? If they hadn't got into trouble with their superiors, they never would have defected to us and—"

"Stop it. Mistrust and hatred aren't going to get us any-where."

It's late and the whiskey is soaking my brain. It's been a long day. Solomon goes off for his call with the Massawa Festival committee. Wolday is getting up to leave too. He hasn't been happy tonight – he didn't have much to say and mostly kept himself company with his drink. He comes over to say goodbye to me.

"You really know Asmara," I say. "Could you take me around, show me the town?"

"I have to leave tomorrow," he says.

"To where?"

"Afabet, to the front."

"When will you be back?"

"After we win, unless I die there."

"You won't die, you're a hero. I hope to get out there soon myself, to cover the military offensive. So I'll see you in Afabet, or maybe Nakfa – I definitely won't go there with anyone else." With that I give him a kiss on each cheek. Of course, I have to stand on my tiptoes to reach that high.

"Don't worry, Tsegaye, victory will be ours." He bends to give me a hug, then leaves.

I turn and look at Fiammetta, the northern beauty, and a smile comes slowly to her face, like the evening moon rising.

"I hope we'll meet again," I tell her.

"I'm sure we will. Asmara is a small city."

"Will you teach me Tigrigna?"

"Yes, but not for free," she says.

"I'll pay whatever price you name."

"But what if you're a moron? Then it will cost you more."

"With a teacher like you, I'll be smart," I say.

Silay comes over to us.

"Tomorrow, the interview, okay?" I ask him.

"Yes, tomorrow," he says. "As long as you don't mention anything about stray dogs."

Tomorrow will be another long day, and then more long days will follow. Tonight, though, the moon is bright and inviting, the air cool and fragrant, all under the North Star.

Do you remember me? If not, that's fine.

In the beginning was the word, the word was the author, and the author was the word.

Tsegaye is asleep now, but his story continues.

Life does not stay still – it's always moving, weaving together one existence with another to make its web.

7

PUBLIC SAFETY

Tuesday, December 29, 1981

Director Betru Tessema is restless. He leaves Solomon Betregiorgis's party and goes back to his office. He spends most of his days and many of his nights in the Public Safety building. His office does not in any way resemble a regular office, but is more like a rich man's living room with a black couch big enough for two people to sleep on. Betru frequently stretches out on the couch and stares up at the ceiling, as if the enemy's movements are sketched on it. When he's in the bathroom shaving, it is not his round and well-fed face that he sees in the mirror, but organizational charts of insurgent spy cells. He gets so engrossed in the diagrams he forgets he's shaving and cuts his face. He promises himself he will pay more attention next time, but it happens more often than he likes to admit. For some reason he refuses to use an electric shaver. He prefers a regular razor with blades, probably because it gives him a very clean and close shave.

When Director Betru arrives at the Public Safety building, the civilians as well as the military people stand to attention.

Even though it is night, there's no office with its lights off or its door closed. Nobody leaves without first getting his permission. They all stay by their desks, cussing, yawning, dozing off, drinking enough coffee to cause heartburn. Exhausted, they smoke cigarettes to stay awake while they write reports they may be asked to present to him at a moment's notice. They all hate him. He's devoted to the job and demands his team be as well. He cares more for competence than personality – he likes anyone who is a hard worker. He draws people close or pushes them away based on how good they are at what they do. People may hate him, but there's no-one who does not respect him, and he prefers respect over love.

He goes down the long hallway, opens his office door and turns on the light. He does not like how his office smells, like plastic. The door automatically closes behind him. It has a one-way window that gives him a clear view of the rest of the floor. He goes into the bathroom, a large opulent room with granite counters, and uses the toilet. He washes his face and sprays himself with a little cologne. In the mirror he sees not his own face but that of Silay Berahi, with his small eyes, his sharp features and even sharper mind. For the first time Betru is worried about his own state of mind. Lately he's been having trouble seeing his own face – all he sees in the mirror is the face of the enemy. He's been in this job too long.

The job is his calling and he has never done anything else. He graduated from Addis Ababa University in 1957 with a degree in political science and was hired by the Internal Security Administration. It was the chief himself, Workneh Gebeyehu, who hired him. Betru had no qualifications or experience relevant to intelligence work, but he was from Gondar, the same as Workneh. Today, after all this time, he's still doing the work his long-departed mentor picked him for.

His memory flows across twenty-five years of spying, but his victories and accomplishments don't boost his ego. Instead he feels empty. Empty heart, empty life, empty existence. He's never married or fathered any children to carry his name – a solitary life in a big world.

And he's getting old, not much time left before retirement. The years have left him behind like a shadow at dusk, and this troubles him. He hates having lost his youth, hates his grey hair. Salt in your hair used to bring respect, but the new generation has no use for old-timers.

He hasn't got very far in his twenty-five years on the job. Four of those years were spent in Alem Bekagn Prison, the prison that ends your world. Accused along with Workneh of collaborating in the ill-fated 1960 coup attempt, he was sentenced to five years. All he had done was his job. "The enemy of the government is the enemy of the people." That was the code he lived by, and he had nothing to do with the coup. Still they did not spare him. After four years he was pardoned and allowed to go back to his old job. Even so, he was never fully trusted, never promoted, never groomed for a higher position. Year after year he was passed over for promotion in favour of people he himself had trained, and his trainees became his bosses. But that isn't what made Betru bitter. What did, what really gnawed at him and drove him into an angry depression, was the fact that the public hated him simply because he worked for a government they detested. He considered quitting, but he knew his superiors would never allow it. They wouldn't let him go because he knew too much, and they wouldn't promote him because they didn't trust him. He was stuck, and the only thing he could do was drift along in an aimless life, an ignoble life.

He drifted and he drank. If not for the Revolution coming

in 1974, blowing up like fireworks all over the country, he would have remained a committed alcoholic. But he hasn't drunk or smoked since, thank goodness. He can't be sure of it, but the onset of the Revolution, the rising of the people, seems to have absolved him of his past sins. The Revolution has given him the sense that he is one with the people, no longer their enemy. Trust and hope has been placed in his profession. To be seen by the people as their jailor, their nemesis, that was what he had been hiding from in the booze and the women. At one point he even considered killing himself. With the Revolution and the renaissance of his spirit, he's ready to live again, ready to serve again.

Betru is a committed socialist now, a loyal operative of the Derg. "Showing mercy or compassion to a class enemy is a reprehensible act. A conscience that puts itself above the class struggle is no better than the empty exaltations of a priest. Spying is an obligation for a patriot. Who said a revolution is a courthouse with fairness to all? The enemy must be destroyed, even if the sword of revolution sometimes lands on an innocent neck. Anything else is the whimpering of intellectuals incapable of seeing the big picture. Revolution is not a game. It is not subject to our whims, but rolls forward at its own pace. Should anyone ask why, the answer is simple. Regardless of our feelings, history is rejecting capitalism. Capitalism is not eternal, it is dying, it is shrivelling not blossoming. Opposing socialism is to deny reality." That is what he says and that is what he believes. Surprisingly, he did not acquire his beliefs by reading, but absorbed them from experience.

Betru abhors those who, in their naïve way, contort themselves in order to pretend to serve the Revolution. He believes they are an obstacle rather than an asset. Many people want to be passengers on the revolutionary train, but how many of them are truly committed to serve the Revolution with honesty and integrity? How much damage will all these passengers do in pursuing their selfish interests? How many homes are broken and how many families are destroyed, how many lives are lost for naught? How sad. Such unscrupulous individuals have given socialism a bad name. And now the Red Star Campaign – how many profiteers, how many seekers of promotions and medals, how many rent-seeking merchants have already boarded that train? The lack of a complete intelligence file on each of the Red Star participants frustrates Betru. It leaves too much to guesswork. He looks at his watch and it is 10 p.m. This annoys him as well, and he leaves his bathroom.

A dozen guns hang on one wall of his office. He takes down a pistol and aims it at an imaginary target. His mind's eye is zeroing in on Silay Berahi. He stands there for a moment, his arm steady, then puts the pistol back, relaxed. Handling his impressive collection of guns, cleaning and rearranging them, calms him, as does playing solitaire. Like Napoleon, a war could break out or an earthquake could flatten the world and he wouldn't move an inch until he finished his game of solitaire.

Through the one-way glass in his door he sees his subordinates lined up in the hall. He presses a button on his desk and the door opens. Four young men walk in, one after another. They have bleary eyes, matted hair, and the look of men who haven't been sleeping much. Even their ties look tired, crooked. One is short with dark skin and seems very proud of himself. Another has lighter skin and a shy look. The other two are tall and carry themselves like big city guys, always on the make. All four are handsome and fit.

Betru looks at each of them and sees how tired they are. He feels sorry for them, and begins to wonder why he's working them to death, but he knows the answer. Serving as the Head of Security for the Red Star Campaign is undoubtedly the most important assignment of his career, and it might be his final assignment. It has taken him twenty-five years of work to get to this point and he knows his bosses expect perfection. He is a piece of gold being tested by fire for his purity and value, and he must deliver golden results. Whether his career goes down as a success or failure will depend in no small part on what these four men do, their hard work and persistence, so he has no choice but to work them night and day. That is not, however, his only motive for keeping them busy.

He sets aside any sympathies he has for them. To hell with them. He knows they need to work hard now if they want to get ahead in this agency. He worked hard, but what did it get him in all his years? He's been loaded with work to no benefit – a donkey can't eat what it's carrying. And now these new graduates are in a hurry for promotions? Forget it, let them work hard.

"Let me hear today's reports," he tells them. "Summaries, nothing too detailed, it's getting late."

"Yes, comrade," says Agent Teklay Zedingl, one of the city guys. He adjusts his glasses on his aquiline nose. "It's only fifty minutes until curfew." His colleagues call him James Bond: he likes pretty women, fine liquor, tailored suits and parties. Beyond that, he is tall and fit, a very good-looking young man. Women adore Agent Teklay, they are his best sources, and he's good at getting information out of them. He claims he can find any secret in the embrace of a woman. The job seems effortless for him, and no civilian suspects he's a spy. But when the situation demands it, he turns deadly serious in a single heartbeat. Betru likes him for the results he gets, but doesn't trust his judgement – Teklay is too driven by revenge. His beloved younger brother was murdered in Asmara by Shabia insurgents, and since then Teklay has been waging his own private war against them.

Betru smiles. "The curfew just means you'll go home to bed early."

"Comrade Director," says Teklay, "man was not created just to sleep."

"So he was created to chase women?" They all laugh.

"It's part of life," says Teklay. "Where do you suppose the best intelligence is gathered? From underneath women's clothes!" Again they laugh. "Don't you think?"

"It comes with risks," says Betru. "I'm afraid that someday you might get lost in a woman. They're dangerous, especially in our work. Don't assume that because a woman spreads her legs for you that she will also open her heart. She might steal yours instead." Betru leans back in his chair. "Anyway, we have no justification for going anywhere yet. Do you know what's going on at the Chairman's office right this minute? They're holding a staff meeting that will probably last until sunrise. The army that has been living in foxholes for the past seven years isn't rushing home to sleep either. You can't go to bed early and then line up in the morning to get promoted."

"Comrade Director," says Agent Seyoum Serekebirhan, the short dark-skinned one, "I do not agree with your assessment." Agent Seyoum never agrees with other people's assessments.

"Which assessment?" asks Betru.

"That women are not good targets for intelligence."

"How so?"

"Contrary to what you think, they do give away their heart

to every man they sleep with. They give away their bodies and they give away their country's secrets. It's money and jewellery they care about, not their country. Really, when it comes to women we haven't done that much, we could do more."

Betru looks at his watch. This is his way of indicating that he doesn't care to waste time on rhetorical arguments. Plus he worries about Agent Seyoum. Even though the young intelligence officer is quite good at what he does, Betru knows that he's in a rush to get promoted. He also suspects him of corruption. Agent Seyoum never has enough money and spends his monthly salary in a week, two at most. Nobody knows how he manages to make it to the next month. So far Betru has not caught Seyoum taking bribes, but one of these days . . .

"So, where do you think women get the secrets they sell?" he asks Agent Seyoum.

"I don't know, maybe from men."

"Don't say 'maybe'. They get 100 per cent of their secrets from men, their lovers, husbands, boyfriends. Men have an inherent tendency to trust women. Remember, Adam was fooled by Eve. But I agree, women are critical for the performance of our duties. The best intelligence agencies use mostly women. It would be better if, instead of insulting our women, we trained them for a change. They are unequalled when it comes to beauty and brains. Have you all read the book *Sex Espionage*? Especially you, Comrade Teklay."

Agent Seyoum hurriedly takes notes. Betru wants to slap him. "Comrade Seyoum, do not trouble yourself. A proposal to train women for intelligence work has already been presented to the top brass, and my hope is that such a school will soon be established. And, Comrade Teklay, you can help us with the recruiting. Let's get on with our work. Who shall we start with?" He removes his watch and places it on his desk.

Everyone understands the Director's remark. Seyoum has the bad habit of stealing other people's ideas and presenting them to their superiors as his own. Teklay raises his hand.

"No, no," says Betru, "let's wait on your report and start with the Government Agencies Security group. Is that okay with everyone? How about it, Agent Ashebir?"

Agent Ashebir, the light-skinned young man, is vigorous and dynamic. He is self-motivated and vibrant, moving so fast that he seems to be everywhere at once. He doesn't smoke or drink, and nobody knows what he does with his money. He is suspicious even of his own shadow and uninterested in anything other than intelligence work. Any piece of paper he sees, he will pick up and study. Anything that is said to him, he dissects for hidden meanings. His colleagues are aware of his tendencies and avoid talking to him. In fact, they dart the other way when they see him coming.

Ashebir's hobby is sitting by the fireplace. Every evening at home he will gather whatever he needs to start a small fire, then sit and watch as the pieces of wood burn, the embers glow, and the flames flare up and burn out. He will not go to bed until the last of the wood has burned to ashes. No-one knows why Ashebir enjoys this. He does not talk about it. Firewood is hard to come by in Eritrea and he has been unable to make his fires since he came to Asmara. Instead, he spends his time playing pool. Even there, it is not the game of pool itself that interests him, but creating chaos. A ball hitting other balls and shooting off in unexpected directions, that is what gives him pleasure. No-one likes playing pool with him.

Betru loves Ashebir for his energy, for his boldness and

cruelty. He is unforgiving. By Betru's reckoning, a good intelligence agent has to be fast, brave and brutal. And it helps to abstain from alcohol. If he has any concerns, it is that Ashebir is quick to anger and does not yet know how to really analyze and put to use the evidence he collects. He thinks Ashebir is gifted but raw, in need of someone who can mould him into a true professional.

"What is your report, Ashebir?" asks Betru.

Ashebir speaks with a very slight lisp. "Overall, security practices in and around government buildings are robust and in good shape. That said, we know the insurgents are trying to create pandemonium among the public and cripple the Red Star Campaign before it begins. In fact, I have obtained evidence suggesting they're planning an attack on either the airport or one of the large factories to discourage—"

Betru interrupts him. "What kind of evidence? We don't have time for speculation."

"It's not speculation," says Ashebir, clearly irritated. "I went all over town today. One farmer confirmed to me that some insurgents with grenade launchers were spotted around Tselot. I don't know what their actual target is. They might want to hit one of the factories out there. But more likely the airport."

This is something Betru must act on. He picks up his phone and dials. He breathes heavily, like a horse, and taps his desk with his fingers as he waits for someone to answer.

"Hello?" croaks a voice on the phone.

"Hello, who is this?" Betru stops tapping.

"Operation Lead," says the voice.

"Okay, so who are you?"

"Colonel Alemayehu."

"Oh, hello, Colonel Alemayehu, this is Director Betru,

Betru Tessema, with Public Safety. What happened to your voice?"

"Fatigue."

"We're just getting started, and there's a long way to go. Listen, Alemayehu, we have intelligence that the insurgents are planning a terrorist attack, probably using grenade launchers. The security forces in Tselot, Godaif and Sembel all need to go on alert right now. This is our joint responsibility, understand? Those are all places the Chairman is scheduled to go, and any attack on him would have serious political repercussions. So listen carefully, Alemayehu. I'm not asking you, I'm telling you – get those forces on alert, right now."

Betru hangs up without waiting for a response. He looks at Agent Ashebir. "Anything else?" Ashebir is clearly happy that his report has been acted on so quickly.

"Another issue is that people are scared," says Ashebir. "They're afraid there will be attacks, so they rush home before dark. The streets stay empty. Stores are running out of grain, prices have skyrocketed, and people are getting hungry. There are sympathizers who secretly support the insurgents and are inciting the public, but we haven't yet been able to identify them. It's a volatile situation." Ashebir consults his notebook for a minute, then continues, "Also, six local officials disappeared today from two districts." He hands over a list of their names and addresses. Betru looks at it and makes some notes.

"Regarding people panicking, grain disappearing and prices escalating," says Betru, "Tsegaye Hailemaryam reported this on television and presented a really good programme to calm people. Reassuring the public is the responsibility of his propaganda unit. That's their work, and they have a lot to do. What we *can* do is to keep collecting intelligence and sharing it with them. State secrets have no value if they stay secret from everyone.

"We also need to be very careful how we operate. We shouldn't arrest people or interrogate them without strong evidence. Nothing alienates the public quicker. If we do that, nobody will cooperate with us and our efforts will fail. Leave cruelty to the insurgents.

"You know, the Eritreans who joined the insurgency after the Revolution, they didn't do it because they were radicalized by the separatists. At least, that wasn't the main reason. Most joined the insurgency because they were tired of living in fear. We share the blame for that. At the time of the Revolution in 1974, Shabia had no more than five hundred active members. In the next three years, we estimate the insurgency grew to between eight and ten thousand members. Why? Because of us.

"The old army, the National Army, they came here with the idea that every Eritrean was a terrorist. If there was an attack, they didn't worry about distinguishing the innocent from the guilty. They retaliated against everyone. They shot first and then yelled 'Stop'. A unit of the 15th battalion was put in charge of internal security for Asmara. They took over part of the exhibition hall and set up their own interrogation centre, their own court, their own prison, and carried out their own executions, right there on the spot. A unit called Union Command had a similar mission, and they began seizing the property of people who had been arrested. It was supposed to be held by the government until their trial was finished, with inventories and receipts to everyone, but that's not what happened. Then the Derg deployed a group here from their Interrogation Centre in Addis. It was called the 'Special Unit'. Nobody was sure who they were or under whose authority they operated. But they were here too, making arrests, carrying out interrogations, imposing sentences.

"Most of the people who were arrested, beaten, jailed, executed – they weren't really enemies of the Revolution. Instead, maybe someone in the Union Command wanted their house, or someone in the 15th battalion wanted their wife. Maybe there was an accusation, that's all it took. If the insurgents wanted to get rid of one of their own, or just someone they didn't like, they would leak the name to one of the security agencies and that would be it.

"Maybe a man is arrested by the Special Unit. Nobody knows the reason. He is interrogated, he is beaten, he is condemned. The execution is carried out on the spot. There is no-one to ask why the due process of law was not carried out. The man is gone and so is his money and his property, no receipts. No-one says a thing.

"In those days there were corpses in the streets of Asmara almost every morning. People who had been hanged, people who had been shot, their bodies left at intersections, at checkpoints. Who killed him? Why was he killed? There was no-one to ask and no-one to answer. Only the god of revolution knows. The dead are silent.

"People were terrified. And those idiots at the 'Temporary Secretariat for Security' only made it worse. So of course people fled to the bush to join the insurgency, especially young men. Even their mothers urged them to go. Better that than watch them be murdered. What should they do when we flood them with terror and panic? When people are faced with mass injustice, mass incarceration and mass murder, they will run away to save their lives. Unless they're a total extremist, nobody who is assured of life and liberty joins the insurgency. Most insurgents are not crazy.

"Am I lecturing you too much? I know this is all ancient history now. Our Revolution has been blessed with a centralized democratic leadership. It obliges us to respect the fundamental rights and liberties of all people. If we do that, there is no reason we can't win the hearts and minds of the Eritrean people. I'm not just babbling away here without a point. By modelling good behaviour we can earn the goodwill of the people. They want safety, and it is our job to give it to them. That's why we changed our name from the Ministry of Public Security to the Ministry of Public Safety."

He looks at his watch and continues. "Some people might think we have come here to resolve the Eritrean problem with one massive military battle. And of course we do have to break the insurgency's back. But the purpose and aim of the Red Star Campaign is long term. Our ultimate goal is to create understanding and trust between our people so we can get to the point where we stop killing one another and instead sacrifice for each other."

Seyoum yawns and stretches. "I have more to report."

"Go ahead," says Betru.

"I am worried about the Red Star people who came from Addis Ababa."

"How so?"

"You see them on every street, in every shop, drinking in every bar. If you go to Babylon Square right now, it will be like a Red Star Campaign party. The high-ranking officials are filling up all the bordellos in town. Who is responsible if something bad happens to one of them?"

Betru shakes his head. "Everyone has to be responsible for himself, they aren't here on holiday. But we still need to do something about that. Each of us needs to follow up those situations with a report."

"But, sir," Seyoum says.

"What?"

"We don't have an expense account here, and information isn't free," says Seyoum. "We can't do much without money."

"Yes," says Betru. He smiles at Seyoum. "Particularly you, you need money. I think your pocket has a hole in it. But don't worry, we have plenty of funding. The challenge is to put it to good use. There's lots of bribery and corruption here, so we have to be careful. People here are thrifty, they won't spend one birr without good reason. If someone buys you a drink, they have an agenda. The next day they'll come and ask for a favour, to get someone out of jail, issue a passport to someone. They seem to think that anyone from Addis Ababa has the ability to solve all their problems. The women especially seem to think this. I warn you, comrades, be cautious. Be suspicious. It's part of our job."

Seyoum checks his notes. Teklay yawns, then looks at his watch. He has settled into his chair, as has Ashebir. The fourth man, Major Garedew Mekonnen, doesn't look like he's listening and rarely speaks. He is Chief of Interrogation, and has been in Asmara for several years in that role. The mention of his name makes people nervous. The orders he gives are usually limited to the phrase, "Hold the prisoner down." With political prisoners, he tries to make them feel like he is their friend. If he doesn't get what he wants with that approach, he becomes unhappy and switches to physical tactics. Prisoners get frightened whenever he starts to look upset. Some even piss their pants. But Major Garedew is a family man. He loves and adores his wife and children, and won't work late. He believes everyone is entitled to a peaceful night, even his prisoners. It is mind-boggling to watch him relax at home with his family after spending the day beating prisoners and having them whipped. Betru wonders whether the Major should maybe take a few classes in psychology.

Seyoum raises his hand to speak and Teklay rolls his eyes.

"Yes, what is it?" asks Betru.

"Comrade Director, I'm not crazy about this 'once and for all' phrase we use whenever we talk about the Red Star Campaign. The campaign is a three-month initiative, right?"

"Maybe, maybe not."

"To openly proclaim that we'll solve the Eritrean problem 'once and for all' in just three months is not helpful, it's not good politics."

"Why not?"

"Putting a deadline on this campaign is a tactical error. If we fail, we lose our credibility, our authority. Ultimately it might jeopardize our ability to govern the country. And I believe it is our duty to point that out."

"I agree," says Betru. "But there's no need to worry. Nobody is saying all the problems of this region will be solved in three months. Sure, there are specific goals we plan to accomplish within that time. But efforts to resolve the issues will continue, and no-one knows how long that will take. That's how to think of it. Even so, you have a good point, and the Propaganda Initiative Section has to be careful about that. Okay, let's hear from our Interrogation Section. Major Garedew?"

Major Garedew's voice is hoarse. Being so aloof, he talks as if nobody else is in the room. His eyes are large and red, and his expression is that of an angry lion. "Today I do not have a lot of information," he says.

"What happened, not enough beatings today?" asks Betru with a sarcastic tone.

"A terrorist will never talk unless they're in pain."

"A bourgeoisie like us, accustomed to a comfortable life, will give away all kinds of information before you even lay a finger on them," says Betru.

"Who volunteers self-incriminating information?" asks Garedew.

"Enough, please proceed with your report."

"According to recent deserters from the insurgent stronghold at Nakfa, the enemy has already learned the deployment of our battalions as well as their numbers and strengths," says Garedew.

"What have the deserters told us about their own forces?"

"They are low ranking, so they don't know much. No details, no numbers. They do talk about the terror, corruption and hunger among the insurgents. If they get the opportunity, most will choose to flee. As a result they are watched very closely. That is the situation. But I did get one piece of worthwhile information that—"

Betru interrupts him before he can finish his sentence. "What is it?"

"The French have provided them with a large shipment of gas masks."

"No way!" Betru is surprised.

"It's true."

Betru makes some notes. "Why would the French get involved? What a mess this Arab oil creates. The Americans might get involved too. I wonder what their spy satellites are telling them. This campaign will have a big impact on our future foreign policy. But for now, what can we do?"

The four men are silent as they have no answers for him. Betru wasn't expecting any. He snorts like a horse, then takes off his glasses and cleans them with a white handkerchief. He is careful to clean his glasses regularly.

"Very well," says Betru. "Teklay, where are you with the other job I assigned you?"

"Which one?" The Director does not assign his agents only one task.

"The Silay Berahi one. Where is he right now?"

Teklay smiles. "He's at the residence of Fiammetta Gilay."

8

THE ARROGANCE OF GOLIATH

Director Betru Tessema stares at Agent Teklay Zedingl, who restrains himself from smiling.

"Okay, so Silay Berahi is at Fiammetta Gilay's house at . . ." Betru looks down at his watch. "At 10.30 p.m. on a Tuesday night."

Teklay adjusts his stylish glasses and lets them rest low on his narrow nose. Silay was a key player in the Shabia insurgency who just defected to the government, so of course Director Betru is eager for every detail. Teklay continues with his report: "Our people followed him from the gathering at Comrade Solomon's residence to Fiammetta Gilay's house in Mai Temenai. His car is still parked in front of her place, but our team did not enter the house to confirm that he was inside. But if you want them to—"

"No, no," says Betru. "That's not necessary. Let's leave it at that for now. But make Silay Berahi your main assignment. Be sure he is followed at all times and don't lose track of him, even for a minute. Under no circumstances should he be aware that he is being followed, not the slightest suspicion. Do the same with the woman, and maybe she'll lead us to someone. Now, let's analyze this together. Why did Silay defect back to us?"

The men are paying close attention. Betru taps his desk. His gold ring with a lion insignia flashes in the dim light.

"Why don't we try turning him upside down?" asks Major Garedew. His favourite tactic is to suspend a prisoner upside down as a prelude to a beating.

Betru looks at Garedew with distaste. "Turning them over isn't reliable." He remembers seeing Silay's battered back at Solomon's party. "Besides, Silay is used to pain. Better we find a different approach."

Garedew, clearly disappointed, falls silent.

Next to speak is Seyoum. "Other extremists in the insurgency have returned peacefully and are making amends for their transgressions. Like Silay, they had leadership positions in Shabia or Jebha. What is so different about Silay's return that we have to worry so much?"

"But why now?" asks Betru. "Why this particular moment? Is he a plant, or a real defector? If he's a plant, then what is his mission? We need answers. Silay is a very smart fellow, and so far he has answered all our questions. The information he's provided has checked out. But for some reason I still have my doubts about him." Betru starts tapping his desk again, this time rather forcefully.

"I knew Silay when I was a kid," says Teklay, feeling the old hurt inside him. "Even then he was adventurous. But also selfish and greedy. He loves money and power and is willing to take risks. I was a teenager and Silay was in his twenties when Eritrea was absorbed back into Ethiopia. He was the one who brought me into Mahber Shewate, the separatist movement. We were all scared of Silay because of how violent he could be. He led us on some attacks against officials, but then next thing we knew, he had exposed us to the government. Six of us ended up in prison, but my father got me out. One of the others, Gebray Tekeste, did seven years. Now he owns the Paradiso coffeebar here. Gebray really wanted to kill Silay for his betrayal, even more than I did. Later on Silay was appointed district governor and got involved in trying to broker a peace deal between the government and the insurgency. But at the same time he was spying for the CIA. That's how he could afford his lifestyle, going out to bars and restaurants every night, always with a new car, a new woman. Spending all that money, we knew it was beyond his government salary."

Teklay again adjusts his glasses and this time thinks to straighten his tie as well. "Then with the Revolution in 1974, everything changed," he says. "We heard Silay fled to the bush to join the insurgency. He has some story about why he switched from Jebha to Shabia, but the real reason is that he saw Jebha was going to lose. He realized that if he wanted power, he would have to switch to Shabia, and they welcomed him with open arms. With his daring and cruelty, it did not take him long to climb the ladder of power there. He became famous, and we all know the abuse and torture that followed. My younger brother was murdered while Silay Berahi was in charge of internal security for Shabia. I have some evidence that the order to kill him may have come from Silay himself. I think I was the real target, but they couldn't find me—"

Betru interrupts Teklay. "We are not discussing personal revenge here. That should not influence our decision-making. Let's get back to the main point. Why did Silay Berahi defect when he did?"

Teklay bows his head and wipes his eyes. He grinds his

teeth, then speaks. "I looked into it and I think there are two reasons for his return. One is that he was unable to get elected to Shabia's politburo, the elite of the elite. The other reason is that he realized there was a growing imbalance of power between the insurgency and the Revolutionary Army, and the insurgents are on the losing side. As I said, he's mercenary. As far as I know, he came back for selfish reasons. If we give him money and privileges, he's ours." He bites his lip, hard.

While Teklay is speaking he is also thinking of ways to avenge the death of his brother. He knows that the Director does not appreciate his intentions.

"You shouldn't forget that the well-being of the defectors is your responsibility, along with tracking their daily activities," says Director Betru. "It's possible we may need Silay, so if he asks for money, give it to him. Also, move him from the Albergo Ciao to the Nyala Hotel, it's nicer. But I don't agree with you about his reason for defecting."

It is Agent Ashebir who speaks up this time. "So why do you think he returned?"

"What if he is an infiltrator, a plant?" asks Betru. "Have you tried looking at the situation from that angle?"

Seyoum purses his lips. "Would Shabia send someone like him, who knows so many of their secrets, and thereby expose itself to such a degree?" he asks. "I seriously doubt it."

"To be suspicious is not a bad thing," says Betru. "Teklay, you need to keep on him, closely. What do you know about Fiammetta Gilay?"

"I know she is beautiful," says Seyoum. "But Major Garedew is the better person to speak about her. She was his honoured guest for a while."

Garedew glares at Seyoum but stays silent.

"Well, Garedew, what do you know about Fiammetta Gilay?" asks Betru.

"She was incarcerated for three months at Hazhaz Prison."

"When?"

"About four years ago, so 1977."

"What was her crime?"

"She was accused of funding the Jebha insurgency," says Garedew.

"And?"

"In fact, she did not. A Jebha agent living undercover here in Asmara was making money with some petty fraud scheme, something with a fake raffle. When he got caught, he claimed that his victims were members of Jebha and tried to trade their names for his freedom. She was one of those falsely accused by him, that's all." Garedew falls silent.

"Did you tie her up, turn her over?" asks Betru.

"I couldn't."

"Why not?"

Garedew laughs. "I never met a female prisoner like her. She came in September, and right away she got busy collecting the daisies that grow on the grounds inside Hazhaz. She wove them into earrings, bracelets, necklaces – she used them as her jewellery. The other prisoners started calling her Princess Fiammetta. Wearing all those daisies, sitting on the floor that she had covered with grass, she really did look like royalty. She played it up, too, made a crown of flowers and wore it. I never saw her depressed. Somehow she took being in jail as fun and never worried about it."

The other men are paying close attention to Garedew now. "I tried to get her to talk by telling her that just contributing money was no big deal, that lots of people gave money because they feared for their safety. Then I tried to scare her. But her answer stayed the same: she said she had never contributed to the insurgency and had never been a member. 'Major,' she told me, 'these things you call Jebha and Shabia, I heard about them for the first time here in prison. I paid that man you arrested twenty birr to enter a raffle for a new house. I did that twice. If I was contributing to the insurgents, why should I pay that much? I hear they're happy with five birr.'"

Garedew pauses, then continues, "So finally I took her to the interrogation room. I tore off her jacket and threw it on the floor and warned her to tell me the truth. You know what she said? It's amazing. She said, 'Why? Are you going to hang me upside down, you rude man? I swear on the name of my father, you're nothing but a brute. Come on, let me see you touch me!' After that, I couldn't turn her over, so I laughed and let her go. I don't know why, but I've always thought of her as an innocent."

Teklay imagines Fiammetta's beautiful body. He longs to discover the secrets hidden between her thighs. An idea occurs to him that puts a smile on his face: even if he can't kill Silay Berahi yet, he knows where he is vulnerable. He will use Fiammetta Gilay and her beautiful body to torture Silay with jealousy and rage. He will burn him.

Betru is still tapping his desk. He closes one eye and aims his finger at an imaginary target.

"Okay, boys, it's getting late," he says. "The information in our files on all these people is not sufficient. Major Garedew, starting tomorrow we have to begin assembling a biography of every individual who resides in this city who might have any sympathies with the insurgency, any connections with them. We need to create a Biographical Intelligence Centre. I know it won't be easy, but we have to have it. Now that so many public institutions keep records on individuals, it should be possible to collect that information. Where were they born? Where were they raised? Where did they go to school? What are they interested in? What have they written? With whom and where do they spend their time? What records are there about their past? And, if possible, what about their character? Don't worry, we'll give you plenty of manpower. Tomorrow give me a report on the personnel and funding you'll need and we'll get the project rolling."

Without pausing, Betru turns to Ashebir. "Comrade Ashebir, regarding the six officials who disappeared from their districts, I will need a report from you tomorrow detailing who they've been in contact with, how they got elected, and who got them elected. I'm still going to need your reports on the security of government buildings, so don't neglect that. And I want you to make sure that Colonel Alemayehu put those forces on alert. Confirm that and report back to me first thing tomorrow morning.

"Comrade Seyoum, tracking the activities of everyone who's here from Addis for the Red Star Campaign is your responsibility. I will need reports on where they go, who they meet, what they do, what they say, plus a short biography on each one of them. It has been announced that the insurgent's radio station, Dimtsi Hafash, will be jammed starting tomorrow. I do not trust our propaganda people to do that, so I want you to follow up to make sure it happens. And let me know what programmes they're putting out."

Betru takes off his glasses and cleans them. "Finally, boys, I have a theory," he says. "And you, Teklay Zedingl, will be the one to prove it true or false. It's an important job. What you uncover could determine the outcome of everything we do here. My theory goes like this: I believe Silay is here for a purpose. If you've been listening to the insurgent radio station, they were smearing him even before we publicized his defection. They never did that in the past, when others left the insurgency. So why do it now? I think they're trying to make us overlook what's really going on. Seyoum, earlier you asked why they would expose themselves by sending him, with all he knows? That's the catch. There is not a whole lot we don't already know about them. What new information can he really tell us about Shabia? Other than a propaganda win, he's not that valuable to us.

"So why did Silay defect? Why now, at this time and under these conditions? What's his mission? We need to find those answers. What we get from him might finally give us some information on The Bureaucrat. Who is he? Does he really exist, or is he a phantom? He goes by different names, and we hear different rumours about him. Is he really pulling the strings for the whole insurgency? We don't know much about him, even with all our surveillance. Now is the time to figure it out. If we can't destroy the insurgency's spying infrastructure now, with all our increased efforts during the Red Star Campaign, I don't think we'll ever be able to.

"The insurgents seem to know everything about us: our troop movements, our strengths, our weaknesses, all of it. That means they're here in our midst. Who are the infiltrators? And now that the Red Star Campaign is starting, I don't think they'll limit themselves to just gathering intelligence. What actions are they going to take? What attacks are they planning? Silay can lead us to the answers. At least, that's my hope. I don't know for sure. He could be clean, but we still need to watch him. Teklay, tracking Silay and investigating those questions is your responsibility. If you need it, you can have a hundred men to work on this and support you. I don't want Silay to have a single private moment, not even when he goes to the bathroom.

"Comrades, I think we're sitting on top of a ticking bomb. A web is wrapping around us, and we must break through it. We should not underestimate anyone – it was Goliath's arrogance that led to his downfall. This isn't going to be easy and we have no time to rest."

Teklay Zedingl yawns and loses all hope of making it to the bars tonight.

9

MISSION

After leaving the party at Solomon's house, Silay Berahi drives Fiammetta Gilay in his Volkswagen along Keren Road towards her house in Mai Temenai. They don't exchange a single word on the way, both lost in their own thoughts.

When they reach her house, he asks her, "Did you enjoy the party?"

"It was good," she says.

"Because you met that journalist. I could see it in your eyes. You're still the same Fiammetta, going after famous men. What do you see in him?"

Mai Temenai has no street lights and the darkness is so dense you can almost touch it. It is cold out and the neighbourhood dogs start barking.

"None of your business." Fiammetta is about to get out of his car when he grabs her arm. "Get off of me!" she says.

"Relax, this is no time for romance. That's for another day. Right now I need to leave my car at your house."

"Why?"

"I have my reasons."

"What kinds of reasons?"

"Is this an interrogation?" asks Silay. "It was your freedom I bled for, all those years."

"So what do you want now?"

"Do you think I'm a traitor?"

"Traitor or not, I really don't care," says Fiammetta.

"I hear you like men from the heartland – the Amhara."

"Heartland, north, south, who cares?" says Fiammetta.

"What do you want to let me leave my car here tonight?"

"What I want is to not get in trouble."

"There is no trouble. The government has asked me to give them a full report on the insurgency, and they want it tomorrow. So I need to go now."

They get out of his car. Silay locks it and heads into the darkness. He walks down the street away from Fiammetta Gilay's house to where another car is waiting for him. As soon as he gets into the waiting car it speeds off. They do not take Keren Road back into town, but instead take the road that goes by Hazhaz Prison and the Tuberculosis Clinic. Silay watches to see if anyone is following them. After a few turns they reach Paradiso Street. The driver is a tough-looking young kid and he drops Silay at the Paradiso, an all-hours coffeebar that shares its name with the street.

Wearing a dark overcoat and hat, Silay heads straight into the coffeebar. He takes a coin from his pocket and shows it to the barista, an old man named Aboy Tekle.

"Our coffee costs more than that," says Aboy in his white jacket.

"I don't need coffee," says Silay.

"Then what do you want?"

"I need a clean bathroom."

The barista gives him a hard look. "Yes, we have one," he says.

He leads Silay to the back and opens a door to show him the bathroom. It's a spacious room with bright white tiles and a large sink built into the floor. Silay is confused and hesitates. Aboy is an old man but he moves quickly. He bends down and presses something under the faucet and the entire sink, which had looked to be anchored in concrete, slides away from the wall. Silay is startled and steps back, then moves forward to look at the gaping hole under the fixture. A lightbulb hangs over a narrow metal ladder. The barista gestures at him to hurry down it and Silay obeys. With another push of the button the vanity unit slides back to its original position and once again looks like any sink in any bathroom. Aboy uses the urinal, washes his hands and goes back to his station behind the bar.

When Silay reaches the bottom of the ladder he finds himself in a large room where three men sit around a table with four chairs. They seem impatient but give him a warm welcome. Silay takes off his overcoat and hat and joins them at the table.

"Now what?" Silay asks them.

"You were just with a woman, correct?" asks one of the men. His consternation is clearly visible on his flat face. His big eyes are shot through with red. He's smoking a cigarette and the movements of his hands are very precise.

"So what, why not?" asks Silay. "What's the big deal if a man who's lived in the bush for seven years, the first thing he does is find a woman, one who smells nice? You all live in Asmara. You don't know how we suffer out there."

The man with the red eyes who asked the question is Gebray Tekeste. He is not swayed by Silay's response. He's a sceptic and he wants a straight answer to his question. "So who is she?" he asks.

"My girlfriend from the old days."

"I'm asking you for her name."

"Fiammetta Gilay."

"Fiammetta Gilay?" Gebray reaches into a box under the table and takes out a large black file folder. He thumbs through the papers in it one by one. After a while he stops and pulls out a photo. "This is her, yes?"

Silay nods.

"Not good," says Gebray. He starts reading from a document clipped to the photo. "She loves associating with people from Addis Ababa, the heartlanders, the Amharas. She was jailed for being a member of Jebha. How come she was let go so easily? What is she doing these days? The photo shows her wearing fancy jewellery, where does she get the money for that? Why did she not go to Saudi Arabia, Abu Dhabi or Dubai like other beautiful women? That's suspicious. She could be an Ethiopian spy. She's often been seen in the company of Colonel Wolday. You know, our women are not like they used to be. They've become whores." Gebray is angry now.

"Colonel Wolday Tariku?" asks Silay. "Since when?"

"It doesn't say. It looks like he spends a lot of money on her. And he hasn't been seen with any other women. Maybe he loves her."

"What about her?" asks Silay.

"Who knows." Gebray's tone has grown harsh. "I advise you to exercise extreme caution with her."

"I know what I'm doing," says Silay.

Gebray pounds the table with his fist. *"Ma guarda un po!"* he says in Italian. "I don't care if you've been stuck in the bush or not. We have discipline here. We are in a life-and-death struggle. The entire city is overrun by Derg security, just look around. Do you understand me?"

Silay slowly gets up from his seat. He turns his back to Gebray and looks at the other two men with his small eyes. His teeth are clenched. Speaking slowly and carefully he says, "I do admire the precautions you are taking. But going forward, you will be taking orders from me. Am I clear?" He loosens his tie and reaches under the collar of his shirt to pull out a folded piece of paper. He turns and hands it to Gebray.

Gebray carefully unfolds the paper. As his cigarette smoke fills the room, he reads it out loud: "Arbate Asmara – For a limited time I am informing you to receive all orders, directives and resolutions from Silay Berahi." It is signed Isayas Afewerki, Chief Secretary and Supreme Military Commander, Shabia. Arbate Asmara is Gebray Tekeste's code name.

"Now burn it," says Silay. Gebray touches his cigarette to it. Silay waits until it's burning, then says, "Starting right now, your orders come from me. My word is law."

Gebray is silent. He thinks about the letter in his pocket from The Bureaucrat in Addis Ababa. The letter instructs him that, should they become suspicious of Silay Berahi for even the smallest breach, they should immediately use whatever means necessary to eliminate him without any delay or deliberation. He wants to take the letter out of his pocket and burn it with the other one, but decides not to because Silay might insist on reading it first. He was surprised to receive an order giving him permission to kill Silay if needed. The Bureaucrat must have his reasons. Gebray doesn't know anything about the person behind that alias, whether he's short or tall, dark or pale, young or old. He only receives his orders.

The four men look at each other. Fire turns the paper to ash.

Gebray Tekeste has long had a grudge against Silay. When

he saw him tonight, the deep loathing returned and he can taste it on his tongue. He realizes how much he hates him. Silay has always used his power to dominate and humiliate his friends. And here he is, at it again. It was Silay who had bullied him into being a member of the separatist group Mahber Shewate. How selfish and arrogant Silay had been then. But Gebray could overlook Silay's narcissism. After all, unless they're crazy, who doesn't love oneself? The hate came from a deeper wound. Silay was appointed a district governor by the Haile Selassie administration, thanks to his influential father, Berahi Dejazmatch. Once he became governor, Silay exposed and imprisoned the six young men that had worked alongside him in Mahber Shewate. Gebray was one of those men, and was sentenced to seven years. Others got out early because they came from influential families, but Gebray's family was poor and he had to serve his full sentence.

After he was released, Gebray was stuck – how could a poor man with no education, no family to support him and no employment find a better life? A man has to earn a living to survive. Life in prison had crippled his spirit but strengthened his body and given him a ruthless heart. He had seen that life was cheap. Now the suffering and crying of others means nothing to him, he saw it all in prison, it's just another day. So who was there to offer him a job after his release, when he did not have anyone to turn to, when the day was as dark as the night and he was lost and alone? It was Shabia. They offered him the kind of job he knew he would be good at, a hired killer. "Killing to make a living" became his motto. And now he is a master of his trade, all thanks to Silay Berahi's betrayal all those years ago.

Gebray looks at Silay through the haze of cigarette smoke.

He smiles at the thought of making Silay laugh. Gebray has made quite a few people laugh in his career. By making them laugh, he means killing them.

Silay clears his throat and says, "Now, let me explain my actions."

Gebray worries that Silay might have guessed his intentions.

"I have good reason for seeing Fiammetta Gilay," says Silay. "I have known her for a long time, since we were at school together. She's still the same, not a whole lot of growing up since then. Fiammetta will go out with anyone who will show her a good time. She just wants to have fun and doesn't think more than two or three days ahead.

"Going out with a beautiful woman helps convince the government that my intentions are peaceful, and that I'm back for good. To give me cover to come here, I told people I was going to spend the night with her, and in fact my car is parked outside her house. That's why I asked you to collect me in Mai Temenai. And I was hoping she'd pick up one of the Red Star men at Solomon's party. She has a thing for those Derg donkeys, and if she got involved with one, that could be helpful to us. I didn't know she was seeing Colonel Wolday. Unfortunately, instead of picking one of the important donkeys at the party, she was talking with some television reporter named Tsegaye."

"Who did you say?" It's Yohannes Asfiha, a tall and skinny young guy with a big Afro. His voice is as thin as his frame and hurts the ear.

"Tsegaye Hailemaryam," Silay says.

"Did you see his programme they broadcast tonight?" asks Yohannes.

"Yes."

"He's dangerous," says Yohannes. "His programme made us look bad. If he continues like that, we'll lose public support."

"That means you haven't done your job." Silay is upset. "You have to incite the public, make them angry about all the injustices. Create in their psyche a state of action, not peace. No-one has the right to an unburdened existence. There is no peace. Going forward, this is one of the main objectives we must focus on."

"You missed my point," Yohannes says. "Tsegaye is no ordinary journalist. He's the Chief of Propaganda Initiatives for the Red Star Campaign and—"

Silay interrupts. "What does he know about Eritrea? Please tell me that?"

"He's been here a few times before," says Yohannes. "He spends time talking with people. He's good at finding things out. He's like a bloodhound that way, persistent. People trust him. He's not like other journalists. Tonight's programme is a good example of that. And starting tomorrow he is planning to block our radio broadcasts. What's the term for that?"

"Jamming," says Gebray.

"Yes, they'll be jam—"

"Where did you get that information?" interrupts Silay.

"We have our people. I have all the orders Tsegaye gave this morning. He's a dangerous adversary."

"If he's that dangerous, then we need to make him laugh right away," says Gebray.

Silay gives Gebray a look of something like pity. "That's your solution to every problem, making people laugh."

"Dead people can't cause problems," says Gebray. "To remove trouble by the roots, making them laugh is the best solution."

Silay frowns and turns to Yohannes. "What have you done with the intelligence you received about the jamming?"

"Nothing yet."

"Stupid, you are truly stupid," says Silay and slams his fist down on the table. "You have critical information in your hands, but you haven't done anything with it? Didn't you realize it was important? What's the point of gathering intelligence if we don't put it to some use, get some benefit from it? We need our Dimtsi Hafash radio programmes to survive, especially right now – I don't know if you realize that. How will the public know we exist if our radio broadcasts are cut off? The jamming could cost us the support of the people.

"So now, right now, I need you to get this information to The Bureaucrat. Confirm with him that they'll get ready to use a different radio band to broadcast on. They should not, under any circumstances, concede that our transmissions will be jammed. Tell him they need to get ready. We need to teach these Red Star donkeys a lesson."

Yohannes looks confused.

"Did you hear me?" asks Silay.

Gebray blows out smoke. "If the transmission tower in Sashemene had been finished on time, we could talk to The Bureaucrat directly."

"Sashemene is so close to him in Addis, he should have made sure it was ready," says Silay. "The Bureaucrat is getting lazy."

"Do you know him?" asks Gebray.

"Yes. But only two other people know his identity. It needs to stay that way because we've been careless before about keeping secrets."

"What does The Bureaucrat look like?" asks Yohannes.

"What do you think he looks like?" says Silay.

"An old man," says Yohannes.

"Thin and dark," says the fourth man, speaking for the first time.

"A chain smoker," says Gebray.

"No," says Silay. "He's young, light skin, good-looking. Doesn't drink or smoke. That's all you need to know."

Yohannes gets up and disappears through a door.

Silay sighs. "Is there anything to drink around here?" he asks. "I'm thirsty."

The fourth man gets him a glass of whiskey mixed with Dengolo. He goes by the codename Zelalem and is the youngest of the four men.

Silay takes a drink. "This is good," he says. "But we have important business. My mission is called Oromay. And from now on you'll know me only by that code name – Oromay." He takes another gulp of his whiskey. His little eyes shine with excitement.

A red light on the ceiling starts flashing.

"What's that?" asks Silay.

"It means Public Security agents are in the Paradiso," says Gebray. "Don't be alarmed. They really like our coffee."

Silay relaxes. "The Oromay mission has four parts. First, if the fighting in Nakfa starts going against us, we'll launch major attacks in Asmara against the Red Star donkeys and open another front. Second, to sabotage their attempts at economic domination. Third, to inform the public of the dire reality of the situation, even if it causes a crisis. Fourth, to intensify our urgent intelligence and infiltration efforts. The day of reckoning is coming."

"Is the situation that bad?" asks Zelalem.

"Yes," says Silay. "Our forces are penned in at all four corners – at Karora, Algena, Afabet and Kerkebet. The

Ethiopian Army is assembling its troops in Keren and will move north from there. Our one advantage is our natural fortress in Nakfa, and even that can last only so long. We thought the government troops were poorly trained, like they were in their Raza Campaign in 1976. So our plan was to lure them to Nakfa, where we could unleash all our forces and destroy them for good. But I think our intelligence was faulty. I don't think this Ethiopian Army is that easy a target. As a result, unless we create hell on earth in Nakfa, they will defeat us. These donkeys aren't like the old donkeys." With that Silay raises his glass and slugs down the rest of his whiskey.

Gebray blows out some smoke. "We fought their 15th division in Nakfa for seven months. We can fight them there for seven years. Do they think we're Somalis and they can conquer us in three months? Let us leave the politics aside for a moment. Like them, we are Ethiopians. The burning spirit to fight the enemy, the willingness to die for one's country – it runs in our veins as much as theirs."

"Correct," says Silay. "But their strength is growing, while ours is declining because of our internal conflicts. We aren't getting much help from the outside either."

Silay lights a cigarette. Everyone in the bush smoked and drank. If the fighting didn't kill them, the cigarettes and alcohol almost certainly would.

"For the Oromay mission, we need a dedicated unit," says Silay, breaking the silence. "To get ready to conduct operations against the Red Star Campaign. That's why I was sent here. From this basement we will unleash hell on their men anywhere we find them in Asmara. The challenge is that we as Shabia are not experienced in launching terrorist attacks inside a big city. And we're short on time, as they're likely to begin their Nakfa offensive soon. We must try to find out the exact date and—"

Gebray interrupts him. "We already know. The third week of February, probably Monday the 15th or Wednesday the 17th."

"And?"

"We've shared that intelligence with the appropriate people."

"Good," says Silay. "How many people do we have in Asmara, what is our capacity here?"

"We have enough people," says Gebray. "Our limitations are money and weapons."

Silay smiles. "Don't worry about either. One million birr has already been budgeted for Oromay, and we're bringing in more weapons even as we speak. The question is how best to use them. We're going to need a strategy, based on good intelligence, to make that happen."

Surprised by the scale of the operation, the other men fall silent while Silay grinds his teeth.

"We need to decide who to eliminate," says Silay. "I need a detailed study of who, why, where, when and how. Start with Colonel Wolday Tariku and Agent Teklay Zedingl."

Gebray sits up sharply, like he's been kicked.

"What's wrong?" asks Silay.

Gebray looks away and does not answer.

"I understand," says Silay. "You were friends with Teklay in prison. And you think maybe it's my fault that you were both there? Old fights are a waste of time – nobody lives in the past. History has brought you and I together here under the same banner. And it's put Teklay on the opposite side. He's a dangerous man. We need to make him laugh."

Gebray shakes his head. "It's better to keep him alive for

now. Since he's my friend he gives me cover for my operations. We talk, we eat, we drink, and because of that, nobody is suspicious of me. And I get information from him about his movements and activities. I can definitely kill him, but he's more useful alive than dead." Gebray rubs his red eyes and takes another drag on his cigarette. "And because of him, our coffeebar here has become a hangout for lots of security people."

"When the time comes, he must laugh," says Silay.

"If he must, he must," says Gebray.

"In addition, add to the potential assassination list the names of Director Betru Tessema, Solomon Betregiorgis and Tsegaye Hailemaryam. Make files for them. And I need the complete list of defectors who have rejoined the government, I need that right away. Also the names and addresses of those who want to cooperate with us, every one of them. We must infiltrate the ranks of every Derg organization in Eritrea, civilian and military. Let's get started – Oromay!"

Gebray pictures the many people he will make laugh and how the streets of Asmara will fill with the smiling bodies of dead Red Star campaigners. All those files and lists to put together: Central Committee members, government officials, high-ranking military officers, internal security operatives, local leaders and potential sympathizers. He grows crazy with happiness, imagining going through all those photos, all those smiles.

I do not believe it is necessary for me to introduce myself again. I have no face and no name. I am not constrained by time or space. This is me: I have been, I am, and I will be.

The story continues.

Life is like a spider's web, spreading out and entangling us.

PART TWO

10

ALL ROADS LEAD TO ASMARA

"Comrade Tsegaye, phone call from Addis Ababa," says Rezan.

My secretary is now almost my boss. She orders everybody around in my name, including me.

Groaning, I grab the receiver and bark, "Who is it?"

"Why are you angry?"

It's my fiancée, Roman Hiletework. I haven't been calling her as often. When women are left alone, they feel neglected. Afraid of her anger, I soften my voice and try to sound nice. "Oh, Romi! Did I sound angry?"

"Yes, Tsegaye, you roared at me like thunder!"

"That's not my fault. My superiors call me from Addis every minute just to yell at me. They want to boss me around from there. Other people call to give me a hard time because they think I'm after their jobs. How are you?"

I look at my watch as we talk – I don't have much time. I'm up to my neck in work. The Asmara Conference begins tomorrow, to formally inaugurate the Red Star Campaign. Everybody is frantic and the city is in chaos, utter chaos. Every road in Ethiopia now leads to Asmara. There are people here from every corner of the country: representatives of the Central Committee, government officials and ministers, military commanders, civic leaders of different ethnic groups, even artists. Asmara's population has swelled so fast, the city feels like it's about to explode. The same is true for me: I'm so overwhelmed with work that I'm about to detonate. I realize that Roman isn't going to hang up the phone easily, so I say a silent prayer that the call won't last too long.

"Why did you disappear like that?" she says.

"I'm alive. Well, not really – it's very stressful here."

"Did you get lost in the palm trees? How are the braided ladies of Asmara?"

"If only that were the case. I miss you."

"So why don't you call?" asks Roman.

"Honestly, if you were here, you'd see that everything has gone haywire."

For some reason I start thinking of Fiammetta Gilay. It's been almost a month since I got her phone number, but I haven't talked to her since. I arrived in Asmara on December 28th and I met her the next evening. The calendar on my desk says today is January 25th. How does time get away from me? She's probably forgotten about me.

"Why are you shutting me out?" asks Roman.

"I'm here," I say. "How is our Addis?"

"Quiet. Empty."

"All the ambitious young guys have probably moved here."

"It's dark and gloomy here for me," she says.

"I can barely tell the difference between day and night, that's how much I'm in the office. Three months will be over before we know it."

"Tsegaye, I'm afraid you've forgotten me. I worry."

"Please, stay strong," I say. "I'm lost in a jungle called the

Red Star Campaign. But when I do think of something else, I think of you – that's where my heart is."

"Stop it."

"It's the truth, I swear." Women don't believe they're loved unless you swear it to them, again and again. Especially Roman. It's that pride of hers.

"Alright then," she says.

"I miss you."

"Me too. I've sent you a cassette tape."

"What kind of tape, my love?" I ask.

"A tape of songs, to explain how much I miss you. I must have listened to it at least a hundred times."

I look at my watch again. Man, time is going fast, but I'm scared of cutting her short. Unless Roman is done with a conversation and ready to hang up, she doesn't like to be rushed. And she's already worried about us. I silently beg the god of love to tell her to end the conversation.

"Wonderful, thank you so much," I say. "I'll definitely listen to it as soon as I get it. And if there's anything you want from here, I can send it to you."

"From Asmara? What else is there other than sweaters? And their sweaters are thin, like cheap straw mats. I hear Asmara is full of cheap sweaters and cheap women."

"Maybe something else?" I say.

"The only thing I want is you. Addis is dragging me down. There's nothing to be happy about here."

"Don't be sad, Romi. I'll be done and back to you before you know it."

"Ciao," she says and hangs up.

As soon as I put down the phone I have the urge to call Fiammetta Gilay. Twice in the last month I tried calling her, but nobody answered. I pick up the phone to call her, but

143

some of my team members rush into my office. They look upset.

"Oh boy!" I say. Nobody brings me anything these days except problems. Transportation is a big one. The radio technicians need to work on the transmitter at Kagnew Station, Reporting Team One is in a rush to get to Edaga Hamus and Edaga Arbi to document art exhibitions, and Reporting Team Two needs vehicles to cover the visitors coming in from Addis. Everybody's going in different directions.

One of the cameramen who just came into my office starts ranting at me. "How can we do our jobs if we have to carry all our camera and video equipment on foot, all the way from the airport to Akriya? We're not officials, so they won't give us a car. But they want us all over the place, like salt. If we're a minute late, we get yelled at, like we're dogs. And these days nobody will even have a meeting without a TV camera running: speakers won't give their speeches, singers refuse to sing, unless someone's filming them. We're not the Almighty, we can't be everywhere at once. I won't be held responsible for the failure to document the history of this campaign. It's unacceptable to order us to go here, to go there, and not give us proper transportation. We're human beings too!" With that he drops his camera on the floor.

His complaint makes perfect sense, but I don't care for his tone. I have to make an example of him to stop this kind of angry outburst from becoming a daily occurrence.

"Your fight is not with your equipment," I say in a calm but determined voice. "I don't want to see this kind of behaviour. Pick up your camera." I can tell he's tempted to leave his camera on the floor until I grant his request. He struggles with his ego for a moment, then slowly bends down to pick up his camera. Honestly, I don't know what I would have done if he'd refused.

I sigh with relief and ask Rezan to connect me to the Regional Transportation Services Centre. When I get someone on the line, I let him have it, yelling full force at whichever Grazmatch I'm talking to – it seems like every local official here is named Grazmatch, Keganzmatch or Dejazmatch.

"What do you expect?" he says. "I have my own problems too."

"It is not like that Comrade . . . Grazmatch?" I guess.

"Yes?"

"I'm not sure you understand how journalism works. It moves fast and never stops. We can't put anything off until tomorrow or the next day. Nothing waits. I need three vehicles here right away. If our job is not accomplished because transportation is not available, someone will be held accountable. It won't be pleasant."

He says he'll send me three cars right away. The people here enjoy their own power, but revere greater power.

I look at the people standing in my office. "Comrades, any other urgent problems?" Nobody answers. "Okay. Remember, don't just complain, but work together to find solutions. And have a little patience." They seem unconvinced, but I dismiss them anyway.

As soon as they're gone I pick up the phone and call Fiammetta Gilay's work number. After three rings, she answers.

"He . . . llo?" she says, almost singing.

Even though I recognize her voice, I ask in Tigrigna, "Who am I talking to?"

"Fiammetta."

"Ah yes, the northern beauty," I say, switching to Amharic.

145

"How are you? This is Tsegaye Hailemaryam. Remember me?"

"Is that you? I thought it was an Agame calling me." As she speaks I can picture her hair bouncing back and forth.

"What?"

"Your Tigrigna makes you sound like you're an Agame," she says. "Your accent."

"Are you insulting some of your fellow Eritreans?"

She laughs. "Are you okay? You disappeared, but I see you a lot on TV. So many lies!"

Before I can answer, I hear an odd sound on the phone.

"Are you eating while you're talking to me?"

There's a pause.

"I'm brushing my teeth," she says.

"In the office?" I ask, imagining her beautiful mouth. Around here, everyone cleans their teeth with the traditional mefaqiya twig, even an old woman with one tooth left, even walking on the street, no matter if it's day or night.

"Yeaah," she says, and I hear her Tigrinya accent come through.

"Yeaaah," I say, copying and exaggerating her accent.

"Stop it," she says and laughs. "Actually, your accent is more like an Adal. And not a smart one."

"So many insults! First I'm a liar, now I'm an idiot."

"You can be both. You sweet idiot."

"How is Silay Berahi?" I ask.

"You haven't heard? What kind of reporter are you? Not a very good one. We're getting married this coming Sunday. In fact, it would have been last Sunday, but the dress I ordered from Abu Dhabi didn't get here on time." She's laughing.

"Abu Dhabi? Eritrea gets everything from there now. But congratulations! Don't forget my invitation."

"Where should we have the reception – the Embasoira or the Nyala?"

"Wherever you can afford," I say.

"Oh, you moron. I'm just teasing. No wedding. I swear, sometimes I lie for no reason. What kind of a woman am I?"

"You're a sweet liar," I say.

She laughs. "How is Red Star Asmara treating you?"

"With all the work, I haven't been able to enjoy her beauty yet."

"We welcomed you to a nice city, but now you're driving us out of it." Her tone is light.

"When can we see each other? Clearly, I need help with my Tigrigna."

"Are you going to the Massawa Festival?"

"Of course," I say.

"Why don't we meet there? I'll be at the festival with my friends. I hear it's going to be a grand time."

"Really?" I ask.

"You don't trust me?"

"Well, you just told me you were a liar."

"You moron. Look for me at Gurgusum beach. I'll be in my bikini. Ciao!" With that she hangs up.

Is she telling the truth? Or maybe that was her diplomatic way of telling me to get lost. The nerve. She's got me agitated. I don't know why confident women have that effect on me.

I don't have time to think more about Fiammetta Gilay – Firew Zerihun and Agent Seyoum Serekebirhan enter my office, one after the other. I'm not happy to see them. I have no time, nobody does. Everyone is fighting the clock and the smart ones find ways to unload their tasks on the unsuspecting.

"What's up?" I ask.

"Work by day, pasta by night!" says my friend Firew. He's one of our news photographers from Addis, but we've started calling him the Mayor of Asmara. There's no spot in the city he doesn't know, including the bordellos. Something about his short stature and big expressions makes him a natural comic.

"I take it pasta agrees with you," I say.

Firew puffs up his belly and pats it with both hands. "You don't like it because you don't understand its language."

"What language does it speak?"

"Italian or Tigrigna, it goes hand in glove with those languages. It speaks beautifully, especially when enjoyed with two glasses of wine. *Pasta, mepesete, pesete* – such a musical lady! Water doesn't work though. When you add water to pasta, it expands. So if you drink water with pasta, the same thing happens and your tummy inflates. But two glasses of wine gives you perfect digestion. That's what the Italians do, *e cosa fatta!*"

"That's a nice theory," I say.

"*Grazie. Ma non ci sono soldi,*" says Firew.

"What?"

"I'm out of money. This city is so expensive. And the women! What can you do? Isn't that right, Comrade Seyoum?"

"I can tell where this headed," I say to both of them. "You better not be here to ask me for money. I have actual work to do."

Seyoum curls his fingers like a leper and begs me. "Please, in the name of Saint Mary of Enda," he cries.

"Let Saint Mary help you," I say.

Imitating a beggar, Firew tilts his head up at me and blinks his eyes. "Please big brother, we have not even one birr."

Nature gave me a heart that doesn't know how to say no, so I take some cash from my wallet and hand it over.

"You wouldn't have to beg if you stopped taking every woman in Asmara to Caravel and treating them to gelato."

"We will not bother you again, Tsegaye," says Seyoum.

"Sure."

"I swear."

Firew smiles. "Gashe Seyoum here has started a nice business—"

"Hush!" interrupts Seyoum, trying to shut Firew up.

Firew ignores him. "How do you think he gets by? He calls Addis and tells girls that in Asmara you can get fancy shoes and purses for good prices. You know how our women are about fashion: they rush to send him money, even if they can't afford it. But Seyoum buys those really cheap shoes and purses you can get at the market and keeps the difference. It's the perfect import–export business!"

I shouldn't indulge such inappropriate behaviour by Seyoum, but I can't help laughing.

"Do you want to know what this idiot did?" says Seyoum, pointing at Firew. Now it's his turn. "His sister was visiting here with her husband back when Asmara got surrounded by the insurgents. Their sympathizers inside Asmara were having a grand time targeting people like them, from the heartland, and they were afraid they would be trapped in the city. His sister promised that she would make a big donation to the Saint Mary of Enda Church here if the revered saint would save her from such humiliation and see them back to Addis safely. Well, they did get home unharmed. So when Firew came here for Red Star, she wired him money to deliver to the church for her. But our man took the money to the bars instead, spent it all on drinks."

"Then what happened?" says Firew. "Tell the rest of the story, Seyoum."

Seyoum stays silent, so Firew takes up the story. "The day I got the money from the bank, you know I always take pity on Seyoum, so I took him out for a drink. After downing five bottles of cold beer, he asked me where I got the money. So I told him, and you know what he did? He said, 'Oh, brother, that's blasphemy! I won't drink with money pledged to Saint Mary! You're the devil himself!' Then he shoved some money at me for the drinks, crossed himself, sprinted out of the bar and ran straight to a church!"

"You guys are incredible," I laugh. "I don't know if the campaign can survive you two running around the city."

"It's just for fun," says Firew. "We all need some amusement, and the campaign won't last for ever. But you, you're so focused on your work. Did somebody promise you a promotion if we win?"

"Journalists are like singers – we never get promoted," I say. "If you start out as a journalist, you die as one."

"People say that we were selected for Red Star because they want to promote us to higher positions when we return to Addis," says Seyoum.

"That's a cow in the sky," I say.

"And what do you think the people back in Addis are saying about us?" asks Firew. "They say that all of us who got sent to Asmara were picked for the campaign because we didn't do much in Addis, so we're expendable."

"The usual lies, creating conflict," I say. Time to change the topic. I turn to Firew. "Have you checked the communication line between Tinsae Meeting Hall and Asmara Studio?"

"Yes," says Firew. "I just came from there."

"And has it been linked with Addis Ababa?"

"Yes, everything on both ends is ready to go for the

convention broadcast. But the Addis office doesn't seem to have much faith in us being up to the task."

"Anything else?"

"I checked everything based on your orders," says Firew. "The banner graphics are ready to be inserted in the TV broadcast, and the voice-over commentaries and songs are ready too. All the production tasks have been listed out and assigned. We are all set and ready. The audio recording equipment, the microphones and cameras, they're all in position. Same with the microwave link, it's all set and ready. The connection between Asmara Revolution Square and Saba Stadium is laid out correctly. We have it all covered."

"Perfect, good job. If everyone was like that, we wouldn't have anything to worry about."

"That's the first time you've said anything like that," says Firew.

"Said what?"

"Praise! You're not satisfied with your own work, let alone other people's. You're always worrying for no reason. Trust people, let them do their job."

"Are there people who can be trusted?" I ask.

"Comrade, trust is mutual. I trust you if you trust me. The Red Star Campaign isn't just your responsibility, it's everyone's responsibility."

"I hope you're right."

"I'm worried about you, my friend," says Firew. "You're really tense these days. Bottling things up."

"We've been ordered to keep ourselves tied down tight, remember? In a campaign like this, there is no such thing as hurt feelings or slowing down. Or sleep."

But Firew is right; he knows me well. I have not been satisfied with other people's work here. And I'm anxious. There's so much to do, all of it urgent, that I'm forced to delegate tasks. But then they're out of my control, and all I can do is pray that they get done right, and done quickly. I don't feel good about it. Making television is an art, no matter what some people think, and like any artist, I hate being coerced. My soul rebels against it. You can't be creative on command, and taking orders exhausts me. I need sleep, but my superiors are merciless.

"There's one thing I am really worried about though," I tell Firew.

"What?"

"The movie cameras and film we ordered from abroad haven't arrived yet. We have what we need for the convention in Asmara tomorrow, and for the Massawa Festival. But if the military offensive starts before they get here, I don't know where I'm going to hide. We won't have enough cameras or film to cover it. It's giving me nightmares."

"Don't fret," says Firew with a smile. "They'll get here. Everything always comes together at the last minute."

Firew Zerihun is the most optimistic person I know. He only sees the sunny side of things.

"Well, I came here for an entirely different reason," says Agent Seyoum.

"What intelligence do you think you'll get from me?" I ask. "Propaganda isn't secret." I like teasing the security people.

"Oh, it has its share of secrets," he says and smiles, showing off his straight white teeth.

"So what do you need?"

"It's about the jamming operation you're conducting."

"Yes, I think it's going well."

"The insurgents are still broadcasting. We suspect there are Red Star insiders who are sabotaging the jamming. We need to find out who they are and eliminate them." He isn't smiling anymore.

"No way! The insurgents can broadcast, but their signal can't reach anywhere because our jamming blocks it." My voice is loud now. "Between the technical collaboration from Addis and the blocking we do from here, our effort is producing the expected results. They change their location and frequency dozens of times every day. You can't just say you suspect an insider without a shred of evidence. That doesn't help the campaign!" I'm agitated and snapping, like a flax seed in a hot pan.

"Why so negative?" asks Seyoum. He is very calm.

"That's how it is! I've been yelled at too many times about this. Our men are fighting a war of bandwidths and frequencies, and it's not easy. It's noisy and nerve-racking, and if they don't get a break soon, they'll end up in the nut house. Go and see for yourself what they're doing. Dimtsi Hafash is already muffled. If you want to totally silence their broadcasts, then we need to destroy their main broadcasting station. And that's not my decision to make!" These days everyone's temper is hot.

"If we knew the location of their station, destroying it would be easy," says Seyoum.

"Can't Silay tell us?" I ask.

"It's portable. It's probably somewhere in Nakfa, but how can we find one antenna moving around all those mountains? It's not like we haven't been trying."

"What surprised me is that Shabia started moving locations just as we started jamming them," I say. "They were prepared, they knew it was coming. So maybe they do have an inside man."

"That's what I said."

"Who could it be?"

"These sympathizers are tricky. They have hearts like crooked roads, hard to follow. Have you been on the road to Keren, with all those twists and turns? They're like that."

"Then it's time for you to go for a drive, comrade," I say. "Security is your job."

"How's Fiammetta Gilay?" he asks, changing the subject.

"Why? Am I supposed to be having an affair with her?"

"She's been asking around about you," says Seyoum.

"Agent Teklay Zedingl asked me about her the other day. What are you Public Safety people worried about?" I'm surprised they're even paying attention to this, with everything else going on. "Anyway, you're better off asking Silay Berahi. I don't know a thing about her. And if I did, that would be my own private business."

"Silay is angry with you because of her."

"Why? What have I done?"

"She has her eye on you. Teklay's angry too – he thinks you beat him to the prize. And when it comes to women, he's used to winning. She's a beauty."

"So, why don't you try your luck?" I ask Seyoum.

"I did."

"And?"

"Unsuccessful."

"Is there anyone in Red Star who isn't chasing after her?" I say.

"You might be the lucky one," says Firew. "Don't worry about your fiancée. She's in Addis."

"Thank you both for all the advice I didn't ask for."

"I don't get it," Seyoum says. "Women fall for you, and you're not even that good-looking. What's your secret?"

I laugh and give him my time-tested advice: "Ignore

them and they will come to you. When they do, treat them with respect and they will love you. Love them, satisfy them, but – following the 11th Commandment of the Good Book – do not trust them. That's all there is to it." I'm having fun with this.

Rezan rings me on the phone. "Comrade Tsegaye, there's a call for you from Addis."

It's my superior. He goes straight to what's on his mind.

"It's about the cameras ordered from abroad," he says.

"They've arrived?" That would be wonderful.

"Listen, I'm here in Addis. I'm not in charge of New York or London or Geneva or wherever they're making the cameras. It's out of my control. But I'm calling to tell you that I just received a telegram saying the cameras won't arrive this week."

"Oh boy," I say.

"On another matter, why are you disparaging the ministry?"

"I'm doing *what*?"

"You were sent to Asmara to represent us, Tsegaye, not to insult us."

"What insults? What are you talking about?" My voice is loud and angry.

"Why are Red Star people calling me and complaining, as if they don't trust that we're working hard back here in Addis too?" He's like a wounded animal when his pride is on the line.

"I don't know anything about that. Why don't you ask the people who are calling you? Listen, comrade, I'm not playing games and I'm not the problem. If you want to doubt me, fine, but you might as well be suspicious of your own shadow."

The phone goes silent. Either he isn't saying anything or

the line is dead. I don't even have time to get angry as there's another call coming in.

"Hello!"

"My ears! Why the loud voice?" It's the Chief of Protocol.

"My apologies," I say in a quieter voice.

"It's okay, darling, you're not the only one who's yelling and screaming these days. It's infected us all. But your presence is requested, urgently."

"Where?"

"Where do you think? Right here! Chairman's office." He hangs up.

I look at my watch and it's past noon. Nobody seems to care about lunch anymore. I wonder why I'm needed. It's probably to do with the cameras and film. My deadline was January 18th, and we're a week past that now. The Chairman doesn't forget a thing.

"Listen, Firew," I say. "Tell our reporters to be at Tinsae Hall tomorrow at six a.m. Exactly at six am. And make sure they dress right. I don't want to see any hippie journalists."

Firew and Seyoum leave. As they do, Suslov comes into my office with his pointy face and regal attitude.

"Comrade Tsegaye, your phone is always busy," he says.

"Everyone calls me. People think a news release is the solution to every problem. If television cameras are pointed at them, they assume they're making history. And if we don't broadcast it, then they think it didn't happen."

"I'm actually here to discuss the progress of the propaganda work." Suslov – real name Yeshitla Masresha – is still standing. He doesn't like sitting in someone else's office chair. He's smoking a cigarette, which I've never seen him do before.

"Alright, but I've been summoned to the Palace."

"This won't take long. The propaganda we're producing should not be emotional. We're here to fight separatism, that's it, not to change existing customs or create new ones. When we talk about unity, it has to be about the unified class struggle of the proletariat as defined by the Revolution. It should reflect both our national character and the international context of our struggle. Scientific socialism requires scientific propaganda. Instead of putting forth one sensational claim after another, we should be rigorous and analytical. Instead of hurling insults, let us show the reality on the ground, the facts as they exist. But don't be too wordy – I hate that."

"Sure, that's fine. We'll try." I say. "I'm like you, I don't care for big stacks of wild words. That's why I hate contemporary poetry. But it can't be too dry. People have feelings. They like things that appeal to their emotions."

From his expression, Suslov doesn't care for my response.

"For all the material you're preparing," he says, "it should be carefully reviewed and edited by experts before it's published or broadcast."

Does he not think I'm already doing that? Regardless, Suslov walks out and I'm right behind him, hurrying to the Palace.

I meet Solomon Betregiorgis going down the stairs, two steps at a time. He's always in a rush but, as usual, he looks like he's been relaxing all day.

"Ready to broadcast the conference?" he asks.

"Everything's ready."

"From here on out, the success or failure of the Asmara Conference depends on how you present it," he says.

"Lord help us then."

"The Lord has no ears for politics," says Solomon and darts away.

I run over to the Palace where the Chief of Protocol, Tedla Regassa, waves me into his office. He's on the phone giving instructions about the seating arrangements for tomorrow. When he finishes, he looks up at me and smiles. "You've been invited for lunch."

"Good, but I hope it's not pasta again."

"No, you'll be wined and dined with our world-renowned delicacy: militia gruel!"

"It's actually not bad," I say. "I spent a week in the Ogaden eating nothing else."

"Yes, it works well for both hunger and thirst. It can also warm you up if you mix some sugar into the porridge and let it ferment for a few days. If we ran out, the army would mutiny." He looks at his watch and grimaces.

"What's wrong?"

"I've been unable to enforce the radical notion that lunch should be served on time."

There's a commotion outside his door and he smiles. The Chairman and a parade of officials are coming down the hallway. We join them and head to the Palace dining hall. The Chairman walks with his head bowed and his hands behind his back, as if buried in thought. We sit at tables set with injera bread and wot stew. I guess Tedla was joking about the militia gruel.

My stomach starts to grumble but no-one is touching the food yet. Instead of eating, the Chairman asks questions and makes comments. It's more of a meeting than a meal. Ministers, commissioners, military commanders – they're all angling to get the Chairman's attention. Did we leave any officials behind in Addis? I question why some of them are here, but then again, a cold wind blows on those who are distant from the centre of power. There's a lot of talk about development projects, hospitals, logistics, construction. I'm really hungry.

Finally, Comrade Chairman reaches over and takes some injera. The rest of us dive in. The Chairman doesn't seem to have much appetite, and I think he could stand to gain a few pounds. I'm just about to take a big mouthful of injera and wot when the Chairman looks right at me.

"How's the media?" he asks.

I set my food back down. "We are good, Comrade Chairman."

"The Ethiopian proletariat must be able to follow the class struggle in this region via newspaper, radio and television," he says. "The Eritrean struggle is our national priority, and the media must show the people that we are winning, defeating the cancer that has taken root here."

"We are ready to do that," I say.

"How about the cameras we ordered from abroad?" asks the Chairman.

I explain that none of them have arrived yet, and the reasons for the delay. To ease his displeasure, I tell him everything will be here by next week, and that in the meantime we can cover all the Red Star activities with the cameras and film we already have on hand.

The expression on his face is alarming me. It looks as though he's about to ask another question, but the Chief Secretary speaks up instead.

"Comrade Chairman, please eat," he says. "We should not bring our work to the lunch table. It is bad for the digestion." The Chief Secretary is such a sweet bag of nuts.

The Chairman gives a little smile and takes a small bite of injera.

As for me, I've lost my appetite.

11

CALL OF THE RED STAR

"It is indisputable that Ethiopia, throughout its long history and by the virtuous courage of its youth, has defended its lands from the Omo River Valley in the south all the way to its Red Sea coast. Even though the challenge we face now in our northern province is unique, this region has suffered for many years from one conflict after another. The Turks, the Egyptians, the Italians – all have waged war on us, attempted to invade our country by using our Red Sea coast as their entry point. Our northern region is the origin of our civilization, giving us our unique character, our cultural heritage, our religion, our alphabet, and these are well-established facts that cannot be repudiated. By the same token, it is also undeniable that we have confronted one invasion after another that attacked our country from this direction.

"We have maintained and protected our historical solidarity: Kaleb ruled the Red Sea route from Adulis, Libne Dingel wandered in the jungle for years, and Yohannes paid the ultimate price by sacrificing his head at Metemma. Alula Abanega stopped an invading army at Dogali, declaring the Red Sea to be the natural border of Ethiopia, and those who dared challenge him learned their lesson from the might of his army's sword and perished in the unforgiving desert. King Tewodros fought valiantly until the last bullet and then took his own life at Mekdela so as to not be imprisoned by any other human being, let alone a foreign invader. King Menelik and Empress Taitu inspired every patriot with a call to victory and turned the battlefield into a raging fireball, decimating the invading Italian army at Adwa. Upon hearing testimonials like these, one after another, it reminds us of who we are, reminds us of our enduring struggle to preserve our independence, reminds us of our centuries-old quest to be left alone so that we may live in peace. This is a country in eternal search of peace, as parched land thirsts for water.

"At this historical conference attended by representatives of the Ethiopian proletariat, the Eritrean Province Red Star Multi-Faceted Revolutionary Campaign and its context, purpose and goals is declared to all Ethiopians on January 26, 1982 from Tinsae Hall located inside Asmara Palace. It is a momentous day and all the cities, towns, villages, mountains and valleys across the country shall remain tuned to the conference proceedings."

Sitting in my office equipped with a specially designed telephone system, I am monitoring the historic speeches via radio link. I coordinate the broadcast of the Asmara Conference proceedings between the temporary studio inside Tinsae Hall and the main studio at Asmara Radio Station. As I work, I imagine the millions of people across Ethiopia listening to us on their transistor radios while at work in factories, offices and fields. I can feel their patriotism. The Chairman's speech is extraordinary and inspiring, clearly laying out the origins of the insurgency and the current situation. He vows that we will resolve the Eritrean problem, once and for all. The Red Star class war is declared, and the Red Star call for peace put forward – war and peace.

For the past eight years, we Ethiopians have been at war with each other. Will the god of revolution relent and grant us peace now? Or will our misfortunes continue with more death? Today, the people of Eritrea are called upon to render that verdict.

Director Betru Tessema comes into the studio and looks at all the radio gear and telephones around me.

"Don't you look like a busy cook, all her pots and pans on the stove," he says.

"Well, we are the household help, right?" I ask. "The staff whose work never ends?"

"Are the speeches really being broadcast to every part of Ethiopia?"

"Definitely. Would you like to hear for yourself?"

"Is that possible?" he asks.

"It's easy."

I hand him the phone that connects us with the News Service Agency offices in Gondar, Gojjam, Mekelle, Addis Ababa and other cities. It's an open line, and Betru listens as reports come in about the broadcast from different areas of the country.

"Are you a believer now?" I ask him after a few minutes. "Thanks to the transistor radio, all of Ethiopia has ears."

Betru nods, but his usual smile is missing and his fair-skinned face has lost its shine. "You look troubled," I say.

"Yes, I'm really worried, Tsegaye."

"About what?"

He looks puzzled. "About what? All the leaders and

high-ranking officials in the entire country are gathered together under one roof. Of course I'm nervous."

"What do you think will happen?"

"Anything can happen. The insurgents are ambitious. They might try something to get the world's attention."

Betru turns and looks out of the window. The sun is shining and the wind makes the palm trees sway like they're dancing to a slow sad song.

"You're right," I say. "We're like eggs in one basket."

I've caught Betru's anxiety. The insurgents have launched several attacks in the city in the past two days. It's not been easy on Director Betru and his internal security team. Last week another security official was unceremoniously relieved of his duties, so Betru has several reasons to worry. The Red Star Campaign has raised everyone's blood pressure.

"We've tightened security throughout the city and the surrounding area . . ." he says, his voice trailing off. He slowly scratches the window glass with his fingers. His back is as broad as a dresser, and tense.

"But you're still worried?"

"What if there's a conspiracy at work? An assassination plot, or some kind of terrorist attack. To create chaos. Probably in the next few days. Here at the conference, or at the festival in Massawa. No, maybe not there – they know security is tight in those places. But somewhere. I can smell it in the air."

Betru pauses, then turns from the window to face me again.

"By the way, do you have the tape of the interview you did with Silay Berahi?" he asks.

We keep old interview tapes here in the studio in case we need to use clips of them. "Why do you need it?" I ask.

"I need it."

"Is there something you're suspicious of?"

"What does it matter to you?" says Betru. "If you have the tape, then let me have it." He is rapidly losing his patience.

"If you're suspicious of Silay, why not force it out of him? Hang him upside down."

"We don't do that, not anymore. We know how to get information without torture. No secret lasts for ever. People rarely take them to their graves. Sooner or later they let it out. You just have to be there at the right time to catch it."

"The insurgents and their sympathizers are good at not letting their secrets slip out," I say. "And they recruit people who have never been under any suspicion to carry out missions. It could be your trusted neighbour, a good friend, a respected official, or even the head of an important government agency."

"You seem to know a lot about them," says Betru.

"I'm a journalist." I start looking for the interview tape in the filing cabinet. "There's nothing new in the Silay tape. If I'd known in advance what you wanted from him, maybe I could have got something out of him. But nobody ever tells us ahead of time." I find my notes from the interview and pull them out, then look again for the tape. "My own opinion is that the last two defectors did more damage to Shabia than Silay. From what I hear, that forced Shabia to change their organizational structure and many of their tactics. Compared to that, Silay's defection is no big deal. I don't get why they keep complaining so much about him on their Dimtsi Hafash radio broadcasts, like he's the first and only defector."

"Interesting. Why indeed?"

"I'm not sure," I say. "Maybe because of how he damaged morale? But when I interviewed Silay, there was one thing he said that stood out for me. He was adamant about it."

"What was it?" Betru asks. I can tell he's in a hurry to get an answer.

I check my interview notes. "This is what he said: 'We claim to be liberators. But truth be told, we are not. Who are we liberating the Eritrean people from? Unless we can convince the people that Ethiopia is a colonizing state like the European powers, then our struggle is misguided and lacks justification. Unlike the Ethiopian Patriots' struggle, or other wars of liberation in Angola, Namibia and Zimbabwe, ours is not an anti-colonialist war. We cannot claim this civil unrest is designed to bring about political change, because it is not. Compared to the civil wars in China, Cuba and Vietnam, or the ones long ago in France, Spain and Russia, or the one now in El Salvador, our struggle is very different and lacks any connection with those, either in philosophy or purpose. Overall, we are not fighting to introduce a new political order. If we were, we would not be raising our swords to fight against the Revolution that is attempting to establish a socialist system in Ethiopia. So what is the foundation and purpose, the motive and objective of our struggle? In short, it is an ego-driven short-sighted adventure without merit.'"

"Do you think he believes all that?" asks Betru.

"How would I know? But regardless of whether he believes it, what he says has some truth." I find the tape and hand it to Betru. "But I don't believe Silay when he says the insurgents have no choice but to huddle together like monkeys in Nakfa."

"Why don't you believe him?"

"Gathering all your forces together in one place? That's suicide."

"So what do you think they'll do?" asks Betru.

"I don't know – that's a job for military intelligence. What

165

if they lure our army to Nakfa and then march on Asmara instead?"

Betru laughs. "No chance. A guerrilla force, once it grows and becomes a conventional army, it can never go back. It's like going back to nothingness, impossible. If they try to become guerrillas again, they will fall apart fighting each other. No, it won't happen that way."

I shrug.

He rubs his eyes. "Do you know a woman named Fiammetta Gilay?" asks Betru.

"Why is everyone asking me about her? I have no relationship with her. I met her one time at a party, and we talked once on the phone. That's it."

"Why don't you arrange to meet her in person?"

"Why should I do that? Please, do tell?"

"She's a beautiful girl, isn't that enough?"

"Okay, I get it," I say.

"What do you get?"

"I think you want something from her."

"If you say so," says Betru.

"Why don't you use someone from your own team? You have some very sharp boys working for you. And I'm a journalist, not a spy. I have no experience with this."

"Anyone with a good nose for news makes a good spy. And I believe you're a true patriot."

"What does patriotism have to do with this?" I ask.

"Anyone who spies for his country, for the Revolution, for the security of the people, they're a patriot. It's not like before. The Public Safety agency isn't the public enemy. Anyway, you think about it." Betru turns to leave.

"Why do you want me to get closer to Fiammetta?" I ask.

"So that, through her, you can get closer to someone else."

166

"What sort of someone else?"

"The Silay Berahi sort." Director Betru disappears through the studio door.

Silay Berahi. The insurgent radio station Dimtsi Hafash denounces him as a traitor on a daily basis. But why are they so angry at him? Is it because he exposed the fact that the Shabia leader Isayas Afewerki has a close relationship with the CIA? The United States will never forget the humiliation it was handed by Ethiopia when we closed their Kagnew Station in Eritrea. It cost the Americans their alliance with us, and thus their staging ground into the rest of East Africa. Somalia is no replacement for that. So now who else can they turn to in this region except the insurgents? I'm sure the Americans would love to get back into their listening post at Kagnew Station, right in the heart of Asmara. And the Red Sea. They held joint training exercises there with Egypt, their "Operation Bright Star". Red Star and Bright Star – coincidence? Did Silay defect in order to carry out the Bright Star mission from the inside? I almost feel sorry for him; he is the colobus monkey caught between two trees.

I lose my train of thought as my staff barges into the studio. It's the television crew with the morning's film.

"So, boys, how did it go?" I ask.

"We're exhausted, but the filming went well," says one of them. "The audio may be spotty here and there though. If we can get it ready for tonight, that would be a miracle."

"Trust me, it will be broadcast tonight from Addis." I turn to the others. "How about it, was it a success?" I had sent a crew around Asmara to film people listening to the speeches and reacting to the conference. The idea is to run that as a segment on the news tonight.

"It was great. We went everywhere in Asmara. We even

interviewed some of the workers at the Melotti Brewery. It was so sad to be surrounded by beer but not be able to drink any."

"The life of a journalist." I hand them some beer money for later. "Listen, after lunch I want you to go ahead to Massawa. Make sure you bring the camera lights, spare batteries, cords – take everything we need to cover the festival. I'll join you there later."

They leave and I box up all the film from the morning, both movie and still photos. I head straight for Army Aviation where a special plane is waiting to take it to Addis. How crazy is that? Filming speeches in Asmara in the morning and sending the tapes to Addis Ababa by plane to be broadcast that night on the news – in this day and age, that's no miracle. A miracle would be broadcasting it live to the public on TV, instead of just radio. As I pass Tiravolo and drive fast towards Sembel Field, the whole situation makes me smile.

One day all the major cities of Ethiopia will be linked by two-way television and radio communications. If we have peace, we can make that happen. With peace, we can put our energy towards creating prosperity. Of course, once we have prosperity, people will probably forget about the media. They'll be too busy eating and drinking. Hungry people solve problems. It's like what Lenin said when asked if Communists have dreams: "You think we eat and spend the night burping? Yes, we dream, but we dream of a better world."

What would our world look like without the media? How are we going to solve our problems going forward? It should not be left up to the battlefield. What is the purpose of life if not to work for harmony, peace and human progress? The people of the planet, with or without the confusion of the media, have been incapable of living as one. What a sorry world! And there is no replacement – she's an only child.

I arrive at Army Aviation at Sembel. Major Koricho Tadesse does not welcome me with his usual smile. He's lost weight and looks stressed. He's probably just busy. Jets, helicopters and small planes take off and land every minute. People and freight are constantly loaded and unloaded. The airfield resembles a mental asylum. But unlike the last time I was here, Major Koricho doesn't seem interested in the planes as they take off and land; he's not even looking at them.

"Why are you late?" he yells at me. It's not really a question.

"Isn't the aeroplane just for this film? The speeches ran long – these things happen."

"Things?" he says, still angry. The man is not well.

"Look, Major, it was entirely out of my control, otherwise I wouldn't have been late." I hand him the box with all the film.

In the past he would always call for someone to take the film and load it onto the plane. Now, though, he takes the box himself and hurries off with it right away. His hustle pleases me and I go back to my car. Fighter jets and cargo planes are taking off and landing. The airfield shakes from their roars and my ears ache. I start the car and remember a roll of film that's still in my pocket. I turn off the engine and run to catch up with Major Koricho.

I find him with a tall skinny young man in mechanic's coveralls. They're unloading a crate from the special plane assigned to deliver our film to Addis Ababa. The plane used to belong to Madame Melotti and is parked away from the others on one side of the hangar. The Major and the young man are focused on the crate and don't notice me approach.

"Comrade Major," I call out.

Major Koricho spins around to face me and the crate he and the young man were unloading slams down onto the tarmac. One side of it breaks open and I catch a glimpse of Kalashnikov assault rifles. They look brand new, straight from the factory. There isn't anything unusual about this, weapons are loaded and unloaded here all the time. But if dropping them caused an explosion or a fire, our film could be destroyed and that would be a tragedy. The Major and the young man look shocked and angry, but I don't know why. I feel like I've seen the young man somewhere before, but I can't place him. He runs and gets a rope and lashes the crate back together.

"What is it, Tsegaye?" asks Major Koricho in a raspy voice.

"This roll of film, I forgot I had it in my pocket."

"Why are you so disorganized? You should have put it with the rest." He grabs it from me.

Something about this situation makes me nervous, so I try to lighten the mood. "Comrade Major, when do you think you might find time for an interview?"

"I don't have the time," he says.

"I understand, you're overloaded with work. But I really want to interview you before you retire. It will be a wonderful story."

"I'll think about it," says Major Koricho, but he doesn't sound enthusiastic.

He has more grey hair now than when we stood here together last month. His skin is darker too. But who doesn't have more grey hair and burnt skin these days? These are the rewards of the Red Star Campaign: getting darker, skinnier and greyer. I'm sure I have some grey hairs myself now.

Before I leave I ask him, "By the way, do my people need to meet the plane at Army Aviation in Addis, like usual?"

"No. Bole Airport." He turns his back to me. "I have no time now." He's basically telling me to get the hell out of here.

I don't have time either, as I think about all that my crew and I have to do in Massawa.

12

FESTIVAL IN MASSAWA

Going from Asmara to Massawa is like diving from a high mountain into the Red Sea, a drop of 7,500 feet. I arrive just before sunset, the January air still cool. The city is filling up with people in anticipation of the festival, all the Red Star officials here from Asmara, everyone wearing sweatshirts printed with the festival logo. Commemorative flags flutter all over town. There's a sense of celebration in the air, a holiday atmosphere. The Red Sea is calm and gilded with the rays of the setting sun, a lake of molten metal. The horizon burns gold and yellow.

The festival has lent some of its brightness to daytime Massawa, but she is a city of the night. She sleeps in the day then wakes at dusk and vibrates with energy until dawn. But I can tell she has lost some of her shine: three years ago she was a battleground, a killing field, and the scars are visible on her face.

This is how the Battle of Massawa happened. Until December 1977, the Shabia faction of the insurgency occupied ten of Massawa's thirteen districts. The city includes the mainland, called Edaga, and a small island several hundred yards off the coast called Taulud. The insurgents were in control of the Edaga mainland from the gas refinery and along the coast from Gurgusum beach all the way to the cement factory. Their main outpost was Saint Michael's Church in Edaga, which they had fortified with three .50 calibre machine guns. The church overlooks the one bridge between the mainland and the island of Taulud, parts of which remained under government control. But with the machine guns, it would be impossible for government troops to get across the bridge. The only other way to get from Taulud island to the Edaga mainland is on foot across the marsh flats at low tide, but that also invited a hail of gunfire from the fortified church.

Thinking back, I'm amazed at how our Revolutionary Army managed to not only hold out on Taulud, but advance and destroy Shabia's fortifications on Edaga. It was a breathtaking operation carried out by fearless patriots. Sword meeting sword, black men bayoneted and bleeding red, breath leaving bodies: a mission of death.

The attack plan was based on careful study of the insurgent fortifications. Shabia believed them impenetrable, but our commanders saw a way. To keep the plan from leaking out, the officers were sequestered in the assembly hall on Taulud until the last minute. At 5 a.m. the officers led their men out in two units, both heavily armed.

One unit started from the naval base and began sneaking across the marsh flats towards the Edaga mainland and Saint Michael's Church. The other unit advanced on the lone bridge between Taulud and Edaga. As they went, they fired shots from different locations to confuse the enemy.

With both units in position, the commanding officer ordered the gunners to fire on the insurgents' machine-gun emplacement in Saint Michael's Church. No shots came. "What are you waiting for?" demanded the commander. "How can I?" replied the lead gunner, pointing at the church and holding up the cross that hung around his neck. The commander drew his pistol and pointed it at the gunner's head. "I order you to fire!" he yelled. The gunner crossed himself and asked for Saint Michael's forgiveness, then pulled the trigger. In a volley of fire, Shabia's machine guns in the church were silenced for ever. Shabia never expected that we would dare to shoot at a church, never expected that we would pay that price to defeat them.

The Revolutionary Army attacked Edaga from both sides, charging in with grenades and bayonets. By mid-morning all of Shabia's fortifications were destroyed and their fighters annihilated. It was the end of the Battle of Massawa. Our commanders had estimated that several thousand soldiers might be lost in the attack, but our deaths were limited to six hundred. The battle decimated Shabia's best fighters and has become a famous example of a heroic attack on a seemingly invincible position.

I walk past Saint Michael's on Edaga, where the road runs along the beach. There I notice two skulls emerging out of a dune. I kneel down and study them. Maybe an insurgent and a soldier, both fallen in battle. I try to figure out who was who. Both skulls have the same shape, the same anatomy. I brush the sand back over them and let them resume spending eternity next to each other. I turn and walk back towards where I parked my car. Before I can get there, a convoy of Land Cruisers roars towards me and I freeze.

"Tsegaye!" a voice calls out from one of the speeding cars. It's Solomon Betregiorgis. He hits the brakes and I close my eyes – I don't want to see the other cars slam into him. But somehow they don't and he's fine.

"What are you doing here?" he asks from the car window.

"Just looking around."

"Why?"

"That's what journalists do," I say.

"Get in," says Solomon.

"Where are we going?"

"We'll go through town, check that everything's ready at Gurgusum."

"What about my car?" I ask.

"Leave it. We have guards all over the city. Didn't you see all the security on the road from Asmara?"

I hop into his Land Cruiser and he accelerates, followed by the three cars behind us. He's smoking a pipe and drives like a maniac. I was right not to get a ride with him from Asmara – if I had, I'd be five pounds thinner from sheer terror. I'm sure he loved speeding down the mountain along the razor-edge cliffs at Nefasit and Embatkala, Dengolo and Dogali. Even going slow, the highway from Asmara to Massawa can make the hair on the back of your neck stand up.

"How did everything go this morning?" Solomon asks.

"It went well. All of Ethiopia was all ears."

"Wonderful!" With his pipe stuck in his mouth he talks through his teeth. "Did you get a room here for the night?"

"Yes, thanks to you. I booked a room at the Dahlak Hotel. But I hear a lot of people left it too late and are upset that all the good places are full."

"Please, never mind those people and their creature comforts. I'm not worried about their complaints – my only concern is the festival itself."

The Gurgusum–Massawa train clangs past us and Solomon

takes the pipe out of his mouth. "Look there," he says and gestures at the train with his pipe. "That's the other miracle. The insurgents stole the rails to use in their fortifications, but we managed to repair it in just two weeks. If people truly want to accomplish something big, there's nothing that can stop them." He taps my arm with his pipe. "There are loud-speakers on the train now, can you hear the song?"

"Yes, I do," I say.

He starts singing along, "'*The train is fast, the train is fast . . .*' – it's that old one by the Lalibela Arts." The train catches up with us, then pulls ahead.

"I'm so amazed by this Revolution," he says. "Enrolling fifty-six thousand students in the Development through Cooperation Campaign. Creating the Tatek Military Academy from scratch and training three hundred thousand soldiers in just a few months. All that, and now for the launch of the Red Star Campaign, bringing in thousands of people from all over Ethiopia, arranging their stay in Asmara for the conference, then to Massawa for the festival. That's big, and it's not easy. It takes determination. Do you know how many divisions the army had before the Revolution? Only four. And how many do you think it has now? A dozen, three times as many. Honestly, the way a revolution makes you super-organized and totally capable of delivering results is just spectacular."

He puts his pipe back in his mouth and again speaks through clenched teeth. "I'm telling you the truth. Those of us who have been in the Revolution and lived through it, we'll be more than happy to help the next generation run their own revolution. We won't be like the old socialist countries – we'll help the youth, whether it's starting a new revolution or protecting this one. We should start our own consulting business on how to run a revolution."

176

We finally slow down when we reach Gurgusum. A lively city of tents in green, red and yellow fills the beach.

"What could we charge?" I ask.

"For what?"

"For what you just said, revolutionary consulting." We both laugh.

"Oh, you cynical journalists," says Solomon. "Really, the history of the human race has been one of progress, even if you can't see it."

He parks the Land Cruiser and turns off the engine. Right away his security entourage is out of their vehicles and taking up positions around us. Solomon gets out of the car and heads towards the beach, but he is immediately met by members of the festival's organizing committee. Everyone wants to be near men of power like Solomon. Soon he is surrounded and I lose sight of him.

The Gurgusum coast is breathtaking. Waves crash one on top of the other like beats of a drum, rolling up along the beach to wipe clean the sand, then calmly returning back into the sea. People from Addis and the heartland stand and stare out at the water in awe. Some have probably never seen the sea before. Out along the horizon a boat bobs up and down in the dusk. The lights of the city trace rays out into the water, bouncing from one wave to the next. Everyone is outside their tents, hundreds of people relaxing in the cool evening. The beach is a kaleidoscope, each cluster of colourful tents belonging to a different ethnic group, a different religious group, a different civic association. Tomorrow is the grand opening of the Massawa Festival, so there are singers and performers and theatre companies all rehearsing among the tents, their songs floating out over the sea, hitting the waves and echoing back.

177

I hear Solomon calling me and I go over to him.

"How does everything look so far?" he asks. "Isn't it going splendidly?"

"No doubt, it's going well," I say.

"Yes, tomorrow we'll have all kinds of food here, drinking and dancing. You know, for the last four hundred years, Ethiopia has not been able to really enjoy this place, even though it's our birthright. It's been all blood and sorrow here. But the Red Sea is our lifeline and our sustenance, and we should realize how important it is to our existence."

We stand and look out at all the tents as the night begins to obscure them.

"I'm sure that most of the people here from Addis had no idea what the Red Sea looked like," says Solomon. "For most of our people, the furthest their thoughts go is the limits of their village, the banks of their river. Honestly, I would be so happy if all of Ethiopia could come here and visit the Red Sea. Then everyone would understand why our ancestors fought so hard for it, and why we need this Red Star Campaign."

Once Solomon starts talking, he won't stop until he's said everything he has in mind to say. I pull out my notebook and start jotting down some of what he's said.

Solomon points over to one side. "Can you see the tukuls?"

Despite the dark I can make out two structures, both round with thatched walls and roofs.

"Yes, I see them," I say. Solomon nods and seems very satisfied. I spot some festival committee members by the tukuls. They appear to be in an advanced state of exhaustion.

"We had to airfreight the straw for them," says Solomon. He's in a hurry and we walk back towards his car. "How come you're not saying anything about the cost?" he asks, but I don't answer.

"Where to now?" I say once we're in the car.

"To Kaleb Hall. I want to check that the photography exhibition is ready."

"It is. I was there earlier and everything's ready for the opening celebration. We're all set for tomorrow. All I need now is some rest."

"Do you have the master schedule for the festival?" he asks.

"Yes, but what time is the ceremony at Dogali tomorrow morning?"

"I don't know the exact time either, but be there at six."

He drives me back to Edaga and drops me by my car.

I go back to the Dahlak Hotel, hoping to get to bed early. From my room I have a view of the sea. In the waves the city lights are dancing and playing their games. The surf booms against the sea wall, then hisses back out to sea. Watching the water revives me and I'm no longer sleepy. Instead, I take a shower and go down to the hotel bar.

I want to get a beer, but the place is jammed and there's hardly room to stand. Everyone at the Red Star launch in Asmara this morning is now packed into the bar. Some are laughing, others are arguing, and some are lost in deep, thoughtful conversations. And, of course, some are camped out at the bar, ordering one beer after another, hoarding them in anticipation of it running out. A few are working hard at complaining about the lack of hospitality arrangements.

Director Betru Tessema is standing in a corner and seems to be counting the officials here one by one. For him, this must be like shepherding jumpy goats. Agent Teklay Zedingl is in another corner talking with a tall man I recognize – the young mechanic I saw with Major Koricho at Army Aviation today. And now I remember the first time I saw him, he was with Teklay then too. I try to shove my way over to them but then I see Silay Berahi making his way through a knot of officials. I manage to grab Silay's shoulder and he stops.

"Hello, my dear comrade Tsegaye," he says.

"Where have you been?" I ask.

"I've been around. I've been working on my presentation for the symposium. You people never give me enough time."

"That's because we don't have time to spare either."

"Here's hoping your haste will lead to success," he says in a sarcastic voice.

"But wait, aren't you one of us now?"

"Me? I'm nothing but a stray dog that's crawled back home."

"We stopped using that phrase," I say. "Now we say you have returned to the community in peace."

"You call it peace?" he asks.

"What else should I call it?"

He just smiles, again sarcastically I think. His eyes dart around the room, as if he's looking for someone. He's anxious.

"What's your presentation at the symposium about?" I say.

"It's about the connection between Shabia and the CIA."

"What purpose will that serve?"

"It will help expose Shabia's reactionary stance. What do you think?" He looks at me intently, trying to read my expression.

"It won't change the Shabia–CIA collaboration," I say. "That's been going on for years. We know the CIA uses Shabia for its own benefit. But do we know that Shabia benefits from the CIA?"

Silay doesn't answer but I can tell he's annoyed. Someone elbows past us and I continue. "And do we know that

Shabia will gather its forces together in the mountains of Nakfa?"

"What other choice do they have?" he asks. His voice is loud, but it's also loud in the bar.

"Guerilla warfare. Disperse their forces. Launch terrorist attacks in cities, sabotage factories, kidnap officials. What would prevent Shabia from doing that?"

"You have a great imagination," he says.

I don't let up. "You defected last month. You were a member of Shabia's Central Committee. You should know their plans. How could you not know?"

We're standing close in the crowded bar, but now he leans in even closer, his face almost touching mine. "Where did you get the idea that every member of the Central Committee has access to every secret? Shabia's leadership is a very small cell. They expect every member to follow orders without asking questions, without making suggestions. You can't always get the information you want. As a journalist you should understand that." His face relaxes and he leans back. "But I hear you're thinking about changing careers, maybe becoming a spy. That's too bad, really. Your suspicions disappoint me."

"I'm not suspicious. It's my professional curiosity. The only way reporters learn anything is by asking questions. And there's no way I'm going to switch careers now. I'm sure I'll die with a microphone in my hand."

Some more people shove past us towards the bar. Silay seems unconvinced.

"Besides," I say, "when a journalist gets tired of the media, they become a diplomat, not a spy. You can be a total failure as a diplomat, but you get to drink on the job and nobody arrests you. Can I buy you a beer?"

181

"Another time. I have to find someone. We'll have another opportunity – there'll be many victories to celebrate together." With that he pushes off into the crowd. I wonder if he's going to meet Fiammetta Gilay.

I shove my way to the bar and find Metshafe Daniel there ahead of me, beer in hand.

"Mr TV!" he says.

He's wearing a light white shirt with a blue tie, stylish as always. His cologne announces his presence from a distance.

"How are you, Mr Economy?"

"Confusion!" he says. "Chaos reigns!"

"What happened?"

"Bad planning. They ran out of rooms. And I thought the beer was supposed to be free? If I knew it was going to be like this, I would have stayed in Asmara."

"Who needs a hotel room? There's a thousand tents set up in Gurgusum just waiting for guests."

"Me? Spend the night in a tent? On the sand?"

For fastidious Metshafe, that's unthinkable. If he could help it, he wouldn't even step on the ground.

"Well then, you may have to spend the night walking the city," I say. "Good thing there's no curfew here. The fun starts once it gets dark."

"Where is there to go? All the women have disappeared." He sounds truly sad.

"You're right, the Eritrean beauties have fled across the Red Sea to Jeddah and Abu Dhabi. That's where paradise is now."

"Hell, more like," he says with a laugh. "How's work?"

"It's a dog's life," I say. "You work like a dog, you run around like a dog, and then you get chased out of places like you're a dog in church." I finally get a cold beer from the bartender and down half of it in one gulp. Sweet relief. "How is it on the economics front?"

Metshafe giggled. He must be in a good mood. When he's not, he avoids people, refuses to talk, doesn't want to eat with anyone. The rest of us who live with Metshafe in the Dr Yohannes house sometimes won't see him for a week. When that happens, we tease him by saying that he's gone off to be with one of his "aunts". He calls the women who run the shops he goes to his "aunts". He has a lot of them.

"My blood pressure is up," says Metshafe.

I point to his beer. "How about your stomach, is it better?"

"You journalists, always making fun of people."

"How about you economists?" I ask.

"People whose purpose in life is to change the world do not make jokes. Do you know who made the world a better place? Adam Smith. David Ricardo. Karl Marx. Men like that. Sophisticated philosophers who don't waste time joking. They just quietly change the world."

"So, what kind of change have you implemented since you've been here?" I ask.

"I've filled all the warehouses with goods, all in perfect condition. The construction work is going exactly as planned. Clinics and hospitals are well stocked with medicines that can cure any disease. Wheat and other grains are abundant. Trucks are available everywhere for transport. Everything you could want, everything is perfect. The Derg is going to give me so many medals." Metshafe is being sarcastic, of course.

"All hail, long may you live," I say.

"I doubt it."

"Why not?" I ask.

"In our position, especially with this campaign, you

always have to say, 'Yes, that will be done and right away.' If you dare say, 'That's impossible,' or 'That's a waste of time,' then you get labelled a reactionary and you're out, you bleed. In the meantime, our economy bleeds."

"What do you suggest we do to stop the bleeding?"

"Diplomacy, my friend," he says. "The world runs on a foundation of give and take. So if we invest heavily in infrastructure, create jobs and provide an environment where people can work and live in peace, do you think the insurgents will still choose to live in the bush, picking ticks off their balls?"

I nod and we both drink from our beers.

"Have you heard the new song the insurgents are singing?" asks Metshafe.

"No, what song is that?" I say.

Metshafe begins to sing:

> Your God, our God
> Can man survive in the bush?
> Is this divine wrath?

He stops and smiles. "That's the kind of song they sing these days. Don't believe that they would rather sit under acacia trees and pick lice off each other. I'm sure in their hearts they're saying, 'Forgive me, Ethiopia.'"

He orders another beer and I finish mine. "Isn't it you diplomats who claim war is what happens when diplomacy stops?" I ask. "The only thing that will make up for spilled blood is spilling someone else's."

Metshafe is silent. I order another beer.

"What happened to the other giants?" I say. The seven of us staying at Dr Yohannes' old mansion in Asmara have been nicknamed "the giants". The group staying down the street from us at the Albergo Ciao hotel is genius at nicknames and making fun of people. All seven of us are short, so they named us "the giants".

I don't actually need Metshafe to tell me. I have a pretty good idea where the other five giants are. Suslov is probably in bed reading a huge book about the theory of something. Giant number two is definitely asleep by now. Giant number three is on the phone to Addis Ababa – he can't sleep unless he talks with his wife for an hour first, chain smoking one cigarette after another. Every morning he says he has quit smoking, and every night finds him finishing his second pack of Nyalas. Giant number four is a playboy, impeccably dressed and always clean-shaven, so he's almost certainly in active pursuit of some young beauty. Giant number five wants nothing more in life than beer. "God made beer" is his mantra.

"They're probably all doing what they most like to do," says Metshafe, startling me.

"What do you mean?"

"Nature's imperative," he says with a sly smile.

"Like you and your 'aunts'! How many do you have again?"

Metshafe laughs. "Have you heard what the locals are saying about us? They say that the Red Star people are here mostly to campaign for the beautiful women of Asmara."

"Maybe so," I say. "Love and war aren't mutually exclusive. We came to save them, not destroy them. They say that Asmara women prefer us heartlanders over the local Tigrinya men. We're supposed to be like the Italians, we respect the fairer sex. While Tigrinya men are always boasting about how this woman or that one belongs to them, even if they've never met."

I have more to say about this, but I see Agent Seyoum and Agent Ashebir pushing their way towards the bar. I go over to them.

"Let me buy you a beer," Seyoum says to me.

"I take it your business is making a profit now?"

"Definitely," he says. "It's a sure thing. Addis women need their shoes and purses."

Seyoum and Ashebir get their beers and chug them down fast.

"Are you in a hurry?" I ask.

"We have two corpses on our hands," says Ashebir.

"Bodies?"

"I'll tell you later," says Seyoum.

The two agents start to make their way out through the crowd.

I hate it when someone begins a story but doesn't finish it. It makes my stomach hurt. I grab Seyoum's arm.

"Are they Red Star?" I ask.

"No, both locals, from Asmara. A man and a woman. The woman was rich, owned a bordello. The man was on the city council, just got elected."

"How did they die?"

Seyoum shrugs. "They were found in the sea. I think they were killed somewhere else and dumped there. Can I go now?"

"Was it a political assassination?"

"That's what we're trying to figure out. That's why we're in a rush." He shakes free of my grip and hurries off with Ashebir. I go back over to Metshafe.

"What were those Public Safety guys telling you?" asks Metshafe.

"That they found two dead bodies floating in the sea. I need to follow up on it, it could be a good story."

"You journalists amaze me, really."

"How so?"

"Saying this could turn into a good story? If you see someone in their death throes, you'd probably ask them, 'How do you feel about dying? What are your thoughts on the matter?'"

I laugh, but he's not wrong.

"Well, my friend," says Metshafe, "I need to find a place to spend the night before it gets too late. I don't want to be found floating in the sea tomorrow morning. Ciao." He heads off through the crowd. I don't know anyone more concerned with their own health and safety than Metshafe.

The beer is working and I'm full of energy now. The night is still young, and Massawa gets better as the night gets darker. Going to bed this early is a mortal sin for me, so I leave the hotel and start looking for the other journalists. I check all the bars in Massawa. The Red Star people have filled every pub, drinking one cold foamy beer after another, but no journalists are with them. I think they might be in Gurgusum, so I drive there, passing many cars going back and forth to the shore.

At Gurgusum I wander through the city of tents on the beach, their colours still bright even at night. There are people singing and dancing in every language and every style: Tigrigna, Amharic, Oromigna, Gurage, Afarina. People are everywhere and nobody is slowing down. Cool air carries the music through me and lifts my soul. A group of young men dance by, laughing and twirling. The stars hang low, almost close enough to touch. Fireworks launch into the sky and explode, their brilliant colours trickling down into

187

the dark sea. The waves sway up and down, dancing to the music. When the surf calms, the water reflects the lights along the shore, the colours spilling and pooling together.

I wander out past the tents to where dark waves crash against the stony shore. A woman in a white dress stands alone on the rocks, gazing out at the far horizon where sea kisses sky. A wave rushes in and washes clean the rocks around her feet before sliding gently back out. The cold breath of the sea lifts and spreads her hair. Her dress is almost sliding off one shoulder, its narrow straps the only thing on her bare back. She looks like a white dove worshiping the god of the sea. I wish I had my camera. More fireworks explode, sending hundreds of sparkling flowers across the night sky. The sound startles her and she turns. I can almost see her face by the light of the fading fireworks, but I can't be sure if it's her. I step closer to see. Yes, it is her.

13

FIAMMETTA ON THE BEACH

"Fiammetta!" My voice exposes my excitement. I make my way over to the rocks where she's standing. I don't think she recognizes me. "It's Tsegaye, remember me?"

"Wa! Is that really you?"

"What are you doing out here all by yourself?" I ask.

"I'm not alone."

I look around the dark beach, but it's just us. "Who are you with?"

"The sea," she says. "No-one is alone when they're with the sea. It makes me happy and it also makes me sad. It's big enough to keep me company." Her heart-shaped lips part to reveal bright white teeth.

"You're right, the sea is life," I say. "Do you come here often?"

"Yes." A gust of wind dances her hair in front of her face and she brushes it to one side. "Or I used to. It's been years since I was here."

I stare out at the dark waves. "I thought you were joking when you said we should meet in Massawa, but surprise surprise, here we are."

"You thought I was joking?" she asks.

"Maybe it was the way you said it."

"No, I was serious. I missed the Red Sea."

"Did you come by yourself?" I ask.

"No, no. I'm with . . . others."

"Silay?"

"Yeaah," she says, stretching the word into a purr with her Tigrinya accent.

"How could he let a beautiful woman like you go off on her own into the dark night?"

She laughs and her hair bounces around. "I'm lying. I just don't know how to give a straight answer. What kind of woman am I?"

"Sweet and devious," I say.

"And you're a moron, a sweet moron."

We laugh together as a wave rushes in around our feet.

"You're a sea goddess," I say.

"Then you better kneel down and pray to me."

I press my palms together and go down on my knees in front of her, the sand wet against my trousers.

She throws her head back and laughs. "I swear, you're a crazy moron. Seriously!"

"Yeaah, seriously!" I say, imitating her accent.

"You! Do I really sound like that? Seriously, you're a moron."

"Where are you staying?"

She stands there silent in the night and the breeze wraps her dress around her. Something has darkened her mood.

"Sorry, did I ask the wrong question?" I say.

"No, no."

"Then what?"

"I don't have a room," she says.

"Yeah, right. You didn't fool me this time."

"I swear, I'm telling the truth. You're not going to believe me even when I'm being honest?"

I believe her now. "You haven't booked a room? Were you going to spend the night right here on the beach, with the sea you miss so much?"

"There was a room booked for me."

"And then?"

"I didn't want to spend the night there," she says.

"How come? Was the room dirty?"

"No, no, it wasn't about the room."

"Then what was it about?"

She doesn't want to tell me at first, but she can sense it's bothering me, so eventually I get the whole story. A good friend of Fiammetta was going to Massawa for the festival with her boyfriend and they invited Fiammetta to join them. When they arrived this afternoon, her friend showed Fiammetta the room they had booked for her. It had just one small bed, and there was a jacket and tie already on a chair. Her friend admitted that she was trying to set Fiammetta up with a relative of hers, an important government official from Addis. Offended and confused, Fiammetta started crying and rushed out of the room. She came to Gurgusum to be on the beach and visit the sea, not caring or worrying about where she would spend the night. When I spotted her, she was standing on the rock thinking about her friend.

"Wa! What does she think I am? A cow ready for the highest bidder?" she asks. "Some women really amaze me, I swear. Does she think I need her help to get a man? What kind of stupid matchmaking is that? If I want to go out with someone, I will. Otherwise, I won't. I'm not some whore." She shakes her head in anger and sends her hair every which way in the dark.

"That can happen between friends," I say. "We think we know what's best for them, but sometimes we get it all wrong."

We walk back to the tents together. The singing and dancing is still going on, even more boisterous than before. Bonfires are burning and we wander around listening to the music and watching the dancing. Everyone seems to be getting along and having a grand time. Without even thinking about it, Fiammetta and I hold hands. We must look like a married couple.

It's getting late so I drive her back into the city. Everyone there is still wide awake and we go to the Ressi Medri neighbourhood to have dinner at the restaurant in the Lena Hotel. Fiammetta orders for both of us, lucky for me – I don't really know much about food, other than how to eat whatever is in front of me when I'm hungry. We have *consumi di brodo in bianco bollito con maionese, insalata verde* and *pane spugna*. To drink, we have a chilled bottle of Bertoli Bianco, a nice white wine. The food is simple and delicious. The owners of the hotel, two old Italians, stop by our table several times, always saying "eat, please eat". One of them has a limp and the other a lump the size of a papaya behind his ear. It seems like the only local word they know is "eat". For them, food is everything. An instrumental version of *Que Sera Sera* plays on the jukebox, also Fiammetta's selection. I've heard it so many times before, but it's still a pleasure to listen to it again:

> *The future's not ours to see,*
> *What will be, will be.*

And if not, it will not be.

After dinner, Fiammetta asks if we can go to the beach that's just a block away.

"What for?"

"I love to visit the sea before I go to bed, to say goodnight. Listening to the sound of the waves is everything to me."

We walk down to the beach and look out at the sea. The lighthouse sweeps its beam across the black water. Waves topped with foam come rushing up and kiss the sandy shore, then retreat into the dark. They sound almost like music, like an Abdelrahim song.

> In the city of Massawa by the edge of the sea
> I remembered the love I had enjoyed

"Isn't it beautiful?" Fiammetta says.

"Very beautiful."

"My soul sings with it. The sea sings love songs, don't you think?"

"Definitely," I mumble.

"The sea is made of salt, and the nature of man is salt."

"Do you like the taste?" I ask.

"Why don't you kiss me?"

I kiss her. We hold each other on the beach in the dark and listen to the sound of the waves. I don't ask her any questions and she doesn't say anything, but we go back to my hotel. I am hungry for her love and she does not withhold anything from me, it is all euphoria. She gives me back twice as much pleasure as I give her. She is stunning.

It is only much later that she speaks. "Honestly, you're a scoundrel!" she says.

"Why do you say that?"

"You just brought me here to your room like that?"

"Would it have been better if I had begged you?"

"If you had begged, I wouldn't have gone with you," she says with a smile. "Get out of here, you really are a scoundrel, I swear."

"Everything about you is so sweet."

"Moron. You are a sweet moron."

"I feel like I've known you a long time," I say.

"Same here. Why is that?"

"They say love and death both happen in an instant. Or do they?"

"Or . . ." she says.

"Or what?"

"Love is like gambling. You win or you lose."

I reach for her again. The god of love is in the mood to be worshipped a second time – he needs to be venerated again to calm his fury. He receives our second offering of love with grace and bestows us with his blessings. All hail the mighty god of love.

"Is there anything here to drink?" asks Fiammetta. "I'm brutally thirsty."

"I could use a cold drink," I say.

I pull on some clothes and go downstairs to the bar, where I get two beers and a Sprite. I step into the lift to head back up and Director Betru Tessema comes in after me. He looks at the drinks I'm holding. Oh boy.

"Well, aren't you the devil," he says.

"Isn't it past your bedtime?" I say, embarrassed. I bet he knows who I'm with.

"Not tonight. Herding goats in the desert is easier than keeping you all safe."

"What's going on?" I ask, hoping the lift will speed up.

Betru smiles at me. "Why do you need two beers and a Sprite?"

"I'm thirsty. I spent the whole day talking. I love beer with Sprite."

"How is Fiammetta Gilay?" he asks.

Betru is an omniscient god, I swear. "She's fine."

"Do you need money?" he asks.

"I'll tell you when I do."

"Women like Fiammetta are very expensive."

I need to set him straight. "Listen, Comrade Director, I know you want my help. I'm only a journalist, but I can tell you that yes, something is going on here. I just need some time to figure it out. Once I have something concrete, I'll share it with you, I promise. Like you said, the success of Red Star is everyone's job. I just don't want to make any mistakes with this. A mistake could hurt innocent people and send you off in the wrong direction. But I'm not hiding anything from you. We share the same goal. Just give me time." With that the lift arrives at my floor.

Betru smiles. "I'm doing this because you journalists somehow manage to find out all sorts of things. But yes, an impatient hyena bites the horn. Though what you consider a bit of trivia not worth sharing might be the key piece we need to complete the whole picture. But take the time you need. And enjoy."

I get out of the lift and go back to my room. This cloak-and-dagger stuff is annoying, as is my inability to put together the big picture of what's really going on. Fiammetta doesn't seem to notice the change in my mood as we have our drinks.

"I swear," she says, "this is the best beer and Sprite I've ever had." She takes another sip. "You know, right after you left I heard someone outside the door. They didn't knock or try to come in, but I heard them out there for a while. Then they went away."

"Maybe it was someone trying to find their room. The hotel is so crowded, there are people everywhere, even at this hour."

Her chest gleams in the dim light of the table lamp, naked and luscious. Her eyes are big and bold, silver coins polished to a shine.

"I thought you came here with Silay Berahi," I say.

"Why?"

"Because you came with him to that party, when I first met you. And he's here in Massawa now too."

"I swear, I don't understand why everyone asks me about him, I'm sick of it. 'What does he say to you? Where do you go with him?' I get questions like that all the time, from—"

"People like Teklay Zedingl?" I interrupt.

"How did you know?"

"Lucky guess. I'm betting he also asked you out?"

"I don't want to be one of his beauties. He changes his women as often as he changes his socks."

"Who says you're beautiful?" I ask with a smile.

"I do, you idiot." She laughs, and her mouth makes my heart throb in appreciation.

"You know you're gorgeous, you really are. A northern beauty. The goddess of the Red Sea." I take a long drink from my beer. "But seriously, that night after Solomon's party – where did you two go?"

"Wa! My house, where else? Where did you think I went? The Nyala Hotel?"

"He spent the night at your house?" I ask.

"You idiot! You think I run a bordello? I live with my parents."

"So where did he spend the night?"

"I don't know! Why are you interrogating me about this? You think I'm a cheap woman? Because I came up to your room so easily?" She is hurt and angry.

"No, Fiammetta, please believe me. It's not that at all."

I kiss her cheek but she pushes me away.

"What, then?" she asks.

"Silay said he spent that night at your place."

"That's totally untrue! Yes, he left his car at our house, but that's it."

"Where did he go?" I ask.

"How would I know?"

We sit there for a minute in silence.

Then, in a quieter voice, Fiammetta says, "He asked me to say he was at my house that night if anyone asked. Begged me, really. But that's it, I'm done. No more questions."

"Okay," I say. "But have you told anyone else what you just told me?"

"No. Why would I tell anyone about my personal business? It's private."

"Why did you tell me, then?" I ask.

"Moron. I swear, you're a moron, seriously."

She trusts me with her secrets, which might be the key to my heart. But where did Silay really go that night? Enough, now is not the time or place to think more about him. Or think about anything except this northern beauty in bed next to me. Fiammetta Gilay – I'm drunk on her beauty. Sometimes life can be generous.

Then I remember Roman. My soul, if I have one, is now condemned to hell. I pray in my heart, "Romi, please forgive me?"

Tomorrow will be a long and tiring day. I pull out my schedule:

6.30 a.m. – Arrive Dogali for dedication of Alula Abanega Memorial Statue

9.00 a.m. – Arrive Red Sea coast for opening ceremonies of Massawa Festival

10.30 a.m. – Public parade for festival

All day – Coordinate and prepare the news of all official activities

5.00 p.m. – Unveiling of photography exhibition at Kaleb Hall

6.00 p.m. – Opening of art exhibition at Massawa Palace

Night – Gurgusum beach for public celebration

Just reading the schedule exhausts me and my whole body starts to tremble. I close my eyes.

Human memory is flawed. We do not even want to remember all that has happened to us, especially the bad things. Life is painful enough once, right?

If you've forgotten, let me remind you – I am the author.

Honestly, I am suffering. To be everywhere at all times, to be engaged with all that is going on, it's becoming too painful for me. I am, I was, I am here, and I will be. But why must I be present for everything and everyone?

To love is to suffer, but to love is also to live, and to live is to love. Tsegaye is in love. It brings him pleasure and pain. That is what Tsegaye wants: a beautiful, sweet life of suffering.

The story continues.

14

FIVE MURDERS

Director Betru Tessema gives in to his rage and slams his fist down on the small table in front of him. He's at the Dahlak Hotel in Massawa, in a large room he booked to serve as both bedroom and office. Lifting his heavy frame from his chair with difficulty, he growls like thunder. This lets the three men in front of him know he is displeased by their handling of the events that are unfolding and growing more alarming by the minute.

"I did not bring you here to tell me the names and addresses and ages of the two dead people!" he says. "We're not traffic cops. I need to know the reasons for their deaths, who murdered them."

Agent Ashebir looks at him with curiosity, while Agent Seyoum seems disheartened. Agent Teklay is sitting on the couch wearing his sunglasses, so it's hard to tell if he's listening or sleeping.

Ashebir breaks the silence. "Right now our people here and in Asmara are doing their best, going all over the place to find out what happened. We're also searching the residences of both victims to identify and gather any evidence. Roads are closed and boats aren't allowed to dock or leave. We've also detained some people identified as suspicious."

The phone rings. Thinking it is a government official, Betru cusses under his breath and picks up the receiver. "Who is this?" he asks.

"This is Garedew, sir."

"Who?"

"Major Garedew Mekonnen, in Asmara."

"Major, I'm in a meeting. What do you need?"

"I'll make it quick. Three more people have been found dead tonight in different locations around Asmara: Mai Temenai, Gejeret, and Geza Birhan. The first victim was the barista at the Paradiso, the second was a farmer and proletariat who was a respected leader of the grain harvesting initiative. The third was a woman, single and a government employee." There is a brief pause and then Garedew reads off the names of the deceased.

Betru jots down some notes. "So what steps are you taking now?" he asks.

"We are following it closely."

"But you haven't found anything?"

"Not yet."

"So what are you waiting for?" Betru growls into the phone. "Or do you suppose the killers will feel sorry for you and take the initiative to walk down to your office and turn themselves in? I want a complete report in the morning. I am so sick and tired of receiving reports that are worse than what I can read in the newspaper." With that he hangs up.

The men in the hotel room seem startled, and Ashebir and Seyoum join Teklay on the couch. The Director makes a fist and looks around, it seems, for a face to punch.

"Have you heard what happened back in Asmara tonight?"

he asks. "Three more people found dead, in different locations. Two men and a woman. So today we have five people murdered, and who knows, maybe ten more tomorrow, twenty the day after, fifty, a hundred. This isn't a coincidence. It can't be. A conspiracy is unfolding right under our noses, and tell me, what are we waiting for, sitting here doing nothing? Could someone please enlighten me? Are we just going to wait for them to kill us all, one by one?"

The three men on the couch look at each other, as if wondering what the Director expects them to do about it here in Massawa. Betru realizes that he lacks anything to give his men to go on, no tangible clue he can put his hands on, other than his hope that something might materialize out of the dark. He picks up the phone and tries the Asmara police commissioner. There's no answer at the office, so Betru tries the commissioner's home number. It rings for a while and he's about to hang up, his rage ratcheting to a new high, when the commissioner answers in a slow and tired voice, "Hello?"

"So you went home to bed early?" asks Betru.

"Who . . ." He yawns. "Who is this?"

"This is Director Betru. So tonight you caught one drunk and one thief, then decided the city was safe? Might as well just go home and get a good night's sleep?"

The commissioner is fully awake now – Director Betru's name has a stimulant effect on officials. "What happened?" asks the commissioner.

"Yes, I'm calling to report a traffic accident," says Betru, his voice thick with sarcasm.

"Where?" asks the commissioner, missing the joke.

"Comrade Commissioner, if you're talking to me while half-asleep, maybe it's better if we continue this conversation in the morning."

"I'm awake! I'm awake!"

"Those who can fall asleep these days are the lucky ones. So, now, listen to me. In the past three hours, five dead bodies have been found at different locations in Asmara. They did not die in car crashes or robberies or falling off ladders. I believe their deaths are related, that there is some sort of conspiracy at work. So I need your help."

"Okay," says the commissioner.

"I want strict security measures put in place immediately, on every street and at every intersection. I am to be notified of any unusual activity, anywhere, anytime. If you become suspicious of anybody, I don't care who, then they should be interrogated immediately. If you hear of any additional deaths, then I need to be notified as well. We'll turn over every stone in Asmara, every pebble, to find out what's going on." Betru does not wait for the commissioner's reply before he hangs up.

He turns to the three men on the couch. "I'm giving you the same orders. Comrades, get going!" The men leave the room together.

In the hallway, Seyoum says, "That man is definitely going to work us all to death before he retires."

"Why is he so ambitious all of a sudden?" asks Ashebir.

"Maybe he wants to postpone his retirement," says Seyoum.

Teklay takes off his glasses and looks at Seyoum. "Are you in a hurry to take over his position?" he asks. "Don't be in such a rush."

Betru steps out of his room and calls Teklay back.

"Where is Silay?" Betru asks Teklay.

"He's on his way to the Lena Hotel to have dinner," says Teklay. "I have men following him."

"Who were those two people who were with him earlier, in the bar? Actually, you talked to one of them too, the tall one." Betru leans against the doorframe.

"Both of them are my friends. The shorter one was with me in prison years ago, Gebray Tekeste, the one who owns the Paradiso now. He came to Massawa to see about opening another coffeebar once the road between Asmara and here is secured. The tall one, the young guy, is a mechanic at Army Aviation."

Betru straightens up. "What did you say the name of the coffeebar was?"

"Paradiso."

"The one whose barista was killed today? Or is there another place with the same name?"

Teklay looks like he's been hit with a rock. "That's the only place with that name in Asmara," he says.

"You think your friend the owner has already heard?"

"I don't know."

"Get on with it then, I want to hear what he has to say. And for God's sake, be tactful. We don't want a James Bond adventure here." With that he slams the door in Teklay's face.

15

THE CONSPIRACY DINES

Silay Berahi is dining at the Lena Hotel with Gebray Tekeste, owner of the Paradiso, and the young Army Aviation mechanic. The mechanic's name is Ikuba Arat, but most people call him Wedi Arat, and sweat is gathering at his temples. Their table is laden with food and drink, they look to be in a jovial mood, and they talk and laugh so loudly that they can be heard throughout the restaurant. Other diners often look over at them to see what's going on. The restaurant is still busy even at this late hour, mostly hotel guests who are mostly drunk. The guests have travelled here from all over the country to attend the Asmara Conference and the Massawa Festival. The two old Italian owners are overwhelmed and very happy about their full house, and smile as they bustle about serving their customers. Silay and his companions talk and laugh at full volume, then drop down into hushed tones for a minute before resuming their loud banter.

Eventually Silay asks his two companions in a quiet voice, "Why were you looking for me? Didn't I warn you in no uncertain terms to stay away from me unless I told you otherwise?"

"You are correct," says Gebray. "But we have an urgent matter." He pauses and looks around the room. "What made you pick this place, anyway?"

"Don't worry," says Silay. "If you make yourself obvious, you also make yourself uninteresting. But I know you don't feel safe unless you're hiding in your cave." He laughs loudly. "Do you have the list of people we're keeping an eye on?"

Gebray is furious. He did not come here to discuss names and lists. But he's ready even so. "Yes, we have the names of 211 candidates. Regarding your questions about when, where, how and by whom they will be dealt with, don't worry about any of that. We're ready to make it happen when you give the order."

Before Gebray can get to the reason why he's here, Silay poses another question: "What's the situation regarding the weapons?"

Gebray speaks quickly and quietly: "We are succeeding there too. True, the security is getting tighter by the day, but we're making progress on smuggling them in. If we can continue for one more month, we'll have a fully armed force inside the Asmara city limits."

"We don't have one more month," says Silay. "Just like the other side, we're short on time. Fifteen days at the most. By then we need to have a well-armed urban fighting force ready to strike. The weapons in Addis Ababa don't help us until they get here. I want the objectives we have to hit first to be given the highest priority. This is it for both sides, our one and only chance. If they beat us now, we may never recover. Or it will take us years." Silay burps and pushes his plate away. "Alright, friends, why do you need me?"

Gebray stubs out the butt of his cigarette in the ashtray with precise motions, then lights another and puffs out a cloud of smoke. Through the haze he looks at Silay and says, "Something unexpected happened."

"What?"

"We needed to eliminate five people today."

"And?"

"We did."

"On whose orders?" asks Silay. He realizes he's talking loudly and looks around the dining room. No-one is paying any attention. Everyone is busy eating their lasagna and their pasta saltata.

"We didn't have time to wait for orders," says Gebray. "It needed to be done."

"Why? What happened?"

"We had to get them before they got us. If I'd waited for your order, they would have betrayed us to the police by now. I couldn't reach you in time, so that's why we came to you now, to inform you."

"Who are 'they'?" asks Silay.

"People who, directly or indirectly, knew secrets. Our secrets. Secrets they were about to spill. Elimination was—"

Silay interrupts him. "If we were more careful about the people we recruited in the first place, this situation could have been avoided. And what do you mean, you had to do this? I'm not your puppet that you inform after the fact. What happens if we get arrested now, before we launch the attacks, because of screw-ups like this? Our incompetence will not be well received in Nakfa. Idiots! *Testa di gallina!*" With the Italian curse he smacks his head with his fist.

"The problem isn't lack of caution," says Gebray. "All five were trusted."

"So where is the problem, then? Is it simple incompetence?"

"One of them, Aboy Tekle—"

"No!" interrupts Silay. "Which Aboy Tekle? The barista?"

"Yes, the old man was about to betray us," says Gebray.

"But why?" asks Silay.

"You know how things are! *É cosí fare!* Times have changed, people want peace. They've given up on us, especially now with the Red Star Campaign. The last twenty years have been hard, one long *marcia indietro*, an unending retreat. Some people are starting to switch sides." Gebray remembers a popular song from a few years ago and sings a few lines:

> *My surprise*
> *I never thought*
> *I would return*

Gebray pauses and takes a sip of his wine. "Do you remember that song, about going back home?" he asks, "It's hard to blame people for wanting peace. They've been chased from their homes, jailed for no reason, hunted down like stray dogs. Some fled to the desert to escape, never to be seen alive again. Some endure a life of hardship in foreign countries. What did they all gain? Nothing. Freedom is like the North Star: we run towards it, but get no closer. What have we offered people other than hope? So yes, the public is anxious for peace. I wouldn't be surprised if they abandon us, if they denounce us. Aboy was about to do just that, and was there anyone in the cause more trusted and reliable than him?"

"You talk as if you too have abandoned all hope," hisses Silay. "This is not what I want to hear from someone like you. Honestly, the weakness of you city folks astounds me. If you'd said that nonsense in the bush, you would have been executed on the spot."

Wedi Arat laughs. "It's too late now," says Wedi. "Our actions were absolutely necessary, like Gebray said. We didn't have any choice but to get them before they got us. Anyway, let God bless the soul of Aboy and the others."

Silay turns to Gebray. "Please make sure Aboy's son is told about his father's death," says Silay.

"Where can I find him?" asks Gebray.

"He's in Nakfa, a brigade commander in Shabia, a fine warrior," says Silay. "Be sure to let him know that it was the Derg who killed his father – those government bastards." All three men laugh.

Silay finishes his glass of wine and lights a cigarette. "For God's sake, though, don't relax just because the dead can't talk. I hope they didn't leave anything incriminating behind. And no more eliminations without my direct order. Final warning."

"What we did was tight and clean," says Gebray. "We searched their houses, checked all their belongings, there's nothing to worry about. But it would be good if you granted us some freedom of action in emergency situations. Such circumstances require urgent solutions."

There is a threat in Gebray's voice. The two men stare at each other. Gebray hopes Silay realizes that he can't possibly be everywhere his orders might be needed, at all times, and thus must grant some part of the request. Wedi wipes sweat from his forehead.

Silay sighs. "Very well, but only in extreme emergencies, and with the utmost care."

"And you do know that Public Security agents are following your every move, right?" Wedi says.

Their table falls silent. New customers arrive looking for dinner, while those who have finished depart. The owners don't seem to be getting tired and give exuberant welcomes to every new arrival. There is no dish that they won't prepare, nothing has run out. They haven't been this busy in years, so they have taken advantage of the situation and raised their prices. And indeed, tonight's customers react with shock when they see the bill and say hushed prayers before paying up.

"Times are tough," says Gebray.

"Yes, and it's our own fault," says Silay. "We don't have a culture of collaboration. We hate each other more than we do our enemies. It's crazy. I think the only allies we have left are the Tigrinya Liberation Front, the same guys we used to make fun of. I doubt even that will last. It's depressing." Silay is silent for a while, then turns to Wedi. "What's the name of your Army Aviation man?"

"Major Koricho Tadesse," says Wedi.

"Is he reliable?"

"We want his help and he wants our money," says Wedi. "He's close to retirement and is always pestering me for more cash."

"Pay what he asks. He's vital."

"We had a little trouble there today," says Wedi Arat. "We were unloading the latest shipment of weapons from Addis when that journalist, Tsegaye, saw us. The Major got startled and dropped the crate."

"And then . . .?" asks Silay. His eyebrows dance around in concern.

"Tsegaye saw the rifles, but I don't think he realized what was going on."

"You don't think so?" Silay asks in a loud voice. "That's the height of arrogance. Do not take Tsegaye for a fool – he's an experienced journalist. He may not be a spy, but it wouldn't take much for him to figure out what's really going on at Army Aviation."

The sweat runs into Wedi Arat's eyes and he wipes his brow with a handkerchief. "What can I do when things are out of my control?" he says.

"Does he know who you are?" asks Silay.

"I don't think so . . ."

"If not, then stay away from him, he's too dangerous for you to handle."

"Do you know where Tsegaye is right this moment?" says Gebray.

"Where?" asks Silay.

"With Fiammetta Gilay at the Dahlak Hotel."

"No way!"

"Room number 13," says Gebray. "Confirmed by our own man."

"Son of a bitch," says Silay. Wedi smiles.

"Why did you involve her in the first place?" asks Gebray. "That was just reckless."

"*State zitto!* Shut up!"

"She might tell Tsegaye that you didn't spend the night with her after Solomon's party," says Gebray. "I don't think anyone else knows about that yet."

"How do you know she'll tell him?" asks Silay.

"I just think she will, that's all."

"Son of a bitch."

"Insults aren't enough," says Gebray.

"What else do you suggest?" asks Silay through clenched teeth.

"Make both of them laugh?"

"That would be another stupid thing to do."

"Why?" asks Gebray.

212

"Because they know Fiammetta and I are friends. They've been questioning her about me. They're not totally stupid, you know. If she disappears, they'll definitely be suspicious, especially if Tsegaye disappears too. Instead—"

Silay abruptly stops talking and starts laughing as Agent Teklay Zedingl comes over to their table. The two other men follow Silay's lead. Teklay pulls up a chair and joins them.

"What's so funny?" asks Teklay.

"Oh, we're just telling some stories," says Silay.

Teklay looks unconvinced. "What kinds of stories?"

Silay realizes that Agent Teklay is sceptical. "The story we were laughing about? Do you know what an old man from the Asmara District did? True story. This old farmer, he lives out in the country, but he came into Asmara and went to a government police station and asked for a rifle so that he could go back and shoot the insurgents. 'What do you want to do that for?' the police ask him. 'Because the insurgents took my land and gave it away,' he says. 'But what if the government wants to make you share your farmland too?' they ask him. 'Wa! Fine, give me two rifles then.'" Silay had invented the story on the spot, but they all laugh.

"Well, I have a sad story to tell you," says Teklay.

Silay waves his hand. "*Cheta!* Who wants to hear a sad story? Life is already full of tragedy. Tell us a funny story. We want to laugh – it really is the best medicine."

"But sadness is the mirror image of laughter."

"*E, dai!* Let's just drink." Silay pours some wine into Teklay's glass, then raises his own. "To the times we spent together growing up, and to the Red Star Campaign." They raise their glasses and toast.

Teklay takes off his sunglasses and swirls the wine in his glass. "Did you hear that Aboy Tekle is dead?"

"Which Aboy Tekle?" asks Gebray. "My Aboy Tekle?"

"Yes," says Teklay and fastens his gaze on Gebray's eyes. "Your barista at the Paradiso."

Gebray leaps up and grabs his forehead with both hands, then sinks back down into his chair and bows his head.

"What?" asks Silay. "What happened to him? When did this happen?"

"We don't know the exact time of death yet," says Teklay. "Maybe three or four hours ago."

"He was at work this afternoon," says Gebray. "I saw him at two and he was fine. Oh my God, Aboy . . ." He wipes tears from his eyes.

"How did he die?" asks Silay.

"We're not sure yet, but he may have been murdered." Teklay studies the other men at the table. To him they seem like actors wearing masks, with rehearsed emotions and memorized speeches. But although he senses they are involved, he has no actual evidence, nothing solid he can point to. This annoys him, and he feels the frustration in his gut. He picks up his glass and softens his anger with one long gulp of the *vino bianco secco*.

"Why do you think murder?" asks Silay.

"His house had been turned inside out, everything thrown all over the place. Somebody was looking for something there."

"Poor Aboy!" says Gebray. "He had an enemy who wanted to kill him? He was like a father to everyone. Poor old man."

Teklay puts his sunglasses back on. "There are no real friends these days."

"Too true," says Silay. "Relying on friendship alone is simply too risky now. You just have to hope none of your friends are really your enemy."

Still showing his grief, Gebray wipes his eyes and blows his nose. "Poor Aboy. Even the espresso machine loved him. I don't think he spent a day away from it for the last twenty-five years. He talked to the machine like it was a person, and I swear it refuses to work right for anyone besides him. Together they made the best coffee in Asmara, no place else could compete. Poor man! The machine is totally useless now without him. It's dead, he's dead, and so is the Paradiso coffeebar."

Silay laughs.

"What's funny about that?" asks Gebray.

"Seeing you cry over your business, your profits," says Silay.

"What is there to laugh about?" says Agent Teklay. "It's normal, everyone feels bad for themselves, isn't that right? The dead are already gone, their graves have nothing to say. Or do you think they might talk after all?"

Nobody answers him. The men sit in silence until Teklay calls over one of the owners and orders another bottle of wine.

"As long as we're alive, let us drink," says Teklay. "To our health, if indeed we are healthy."

"Are you sick?" asks Silay. He raises his glass.

"No," says Teklay. "But nobody lives for ever."

The four men clink their glasses and drink their wine. Outside, all along the Red Sea, it is almost daylight.

215

16

RETURN TO ASMARA

Wednesday, January 27, 1982

A day of revelry at the Massawa Festival. But I have no time to celebrate. The hours rush by on wings as I run from event to event. I can live with all the work on my own plate. The hard part is dealing with other people, gathering up all their recordings of the festival activities, sorting them and getting them back to Asmara for the flight to Addis Ababa.

I finish covering the last event, the opening of the art exhibition at Massawa Palace, and return to my hotel room just as the sun begins to set. Fiammetta is relaxing on the bed and strikes a bewitching pose when she sees me. The sight of her melts away my stress like a cloud on a hot summer's day.

"Well, how do you do, Fiammetta?"

"I'm doing very fine, and you?"

"Great, my northern beauty."

She leans back and her breasts tilt upward, ready to take me captive and claim victory. She stretches her hand towards me from the bed.

"I'm hot," she says. "Could we order up some cold beer? I'm sweaty."

"Go ahead," I say and smile.

I go into the shower. The cold water invigorates my soul, and after that the cold beer refreshes my earthly body.

"You are quite rude," says Fiammetta.

"What have I done now?" I ask, alarm in my voice.

"Why did you wake me up this morning? I'm really serious about getting my morning rest. So rude."

"Perfect! I'm the same, I love sleeping in. If we get married, well, they'll probably find us in bed one day, dead and rotten." I wonder how marriage got into my thoughts – strange. "Don't tell me you spent the whole day here in bed?"

She didn't, I know. I noticed her at some of the festival events. Always standing a little way apart from the crowd, she was like the North Star, bright but solitary. When I spotted her, I prayed that she would be spared from roaming lecherous eyes – every man who notices her imagines kissing her.

"It's a bad idea to marry a journalist," she says.

"Why? What makes you say that?"

"Who wants to sit around and wait for him, day and night?"

"Ah, you'd get used to it. Eventually we get used to everything."

"Me? Never. Especially not a husband who comes home all sweaty. Why should I?" Her face takes on a serious look. "Do you have a wife?"

"No, I do not," I say. Steering away from that steep cliff, I continue on about journalists. "But there is some truth in what you say. What kind of woman wants to marry a reporter?

He won't have any time for her, or money. Journalists always struggle financially. To top it all, he'll never get promoted. Once a journalist, always a journalist. So yes, who would want to marry such a poor, hapless creature?"

"So what's with that ring on your finger?" She's not letting go about my marital status.

"What? Can't a person wear a ring just to look good?"

"What's with the double-talk, hiding gold under wax?" she says.

"Do you want me to write a love poem for you?"

"I want you to tell me the truth," she says. "Swear on your father's name."

"Please, let me compose a poem for you! May I?" Before she can answer I plunge right into one:

On the shores of the Red Sea, across from Marib
A northern beauty, a northern star, resting by the palm trees
You are God's pleasing bouquet, where he can rest his eyes
Flower blossoming from dark virgin clay, wrapped in brilliance
Your beauty alluring even at a distance
Like the morning sun
You, a stunning northern blossom
Sahel's noon passion
Asmara's dawn dew
A splendour of creation time will never wilt
So, my dear, why is it a sin if I pluck you for your beauty?

"Isn't that wonderful?" I say. "The lines came to me so easily. I think it's pretty good. Fiammetta dear, you're making a poet out of me."

Fiammetta just looks at me.

"What's her name?" she asks.

This conversation is going in the wrong direction, but she is not one to be fooled. "What will knowing her name do for you?" I ask.

"Why won't you tell me?"

"Her name is Roman, Roman Hiletework. Are you happy now?"

"Is she beautiful?"

"Yes, she is very beautiful – a rose from the heartland." I watch Fiammetta's face closely. I don't know how this is going to go. She smiles.

"I swear, this is good," she says.

"Really?"

"I like men who are married, or engaged at least."

"Interesting. Why?"

"Oromay! Enough! It's for the best. Suffering is part of love anyway."

"And if I didn't have a fiancée?"

"I would have pushed you away, I swear. But, Tsegaye, what kind of woman am I? Please tell me."

"You are sweet."

"You are a moron, really," she says.

"Woman, you better stop calling me a moron."

"Why shouldn't I call you a moron?"

"Don't they respect men where you come from?" I tease her. "I deserve the same respect."

"Yeaah, who told you that?" she asks.

"I know these things."

"Moron. I swear you are a moron. But why do I keep calling you that? What kind of woman am I?"

"Again, you are sweet," I say.

And she is sweet late into the night.

*

I wake up before dawn, Fiammetta still asleep next to me. Even though the festival continues today, I have to get back to Asmara this morning before the Red Star conference resumes there. All kinds of work is waiting for me. Starting today, and then for the next three or four days, the conference meetings in Tinsae Hall have to be recorded and broadcast throughout Ethiopia – every speech, comment and statement made by every participant. Then the final agreement passed at the conference that describes the objectives of the campaign must be printed and distributed to everyone as the operating manifesto. That much I'm used to; for the past few years January has been a busy month with congresses and conventions to cover. What worries me is that the movie cameras and film we ordered from abroad have not yet arrived. It's a constant source of anxiety, and my prayers to the Almighty for a timely delivery have not been answered. Unlike Saint Haymanot, I can't pray standing on one leg for seven years straight – I don't have that much time.

If the military offensive launches right after the conference ends, where will I be able to get enough cameras and film to document three different combat units advancing on Nakfa? We've used up most of the film we brought with us from Addis. We'll be lucky if we have enough to finish covering the Asmara Conference and the Massawa Festival. The cameras we have are old and not designed for the rough-and-tumble demands of war. History will happen, I won't be able to record it, and the future will laugh at me. As the sun rises, I send up a prayer for the cameras and film to be delivered. Fiammetta wants a lift back to Asmara with me, so I shake her awake.

"I swear," she says without opening her eyes, "you are very rude."

I pull all the blankets and sheets off the bed in one quick motion. She is stark naked on the mattress.

"What can I do for you?" she whispers, eyes still closed.

Thank you, Lord, for letting me partake of your most magnificent creation.

"Kiss me?" I ask, hoping for one more chance to love her.

She leans up from the bed and her kiss is sweeter than a wild rose. Then, reluctantly, she gets up and gets dressed. It doesn't take her long, maybe because she's still young. She can look good without much effort. Not much make-up or jewellery, simple clothes, nothing overdone.

We go down to the hotel restaurant to have breakfast before our drive back to Asmara. Director Betru Tessema is there and winks at me. I think he's happy to see me with Fiammetta. I ask her to excuse me for a minute and go over to say hello to him.

"You look as if you haven't slept," he says.

"Look at her. Would you? Even a short nap?" I smile at him. "By the way, Silay was not with her after Solomon's party that night. Don't ask me where he was, because she doesn't know and neither do I."

Betru smiles. "Now do you see?" he asks quietly.

"What should I see?"

"That love is a vital part of gathering intelligence."

"I don't want any harm to come to her," I warn him.

"Don't fret. Like the Americans say, nobody wants to kill the goose that lays the golden egg. I appreciate the information. And, comrade, please continue your efforts. Who knows, maybe she will lead us further. But don't let love blind you. Keep your eyes open." With that he turns and leaves the restaurant.

I go back and sit with Fiammetta. They're out of orange

juice so I order a cold Fanta. This outrages her: "*Via!* Fanta is *scalogna!*"

I look at her blankly.

"Bad luck," she says. "Fanta is bad luck."

I laugh. "How can orange soda be bad luck?"

She shakes her head and her hair bounces back and forth. "It's bad luck. Because it was a date over Fanta, that's how I lost my virginity. A first date! I couldn't even finish the Fanta, I swear. I left it half-full."

I laugh. "Come on, tell me the whole story."

Brushing her hair out of her face, she tells me how she came to despise Fanta. She had fallen in love with a man, Dr Abel. He was educated, handsome and wealthy. But she was young and had only kissed a boy once. Her best friend at the time, Samira, was older and more experienced. Samira enjoyed toying with men, drawing them in with a flirty smile and then playing them off against each other. Samira would often go with Fiammetta to visit Dr Abel. Eventually Fiammetta started hearing rumours that something was going on between Samira and Dr Abel. At first she didn't believe it, but one Saturday night she decided to show up unannounced at Dr Abel's house. Sure enough, she caught Samira there with Dr Abel and it was obvious the two had just been in bed together. Fiammetta fled in tears and refused to see Dr Abel or Samira again.

Later, Fiammetta met another man and eventually got engaged to him, but he was religious so it was a chaste relationship. Not long before her wedding, she heard that Samira was also engaged, not to Dr Abel, but to a man named Afewerki. As it happens, Fiammetta knew Afewerki – there was a time when he had pestered her for a date. She had never gone out with him, but she had his phone number. She called him and made a date for that same night. Fiammetta and Afewerki ended up back at his house and he offered her a Fanta – it had just been introduced in Eritrea, so it was the cool, popular thing to drink. With her new drink in hand, and the memory of Samira and Dr Abel still bitter in her mind, she took her revenge by sleeping with Afewerki, Samira's fiancé. The whole thing didn't last long; it was over before she finished the Fanta. She had guarded her virginity carefully, turning down many men she liked but considered unworthy. And then she had squandered it.

"I swear I traded it for half a bottle of Fanta," she says.

But the story didn't end there. Some time after her date with Afewerki, she started feeling nauseous any time she was around food. Only spicy dishes tasted good. At first she thought she had cholera, but it was her mother who realized Fiammetta was pregnant. This threw her family into turmoil. Her brothers thought she had brought dishonour on them and seriously considered doing away with her, but her parents protected her and stood by her side. They understood her dilemma, as it was under similar circumstances that they themselves had married. With their help, Fiammetta's previous engagement was broken off, as was Afewerki's, and the two of them married in a hasty ceremony. Unfortunately, the marriage did not work, the pregnancy was aborted, and they divorced after only a few months as husband and wife. And that was the story of how Fiammetta came to detest Fanta, lost her virginity, got pregnant, married and divorced.

"Yeaah, I swear, being stubborn could really have killed me, you know? But what kind of woman am I?"

"You are stubbornly sweet." Whenever she asks me what kind of woman she is, the first thing that comes to me is always that she is sweet. And she is, a sweet girl who is also the salt of the earth.

"Trust me, I'm stubborn," she says. "I drive men crazy. You'll see."

"Yes, yes we will."

"And I don't stay very long with one man. I get bored and fly away."

"We have three months, at most," I say. "Then Red Star will be over and we'll go our separate ways."

We finish breakfast and leave for Asmara. Driving from Massawa to Asmara is like flying straight up – it's so steep, you think you're going to bump into the sky. When we get to Asmara the city is quiet, as if everyone is still in Massawa. Fiammetta guides me through a maze of little streets to Mai Temenai. The houses here were built according to a master plan, with most sitting along a row, connected like links of a chain. They look Arab, but Fiammetta says most of the residents are Eritrean. Red Star Campaign people generally don't have any reason to come to this neighbourhood.

As we pull up to her house, we hear wailing and the cries of mourning. Fiammetta grabs her head with her hands and moans. "Ohhh, what happened?"

"What? What's going on?" I say.

"Do you think it's my mother who's died? What should I do now, Tsegaye? I swear I'm not getting out of this car if she's gone."

"Has she been unwell?"

"Yes, she has something with her heart."

I get out of the car and walk back and forth along the street until finally I find a neighbourhood kid who tells me what's going on. I return to the car.

"Let's go, but don't jinx your mother. She's fine. The person who died is somebody called Aboy Tekle."

"Oh no, Aboy Tekle!" she says with great sadness in her voice.

I feel awkward. For all I know, Aboy could be her grandfather or her favourite uncle. They say Eritrean family trees are always complicated, like tangled chains. Her eyes swell with tears.

I heard this story once. A Menze guy standing on a hill yelled down to another Menze tending his farm in the valley below, telling him to be ready in the morning because he would probably be coming to his house to tell him of the passing of his dear mother. The Menze in the valley, overwhelmed by grief at the prospect of his dear mother's impending demise, started crying. This surprised the Menze on the hill, who called down to him again and asked, "Since you're already crying, do I still have to come in the morning?"

"Do you know this person who just died?" I ask Fiammetta.

"Aboy? Since I was a child. He used to bring me sweets. I adored him. He was the barista at the Paradiso for ever." Tears speed down her smooth cheeks.

We had planned to meet later that night, but we put it off. The dead deserve their due.

PART THREE

17

THE MANIFESTO

The Red Star Campaign has returned from the Massawa Festival to resume the Asmara Conference at Tinsae Hall. The day flies by like one of our MiG-23 fighter jets, and I'm almost surprised when the meetings finish and the day ends. I have no news about the cameras and film we ordered from abroad. All I know is that nothing has arrived yet. Everyone is tired of hearing me complain about the cameras.

My day consisted of running back and forth across Asmara: Revolution Square to Saba Stadium, Saba Stadium to the radio station, the station to Tinsae Hall, to other places I can't even remember now. These days I run to survive, sprinting all over like a mad man. Nights are the same, passing by in an instant. The Red Star Campaign has finally managed to alter the progression of time. I sleep the whole night in the same position, laying on one side like a fallen tree, dreamless.

First thing the next morning, before the start of the conference sessions, I attend the dedication of a memorial statue of Zerai Deres. Then, at the conference, one speech follows another, applause for one speaker follows applause for another speaker, and the hall echoes with over-the-top patriotic declarations by, it seems, every single attendee. All this is chronicled on thousands of feet of precious film ripping through burning-hot cameras. The voice of Revolutionary Ethiopia broadcasts the conference activities from Tinsae Hall in Asmara throughout Ethiopia, the radio waves trekking through the valleys and mountains, across the lakes and rivers, and over the fields, farms and forests to reach every corner of this vast land and pour into the ears of millions of proud but anxious Ethiopians. Hundreds of eager journalists commit ink to paper; radio and television announcers speak till their vocal cords snap; attendees listen until they wear out, some falling asleep in their chairs, tired knees buckling and taking them down to the floor, their ears ringing with more words than they can process, their overworked brains barely functioning. Today only twenty speakers are scheduled, but there are almost fifty still to come in the remaining days of the Asmara Conference. I hope all of us will stay strong enough, and oil our eardrums well enough, to make it to the end.

History marches like this for three days and nights. Each morning before the speeches we break ground for more memorial statues. One is for the Eritrean patriots who struggled for unity under the banner "Ethiopia or Death", and received the latter. Another is for members of the Armed Forces who fought hard for the cause of Revolutionary Ethiopia, and also died.

On the final day of the conference, February 1st, the Chairman declares a holiday, a day of triumph, and we issue the Asmara Manifesto with seven resolutions:

1) Our visionary, resolute and revolutionary leader Comrade

Chairman Mengistu Haile Mariam, Head of the Provisional Military Administration Committee and the Commission for Organizing the Party of the Working People of Ethiopia, Supreme Commander of the Revolutionary Army, on January 26, 1982, delivered a historic speech in the city of Asmara to the people of the Ethiopian nation. This highly venerated speech focused on the impact of international geopolitics on the region, our neighbours and the current Ethiopian situation, particularly relative to the ongoing problem of the Eritrean province. Comrade Chairman introduced the Red Star Multi-Faceted Revolutionary Campaign, a campaign which has as its principal goal the liberation of the Eritrean people and a complete rehabilitation of the regional economy that was devastated by the secessionist insurgents. To this end all of us in a single voice proclaim our unconditional support, and we hereby attest our readiness to boldly pay any sacrifice required of us even at the risk of death, and stand firmly behind these and any forthcoming resolutions the Revolutionary leadership deems important.

2) The forces of anti-freedom, anti-union, anti-people and anti-peace have been consistently rejected by the people, and have time and again failed to represent anyone other than evil imperialists and reactionaries. Consequently, going forward, their destructive messages should not be allowed to continue and must be wiped out once and for all by the greater public. We want to confirm that anyone found to be providing support to these insurgents, internally or otherwise, will be considered an enemy of the people and we will permanently terminate their activities. In consideration of all the defensive battles our Revolutionary Army will undertake, we hereby pledge our resolve to support and stand alongside them in the performance of their patriotic duties.

231

3) For the oppressed among us and for Ethiopians under persecution in a foreign land, who naïvely but mistakenly participated in this destructive endeavour, or were forced to do so, your Revolutionary Government is granting you a full amnesty to fight off and unequivocally reject these criminal insurgents who have been spilling blood in your good name. This Congress is asking you to return to your homeland immediately and stand together with your fellow Ethiopians in the service of your beloved country.

4) The establishment of effective governing bodies will ensure that the people will not again sink into a socioeconomic abyss, and in line with the socialist economy that is currently under construction in Revolutionary Ethiopia, we find it imperative to follow strictly the directions as set forth by our revolutionary leader Comrade Chairman. These directions and the programmes necessitate all farmers to immediately organize under communal farming associations. We are ready to provide the material and technical assistance required.

5) To those outside forces and espionage agencies that have been collaborating with and helping the mercenaries identified by the Ethiopian people as holding anti-freedom, anti-union and anti-peace stances, and trading in the blood of oppressed people, we strongly condemn their actions and hereby demand that they cease and desist their support of the aforementioned mercenaries.

6) Colonial and imperialist influences are contaminating a noble heritage and history that we have proudly and stalwartly sustained for thousands of years. This revolutionary administration, after an exhaustive study and analysis of Ethiopia's historical struggle to remain a free and peaceful nation, is now reversing the trend set by the failed feudal bourgeois social order of the past that managed to put a stranglehold on

our proud history and for too many years kept it from being told, taught and celebrated. As part of the initiative to ameliorate this condition, a memorial for those heroic Ethiopians who sacrificed their lives for the unity and freedom of their country will be built. Accordingly we admire the initiative by Comrade Chairman Mengistu Haile Mariam, the Provisional Military Administration Committee and COPWE Chairman, Supreme Commander of the Revolutionary Army, to dedicate the following memorial statues: in Dogali for the famous patriot Ras Alula Abanega; in Asmara, the Zerai Deres memorial; in Asmara, for those who fought and died under the banner of "Ethiopia or Death"; in Asmara, for the fallen soldiers and members of the Revolutionary Army who valiantly fought to keep alive the spirit of Revolutionary Ethiopia. Going forward, we cordially request the Revolutionary Government to pursue a critical understanding of the region's history so that the naming of places and streets as well as the overarching cultural influence and hegemony of the colonial power is reversed and replaced by the plentiful and proud history of the region and its heroic people, distinctively expressed in its true and accurate form all across the region.

7) Our class struggle takes place in the context of the clash between imperialism and socialism relative to the current geopolitical realities of the Red Sea and the Middle East, and when examined from this perspective it is undeniable that the ongoing imperialist conspiracy against the Ethiopian Revolution is an effort designed to alter the power equilibrium of the region to benefit imperialism. Victory of the Ethiopian Revolution is victory for anti-imperialist forces. By the same token, defeat of the Ethiopian Revolution would be a setback for the anti-imperialist movement. Therefore, we clearly grasp and comprehend the burden our struggle is shouldering and the

significant ramifications it has for the region as well as in the international arena. In view of these complex realities and the bitter struggle we are tasked with, to fight as part and parcel of the global initiative against imperialism, we are hereby dispatching our summons to anti-imperialist forces worldwide, that just as they have stood with us in the past, we again call upon them to renew their commitment and form with us an even more potent united front.

The manifesto is a call to duty for the entire proletariat, with an inclusive vision and a national plan of action. If the insurgents hiding in the mountains of Nakfa have ears that hear and hearts that feel, then they will do the right thing, or else face oblivion. The manifesto is a denouement of one chapter of Eritrea and the prelude to the next. It is the beginning of an end. After the conference secretary reads the manifesto aloud, the room breaks into song:

The Red Star Campaign, banner of our perpetual struggle
The universal truth of socialism
The Promised Land with hope, progress and unity
Fathers and mothers
Peace be unto you
Fathers and mothers
Welcome to you all
Our hands filled with palm fronds
We the blossoming children of today
And the bright future of tomorrow
Join us in the celebration of victory

The whole hall reverberates with song, people toss flower petals into the air and everyone applauds. Then, as is my habit, I grab all the film, photos and tapes and speed off to Army Aviation.

When I arrive I go and find Major Koricho Tadesse. He is a changed man, an angry man. I have no idea why, but he doesn't want to deal with me at all.

"Why are you always so late?" he yells at me, as if I'm his personal servant.

My misgivings get the better of me and my patience ends. "What is your problem? There's a plane assigned exclusively for this purpose. Without my order, it won't be flying anywhere. If anyone is tight on time, it's me, not you."

He doesn't look at all like the person I used to know. Anger is burning in his eyes. It's obvious that he's under serious emotional strain. If he's that badly overworked, I can sympathize. It's becoming a trend here for us to bottle up our troubles, then suddenly explode. The tall young mechanic stands nearby, looking at us.

"Major, could you please hurry?" says the mechanic.

Major Koricho reacts as if ordered by a general. He picks up the box of film and is about to take it to the plane when I ask him, "Who is that man?"

The Major ignores my question. "Did you give me all the film? Or did you forget some again?"

The Major has spent years as the king of this airfield, striding around in control, with power. Look at him now, full of anger and stress, cowering in front of his mechanic. Something is wrong.

"Oh, wait, I did forget something," I say.

"What?" he asks and glares at me.

"There is one more roll of film."

"Where is it?"

"It's on its way. I'll have to wait for it. My apologies, Major, but we'll be here a bit longer."

The young mechanic, clearly impatient, walks over to us. I feel like a dwarf, he is that tall.

"What are we waiting for?" he asks.

Major Koricho explains the situation. The young man tries to hide his frustration, but I can tell he's upset.

"Comrade," I say to him, "I'm glad to meet you. My name is Tsegaye Hailemaryam."

He pauses for a second, then gives a little smile. "My name is Ikuba Arat," he says.

I don't like the look of him. He's like some reptile with too many teeth.

"What's the hurry?" I ask. "The aeroplane is reserved just for our use, right?"

"True, but it still has to leave and fly back here before it gets dark," he says.

"You're a mechanic, correct?"

"I am, so what?"

"So what business do you have dealing with air traffic control?" That should put him in his place. Major Koricho looks very nervous.

"Is it a sin to cooperate and help each other out?" says Ikuba. "I can't start working on one plane until the other one is in the air, in case we need to switch planes. And who has enough time?"

Something in Major Koricho's expression tells me that Ikuba is lying. I know the tall young man is trying to fool me, but I don't know why. They were so alarmed when they dropped the crate of rifles last time. That gives me some idea of what might be going on. The speech we got from Director Betru when we arrived echoes in my ears – he warned us that the insurgents would look to exploit people under financial strain, especially if they were near retirement age. But is that possible here? A hero like Major Koricho would never sell his honour, his integrity, for monetary gain. But his extreme reaction, and Ikuba's, to my invented delay – that confirms something is really wrong here. Now that I know this, I need to figure out how to safely extract myself. Major Koricho and the mechanic glare at me. Ah, a solution.

"Is there a phone nearby?" I ask.

"Yes, what for?" Major Koricho speaks quickly.

"I need to call and ask whether the delayed film will get here soon. If not, then we shouldn't wait and the plane can go."

Major Koricho relaxes and Ikuba takes a deep breath. The Major shows me to the Officer's Club where a group of pilots, all in flight gear, are eating at the buffet. They look to have a hearty appetite – I've heard they really fuel up before and after each flight.

I dial my office and my secretary Rezan answers.

As soon as I say hello, she says, "Yes, Comrade Tsegaye, I was also looking for you."

"Why, what happened?"

"I just got a call that the cameras and film have arrived."

I've been waiting for this news with intense anticipation, so I go a little overboard in expressing my delight: "That's such wonderful news, I could just swallow you whole!"

"What did you just say?" she asks, alarmed.

"I mean, that's great news, thanks for letting me know. Please see that they're brought immediately to my office."

"Also, Comrade Director Betru was asking for you, urgently," says Rezan.

"I'll be there right away," I say and hang up.

I inform Major Koricho of what I am sure he'll be relieved to hear: "The film is still delayed so the plane can leave now, as scheduled."

I drive back into the city, happy and whistling the Red Star Campaign song. The palm trees look even more graceful and more beautiful than before. Braided ladies are leisurely strolling everywhere. It's as if everyone has left their homes and is out on the streets, enjoying the evening.

When I get back to the office, Rezan connects me with Director Betru Tessema.

"Were you looking for me?" I ask.

"Yes, it's about the jamming," says Betru.

That's not what I wanted to hear. My ears ache at the word "jamming", that's how often I get questioned about it. "What's happened now?"

"The insurgency's broadcast is still on air. This time they're using the forty-one-metre band. What are you all waiting for?"

"What are they saying on the broadcast?"

Betru adopts the voice of a radio announcer: "People of Eritrea, the Derg government's strategy in this campaign, its sixth one here, is to finish you off once and for all. Since this is the Derg's ultimate and decisive campaign, you must know that it is critical to defend your own existence. Stand up and fight for your life." Then he switches back to his normal voice. "That's how they're inciting the public. But could you help me understand something here? With all the military might and manpower under our command, why is it that we have so far been incapable of capturing and destroying the insurgency's radio station?" I can hear his distress.

"I have something for you," I say.

"What?"

"Do you know a Major Koricho Tadesse, stationed at Army Aviation at Sembel airfield?"

"Yes, why?"

I give him the details of the suspicious activities, both what I saw a few days ago and today's incident. I'm still not sure about it though. "Listen," I say, "this may just be my own misplaced intuition. I could be wrong. But both were strange situations, so it might not be a bad idea to look into them, cautiously."

"Don't you worry, it'll be done tightly and carefully. This is good work. Actually, this is fantastic work." Betru hangs up.

My phone rings again and I answer. The Military Affairs Political Bureau is calling to yell at me. It's the usual anger of a military officer towards a civilian like me.

"Dimtsi Hafash is still transmitting! What are you waiting for?" he yells. "You're sabotaging us."

Oh boy. I understand that the Military Affairs Political Bureau is taking a lot of heat for the insurgency broadcasts, but I still get angry whenever I hear the word "sabotage". If you're not wearing a uniform, your loyalty is always in question.

I phone the technical supervisor and he tells me that, from Asmara, it's impossible to block the insurgent programmes being broadcast on the forty-one-metre band.

"Why didn't you tell me about this earlier?" I say. It's my turn to get angry at someone.

"I was just about to call you, Comrade Tsegaye, but you beat me to it."

"So what do you suggest we do now?"

"Unless engineers are sent here from Addis to upgrade and repair our Tract B transmission antennas, there's not much we *can* do at this point. Regardless, we definitely need more technicians. We're all just about dead here. It's too much work keeping these old antennas transmitting the jamming signal all day every day."

"Isn't there anything we can do in the meantime?" I ask again.

"Nothing at all," he says. "We don't have an antenna for forty-one-metre short-wave signals."

"Shouldn't we have anticipated this and been prepared, so it wouldn't be an issue now?"

"How? How could we have known something like this would be needed?"

I start cussing like an old sailor. Rezan connects me with Addis Ababa. Our communication engineers at the Voice of Ethiopia radio station aren't known for being helpful. Regardless of their expertise, their first response to any issue is to complain about how difficult or impossible it will be. The "can-do" spirit is just not in them. So straightaway I go on the offensive and explain how critical the situation is, that it needs to be resolved immediately.

"There's no budget allocation for your request," the engineering manager tells me. "And even if we had the budget, it would be a big job. Refurbishing an antenna is not a trivial thing."

I'm getting aggravated. "Listen, comrade, right now I'm not worried about budget or effort. To me, those are non-factors. I'm telling you that this needs to be resolved right away, immediately, now! We're in a war of radio waves, meaning we're not going to sit down with our hands folded and have polite meetings to discuss budgets and procedures and other trivia. This is war and we will fight."

"Maybe there's an alternative until the antennas are refurbished . . ."

At last I'm getting through to him. "What do you have in mind?" I ask, my voice calmer.

"Attempt the jamming from Addis."

"Then do it." Ideas are like coffee and love – best while still hot.

"It would be tricky, and hard. For example, what are we going to do about the regular programmes being broadcast at the same time as the insurgents'?"

"Cancel them."

"I'll need authorization from upper management," he says.

"Comrade, get whatever authorization you need from wherever you need it. Regardless, the jamming needs to start right this minute. I'll have a technician here call to give you the specifics. And the work on refurbishing our Tract B antennas should get going right away too."

After I hammer him with one order after another, he starts his whining. "You're off in Asmara, I doubt you have any clue about the fire drill I'm subjected to here in Addis every day. I don't see why I have to be in the hot seat all the time because of you all over there."

"What good will come from talking about Addis or Asmara? Regardless of the location, we're still the ones responsible for getting the job done, right?"

The jamming dealt with, at least for the moment, I spend the rest of the day preparing to cover the big parade tomorrow. The people of Asmara are supposed to come out to Saba Stadium for a parade and rally to show their support for the Red Star Campaign and the Asmara Manifesto. In the evening I learn that the jamming has started from Addis and seems to be working. I inspect the new movie cameras lined up against the wall in my office with their 300 mm lenses, and I feel like a military commander reviewing his troops. I know we're ready for battle now. All in all, it wasn't a bad day – hard work never killed anyone, and even the arguments and confrontations happened in the spirit of progress, not malice. With all that was accomplished, I make peace with myself and the world. The beautiful sun that has been out all day begins to set, a ripe orange sitting on the horizon.

18

OUT IN THE CITY

I call Fiammetta and explain that the Asmara Conference has consumed me for the last three days. She understands.

"I watch TV," she says. "I can see that you've been busy."

We arrange to meet in front of the Nyala Hotel at 7 p.m. I'm there right on time. It's a pleasant evening, a little chilly. A full moon hangs in the night sky surrounded by twinkling stars, a silver plate on a table of candles. People from the just-concluded conference crowd the streets, their mood celebratory.

Fiammetta jumps into my car and leans close to me, her hair swishing about.

"Tsegaye, how are you?" she asks with a big smile. "Okay, my three-month lover, let's go."

She poses adorably in my car, an art she has mastered. Her face is turned slightly towards me with one shoulder against the passenger window, her chest pointing forward and her legs slightly apart. She tosses her handbag onto the back seat, then lifts her skirt and bends over and inhales. I have no idea what she's up to.

"What are you doing?" I ask.

"I want to make sure I smell okay. Moron."

"You're bold."

"How are you, three-month lover?" she asks again.

"Who knows, I may stay longer than that."

"Yeaah, that was obvious before we even started."

"Really?" I say.

"You think Nakfa will fall in three months? Never."

"Why shouldn't it? The terrain is tough, but Shabia isn't."

"Wa! I swear, between you Addis men posturing and us Eritreans lying, this place is doomed."

I laugh and start the engine. "Where shall we go?"

"Wherever your desire takes you."

"No, you decide – Asmara is your city, I want to see it through your eyes."

"Oh please, stop joking," she says.

"No, I'm not joking."

"As if you don't already know Asmara inside and out? Is there any place you Red Stars don't go? You guys are everywhere."

"What do you mean, everywhere?" I ask.

"Wa! You have the city entirely under your control. And at night you go everywhere on your Campaign of Love."

"The Red Star Campaign embraces the women of Eritrea." I smile at her. "Seriously, where shall we go?"

"Caravel."

The restaurant isn't far from here. I've heard about its reputation for lasagna al forno, baked right on the serving plate. I pull away from the curb and turn to take us there.

"I really do want to see Asmara through your eyes," I say. "The greatness of a city is not in the grandeur of its buildings or the efficiency of its streets. I think the beauty of a city, what makes it beautiful, are its people. An uninhabited city is nothing, it doesn't even make sense. It would just be a wasteland of buildings, a desert of pavement. Lifeless and heartless."

I remember a poem about Asmara, though I can't recall who wrote it. I recite it for her:

> *I say it once, twice*
> *My city holds its beauty*
> *My city holds its children*
> *Buildings with cold granite skeletons*
> *Streets of silent stone*
> *Grace a birthright in my beautiful city*
> *Where human hearts beat*
> *Boundless and unbordered*
> *Tall buildings stretch for meaning*
> *Houses scrubbed of significance*
> *Wide avenues dream of footsteps*
> *Human breath my city's sustenance*
> *Its value measured*
> *In heartbeats, the rhythm of our joy*
> *My shining city sparkling in every eye*
> *Streets a river of lights*
> *A thousand glowing stars reflected on empty waters*
> *Steering no sailors, beguiling no lovers*
> *Good light illuminates what people see*
> *A city residing in its hearts and souls*

"That's beautiful," says Fiammetta. "You should be a writer."

"I would, if I had the talent. But even if I did, it still takes sweat and blood to be a writer. That's why most people take their stories to the grave."

She looks out of the window as we round a corner.

"It's hard to get to an Eritrean's heart," she says.

"Everyone can be moved by something."

"Bravo, Red Star," she says. "That something is usually food, right? Unless the stomach is full, the heart is distant? That's what we need, teff not talk, rice not rhetoric."

The Caravel is flooded with cars. It's a drive-in restaurant where you order from your car and eat there as well. I park and turn to Fiammetta.

"So can I get you some Fanta?"

"*Via!*" she scolds me.

She isn't hungry so we get beer and Sprite for her and a whiskey for me. The waiters are not as friendly as the ones in Addis, but they're faster. They have a system here, and serving customers is considered a real profession. But if something goes wrong with the system, everything stops. Nobody wants to risk breaking a rule.

I take a sip of my whiskey. "You really look marvellous tonight." She's wearing a traditional skirt, short with colourful striped edges, and a shawl that goes with it.

"What, my outfit?" she asks.

"Yes, it's lovely."

"It's only after the Revolution came here that we Asmara women started to get dressed up and go out like this."

"Not before?" I ask.

"Yeaah, who would want to look good and go out in those days?"

"Why not?"

"So we could get rounded up and marched to the Lion's Hotel?" she says, using Asmara slang for prison. "Before the Revolution, if we wanted to go out, we had to be very careful to avoid attracting any attention from the Public Security spies. We'd dress shabbily and wrap ourselves in an old scarf before we left the house."

She is shaking, from her memories, I think.

After a deep breath she continues. "But since the Revolution we dress how we like, and then we go out. That's definitely a sign of peace and prosperity, when women start dressing up and going out on the town."

"You're right. And it's getting even better."

"Oromay! Better now that we have Red Star? There's so much goodness now that every place is crowded with heart-landers! Yeaah."

She's being sarcastic but I don't take the bait. "That is what we want. For both women and men to walk without fear. To all be equally proud to be Ethiopian. That's the real objective of Red Star." I'm happy with my little campaign speech.

"I just hope things don't go back to the way they were," she says. "But if they do, if there's another war, *via*, I'm gone."

"What kept you here last time?"

"I swear, I don't know. Maybe I'm used to being in my own home. Of all my friends, I'm the only one who stayed. I think I would rather die here than end up as a maid for an Arab family."

I smile. "Fiammetta, really, you deserve to be honoured with the Faithful Citizen Medal."

"With so many American dollars inviting me to go to Jeddah or Abu Dhabi, what kind of woman am I?"

"You are the sweet and proud kind," I say.

I order another glass of whiskey. She doesn't want anything else, and doesn't want to go anywhere else. She takes out a mefaqiya twig from her handbag and starts to clean her teeth. Then suddenly she starts peppering me with questions.

"Your fiancée, what's her favourite colour, to wear?"

"Why would you want to know that?" Her question has reminded me of something I need to ask her.

"Because I really want to know. Please?"

"I think she likes green dresses. And black."

"I swear, from now on I'll stop wearing green and black dresses."

"Oh boy."

"What kind of perfume does she wear?"

"Chanel No. 5," I say.

"No more Chanel No. 5 for me. Or, wait, maybe I should wear it for you?"

"Please, for the love of God, stop asking me about her!"

"Why? Are you missing her? Don't be sad, you'll go back to her. After three months. Okay?"

She's serious and her voice is sad. The full moon is partially hidden behind the palm trees. It looks low enough to get caught in their fronds.

"Fiammetta, can I ask you one thing?"

She stops cleaning her teeth with the twig. "What?"

"What happened between you and Colonel Wolday Tariku?"

Wolday has already left for Afabet, the staging point for the assault on Nakfa. I saw him at Sembel as he was waiting for his flight. His hair had grown even longer, so I asked him why he hadn't got it trimmed. "After the victory," he told me in a cold tone. I don't know why, but he clearly didn't want to talk to me. Later I remembered the intense looks between him and Fiammetta at Solomon's party. I had meant to ask Fiammetta about it, but kept forgetting until now.

"Nothing," she says. "But why are you asking me that?"

"Do you remember the party at Comrade Solomon Betregiorgis's house?"

"Of course," she says. "That's when I met you."

"Or could it be that's when I met you?" I ask, trying to flatter her. "Anyway, back to my question. That night you and Colonel Wolday gave each other some intense stares, and I couldn't tell if it was from love or hate. That's what I wanted to know."

There are two rules I live by when it comes to women.

First, I have to know the history of the woman I'm going out with. If I don't, I feel sick to my stomach. That's why Addis women aggravate me. They stay silent, keeping their pasts to themselves. Their commitment to discretion offends me.

Second, I always make them feel like I chased after them. If a woman stays with me, I want her to feel cherished and proud. I sincerely believe that women must be politely respected, in both love and hate.

But my question for Fiammetta does not come from those two rules. It's deeper than that. If she's involved romantically with Wolday, I'm not sure what I'll do. Probably say goodbye. Wolday is a hero who, for the unity and honour of Revolutionary Ethiopia, lives in foxholes. He is blistering under the torrid Nakfa sun in the day, then freezing at night in the same godforsaken place. My conscience won't allow me to run around Asmara having a good time with the girl-friend of such a patriot.

"Tell me the truth, Fiammetta."

"I am. I don't have any relationship whatsoever with him."

"Swear on my palm," I say raising my hand, and she does, hitting mine with hers.

We're both quiet for a minute.

"Okay, Fiammetta, I have to ask—"

"Enough!" she says, interrupting me. She can turn on the outrage when she wants to, and this is one of those occasions. "If you want to get rid of me, tell me and I'll leave, I swear. Not every man who stares at me is my lover, believe it or not."

I believe her completely, and from then on we meet every evening after work.

We are inseparable and Asmara can barely contain us. For sweet gelato we go to Ugo. For drinks and Italian food it's Caravel. For a good Caportona and whiskey, it's Shell or Agip. For a nutritious fruit shake – papaya, orange, or mango and banana – our choice is May Jah Jah's. Tre Stelle is our new place for coffee.

On Sundays we enjoy the scenery along the road out of the city past Sembel Airport. To relax, we take leisurely drives to Keren, down to Massawa, or through the streets of Mendefera. The world is a stage for our pleasures, or so we think. When we get tired we rest in the shade of the majestic palm trees. When we feel energetic, we hold hands and walk through the park. In quiet moments we sit under a palm and admire the Asmara sunsets. Most evenings the setting sun resembles a ball of molten metal, decorating the sky with traces of a thousand vibrant colours.

We get used to the daily presence of each other and come to require it. The origin of love is habit. But habit can bind us and become a prison sentence. Love is a prison of sweet suffering. Fiammetta and I become prisoners of each other. We have no covenant, no certificate of marriage, but our love thrives. The world belongs to us, the two of us its only citizens. Love is blind, and we are blind to anyone who isn't us.

*

Fiammetta and I meet again one evening as usual, the sun low in the sky. It's February and the nights are humid.

"What happened to you today?" she asks. "You look happy."

"I'm in love."

"How reckless!" she says. "With whom?"

"Asmara!"

"Well, then I'm in love with Red Star," she says. "But you know, love doesn't always bring peace."

We drive out towards the airport to watch the sunset. The day fades, stars begin to appear in the indigo sky and the horizon turns to flame. Another mesmerizing Asmara sunset. On our way back into town I head towards Paradiso Street.

"Where are you going?" she asks.

"The Paradiso. I miss their coffee."

She shakes her head, her hair moving one way and her head the other. "No, no, we're not going there. Let's go to Tre Stelle." The twig teeth-cleaner is now in use.

"Why can't we go to the Paradiso? They have the best coffee."

"Not since Aboy Tekle died. And I'm not going to sit there drinking coffee, remembering Aboy and being sad. I'm not built for sadness." She is insistent.

"So what were you made for?"

"For fun. To love and be loved."

"Ciao, Paradiso," I say and head towards Tre Stelle. There aren't many people out and the streets seem wider.

Fiammetta is absorbed in cleaning her teeth, but eventually she breaks the silence. "These days I have no happiness or peace. My heart is sad. Sometimes I cry, and I don't know why. I was never like this, I swear. What's happened to me?"

251

"Something changed," I say.

"Yeaah, you're not from here – what do you know? Moron."

At Tre Stelle she doesn't want coffee but instead orders tea with lemon. Coffee isn't the most popular drink in Asmara. Most people here prefer tea, at least eight cups a day.

I give in to my unfortunate tendency to interrogate her: "So what kind of woman were you in the past?"

"Never serious about anything. Always carefree, happy. But now I don't recognize myself. Forget it, you'll never understand. I swear, you're a complete moron." She's restless now, and rambling. "Please, could you tell me about your fiancée? Wait, no, don't worry, I don't want to know anything about her. Who cares about her? I don't. But what am I going to do if she comes here? I have no idea! Oh, why can't you just die now? I'll carve a Red Star on your grave, seriously. On second thoughts, please don't die. Who'll tell all the lies if you die?" She goes on like that, zig-zagging between humour and complaint. Then: "But what will happen to me the day you leave? Where will I go?" The question is directed more at herself than me.

"Why are we talking about this?" I ask. "Let's talk about something else. Something more cheerful."

"Do you love me, Tsegaye? Tell me, okay?"

"Do you think my heart is made of Nakfa rock?"

"I swear, I can't decide," she says. "I used to be able to treat everything like a joke, take everything lightly. But where did that get me? *Senza casa, senza marito.* No house of my own, no husband. Who am I, a woman who cannot make even a simple decision?" She falls silent.

I see this getting worse. Our relationship is tangling into a knotted clump of yarn. We got into it for simple fun, but now she is overwhelmed. I am too. It's sink or swim, but neither of us can decide. Instead, I just float on the surface and let the currents take me. Where? I don't know.

A waiter, different to the one who brought us our drinks, comes to give us our bill. He brightens at the sight of Fiammetta and they talk in Tigrigna. I can tell they're talking about Aboy Tekle.

"Who is that?" I ask after he leaves.

"He's Aboy's nephew, the son of his brother."

"You know, I meant to ask you, did they ever find out how he died?"

"It wasn't only him! They found his older sister dead the next week. He'd lived with her for years, after his wife passed away, and they were very close. It's so sad, *poverini*." She lowers her head in what looks like a silent prayer for her friends, then looks back up after a minute. "Aboy was shot by the insurgents, by their fedayeen, but as for his sister, nobody knows. Maybe a heart attack, but Adey Lemlem was a healthy old lady. She and my mother were very close, in good times and bad. So sad that Adey Lemlem is gone. She loved good food and drink, and the way she kept her house so clean! You could eat injera off the floor there. We used to go over there almost every Sunday when I was little. She would feed me such good food and then even give me some money to go to the cinema. It was always better going to Adey Lemlem's house instead of to my relatives. She never asked you to clear the table or do the dishes. You know, I was lazy even when I was a kid, so I really liked her, I swear."

I want to hear more, so all I say is, "Okay."

"A day before Adey Lemlem died, she told my mother what happened to her brother."

"Oh, what did she say?"

"That Aboy had started seeing things at work that he

didn't like. He was worried about what was going on. But he was afraid to quit, so he didn't know what to do."

"What do you think he was so worried about?"

"I don't know. He was always a happy person." With that she falls silent.

Fiammetta Gilay has a bad habit: she loves to mix the truth with the lie. She'll take a little truth and then expand on it with her own inventions. She doesn't do it out of malice, really, but to make conversation.

I remember a discussion like that from last week, when she called me from her office:

"Tsegaye, my mother just called me," she said.

"Why?"

"Our house is surrounded by soldiers."

"What?"

"Yes, you remember Alganesh, right?"

Alganesh is Fiammetta's long-time neighbour and close friend. We've taken her out with us for drinks a few times. Alganesh returned the favour by having us over for a tasty shiro wot.

"Yes, what's happened to her?" I said.

"They found guns and bombs in her basement."

"No, really?"

Sitting there in my office, remembering the delicious food I'd had at Alganesh's house, I got scared. As I was eating shiro wot, I had been sitting on top of Shabia's crates of dynamite.

"Oh yes, they got her," said Fiammetta.

"So what are you doing?"

"They're after me as well. I'm calling you from where I'm hiding."

"Why are they after you?"

"I knew about the guns and bombs in her basement, and

254

I'm sure she's told them about me. So I'm running away now – I don't want to go to jail again. Farewell, I love you my dear. Ciao!"

"Stop, Fiammetta, don't hang up! Don't do anything crazy. Where are you? Tell me!"

She hung up as I was yelling at her. I was distraught and wanted to help her, but I didn't know where she was. So many wild ideas came to mind, I didn't know what to do. Finally she called back.

"For God's sake," I begged her. "Please tell me where you are so I can come and get you."

She was laughing. "I swear on my mother's name, I made it all up. I'm fine, you moron."

I was so angry I hung up on her, slamming the phone down. I was livid. She was lucky we weren't in the same room.

Later she apologized. "I swear, I don't know why, but I like to make up stories. What should I do? What kind of a woman am I?"

"You are a sweet liar."

So now, sitting in my car at Tre Stelle with Fiammetta and talking about people being murdered, people dying, I need to know more.

"Who owns the Paradiso?" I ask.

"How would I know?"

"Asmara is a small city. Everybody knows everybody else. And everybody knows the Paradiso."

Fiammetta shrugs, but I have more questions. "Is what you said about Aboy true?"

"I swear on my mother's life, it's the truth." When she swears on her mother, she is telling the truth.

This discussion started out as nothing, really. Now it has me worried. What was going on at Paradiso that scared Aboy? What did he know? What got him killed by the insurgents? The more I think about it, the more anxious I get. And I'm worried about how easily Fiammetta shared that information with me. She's carrying around a dangerous piece of evidence and doesn't realize it.

"Fiammetta, listen to me," I say in a serious tone. "What you just told me about Aboy, you can't mention it to anyone else. It's dangerous. Do you understand? This is no joke. Our lives are at risk. And tell your mother to keep quiet about it. It's very dangerous."

"Why? What's this all about?" she asks.

"Right now, I'm not certain. But I'm sure I'll figure it out soon. Until then, please promise me you won't say anything about this to anyone."

I drive her home. For the first time, driving at night in Mai Temenai frightens me, but I don't want her to notice that. There aren't any street lights in her neighbourhood.

"You're telling me to be careful," she says, "but what about you?"

"What about me?"

"You go wherever you want without security, unlike the other Red Stars. Moron."

"Who knows the day of their own death? I live freely and I'll die freely. It's not something I think about."

"Don't disappear on me, agreed?" It's how she always says goodbye to me.

"As long as you don't either." It's how she's taught me to answer.

19

COFFEE CEREMONY

I drive home from Mai Temenai – fast – and when I get there my phone is ringing.

"Hello," I answer. Thinking it's Fiammetta, I almost say her name. And that would have been a disaster, because it's Roman, my fiancée.

"What happened to you, my love?" she says. "Where have you been? I've been calling you the whole day."

"Too much work, you know that."

"You just got home from work?"

I look at my watch. It's 9.30 p.m. and I remember our routine back in Addis. "I miss your coffee so much."

"I've stopped making it," she says.

"Why? It always smelled so good, with the incense, and you would ask the adbar spirits to look after me."

"I liked making coffee for you, Tsegaye. When you're not here, it's not worth it."

"I feel sorry for your jebenas!" She has a wonderful collection of ceramic coffee pots. She fusses over them and always keeps them ready for the next coffee ceremony.

"I'm out of practice now," she says in a sad voice.

Roman doesn't make coffee because she's addicted to it, or because she wants the good luck it brings. For her, it is artistic expression, her talent and joy showing in every step of the ceremony. She is proud of her abilities. "Great coffee only requires patience, diligence and practice," she says. "Nobody should make it in a hurry, that's sad. Coffee is about slowing down." Rushing robs the pleasure that comes from following the old ceremonious ways.

Before she begins, my queen of coffee washes and puts on one of her full-length traditional dresses, drapes a netala shawl over her shoulders and takes out the berchuma stool she reserves just for making coffee. The best coffee requires red-hot coals in a stove, so she'll have someone bring them to her. Some good music sets the mood and she begins by roasting the beans. The flowing music guides the movements of her hands as she stirs and swirls the green coffee beans in the pan. They are done when each bean is uniformly dark and shiny, as if coated in oil. She carries the pan around to fill the room with the aroma of freshly roasted coffee. The smell alone is delicious. Unlike most women, Roman doesn't hand the roasted beans off to someone else to grind; she grinds them herself to make sure it's done evenly.

Her prized jebenas are waiting, all clean and arranged in a line on a special shelf. The coffee queen picks one of them for service and pours in a precise amount of water. The coals will be re-lit so they again glow red-hot, new music put on, and the jebena pot placed carefully over the newly hot coals. She will not take her eyes off the water until it has reached the right temperature, which somehow she recognizes by sight. Then the ground coffee is carefully added using a small silver spoon. Even at this stage her timing is precise, so that the water stays at the proper temperature even while the coffee is being added. She adds a little more water and waits the right amount of time, just a few minutes, until the coffee is done.

The traditional sini coffee cups – always six, even if it's just the two of us – are placed on the little rekebot table, always covered with a red tablecloth. The jebena will be taken carefully off the coals and placed on its round holder as its hot contents bubble away with gusto. She lights incense in a special vessel, its white smoke and aroma reaching into every corner of the room. The duelling aromas, incense and coffee, are a heady mix. At this point she always pauses for a moment and smiles, becoming even more beautiful. The coffee is ready, she is ready, and life has been elevated. She changes the music to a song with a slow tempo. She raises the jebena high in the air above the table, always to the same height, and slowly pours the dark precious liquid into each sini. Her coffee is so perfect that one cup is complete satisfaction.

Even here in Asmara, more than five hundred miles from our little home, I can picture in vivid detail the proud, beautiful coffee queen visible through the incense smoke. I love her coffee, how she moves in the ceremony, how she will refuse to begin until I am sitting quietly right there in front of her.

"Why are you silent?" Roman asks, and my remembrances are interrupted.

"I miss your coffee."

"Those memories make me sad," she says quietly.

Both of us are silent for a minute.

"How is Asmara treating you?" she asks. "You don't even call me anymore."

She is upset. We might fight.

"It's fine, other than all the work. With the way they feed us here, I won't starve, that's for sure. Every room smells like pasta. I even look like pasta." I'm saying anything that comes to mind, whether it makes sense or not, hoping to steer away from an argument.

"When I see you on TV, you look like someone who's being fed by the braided ladies of Asmara." No such luck.

"You think I have time to chase after other women?" I say.

"Tell me the truth, Tsegaye."

"What?"

"You haven't been with another woman?"

"Please, enough, okay?"

"I don't know what I'll do if I hear about you and another woman. Are you mine? Or do you belong to everyone? The least you can do is to tell the other women that your heart belongs to me. Such injustice. Ech!"

Roman goes quiet for a minute, then asks, "When are you coming back to Addis?"

"Based on what I've been told, I have almost two months to go."

"From your talking points on the news, it sounds like you'll be back in two weeks."

"My love, combat operations haven't even started yet. We have a long way to go."

"But victory will soon be ours, right?" she asks.

"Africa's longest conflict isn't going to be resolved overnight. It's complicated. Nakfa will require incredible struggle and sacrifice. I'm probably going there soon myself."

"What would you do in Nakfa? You're not a fighter."

"A journalist fights in his own way. A soldier shoots and a journalist reports. Both are part of the struggle."

"My bad luck," she says and starts to cry. Roman's tears are never far away.

"There you go, why are you crying?" I try to console her. "Don't worry, nothing bad is going to happen to me."

She cries for a while, then stops. "I sent you the new Aster album on cassette. You should get it tomorrow. Also, I have time off in a few weeks. I want to come to Asmara and be with you. Long distance isn't good for romance."

Fiammetta has given me a tape of Kuku and I've probably listened to it a hundred times. Two tapes from two lovers.

"How is our little house?" I ask.

"It's getting there. I made some nice curtains. All I have to do now is get a new bed. I still don't like the one we have. Maybe we can look for one together in Asmara."

I finish talking with Roman and immediately the phone rings again. It's Fiammetta Gilay and she's not happy.

"Who were you talking to for more than a half hour? You idiot!"

"Who do you think it was?" I ask.

"Your fiancée?"

"Correct."

"What's she saying? What does she want? You dropped me off at my house so you could talk to her, right? How humiliating. And scandalous."

"Oh boy," I say. "I asked you to come back here with me, but you said you wanted to go home." Recently she's been moody, something I hadn't seen in her before. When I ask her to spend the night here with me, she says no. But if I take her to her home, then she's distant and refuses to talk.

"So what if I asked you to drop me at home?" she says.

"Well, what are you asking me to do now?"

"Nothing, idiot."

"Can I please come and get you?" I ask.

"Nope."

"So, what am I supposed to do?"

"How should I know?" she says.

"Okay then, if what you want is for me to beg you, then here, I'm begging you."

"After you took me to my house and threw me away like a broken pot? Ech!"

She hangs up on me.

I'm about to call her back, but my pride gets the best of me and I don't. I know she expects me to call back, but I'm determined not to. I go to bed. But I can't fall asleep.

I don't know what's happening to me. I've never felt rattled like this before. I can't blame it on falling in love – I'm too old to be lovesick. Or is age no protection against love? I don't know. My problem is not love, exactly, but the problem of loving two different women at the same time, and equally. How is that even possible? Life is strange. I can't choose between them. By failing to decide, and decide promptly, I'm asking for trouble.

When I think of the bond I have with Roman and the disaster that's speeding towards us, I feel like I'm being whipped with thorns. Then I bleed with remorse. With Fiammetta, I allowed myself a new romance. It soared into the heavens with the help of wonderful evenings spent relaxing under palm trees and watching the beautiful Asmara sunset, usually followed by a hot night in each other's arms. Now I can't give it up. But when I think of what it will do to Roman, my heart is squeezed in a vice.

I love Roman, but the danger that hangs over Fiammetta's head from whatever happened to Aboy Tekle troubles me. I can't abandon her now, can I? I'm simply not capable of loving someone, and being loved by them, and then abruptly cutting off the relationship. You have to be strong to do that, and I'm not. I'm weak that way. To love someone and then end it? I can't do it. I can't forget the memories of our time together. Everything I do comes from my heart, so I have a habit of trying to keep everyone chained to me. The problem with this tendency of mine is that it's idiotic. But what can I do? I am an idiot.

I give up on sleep and decide to check something with Director Betru Tessema. He often works late into the night, but I can't reach him by phone. I call the Embasoira Hotel, the Nyala Hotel and all the usual spots, but he's nowhere to be found. It's like he's vanished. I try another round of calls with no luck.

I hear an explosion in the distance. Then the night becomes very quiet. I hardly sleep, tossing and turning.

I go to work in the morning tired and in a bad mood.

Right away the phone starts ringing.

I answer and it's Colonel Ambelu from the Army's Political Administration division, looking to ambush me. He's angry and demanding to know where the reporting teams are, but I plead ignorance.

"Comrade Tsegaye," says Colonel Ambelu, "the army cannot hold up its mission waiting for you. The journalists must report this afternoon to be ready to travel overnight to the front. That's an order."

Fortunately, I'm prepared for this. I had already decided which news teams would join the troops to document the coming offensive and I've made the necessary arrangements.

"We're ready," I tell him. "When should we arrive at Army Aviation?"

"At 1400 hours exactly."

"Comrade, I have accepted the order," I say, using the military lingo.

"Have the imported cameras arrived from abroad?"

"Comrade, everything is here and ready."

"And the leaflets that will be dropped from the planes?"

"Ready for delivery," I say.

"I will call you back at 1300 hours."

"Yes, comrade, I have accepted the order."

Colonel Ambelu hangs up. He's a military intelligence officer with long experience in propaganda and incitement, and a detailed understanding of Eritrea. He rarely leaves his office, like he's nailed to his chair. Still, he works hard and says little. He hardly smiles or laughs for fear of revealing his false teeth. His mouth rotted during those horrible days when Asmara was surrounded by the insurgents and food was scarce. Now he seems determined to stay in his office until he drives Shabia out of Eritrea.

Rezan has summoned the journalists who will be joining the army in the three main battle zones. Their expertise covers radio, film, newspapers and photography. They're young and, in their fatigues, look like fresh military recruits.

"Welcome, comrades," I address them. "Each of you should know which battle zone you're assigned to."

They do. I announce the names of the team leaders. Nobody objects and each leader gets a round of applause. I'm moved by their love of country and their commitment to its cause. They are young and eager to do their duty for Revolutionary Ethiopia. I start to get emotional.

"Wonderful comrades," I manage to say. "You are journalists and now also soldiers. You know your responsibilities, so no need for us to waste time here. But take care of yourselves and each other. Don't get carried away. Be careful. Victory is ours! Ciao."

Look at me, talking like I'm a commanding officer, but trying not to tear up.

Firew Zerihun hangs back after the others leave.

"I hope you're not about to ask me for money," I say with a smile.

"No need, plenty of militia gruel awaits me."

"Then what is it?"

"I want to tell you something before I leave," Firew says.

"Continue."

"I'm worried about you."

"What exactly are you worried about?" My eyes, red from lack of sleep, are probably revealing a lot that might make him worry.

"You're spending a lot of time with that girl, Fiammetta Gilay."

"You know her?" I ask, surprise in my voice.

"The whole town knows her. She befriends every new arrival, gets his money, then moves on to the next guy. She's broken up marriages. Men have gone for their guns on account of her. Some have even gone crazy. She used to be with Americans. Now that they're gone, she targets Red Star officials. She can be dangerous, so be careful."

Now I'm curious. "What else do you think you know about her?"

"I'm an expert on Asmara women," says Firew.

"You're the Nightlife Mayor of Asmara."

The Mayor doesn't hesitate. "Listen to me. Asmara women don't know true love. All they want is to use you and brag about it to their friends. They're expert liars. One day they'll be loving, the next they provoke you, turn you into a jealous monster. They nag you, question you, and make your daily life a misery. They attach themselves like leeches and whine about how awful it will be after you leave. So you start to feel sorry for them. Your heart gets divided between them here and your lover back home. They say things about your wife, your fiancée. They create a rift.

"And they spend. Spend spend spend your money. They bring their friends to dinner like a pack of hyenas, until you're a pile of broken bones. And then there are the favours. A passport for this friend, a job for that friend, release this relative from prison. Us heartlanders, we worry about how we look to others, so we go along. The dumb ones abandon their lover back in Addis, split from their families. If they don't, Asmara women will do it for them, calling people in Addis to spread stories there. And when they find out your mission in Asmara is ending, they have this whole act they do to extract every last coin from your pocket. But they'll never actually dump you until they have the next sucker lined up. Some will pretend they love you even after you go back home. Do you know why?"

I shake my head. Firew is really agitated. He's not usually like this.

"I'll tell you why. Christmas. New Year's. Their birthday. They're hoping you send them gifts. They don't care about love. They don't even know what it is.

"Now, Addis women? They have integrity. They may love you or they may hate you, but it's real, not fake. And if they love you, they'll share what they have, try to help you with your troubles. An Asmara woman will never do that. At most, she'll make you some shiro for dinner one night, if you're lucky, if you beg them. Their fists are always clenched, and so are their hearts. I swear, I should write a book called, *Beware of Asmara Women!*"

That's Firew's lecture on the women of Asmara.

"You have been hurt," I say.

"I watch them in action. I get mad when I see what they do to men, especially gullible men. But I've haven't fallen into the trap. They're selfish, they don't know what love is."

"We shouldn't generalize like that," I say. "Maybe some women do that, but not every one in Asmara. That's not how it is."

"You'll see for yourself, especially with your girl. She's famous for how she traps Addis men. Pardon me for being so blunt, but I don't want to see some woman walk all over you, that's all."

I listen to the Mayor while he talks, but I also think about Fiammetta. It's true that we fell in love fast, before I had a chance to think about the risks. Now we're attached to each other, with our phone calls during the day and with our bodies at night. If I'm addicted to her, then I'm trapped under her control. Love is familiarity, knowing each other, so of course there's a tight bond between us. But is the Mayor right, did she lasso me like a horse? The memories of our times together make it too painful to think about breaking up. And that's when jealousy enters the picture. It traps you.

Is Fiammetta playing a cruel hoax on me, like the Mayor says? That's hard to believe. But it's true that she has changed recently. She doesn't call her friends anymore. She doesn't eat much, doesn't want either of us to drink alcohol. She scolds me when I spend money. Is she upset that I'm wasting it, or does she want me to save it so I can spend it all on her? Is she attached to me for real, or does she just want to steal me away from Roman so she can brag about her accomplishment, about how she destroyed an Addis man? It does feel like there's something she's not telling me, between her strange silences and the way she seems lost in thought. It's a mystery I need to solve.

I turn to Firew. "You don't actually know Fiammetta. 'They say.' 'People say.' 'Everyone knows.' Those are phrases people use when they're making things up. It's rumours and slander. Asmara is famous for that. I know Fiammetta. She's no virgin, she's no saint, but she's not just any woman."

"Fine, have it your way," says Firew. He shakes his head. "Meet them, date them, screw them, leave them. That's what I do. But maybe some are the salt of the earth."

I think Firew would love to find a woman he could call the salt of the earth.

"What will happen to this city without you here, without the Mayor?" I joke.

Firew smiles. "Make a radio announcement to all the women of Asmara that I've departed for the front. Tell them that their Mayor will return in glory after victory. Ciao!"

"Mayor, please be careful," I say, but he's already gone.

20

WAR AND PEACE

Firew Zerihun's lecture on Asmara women leaves me uneasy. I want to take Fiammetta's side, but the Mayor's suspicions are hard to dismiss. People do talk about her. Can there be smoke without fire? But the game we started, if it's a game, is one I want to keep playing. I know our love is blinding us. Love does strange things. It can humble the proud, make the courageous cowardly, the greedy generous, the wise crazy, the dull witty. What is love doing to me? My mission now is to understand that, to know myself better.

Oh yes, my mission, the real mission. I call Director Betru Tessema's office at Public Safety. His secretary tells me that he has flown to Addis Ababa to deal with an urgent matter.

"When will he be back?" I ask.

"Sir, I do not have that information."

"It's very important that I talk to him."

"Sir, he did not tell me when he will be returning."

Public Safety assumes everything is clandestine. You can send them a newspaper and they'll file it as 'Secret'. But I need to report what Fiammetta told me about Aboy Tekle, that he was murdered by the insurgents because of something to do with the Paradiso. I'm not sure who I can trust to keep that information secret and not have it get back to Shabia. That would be fatal for Fiammetta, and maybe me as well. I think Director Betru is my best bet, even if I have to wait for him to get back from Addis.

That night Roman calls me with two things on her mind. One is to make sure I received the Aster tape she sent me, and yes, I did. The other is to give me the dates she'll be coming to Asmara. I tell her that some of my journalists have just left for the front, and that I'll soon be joining them. It's the truth, I'm not lying to her.

Everybody's eyes have turned towards Nakfa and the atmosphere in Asmara is uneasy. Us Red Star people are anxious, everyone studying the Chairman's expression to gauge how things are going. His face is a public display of the status of the daily struggles of Revolutionary Ethiopia, its triumphs and defeats, its joys and sorrows, its hopes and despairs. Nobody is sure how much the locals know about what's going on, but lately they all head home before dark like nervous chickens to the coop. The city is silent and the streets of Asmara belong to Fiammetta and me. There's hardly a car at Caravel.

The only person around is the crazy woman Itagegn and her pack of dogs. They hang out behind Caravel. She carries the puppies in a basket and the other dogs follow right behind her. At night she walks around and yells "Dogs are better than humans!" at people. When she lies down to sleep on a street corner, her dogs lie right by her side. They guard and protect her with ferocity. The story is that Itagegn was once very much in love with a man, cared for him more than anything else in the world, but he left her. The loss drove her insane. "I don't like people," she says in a surprisingly beautiful voice. "Call me a mother to dogs." People are generally kind to her and will give her a few coins as they pass by.

"Why are you ignoring me, when I'm not ignoring you?" asks Fiammetta. She also likes to say that dogs are better than people, but she clearly needs other people. We all do. Would God even exist without humans? What would crazy Itagegn or an existential philosopher have to say about that? Fiammetta doesn't like it when I'm quiet. She would prefer that all my thoughts and deeds orbit around her. When I'm quiet she thinks my mind is with Roman and she'll use that to start an argument.

"I'm not ignoring you," I say.

"I've been keeping track of the days until you leave," says Fiammetta. "I swear, I'm tired of counting down the days like a pregnant woman. I really hate the Red Star Campaign." She used to always be happy, but now she's a stranger in the country of grief.

"And then?"

"I need to find a man to help me get over you. Off to your fiancée you go."

"So that's it?" I ask.

She is bitter, sad and still. She expects me to talk to her, but she gets lost in her own thoughts. Then she'll look up at me like she's seeing me for the first time. I hope it's a look of love, but I don't know.

"Are you breaking up with me?" I ask with a smile. "I guess I should expect that. After all, you Eritreans keep trying to break up with Ethiopia."

She laughs at my joke.

"It's good when you laugh," I say. "Being sad doesn't suit you."

"I'm not going to laugh anymore from now on, Tsegaye," she says.

"Fiammetta, why?"

"You don't understand. This is so bad." She bites her lip. "Do you really think I would betray you?" Her voice is sad. "Let's swear – hit my palm."

I gently slap her palm with mine to make the vow.

Again I try to get her to tell me what's bothering her, but she refuses.

"This is my own problem," she says, "and I have to solve it."

"There's nothing I can help you with?"

"Nothing." Tears begin to fall from her big round eyes.

I don't say anything, but instead take her back to my place. It's better not to ask her to make decisions. She won't answer, but she doesn't object if I decide. On the drive she is quiet, worried about whatever her problem is.

We go to my room and suddenly she is voracious in bed. It's like she's hungry for life itself – insatiable, savage and cruel, all at the same time. She cries tears of both passion and anguish. It's a night I know I won't forget.

Afterwards, Fiammetta wants some music. She gets up and presses play on my little stereo, then comes back to bed. It's Aster Aweke's new album. I shouldn't have left Roman's cassette in the stereo – thinking of Romi breaks the mood:

> I don't want to share you
> But it is you they want

Fiammetta is lost in the song. It ends, and the next one begins:

As I feared, Fiammetta asks me, "Where did you get this cassette?"

I can't lie to her. "My fiancée sent it to me."

She jumps off the bed and yanks the cassette out of the stereo. She cracks it open and tears out the tape, letting the thin ribbons fall to the floor. Then she picks them up and throws them at me. Naked, she stands there, shaking with rage. Then she starts pulling on her clothes.

"Where are you going?" I ask.

"Home."

"What about the curfew?" Unless you have official security, it's too dangerous to go out after the 11 p.m. curfew.

Fiammetta pauses, then pulls out a chair and slumps down into it. There's nothing else she can do.

Both of us sit there, suffering. I'm wondering how I got into this mess. She's probably cursing the day we met. We sit there like that for a while, in silence. My mind wanders, lost.

Finally, I take one long sigh and break the silence. "Please listen to me, Fiammetta. Give me some time. I haven't had any time to think. I really don't even know what to think. Please give me some time, so I can figure it out."

"I wish I had time to give you," she says. "But I don't, I don't have it."

"What do you mean? We've had so many good times together. How can you just forget all that, throw it away like it doesn't matter? Are you really going to do that?"

She doesn't say anything. Then she asks me, "When do you leave for the front?"

"I'm not sure. Soon, probably."

"Soon is good. Soon solves my problem."

"So I'm your problem?" I ask.

"Moron."

"Maybe it's for the best. I'll have time to think. And a little distance can be a good thing. It either strengthens love or tells you it's not true."

"Moron."

I try to get at what's really bothering her from every angle I can think of, but she won't tell me. Eventually we hold each other again – war and peace. Maybe we will be like this together, always, for life.

PART FOUR

21

IN UNIFORM

My orders to go to the front come suddenly, leaving me only a few hours to report to Army Aviation. That's how the military operates: curt orders issued with no warning and inadequate time to prepare. I prefer a more methodical and deliberative approach, but I've barely got enough time to pack. I put on my uniform as best I can and dial Fiammetta Gilay's number to say goodbye.

We spent last night together, but lately her behaviour has got even stranger. She doesn't want us to go out in public, or even for me to give her a ride home. She makes excuses, says it's because I'll be leaving soon, but I know she's hiding something from me. I push her to tell me, but it's in her Eritrean blood to be stubborn. She's always looking over her shoulder, or out of the car window, and she startles easily.

"Are you looking for someone?" I ask her sometimes. "Who are you looking for?"

She answers with her standard response: "Why do you care, moron?"

On the third ring she picks up.

"Fiammetta, how are you?" I say.

"Why are the soldiers standing with their backs to us today?" she asks.

Our soldiers posted around Asmara don't usually assume any particular formation. So when they line up in a row on the sidewalks, facing the streets, people know that there's a high-ranking dignitary either arriving or departing the city.

"They must have heard that Tsegaye is leaving," I joke.

She doesn't laugh or say anything.

"Really," I say. "I'm going to Afabet. They just told me, so I'm calling to say my farewells."

"Right," says Fiammetta. She doesn't believe me.

"Really. You should see me in my military uniform. I look quite distinguished."

"I swear, I do not want to see you in uniform."

"You don't want to see me?"

"If someone is in a uniform, that always means goodbye."

I get a flash of jealousy. "So you've had a lot of soldier boyfriends?"

"Why do you care about anything that happened before I met you?" she says.

She's right. I shouldn't care what she did before. But I do – jealousy is poison. It's hard to forget that she's been with other men, and hard not to wonder if she prefers the pleasure she got from them. It is a torment I have no answer for, love and jealousy.

I return to my eternal question. "Fiammetta, wouldn't you rather tell me what's been bothering you?" Since I'm leaving, maybe she'll tell me now. I have a pit in my stomach.

"You go to your war, and I'll go to mine."

"And what is your war?" I ask.

"The war of love."

"Wonderful, we will meet on the love front," I say.

She pauses. "I doubt we'll ever meet again, Tsegaye."

"What?"

"Victory is ours!" Suddenly her tone is sarcastic, mocking. "The Asmara women have been occupied, conquered by the glorious Red Stars! The Addis men can leave as heroes now! Victory!"

"Enough, Fiammetta. No more jokes. I want the truth."

"You'll get it when you return." Her breathing becomes heavy.

"Get what?"

"Victory," she says in a soft voice.

"Without a doubt," I say, but my heart gets heavier in my chest as I speak. "Don't disappear on me, okay?"

I hang up and immediately head to Army Aviation at Sembel. I can't get Fiammetta out of my head. When a man can't stop thinking about a woman, either they're in love or he's a complete fool. I think I'm both, completely in love with Fiammetta and a complete fool for allowing that to happen. Driving to Sembel, I realize I'll be leaving behind my beautiful Asmara as well, my charming city of palms. I think I'm in love with Asmara along with Fiammetta. Asmara and Fiammetta, Fiammetta and Asmara – they blur together in my heart.

The Army Aviation airfield is bursting with activity. One fighter plane takes off as another comes in to land. A line of massive Antonov cargo jets shuffle out to the runways and lumber up into the sky. Weapons of all kinds are lifted and loaded into cargo bays as soldiers march up ramps into planes. Mechanics are rushing about while Air Force pilots inspect their aircraft. Military commanders flanked by top government officials watch over it all, trying to keep this organized chaos on track. I look for the plane that will take me to Afabet, the staging area for Nakfa.

"Tsegaye, my friend, you look good in uniform." I turn around and am happy to see it's Director Betru Tessema.

"I've been trying to reach you for days," I say.

"I was in Addis, I just got back. Where are you heading?"

"Afabet. I left a letter for you at your office. It has some information that might help you, but I'm not sure where it may lead. It has to do with the Paradiso coffeebar."

"Paradiso, Paradiso . . ." he mumbles the name to himself a few times. "Isn't that near where I'm staying? What did you find out?"

"It's all in the letter. I don't have time to explain now."

Betru's eyes look heavy and he carries himself like someone who hasn't slept. He's beginning to show his age. He leans in close and lowers his voice. "Have you heard of someone called 'The Bureaucrat'?" he asks.

"Yes, of course. Every ministry is full of them."

"No, as a code name. For the . . . for a very dangerous man. His real name might be something like Girmay, Goitom, Neraye or Afeworki. Or he might go by more than one name. It might be someone in government, maybe even right here at Sembel. He seems to be a man of many faces."

"What does he do?" I ask.

"It's enough for you to know that he's dangerous."

I thought of Ikuba Arat, the tall young mechanic. Could it be him? Or maybe Silay Berahi. The murder of Aboy Tekle, what was scaring him before he was killed, the strange relationship of Major Koricho and Ikuba, all this tangles together. I don't know what it adds up to.

"The information I gave you on Major Koricho Tadesse,

has anything come of it?" I ask. The aircraft are loud enough that we won't be overheard.

"We're monitoring the situation. It requires great care. Until we understand the bigger picture, arresting one man just tips off everyone else. Don't worry, leave it to me."

"I appreciate your leadership."

"How is Fiammetta Gilay?" he asks.

"She's fine. But she's different lately. Something's bothering her, but she absolutely refuses to tell me what it is. I hope nothing bad happens to her."

"Don't worry, she'll be safe," he says to reassure me. "How about Silay Berahi?"

"I haven't seen him lately."

"He's like a fox. Smart, elusive, tricky."

"You're very observant about Silay," I say. "Very zealous."

"He might be the key to all of this. Maybe . . . maybe . . ." He stands silent for minute, then looks at me. "Have you heard of 'oromay'?"

"Of course. 'Oromay' is a common word here in Asmara. People use it at least ten times a day."

"Yes, but what does it mean to you?" asks Betru.

"Done, finished, the end, it's over."

"That's what I thought too."

This is making me curious. "What are you getting at?"

"Have you heard it used in some other way? For example, to refer to a mission or an operation. The Oromay mission?"

"How would I know? The Bureaucrat? Oromay? Comrade, my assigned job is not 'spy'."

"I know that too," says Betru with a smile. "Gathering information about the enemy is a public responsibility, not just a job for our intelligence agents. Everyone must be a spy for the Revolution, for our homeland. It's not enough to say you're a revolutionary. Right now, action is what counts."

"Thanks for the lecture," I say. "I hope the letter I left for you is helpful. And take care of Fiammetta. Ciao!"

I march off to the plane that will take me to war.

22

THE AFABET BRIEFING

After a thirty-minute flight we arrive in Afabet to suffocating heat and swirling dust. There's nowhere to hide, you just stand there and suffer. The dust coats your skin and clogs your nostrils. Then I hear some soldiers talking about how Afabet is heaven compared to the front, which just about kills my enthusiasm for covering the war.

That night the force commander, a young Brigadier General, gives a presentation on the impending offensive. The audience is a mix of military commanders just arrived in Afabet from Asmara, along with government bureau chiefs and political commissars. Even though most of them are already familiar with the war plan, they're expected to sit and listen patiently. But it's all new to me. I'm lucky that I got here in time for the briefing.

The Brigadier General looks around the room and begins his speech. "This is the high-level structure and attack plan for the offensive. Our Second Revolutionary Liberation Force will commence operations on three main fronts: Kerkebet, Algena, and here at Afabet. The force that is to advance on Kerkebet will be composed of two battalions plus Sentek, our powerful tank regiment. That combined force is code-named Lightning. Three battalions will be dedicated to the Algena front, and they're code-named Reaper. The operational mission of both Lightning and Reaper is to surround, contain and prevent the enemy from breaking out of Nakfa and to stop any reinforcements from coming in. The task of breaching Nakfa, the mountain fortress that serves as the main headquarters and base for the Shabia insurgency forces, is assigned to a combined force of four battalions: the 3rd, 17th and 22nd, plus the elite Red Boots battalion. This joint force is code-named Dagger. The invasion, our D-Day, will begin in three days – February 16th at 0400 hours. Accordingly, joint force Dagger is departing Afabet today and tomorrow, heading north to get into position at the front."

I arrived in Afabet as the 22nd battalion of joint force Dagger was leaving. Most of the soldiers were young and they didn't act like they were marching into a war. They were laughing, having fun, joking around. I don't recall every face, but they all looked like me. They had my face, an Ethiopian face.

The Brigadier General continues his briefing. "Joint force Dagger has their work cut out for them. They are to blockade the highway that connects Nakfa to Algena, follow the River Mihon to obtain a staging position to the southwest of Nakfa, and capture enemy positions at Peaks 1725, 1755 and, most critically, Peak 1702. That will allow joint force Dagger to encircle most of Nakfa, 270 degrees of it. Then they can attack and destroy the main Shabia force there.

"As for the enemy, we believe they have organized their defences into three rings. The outer ring begins not far from here in the hills of the Seseneb Mindab all the way through the outskirts of Kubkub and the port of Mersa Gulbub. Some

distance inside that ring is another, with defensive fortifications in the hills from Bashara, Ras Armas, Rohoret and
Gadud. The enemy strategy is that if the outer ring fails,
they will retreat to the next line of defence, the second ring,
and continue to wage war from there. If the second ring is
broken as well, we believe their plan is to continue the fight
from several strongholds in the Nakfa mountains: Nakfa
Gate, River Mahon, Denden Plateau, Adhoba Valley and the
Harewa Range. Those are formidable natural fortresses, and
that's where they will make their last stand. The Adhoba
Valley is their only escape route. Our intelligence indicates
that they have stationed their most capable forces there to
defend it at all costs."

That gives me a good understanding of the arrangement
of the two opposing armies across the combat zones. The
Brigadier General will be leading joint force Dagger, and he
goes on to explain more about what to expect in the battles
to come. The enemy has some advantages, to be sure. Our
forces have to assault their positions, and military doctrine
calls for the attacking force to be at least three times the
strength of the defending forces. It's understood, though,
that this three-to-one ratio applies only if the terrain is neu-
tral. But the Nakfa region is one of the harshest and most
demanding environments on the planet. Its peaks freeze, its
valleys boil. The rugged mountains and hidden caves make
it difficult if not impossible to carry out reconnaissance to
determine the location and strength of enemy forces. In such
a circumstance, nobody can say how many troops might be
required for success, or how long it might take.

I saw the deadly Nakfa mountains for myself on the flight
here, a chain of peaks that spring up suddenly from the
earth and climb straight into the sky. Between the mountains

are deep arid valleys and canyons, hellholes of creation. If God got angry when he was creating the world, the Nakfa Range is where he lashed out. You can picture him clawing the earth to make these jagged rocks in preparation for the Second Coming, their sharp serrated edges ready to receive and torment the damned.

Monkeys can't climb these mountains, let alone men. If you manage to get past one craggy peak, you'll immediately be confronted by another even more hostile and rugged than the first. Debre Emen, Megzaiti, Tamiru Terrara, Denden, Galdenden, Katar, Guwa, Hilmit, Gerger, Hatseynet, Rora Tselim. From a distance these mountains look like a circle of mourners dressed in black, their tears flowing down the limestone channels of their slopes. More distant hills loom up through the fog, ominous, like rebel assassins cloaked in white gabis.

The enemy made these mountains their fortress for good reason, forcing our troops to fight on a battlefield not of their own choosing. Not content with the formidable natural fortifications, Shabia has spent years digging foxholes and trenches. These defensive fighting positions are spread out all over Nakfa, each a purveyor of death to the unwary. Tanks, artillery and aircraft are of limited use in such terrain. What is needed are soldiers with the bravery and determination required to engage in hand-to-hand combat. It will be a battle of man against man, man against nature.

By taking advantage of the natural terrain, the enemy also hopes to prevent our Revolutionary Army from moving freely across the vast zone of conflict. This they can accomplish simply by mounting .50 calibre machine guns on the ridges overlooking key passes. Operating those guns requires considerable manpower, however, but Shabia is rumoured to have assigned that task to a special unit of disabled fighters. Most of these men have lost their legs, making it impossible for them to keep up with the rest of the enemy force. But a single disabled soldier can stay put in his foxhole and hold a whole regiment at bay with his machine gun, fighting on until he is overrun.

Otherwise, the enemy is counting on their ability to manoeuvre swiftly. They know the area, its trails and passes, entrances and exits. They are used to the oppressive heat of its valleys and the cold of its peaks. Their men need only a little water to survive, like camels, and they know where to find more when it runs out. Water is life, and part of the enemy's strategy is to maintain control of water sources.

In contrast, our Revolutionary Army only knows the Nakfa mountains as a feature on a map. And even on maps, some of the names and locations of key landmarks are missing or widely thought to be incorrect. It's easy for soldiers to lose their way, become separated, get picked off by snipers. The steep peaks test the skills of even experienced climbers with light packs and free hands. The mountains can fight without needing food, water or ammunition. They will not be defeated. The enemy can just wait on the mountaintops, barely needing to defend themselves, occasionally raining fire down on the invaders struggling up the slopes. This is the battle that awaits our Revolutionary Army. But they know their mission and are ready to make the ultimate sacrifice. I can see it in their faces and it makes me proud.

The Brigadier General giving the briefing is tall, thin and handsome. He's still a young man, newly promoted to his rank, but his once bright and smooth skin has already been scarred by the desert. He chooses his words carefully while rummaging through his long beard with his fingers and gesturing at his aides with his black swagger stick.

I am moved by how he ends his briefing: "If we could stand hand in hand with our opponents, no foreign power could ever invade us. Both sides are the children of Ethiopia, famous for our patriotism and courage. We know and understand each other well. That makes this war tragic, brother killing brother."

Then Colonel Wolday Tariku takes over and leads a discussion of the enemy's tactics. Wolday looks gaunt and dark. His beard is bushier than before, covering most of his face. He concludes his portion of the briefing by saying, "The battle we are about to engage in will require the ultimate sacrifice. We are ready for that. Our victory flag will fly over the noble bodies of many loyal soldiers of the Revolutionary Army."

I don't doubt him – Wolday is a man of his word. But he's still avoiding me and I don't know why. I've seen him a few times today here in Afabet, and each time he has hurried away. He leads the Red Boots, a small elite battalion that everyone here is excited about.

The Red Boots are made up of men who fought with Colonel Wolday in the Ogaden Campaign of 1977. Now they have reunited here for the assault on Nakfa, some three hundred strong. They love the Colonel as a brother, and he in turn loves them as his own. He knows every one of them by name, knows their families and their battlefield specialities. And now, with one heart and one spirit, they are ready to march on Peak 1702.

23

WHISKEY TALK

Peak 1702 is not the tallest mountain in the Nakfa range. Peak 2059 is higher, and others may be as well. What makes Peak 1702 so critical is its strategic location – it's the key access point to Nakfa, only three miles from the airfield. To control this crucial mountain is to control the gateway to Nakfa. Capturing this peak from the Shabia insurgents is the paramount goal of Colonel Wolday Tariku. People say he thinks and talks about nothing else, day and night, and sometimes sleepwalks, still mumbling about Peak 1702. He is a man obsessed.

But that's not why Wolday is avoiding me. My gut tells me it's because he has feelings for Fiammetta Gilay. What else could it be? There's no ill will between us, nothing in our past to put us at odds. We were childhood friends, though our careers have taken us in different directions. Has the passage of time soured things between us? People change with age, friends can become strangers. I need to talk to Wolday to figure out what's going on, and also because I want to accompany him and the Red Boots to document their battle for Peak 1702.

The briefing ends well after dark and I begin searching Afabet for Wolday. Thank goodness Firew Zerihun is here. He'll come with me to Peak 1702 to handle the photography. Another journalist, Yonas Darge, will be our television cameraman. Both joke about me leading them to the very ends of the earth. Firew's fame has preceded him, and he's already managed to make friends with everyone here, adding the unofficial title of Mayor of Afabet to the portfolio of cities he has made his own. So it's not long before Firew points me to where Wolday is camped out with his men.

The Red Boots are billeted near the Afabet hospital and have a bonfire going. They're drinking beer, singing and dancing around the fire. One of the Red Boots shows me to Wolday's tent. Inside, a lantern is the only light. He's sitting on a small stool, a bottle of whiskey in front of him, absorbed in cleaning his rifle.

There's another stool in the tent and I sit down opposite him.

"Are you planning to finish that bottle by yourself?" I say.

He's not happy to see me, but nevertheless he fills a canteen cup with whiskey and offers it to me. I take it from him.

"To victory," I toast. "And to the memory of our time together as kids."

We clink our canteen cups and drink.

"This might be my last bottle," he says. "My last cup, my holy grail."

"Why so grim?" I ask.

"I'm leading men to death."

"I know. And I know you will return victorious. We will share more drinks together, many more."

"I hope so," says Wolday.

He sets his rifle aside and takes out his pistol. He checks

it over and then, satisfied, returns it to its holster. It's obvious he doesn't want me here. The whiskey has given me courage, so I ask him straight out.

"Why are you avoiding me? What have I done to you?"

"You think I'm avoiding you?" he asks.

"Give me the truth, Wolday. I need to know."

"What are you talking about?"

"Is the problem Fiammetta Gilay?"

His face suddenly changes. "Who is Fiammetta Gilay?" he says, but his expression betrays him.

"Come on."

He's silent for a minute. The lantern flickers.

"Best we don't speak of it now," he says in a cold voice. "Instead, we should talk about the war. How did you get dragged into it?"

The topic of Fiammetta is closed, and I decide to respect his decision.

"Journalists have a part to play in war. We record it for history. And so I decided that I'd go along with you."

"Where do you want to go with me?"

"Peak 1702."

"Have you lost your mind?" he asks.

"Why? Have you lost yours?"

"Many of us will not return from this mission," he says.

"I know that. But who says my blood is more precious than yours?"

Wolday picks up the bottle and refills our cups.

"Besides, I'm too small a lamb for anyone to bother sacrificing," I joke.

He smiles. "Maybe it's not a bad idea. Your determination is impressive. But it's not up to me. You'll need to get permission from high command."

"Like who?"

"The Brigadier General." He takes a sip of his whiskey. "But this is a military operation. In combat, my unit won't have the capacity to protect journalists."

"We can take care of ourselves. And I'll ask the general. But if you support me, he won't refuse. I bet he wants the fighting documented for posterity even more than I do."

"Many of those in command now are young officers," he says. "Inexperienced but very ambitious. Most of them shouldn't command anything bigger than a platoon. But now a weak officer gets made a battalion commander when he can barely lead a squad. It's the same in government. Thanks to the Revolution, people who lack the training, skill and character to be anything more than low-level administrators are now in charge of whole departments. Is the Revolution a class struggle? Yes, it is. But if it just creates paths for undeserved advancement, it will end badly. Very badly."

I nod. The whiskey has got Wolday going now.

"Three reasons," he says. "There are three reasons why this is dangerous. First, incompetent leaders will band together, united by their shared knowledge that they're unqualified for their posts: 'I know you, you know me, we cannot advance by merit, so instead let's scratch each other's backs.' But running a country is no game, and incompetence can bring it all to a halt.

"Second, this creates a new class of opportunists, greedy reactionaries. Milovan Djilas predicted this in Yugoslavia. This new class will grant themselves special privileges because of their administrative monopoly.

"Third, power always corrupts. We can no longer feel superior to others based on personal wealth, based on our bourgeois lifestyles. The Revolution eliminated those things, but it hasn't eliminated the desire for them. So what do people do to satisfy their desire for a comfortable life? They do whatever it takes to get the quick promotion, exaggerate their experience, pretend they have the skills. Being rational and honest won't get you that powerful position. Once they get power, they can abuse it to obtain personal luxuries. The black market thrives that way. Our unfortunate history of corrupt officials is returning, despite the Revolution."

The dim light of the lantern casts faint shadows around the tent. Wolday looks genuinely troubled as he speaks. "We brought the Revolution in the name of the people. Now we're alienating ourselves from those very people, the people we promised to lead to freedom and prosperity. They're going to end up hating us. We need solidarity! We get so focused on personal advancement that we forget to cooperate and our revolutionary unity is lost. That's a very dangerous situation for a wartime government, for an army heading into battle. It frightens me more than Shabia in their Nakfa foxholes."

"What can we do?" I ask. It's my turn now. "This is a revolution. It's going to take time for it to stabilize. Until then, some reactionary practices are inevitable."

Wolday looks up at a traditional painting he's hung on the wall of his tent, a church scene. He takes a sip of his whiskey and studies it.

"Revolution was never meant to elevate the petite bourgeoisie, the greedy merchants," he says. "We must live and die like the people, the masses. Learn their struggles for the basics of life. Have no wish, no desire, that is beyond the means of the masses."

Wolday pauses and refills our canteen cups.

"Comrade," he says, "let us leave this sad topic behind and attend to our drinks."

We raise our cups. Through the canvas walls of the tent we can hear the singing of the Red Boots. Tonight is drinking, singing, dancing. Tomorrow is war, destruction, death. That's the life of a soldier . . . everyone's life, actually.

"Do you remember when we were kids?" I say. "You would make us play soldiers, all day long."

He smiles. "It was good training!"

"And now we're going to play the real game. It's a good life."

"Yes, it's been a good life." He pauses, then asks me, "How is Asmara these days?"

"She's the same. Still beautiful, still sad."

"Eritrea is like that, beautiful but tragic."

"I hope it will be rejuvenated by our Red Star Campaign," I say.

"That's my hope."

Our whiskey bottle is empty. Outside, the dancing and war chants are still going strong.

"The tragedy is that it was foreigners who planted this idea of separating Eritrea from Ethiopia," I say. "It divides Eritreans themselves. Some are stripping this region to its bones, but more are fighting with us to preserve Ethiopia. People like you, people from Eritrea who know they are Ethiopian citizens. People who understand that it would be a disaster for all of us if Eritrea split off from its motherland. Ethiopia's survival depends on its unity from north to south, east to west."

"I won't accept anything less than a united Ethiopia," says Wolday.

I remember a question I've had for years about the army, but have never had the courage to ask. "Back in 1979, when we were winning the war here, our soldiers chasing the insurgents into their mountain hideouts – how come they were not allowed to finish the job? Allowed to follow them and keep fighting and destroy Shabia for good? Maybe then we wouldn't have to be here now."

Wolday shrugs. "Maybe they thought Shabia would realize it was doomed and do the sensible thing and negotiate. I don't really know. But I doubt anyone wants the Eritrean problem to remain unsolved."

We both fall silent. After a while I sense he is done talking. His heart is with his Red Boots, outside in the dark around the fire. I get up to leave. My chance to learn what's going on between him and Fiammetta is over.

24

THE RED BOOTS

It is a battle to convince the military brass to permit three journalists to accompany the Red Boots battalion on their campaign to capture Peak 1702. Among the many points of contention is who will be responsible for keeping the journalists out of harm's way. However, it is also agreed that, insomuch as it is the duty of journalists to chronicle the progress of the Red Star Campaign for the sake of history and the instructive benefit of future generations, it is also obligatory that journalists see to keeping themselves safe from harm.

The next source of acrimony is our desire to embed with the Red Boots. The commanders point out that the Red Boots have the most dangerous assignment, and it is preposterous to think that mere journalists could survive such a mission. Especially when there are so many other units – their own, for instance – in greater need of having their exploits documented for posterity and the Ethiopian public. If we accompany a battalion operating in a somewhat less deadly environment, then we will have a better chance of getting the story of the Red Star Campaign and, importantly, living to tell it. Some commanders are sincere in making this suggestion.

Others openly lobby for their units to be the ones featured in our stories. Unfortunately for them, and maybe for us as well, I am determined to accompany the Red Boots battalion to Peak 1702.

There is a meeting about it, of course. And it's the young Brigadier General with the long beard who harangues me the most, pointing at me with his swagger stick. "Comrade Tsegaye, being stubborn simply has no place on the battle-field!"

My frustration is probably obvious to all. "We have the right to carry out our work in the manner and place of our choosing," I say. "We have the right to make sacrifices. We will be going to Peak 1702. Understand that I have the authority to make that decision and I have made it. Any further debate is a waste of time."

In the end, nothing changes my mind. My heart is set on Peak 1702, and I know it's the same for Colonel Wolday Tariku and his Red Boots. Their zeal is now my zeal, their dream my dream, their victory my victory. And if need be, their death my death. I dream about standing on the summit of Peak 1702. It is becoming my constant companion.

The meeting finishes with my decision intact. I walk out with Wolday.

"How come you kept quiet?" I say to him. "You should have said something to support me."

"What could I have said?" he asks.

"That the mission of the Red Boots is important and worth us documenting."

"And have them accuse me of arranging this to benefit my own legacy?" he says.

"So what if they say that?"

"I don't worry about my legacy, what history says." Wolday

stretches his long arms, as if he's looking for a place to put them. "I hope you're happy that you got your way. But as of now, you're under my command. And trust me, it's serious business. There will come a time when you start wondering why the hell you wanted to do this."

He leaves me with that warning and strides off, then stumbles a bit before recovering. Wolday is clumsy in peace, graceful only in combat. Put him on a battlefield and his awkward appendages become a coordinated set of killing limbs, carrying him from one firing position to the next with the speed and stealth of the legendary Ethiopian leopard. No setback rattles him, and the only time he cries is for the memory of fallen comrades. It won't be long now until he returns to war – the Red Boots battalion is scheduled to depart at 1300 hours.

We start moving out of Afabet exactly on schedule. Firew Zerihun snaps photos while his loyal Afabet subjects wave farewell. Yonas Darge struggles under the weight of his film equipment. A few heavy trucks carrying supplies for the 17th battalion are also part of our convoy, and their safe transit is an additional part of our mission. The Red Boots are carrying only light weapons, allowing them the speed and freedom of movement needed to ascend Peak 1702. As we leave, we learn that the 3rd and 17th battalions, part of our joint force Dagger, have succeeded in the first phase of their mission. The Red Boots depart Afabet in a good mood, confident and filled with enthusiasm.

The 17th battalion had cleared the road for us, to keep us at full strength for our assault on Peak 1702. They had routed the enemy so we can move forward quickly. We speed up our progress by forgoing the reconnaissance team that usually scouts the area ahead and reports back.

The overall strategy for joint force Dagger is to capture the roads into Nakfa, then take a series of key peaks that will lead us into the heart of Nakfa, where Shabia lurks. The first and most critical of these peaks is the objective of our Red Boots battalion: Peak 1702. The enemy is keenly aware that losing this peak would be a major defeat. Our intelligence indicates they are going to devote significant resources to its defence, vowing "Peak 1702 or death!"

Every Red Boot understands that the success or failure of the entire offensive depends on them capturing Peak 1702 and destroying the enemy dug in there. They are eager for the challenge and periodically break out in war chants.

Our compatriots will be proud of us, we will never let them down!

We will destroy the enemy even if we have to die to do it! Our comrades will march victorious into Nakfa by using our bodies as stepping stones!

Never surrender! Stomp your foot on the chest of the enemy and seize victory! Be courageous even in the face of death!

With Colonel Wolday, our courageous patriotic leader, no insurgents dare stand in the way of our triumphant march! We will destroy them, we will obliterate them, that is our destiny!

On Peak 1702 we will show the Red Star Campaign's bloody teeth and nails!

We advance along the dirt road with the only resistance an occasional section of soft sand that slows our convoy. The road snakes through the low valleys so there is no breeze to give us even the slightest relief from the merciless sun. With the humidity, the air becomes denser and harder to breathe. Our clothes soak with sweat, as if we've been through a rain shower. The humidity rises along with the temperature, and it feels as though we are breathing steam.

Two of the heavy trucks get stuck in the sand. Some soldiers spread out and take up positions in case of enemy snipers while others start pushing the trucks out of the sand. A group of about a dozen men head out to patrol our immediate surroundings. The landscape is scorched rock and scalded sand, a forsaken land. The only plants are a few stray acacia trees, and Yonas sits under one while Firew takes some photos. Colonel Wolday is working with the men trying to free the trucks from the sand. He never asks his men to do anything he would not do himself. And yet somehow his uniform stays as dry as summer firewood.

Loud bangs come from the direction our patrol went. The soldiers all hit the ground, everyone down on their bellies. I stand there, frozen and confused.

"Tsegaye!" shouts Colonel Wolday. "Get down! Get down!"

His simple message of survival releases me and I immediately drop to the ground. Colonel Wolday remains standing, AK-47 in hand.

Explosions shake us. I feel the earth move underneath me. Is this what the end will be like?

Everything goes quiet. A few minutes pass and everyone gets to their feet.

Our patrol comes back into view carrying five badly mangled men. From what's left of their clothing, I can tell they are insurgents. Three are dead and two are almost dead. This is the first time I've seen what the mayhem of war can do to the human body. I quickly turn around and hunch over so nobody will see me as I vomit.

The two badly wounded insurgents are still alive, but beyond saving. Colonel Wolday strides over to them, draws his pistol, and shoots both men in the head. I have never seen a human brain explode before. The pieces are pink. Is this real?

Colonel Wolday turns to me.

"How's that for history?" he asks.

It's very hot. I feel like my blood is draining from my body. I have no answer for Colonel Wolday.

"You will see worse," he says. "It's part of the daily routine, death in a war zone. Like breathing or eating. I hope you get used to it. And I hope you don't throw up next time." He laughs at me.

I wipe my mouth. The Red Boots have already dug a grave for the dead insurgents and are piling dirt over their bodies. Firew and Yonas are watching this, no cameras in hand.

"Did you have to do that?" I ask Colonel Wolday. "Those two men?"

"They were going to die," he says. "Better to not suffer. And better to die than live with a body mangled by a grenade. That would be bad for them, and for the country."

"Do you really believe that?" I ask.

"I'm always thinking of Ethiopia."

The executive officer comes over to us and gives Colonel Wolday a full military salute. "Comrade Colonel," he says, "it's water time." Colonel Wolday's executive officer is Captain Gasha Tena. He is an intense man, slightly older than his colleagues and just recently promoted from an enlisted soldier to a captain in a single leap. He's fond of chanting, "Never surrender, stomp your foot on the enemy's chest and seize victory. Remain courageous in the face of death." Captain Gasha has received numerous medals for his battlefield courage and patriotism, as have most Red Boots.

Colonel Wolday nods and Captain Gasha blows a whistle.

301

"Attention!" shouts Captain Gasha. Instantly every soldier is lined up and standing to attention.

"Prepare canteen!" The soldiers take their canteens from their canvas holders, open them and hold them straight out.

"Raise canteen!" Moving in unison, the soldiers raise their canteens to their mouths.

"Drink!" They do so without making a sound.

"Return canteen!" In swift coordinated moves, each soldier closes their canteen and replaces it in its canvas holder.

"Forward!" Everyone heads to the vehicles, the heavy trucks now freed from the sand.

Colonel Wolday turns to me. "You journalists can drink your water anytime you want," he says with a smile before he walks away.

I take out my canteen and gulp down the warm water. I would spend my ministry's entire budget for one glass of clean cold water.

25

IN CAMP

At 1700 hours we stop to camp for the night. The site swarms with activity. Sentries stand guard as a camp rapidly materializes around us. We are all told a passphrase to use with the sentries at night: "Fork and spoon." It's the same campsite the 17th battalion used last week, and they clearly tried to make some improvements to this arid hellscape. Someone has carved "Embasoira Hotel" on the one sizeable acacia tree, and next to it on a smaller tree is "Nyala Hotel". I admire their creativity in assigning the names of Asmara's fancy hotels to the only two patches of shade, but it's sad that they have to be in a place like this at all.

The Red Boots have an impressive number of ways to cool off the hot water in their canteens. Some wrap it in wet burlap and hang it from a tree branch, others bury it in the sand by a dry riverbed. Captain Gasha takes my canteen and I'm not sure what he does with it. To them, we journalists are soft creatures who need to be protected like eggs, breakable at the slightest shake. Every interaction seems to involve them sighing and shaking their heads at us. I can almost hear them wonder: "Why in the world are these guys here? They don't have the training or the weapons to take care of themselves! Lucky for them, we do."

Some Rashaida nomads gather just outside our camp at sunset. The men sit in front, and behind them are the women, completely covered in black from head to toe. Not even their hair is visible. I've heard that after a Rashaida woman marries, at the age of ten or twelve, no man other than her husband will ever see her face again. I'm tempted to lift up a veil to see what a Rashaida woman looks like. But the chicken that scratches the ground uncovers the butcher's knife – anyone who tries to lift the veil of a Rashaida woman will lose his hand to the blade carried by every Rashaida man. I curb my appetite to learn about other cultures and marvel at their appearance from a safe distance.

Our cameraman, Yonas Darge, seems to have a different idea though. He's among the Rashaida and, from his gestures, seems to be asking a woman to lift her veil. I sprint over there and grab him to stop his ill-advised inquiry. He struggles and asks what's wrong with me. Then he sees the Rashaida husband, a rather stout young fellow, holding a scimitar. At this point our befuddled cameraman, more curious than bright, backs off. As we walk towards camp, I explain about covered faces and jealous husbands. This panics him and he tries to run back to the safety of the Red Boots, almost dropping the very expensive and currently irreplaceable movie camera he's carrying. I catch the camera, and then him, and we make it back to camp with all appendages and equipment intact.

There I go over to the unit's political commissar, Commander Wallelign Yirga.

"What do the people want?" I ask him, pointing at the Rashaida. "Why are they here?"

"They want malaria tablets," he says.

"Are they sick?"

"Not really. Most of them just want the drinking water we'll give them along with the medication."

That's how dire it is here for water. Why do people try to live in such an inhospitable place, a land even the gods seem to have discarded as worthless? Where do they get the food they need for themselves and their animals? It is beyond my understanding.

Commander Wallelign arranges for the Rashaida to receive a ration of food and drinking water, a certain amount per person. To distribute it in an orderly manner, he invites the women to come forward first to receive their rations. The men sitting in the front of the group consider this a joke, nodding and laughing at each other. Commander Wallelign gets angry and orders the women to come forward first. The Rashaida men turn serious as well and adopt more aggressive postures, waving their arms in anger. In Rashaida culture, a woman should never walk or sit ahead of a man. The Rashaida men have a surprising amount of trust in the restraint of our Revolutionary Army, given that we outgun them by a considerable margin.

The commotion attracts the attention of Colonel Wolday Tariku, and Commander Wallelign explains the situation to him.

"Leave them alone," Colonel Wolday orders. "Accept their customs. Don't cause trouble."

"We should not let such backward practices continue," says Wallelign. "How long should these women remain as slaves of the men? We need to empower them. Isn't the mission of the army to guarantee the Revolution to all?"

"Yes, comrade," says Colonel Wolday in a calm, controlled

voice. "But the Rashaida have lived by these traditions for centuries. Changing them will take time. Empowerment and mobilization should not be beyond what a community can deal with, otherwise it won't work. We can't force it on people from the outside. To create an awakening in people, you must understand them and relate to them."

For our own dinner we are offered tinned food with a choice of stew, either shiro, zigni or vegetables. But the best choice is militia gruel, a concoction of barley flour mixed in water. When mixed with sugar and left overnight, it ferments enough to turn into a warm and slightly alcoholic porridge that satisfies both hunger and thirst. Every soldier has their own proprietary way of mixing up militia gruel, and they offer us journalists samples to impress us. "To satisfy your hunger! To quench your thirst for water or booze! Forever militia gruel!" or so goes one campground commercial. Firew Zerihun, still the Mayor out here and friend to everyone, is touring the different "hotels" of the camp – the Embasoira, the Nyala, the Keren – and sampling the competing versions of militia gruel at each stop.

Tired and full of gruel, we all go to bed early. There's no need to take off your clothes or shoes. With snakes and scorpions about, it's best to sleep with clothes on out here. You spend the day in your uniform, you go to bed in it, you may even die in it. Eager for sleep, I flop down on my sand mattress. The men around me seem restless, and I am as well. I try to count stars. The sky looks close tonight, dark and clear with the most stars I've ever seen.

As tired as I am, I can't fall asleep on the hard ground. I once spent a year sleeping on a concrete prison floor, but I was a young man then. That year felt like a decade. Instead of taking my place in the adult world, I was stuck in a prison cell with hardened criminals. Their lives were devoted to killing and stealing.

My crime was also stealing – I ran off with a beautiful girl, Hirut Agonafir. She was seventeen, I was twenty, and we were in love. The world was ours and it was a wonderful world, except for her parents. Hirut was from nobility and her mother was related to Emperor Haile Selassie's wife, Menen Asfaw. I was from nobody in particular. We were supposed to be studying for exams, but running off together seemed like a better idea. We got away with it for a month, until her family tracked us down and had me arrested. Threatened with beatings by her father, Hirut swore in court that I had abducted her against her will, by force. The judge said I was a threat to the civilized residents of Addis Ababa, especially the women. They shaved my head and off I went to spend a year in prison. It was a high price to pay for love.

Now I am again facing punishment for loving a woman. Two months ago, I was sure that I would marry Roman Hiletework and that our life together would be a good one. Now I don't know. The Red Star Campaign brought me to Fiammetta Gilay and she captured my heart. It's hard to compare Fiammetta and Roman. It seems wrong. And yet, Fiammetta's unrestrained personality, her charisma, her intense love of life – all weigh in her favour. But Roman has a deep fundamental goodness, purity and wisdom. Maybe I will get over all this, somehow. Being in the middle of a war might actually help me figure out who I am and what I want. Or maybe I'm a lost cause.

I still can't sleep and instead have a silent dialogue with myself. "Is anything constant in life, other than change?" The reply: "Nothing is permanent. Everything in life – love, politics, religion – is in perpetual motion, moving and transforming. So why worry?" I roll over on my side. There is nothing to be scared about in this world. You're alive until you're dead, so why be frightened while you're alive? What does it matter? Try to lead a good life, that's all.

"Can't sleep?" says a quiet voice. Captain Gasha Tena is lying next to me on the sand. Apparently he's noticed my tossing and turning.

"I need a roof over my head."

"The sky is our roof, the dirt our bed. We can sleep anywhere – as long as nobody's shooting at us."

"It takes some getting used to," I say.

"No question. For the past eight years my roof has been the skies of Ogaden and Bale, and now the Eritrean sky," says Captain Gasha. Then, quietly, "Do not ever surrender. Stomp your foot on the enemy's chest and seize victory. Remain courageous in the face of death."

"So you've been a soldier your whole life?" I ask.

"Yes, all my adult life. I don't know how to do anything else. We fight, we kill, and we get killed. We gamble our life away. The one sure thing is refusing to surrender."

Gasha starts telling me about his life as a soldier. He joined the army when he turned twenty. At school he was one of the brightest students and he doesn't remember why he chose the military as a career. It could be the nice uniform, but then why an infantry man? No clear answer there either. He could have picked the Air Force, the Navy or joined a mechanized division as a tank driver or a gunner. If he had done that, he would at least have a roof over his head when he goes to bed. He understands why people say that being an infantry man is like being a donkey. But he can't imagine a life other than his chosen one, a foot soldier. Being in the infantry has served as a training ground for him, making him the kind of tough-as-nails person he is now, and satisfied his inner long-ings – it's his calling in life. Above all, he likes being a soldier. That said, he can't help but agree with the comparison of the life of an infantry man to that of a donkey, the most useful beast of burden but also the one we abuse the most.

Military campaigns typically have the objective of con-trolling a certain piece of land. Achieving that control requires the direct physical presence of infantry troops on that ground. The history of warfare has shown that ground troops are an integral part of victory and a requirement for military success. Bombardments from the air, artillery and rocket attacks from ground and naval forces – they all have the ability to deliver heavy payloads of firepower on the enemy and its strongholds. But without ground troops engaging the enemy in a life-and-death struggle at close quarters, without their sweat and blood on the battlefield, killing and being killed, everything else is to little or no avail and the objective will not be attained. The men who carry out close combat are people, not animals or spirits. Even though they chose the infantry as their career, nonetheless they are still human beings like everyone else. As humans, it is inherent in their nature to want to live and enjoy life, to get married and have children, to laugh when happy and shed tears when sad.

It is the foot soldier that points his bayonet forward and goes after the enemy, charging ahead with the aim of killing but with the chance of being killed. It is the foot soldier that crawls across the mud or dirt, rocks or grass, his chest on the ground, carrying his rifle and his grenades, careful to avoid being detected by the enemy as he creeps forwards, ready to spill the enemy's blood or, if the goddess of luck is not on his side, spill his own blood for his country and his people. Do you really suppose history will remember him, this foot soldier? Not really. Yes, battles will be chronicled, and from that history will be written. It will be in the news, on television and even in books. People will talk about it in bars and coffeehouses. However, the focus will be on the progress of the war, the strategy and tactics, with maybe a mention or two of the commanding officer and how bravely, courageously and strategically he coordinated his troops to wage the battle. But when it comes to the regular people, the foot soldiers, it is a different story. For them, history is unforgiving and merciless. Who do you think will even care to know who Captain Gasha was? His accomplishments on the battlefield, his aches and pains? No-one will care, history does not bother about minor details. Captain Gasha is only too aware that he is a fleeting speck in the annals of history, his name remembered by no-one.

At some point, Captain Gasha says, he ceases to exist as a person and, sadly, is replaced by a different entity – a number. From that point on, individuals no longer matter. The decision-making process becomes an accounting exercise, with tallies of the numbers of soldiers killed, wounded, captured, missing in action, and so forth. With those numbers in hand, the army strategists will move to the next phase of the war plan by reinforcing what has already been achieved and regrouping for the next battle. You advance to battle the enemy and, when the situation demands it, draw back to reassess where you stand, and the whole process of marching, fighting, killing and dying starts all over again. That sums up the life of the foot soldier, whose career starts and ends in total anonymity, just a footnote to the march of history, no more, no less.

He is still unable to tell me why he volunteered to join

the Red Boots battalion, a unit which, by the very nature of its missions, lowers your chances of returning alive. He is not doing it to leave behind a legacy. He knows no-one will ever remember who Gasha Tena was. He is not doing it to advance his career. As long as he earns enough to cover his few expenses, Captain Gasha is not the kind to worry about money. He does not have a death wish – like most, he loves life and enjoys being alive. He is not doing this because he is more of a patriot than anyone else. His sense of duty and passion for the honour of his country and the ultimate success of the Revolution is no greater than anyone else's. What is driving him is the time-honoured creed that the country's existence depends on a few being willing to die for the many. I understand where he's coming from. Love of life is not, by itself, good enough – that's a selfish thing, the opposite of love, really. What is needed is to spread love broadly, love others beyond yourself, even if that renders you the sacrificial lamb for the greater good of your country and your people. After all, how did Christ himself teach humanity about love? He did it by sacrificing himself on the cross.

Captain Gasha and I keep our quiet discussion going in the night air, the conversation distracting me from the hard ground. We talk a little about Comrade Chairman Mengistu Haile Mariam.

"We worked together in Ogaden," says Captain Gasha. "That was before the Revolution."

"You don't say?"

"Oh yes. Even then he was courageous and decisive. Just like he is now. I admire brave men."

"So you knew him well then?" I ask.

Rather than answer, Gasha tells me a story. "One time

a young engineer was tasked with a project to build some housing for the Army. He planned well, did everything by the book, paying careful attention to the details and the expenses. The project was concluded on time and below cost. Not only was the quality of the new housing superb, but there was some unused money in the budget. As icing on the cake, he used the leftover funds to build a recreation centre for the soldiers. Everyone in the camp was happy with the results. Then a general came with a team of auditors to carry out the final inspection and evaluation of the building project. People were expecting the general to be excited about how well the work had been done and glad for the much-needed recreational facilities that had been built.

"To everyone's disappointment, the general was angry. He reprimanded the young engineer for building something not specified on the original request without first getting permission from the top brass. Some officers who had initially been excited about the new recreation centre did an about-face and joined in castigating the young engineer, adding insult to injury. By now the engineer, frustrated at the unexpected turn of events, was about to break down. The only person who spoke up about the injustice that was unfolding was Comrade Chairman, at the time Commander Mengistu Haile Mariam. He told the general, 'If the leftover money was taken for personal gain, nobody would have found out about it and we would not be talking about the recreation centre or why it was built in the first place. He gave us the recreation centre through honest and smart work, from savings that no-one here expected we would have, and it would be very unfortunate if that earned him a reprimand.' That was how Comrade Chairman cut the general down to size and restored the young engineer's confidence.

"A different time, when Comrade Chairman was working as the inventory officer of the Lion's Brigade, a general sent him an urgent message requesting a spare part for his car. The Chairman's reply, and it was a quick one, was to inform the general that, as it was, the army didn't even have the required level of inventory to meet its own military needs, let alone to send parts for his personal use.

"There's more. Another time, as an inventory officer, Comrade Chairman was told that the Emperor would be arriving on such and such a day for a tour of the facilities. The orders from his superiors were very specific. His main task was to hide or get rid of the old weapons and broken vehicles before the Emperor arrived, so that he would only see equipment that was shiny, new and in good working order. Comrade Chairman was troubled by this misleading and dishonest request. The Emperor arrived for his royal visit and Commander Mengistu did as his superiors requested by leading him first to see the weapons and vehicles that were shiny, new and in good working order. At the end of that parade, though, he also brought the Emperor to where all the old, unusable and broken equipment was stored. The Emperor did not care for the last phase of his visit, pulled his royal cloak up over his shoulders, got visibly irate and hustled out of the compound.

"As an officer, Comrade Chairman earned a reputation for being a straightforward and honest broker, but his superiors were not happy with him at all. He was considered unco-operative and dangerous, and for a while it undermined his progress in the military. Year after year he was passed over for deserved promotions. Well, look where he is now.

He's a brave and courageous soldier, and to stand alongside someone like him, to fight and die, truly that is an honour of the highest regard."

These are the stories Captain Gasha Tena tells me, and while he is talking I somehow manage to fall asleep.

26

LETTERS HOME

The good Captain Gasha Tena shakes me awake at five in the morning. If not for him, I would have kept sleeping and been left behind as the Red Boots marched off. The men are getting geared up and ready to move out. Firew Zerihun and his ever-smiling face comes over to me and says, "Oh my God, Tsegaye, it was almost the end of us last night."

"What happened?"

"Yonas and I went out of camp to relieve ourselves, and when we came back a sentry stopped us and ordered us to identify ourselves. It was pitch black and we were definitely a little tight from all the militia gruel, and maybe a little unnerved at being in such a strange place. Well, you can imagine, with a fierce soldier staring at us, ready for his first kill of the night with his shiny bayonet, neither Yonas nor I could remember the password. For the life of us, as it were. The sentry was just about to blow us away when Yonas finally remembered the code and shouted, 'Forks! For the love of God, we are forks!'"

I laugh and so does Firew. "You should have just told the sentry that you're the Mayor," I say.

Colonel Wolday Tariku comes over and greets us journalists. "Good morning, forks," he says with a smile. I guess the whole camp knows the story.

"It looks like the battlefield suits you," I say to Colonel Wolday. "You look like you slept well."

His face brightens. He's in his element now, moving with agility and confidence, a Kalashnikov slung over each shoulder.

"A soldier comes alive in his work," he says.

"It will be the same with us forks," I say. "You'll see."

I haven't washed since I left Asmara. I must stink. I don't how I look, but probably bad as well, unshaven in dirty clothes. Comfort, appearance, all those normal things in life have lost their importance here. What is important, and increasingly real, is Peak 1702. It's all I think about. Everyone's in a hurry to get there, to our final goal.

Our convoy moves fast, taking only one quick break for water. I no longer mind the warm water from my canteen. I even enjoy it. We try to cover as much distance as possible before darkness and we arrive at Peak 492 as the day ends. This is the staging point for the 17th battalion. They're happy to see us and welcome us with much fanfare.

The Red Boots do not have much to do at this point, other than getting themselves physically and mentally ready for the task ahead, so they volunteer to run the 17th battalion's camp for the night. The Red Boots serve food and water to the men of the 17th, wash their clothes and assist with any housekeeping chores they can find. When all that is done, the Red Boots are ordered to go and wash. Us three forks follow along.

We watch from a hill as the Red Boots shower from

buckets of water. They look like men baptizing and purifying their bodies in preparation for martyrdom. I struggle to understand what is in their souls that makes them embrace dangerous missions. Their love of Ethiopia is not so much greater than anyone else's, but they've crossed the great divide between love of country and noble action at risk of life. Even in the fading light, I can see that a fire burns in them. They have the beauty of free men. The sun sinks behind the Nakfa mountains and my heart sinks with it – they are about to walk into the lion's den. The sky turns blood red.

When they've finished washing, Colonel Wolday asks the Red Boots to write a letter to someone – their families, a friend, anyone they wish – before they enter combat. It's a military tradition before going on an especially dangerous mission. Curious, I ask some of the men if they would show me what they've written. Everyone I ask is happy to share their letter with me.

The letters are written to wives, children, brothers, sisters, parents, aunts, uncles, grandparents. Some describe where we are now, our experiences on the road, and what awaits us. Most request the readers to stay tuned for future letters. The usual platitude of, "Don't worry about me, I'm doing fine" is part of most, along with the standard scolding of, "Why don't you write back more often? I miss you!"

Several letters say, "If I'm killed, please donate my savings to the Red Star Campaign." The dedication astonishes me. There is also optimism about the campaign. One letter says, "We are now in Nakfa and based on progress so far, this war will be over much sooner than we thought. However please send some money. I will use it to buy cassette tape players and radios at the Algena and Afabet markets. You will be amazed how cheap they are here."

Some letters discuss their hopes for life after they return from the war. "I'm going to spend the money I've saved to expand my farm. I will work to harvest more barley and teff. I will fix the broken tukul for my family to live better." Some who left school to join the army write about how they'll resume their studies once the war is over. They describe the kind of classes they want to take and how far they intend to go in school.

Many write that the campaign has changed them. One letter in particular catches my attention. It's from a young foot soldier to the wife he left behind. "Being in this war has been like going to a speed-learning class about what is important in life. From now on I will take life very seriously, no more fooling around and above all no more of alcohol as the days of getting drunk at every opportunity is no more for me. It is a waste of my valuable time, money and all this reducing my chances of being a better person for me and my family. I swear my love, this war has calmed me down and gave me the best chance to know who I am. I do not get upset about every little thing and gone are the days of jealousy. The only thing I am jealous about these days is life itself for I miss it so much. What I am thirsty for and what I am wishing for is to live a happy life. Doing the right thing by you every day so that our life together as a family is good and safe for you and me and our daughter. Please hug and kiss little Meseret for me and upon my safe return I will make it up to you for all the pain I have caused you all these years. I miss you a lot."

The letters are evidence of the fundamental human hope for a better future, even if the writer doesn't expect to be around to see it. "I have sacrificed myself for the campaign to be victorious." "Nakfa will be where I am buried and where the Revolution springs to life." Some read as if the author were already dead. One, from an officer, stands out: "Death is assured for all, but blessed are those who can pick where and how they die. I am a simple ordinary soldier, not a rich man with an estate to be preserved, so I bequeath you the Nakfa Mountains. Care for them. I have heard Eritrea is essential for the existence of Ethiopia and so I am content to sacrifice myself for Ethiopia's well-being. I do not possess anything of value other than myself to give my beloved country. I have nothing to ask of you, my dear countrymen, other than to keep my country safe from the jaws of her enemies, as they are everywhere and all around waiting for us to relax our watch, so stay awake and stay alert. My dear Ethiopians, when the time comes for me to lay here broken and dying, shedding my last breath for my country, I will be no more, but my bones and my blood strewn all over the hills of Nakfa will not be for naught but will be forever here as a reminder, so you take the torch from me and keep Ethiopia alive, united and prosperous. If you do not, if you fall short, you will have to face me on judgement day, for I will not pardon your failures."

These moving letters make me realize that, to my surprise, I don't have anything like that to share. It hadn't even occurred to me to write to anyone. It's just not me. I don't think about death. It exists, but I don't worry about it. My career is based on what is happening right now, in the moment. The future is not my concern. It's a mystery to me why people waste time thinking about death. Better to devote yourself to the life that is happening in front of you. A flower, freshly bloomed. Holding hands with a loved one. The sweet aroma of a beautiful woman as she unbuttons her shirt.

Maybe I'll think about death more as I get older. But right now, no. There's a joke I heard once, I can't remember where, that if you die, there are only two possibilities: you'll go to heaven or you'll go to hell. If you go to heaven, of course you have nothing to worry about. And if you go to hell, you'll be so busy catching up with all your friends that you'll be too damn busy to worry.

Right now, all I'm worried about is Peak 1702. Even there, what do I have to fear? Either we'll capture it or we'll fail. My main concern is how to report what happens. Actually, that shouldn't trouble me either. One of two things will happen: the news will be reported, or it won't. That's all there is to it. It's not worth worrying about. Why do we place so much value on tomorrow? The day after today could be an illusion. The only reality is today, is now. I am here now. I am okay. I breathe. I look up at the night sky and count the stars and see their beauty, right now. That's enough, so what's all the worry about to be or not to be?

I wake up twice during the night, both times from nightmares. In the first dream, I'm being chased relentlessly by a single bullet. I run away to avoid getting hit, but it follows me everywhere. I sprint as fast I can and zig-zag to dodge it, but the ruthless bullet stays right behind me, about to pierce my spine. Eventually I reach the edge of a cliff, no way out. I wake up, scared to death, shaking like a leaf in the wind and soaked with sweat.

In the second dream, we have climbed Peak 1702 and are scanning the area. No enemy insurgents are in sight. Instead, the mountain itself is throbbing, like a beating human heart. The beats get louder and stronger. I stand there, petrified with fear. Without any warning, the ground underneath me shakes violently. The surrounding mountains begin to explode like massive bombs. The ear-shattering beats of the throbbing mountain, the reverberating explosions, a hail of granite shrapnel raining down from the sky – it feels like the end of the world, the second coming. Again I wake up, scared to death, shaking like a leaf in the wind and soaked with sweat.

27

PEAK 1702

At exactly 0400 hours our unit leaves the camp at Peak 492.
The Red Boots had formed a bond with the 17th battalion
while sharing the site. Even though soldiers usually avoid
goodbyes, the men exchange quick handshakes and hugs
in the dark. We'll be on foot for the rest of the way, and
we march fast out of camp. As we approach Tiksi the sky
begins to glow pink. We stop for a quick breakfast in Rora
Tselim and watch the sun rise in striking hues of red and
gold. Nature has chosen here, of all places, to stage the most
magnificent dawn.

Captain Gasha Tena points out a distant mountain to me.
It's Peak 1702. I'm seeing it for the first time. It's not the biggest mountain in view, but it is majestic. It has steep slopes,
a sharp spire stretching from earth to sky. It sits among the
other mountains like a proud monarch on his throne, out-
shining all his subjects. Everyone is fascinated by the sight
of Peak 1702. The Red Boots point at it in admiration. They're
excited to get there and carry out their mission to subdue this
proud king of Nakfa. I think I can hear their hearts beating,
but then I realize it's my own.

I spot Colonel Wolday Tariku. He's wearing a fresh uniform and looks alert, agile and nimble.

"You're looking good today," I say.

"Today is a day for my formal uniform," he says. He gazes at the distant peak. "It's a terrific mountain. I wouldn't complain if my grave was there. It's close to heaven, don't you think?"

"I'd rather be buried in Addis, surrounded by flowers and green grass. It's too dry and harsh for me to spend eternity here."

"We chose the mountain," he says.

"No-one can choose where they die, not even you valiant Red Boots."

"We're almost there now."

He tells me that the journalists are to follow the infantry squads, but that we must stay behind them at all times. He assigns a squad leader named Damte to be our escort. Damte, who's also a medic, will give the three of us our orders, which we must follow exactly, immediately, and without question. The roads leading to Peak 1702 are mined, the trails heading up it booby-trapped. There is no room for error.

I need to act brave and knowing. "No sweat," I say. "You don't have to worry about us, really."

He's not buying it. "Look, I don't want you to die here. Better you forks stay alive, observe the battle, and make it back to tell the story. That's my request."

"Wolday, tell me, do you ever think about death?"

He takes off his helmet and his long hair spills out. He tries to untangle it with his hand, then gives up and looks at me. "A soldier in battle never indulges in thoughts of death," he says gently.

"How is that possible?"

"You're digging a foxhole, rifle on your back, grenades on your belt. You're sweating in the heat. It rained last night so you're wet and muddy. The enemy is close by, watching for you, waiting for you to slip up just once so they can slaughter you. Where in all that do you have the time to stop and worry about death? When you're in that state of mind, all you think about is how to kill the enemy. How can I explain it? You know death is a possibility, but you don't think about it."

He pauses for a few seconds, lost in thought. Then he says, "Life is what matters, not death." He looks at his watch. "It's time to get the fighting started. Don't take any chances, Tsegaye, and I'll meet you at the top of Peak 1702. Ciao!"

For him, starting a war is as mundane as me picking up my office phone. He gives me the victory sign and walks away. But after a few steps he stops and turns around. He looks right at me. I'm sure he's about to tell me something, but he changes his mind and walks off again without saying anything. What was he going to tell me? I hate cliffhangers.

We get to the end of the road and continue on a trail towards Peak 1702. The trail gets ever steeper as it ascends, and we hug the side opposite the sheer drop. We stay quiet as we walk now, trying not to betray our position. Around us is only rock and dirt. It is as silent as a grave, and easy to imagine that time has stopped and there is no longer any life on earth. We are alert and, realizing we have little control over what happens, very anxious.

We reach a place where two platoons of the 17th battalion have taken up positions on either side of the trail. They've been here for a few days and are dug into their foxholes, ready to fight. War doesn't always mean shooting. Colonel Wolday told me that once. He said most of the time you're sitting in a foxhole, waiting, hoping to not get shot. Other times you lie on your stomach and wriggle forward like a snake, looking for an advantageous position to attack the enemy, waiting for the right moment to strike. Or you might get outmanoeuvred by the enemy and have to retreat. War is like chess, Wolday told me. You evaluate not just your own position, but also your opponent's. You gauge the strengths and weakness of both and, based on that, decide on your next move.

Maybe your enemy is stronger and in a better position. In such instances, your choices are limited. Retreat, recover, and get ready to fight another day. If you're surrounded by an enemy about to overrun you, you surrender. Those are the rules of battle as Wolday explained them to me. But those rules are not always followed. Soldiers are human. Some have too much pride to surrender, others might not realize they are doomed, and so fight on even though the battle is lost. On a battlefield, blind bravado often takes over from logic. The survivors become heroes, and to the war dead goes the glory.

War is ugly. War is horrible. And war has always been with us, from the Bible to now. History is war. Will this ever change? A global armistice declared, every weapon abandoned, destruction forsworn, a world of peace and plenty. Or am I too much of an idealist and war will endure, birthed again and again by hate?

The silence is broken by explosions and my thoughts of war are replaced by the reality of it. The reality is absolute pandemonium. Mortars thunder and Katyusha rocket launchers bellow, their projectiles screaming over us into the hills. Heavy machine guns boom and Kalashnikovs add their repetitive braatatata-braatatata sound. The entire mountain has become chaos. The air fills with smoke and the smell of

325

explosives. Fighter jets dive down like hawks and bomb Peak 1702. Our heavy artillery pounds the slopes. The mountain is on fire. The enemy fires back with their machine guns. Explosions thunder. Now the hills and valleys are on fire too. The time has come.

Our escort Damte leads us three journalists to a rocky area that's relatively safe from the fighting. He identifies each explosion for us by its sound: bomb, mortar, rocket, anti-tank, rocket-propelled grenade, anti-aircraft. We get the cameras out and start recording the battle, Yonas with the movie camera and Firew with still photos.

"How's it going?" I call out to Yonas.

"I'm getting good footage of the mountain," says Yonas. We're all shouting to be heard above the explosions.

"Can we get closer?" asks Firew.

Our escort gives him the answer: "No, we can't. Even for the soldiers, that mountain is death right now."

"What happens next?" I ask Damte.

"The Red Boot forward units are heading towards the middle of the mountain. At the last moment, while the platoons from the 17th cover them, they'll veer to the left and climb the mountain on that side."

"Why go left? The mountain looks steeper there."

"Exactly," says Damte. "The enemy isn't expecting us to go that way. We can surprise them and gain the initiative."

"Let's hope so," I say.

Our intelligence is that the enemy force on Peak 1702 is made up of experienced and highly skilled soldiers selected from two of the Shabia insurgency's toughest battalions. Damte points out to us how their artillery fire is targeting all three groups of our forces: the forward unit approaching the mountain, the support group behind them, and then the rear guard, where we are. Our military planners expected this.

The fighter jets and heavy artillery continue to pound the Shabia positions on the mountaintop, igniting fires and leaving craters. The noise is deafening, even louder as it echoes off the surrounding slopes. We are at the very gates of hell, the demons are loose, and they're turning the world inside out.

A different sound comes from the sky and I look up. Large transport planes are circling overhead. Paratroopers begin to drop from them towards the main slope of Peak 1702. The enemy concentrates their fire on the figures parachuting down. One paratrooper is ripped in half, and then two more. I am frantic.

"It's a massacre!" I yell to Damte, pointing at the paratroopers.

He shakes his head. "Don't worry! They're mannequins! It's a diversion."

At this distance they look real, but I'm relieved.

Damte gets a call on his radio, but it's too loud for me to hear what is said. I can tell that Firew is eager to get closer to the action.

"That's it," yells Damte. "It's time to go!"

28

MOUNTAIN OF BLOOD

The moment Damte says it's time for us to move, Firew takes off running up the trail. I yell at him to wait, but he doesn't so I sprint after him. If I catch up with Firew, I don't know if it's to stop him or join him. As I run, men of the 17th battalion leap out of their foxholes and charge up the slope. The ground itself seems to be exploding now. I run faster and gain on Firew. Not far ahead, the Red Boots advance team is climbing the steep ridge on the left side of Peak 1702. Colonel Wolday Tariku, pistol in hand, leaps from one rock to the next, then turns and urges his men on. Captain Gasha Tena is at his side, the two of them moving in sync. The Red Boots are yelling and shouting as they climb the ridge, and the sound is as terrifying as the gunfire.

I catch up with Firew but don't tell him to stop. We're behind the Red Boots, grabbing onto rocks and shrubs to pull ourselves up the steep ridge. Rocks tumble down on either side of us, explosions are going off everywhere. We're getting close to the enemy machine guns and their bullets sing by us. Firew and I dive behind a cluster of sharp rocks and take cover there. The insurgents are now concentrating their fire on this ridge. A little higher up the mountain we can see the initial wave of Red Boots reaching the first line of enemy fortifications. They charge into the machine-gun nests, bayonets and grenades at the ready. It's hand-to-hand combat up there. Smoke from the gunfire and explosions makes the air more like tear gas.

From where we're crouched I spot one brave Red Boot crawling on his stomach towards an enemy machine gun firing from a trench. He moves in short quick spurts, like a stalking tiger. His bravery stupefies me. I hold my breath as I watch him from our hiding place. Firew sees him too, but his view is partially blocked by the rocks we're sheltering behind. Camera in hand, he stands up and takes a photo.

"Stay down!" I yell at him and pull him back. "Are you crazy?"

He turns to look at me and there's blood on his face.

"Firew!"

He ignores me. Cradling his camera, he jumps over the rocks and dashes up the ridge, then stops to snap a few photos. Just above him, the brave Red Boot soldier tosses a grenade into the machine-gun trench. As the explosion kicks up a flare of fire and dirt, he jumps in after it. Firew climbs up towards him, camera at the ready, then stops and crumples to the ground.

I come out from behind the rocks and run to him, yelling, "Firew! Firew!"

He's still holding his camera but he's beyond hearing. He's almost smiling, his face still bright. For a second I think he's making one last joke. I cradle his head and hug his lifeless body.

Like a madman, I get up and dash towards the now-silent machine-gun trench. Other Red Boots are leaping into it and

I jump down after them. The brave Red Boot's grenade has turned the enemy machine-gunner and his weapon into a single smouldering mass. The brave man himself is lying on the ground, rifle to one side, his hand reaching for the throat of an insurgent. Both are dead. Nearby, another enemy gunner that had been legless is now lifeless. The Red Boots move on to clear the next trench.

I pick up the dead Red Boot's rifle and with its bayonet I stab the bodies of the dead insurgents. I thrust the bayonet into them and yell and curse as loud as I can. Shouting and yelling, I drive the bayonet into the bodies over and over again until I'm exhausted. I drop the rifle and start crying.

I stumble through the land of the dead. Bodies are all around me in this fortress turned graveyard. A man missing his forehead. A decapitated torso with blood pumping from where a neck once was. A man missing his left arm and right leg, bleeding to death or already gone. A bullet-ridden corpse with an open mouth and unblinking eyes staring up at the red sky. Some insurgents are torn to shreds but are still alive, just. A few of them beg for water, the rest to be blessed with one more bullet to the head. This shattered mountain fortress destroyed its own defenders along with many who came to subdue it.

I move through the captured fortifications like I'm touring hell. Most of the enemy are dead or badly wounded. There are some captured insurgents, their heads bowed in shame, their bodies shaking in fear. The rest have fled, leaving their weapons behind. Peak 1702 is now under our control, though I still hear occasional gunfire.

Yonas is filming, but I don't want this documented. I have no interest in recording the mayhem of war, the absurd suffering humans inflict upon each other. It's offensive and beneath the dignity of humanity, worthless to future generations.

The carnage overwhelms my mind and my heart is filled with hatred for the vicious enemy. I spot several Red Boots handing out food and water to the captured insurgents. Nearby, Damte is bandaging the wounds of an enemy fighter, telling him that he will be okay. This breaks me. Firew is dead, Red Boots are dead, killed by these very men. I go berserk.

"Why are you helping these bastards?" I yell. "Kill them! Kill them now! Now!"

Nobody listens to me. I'm a crazy man in an even crazier world.

"Why are you looking at me?" I yell. "No, no, not me. You're the crazy ones. I'm telling the truth. These bastards, did you forget? Five minutes ago they were trying to kill us! To them, we're not human. We're donkeys, kitfo-eating idiots, colonizers and invaders, stupid beasts. That's what we are to them. First chance they get, they will annihilate us, no mercy. They're worse than hyenas in the jungle, they—"

Someone grabs my shoulder and pulls me away from the Red Boots and their captives. It's Wolday.

"Easy," he says in a calm voice.

"Don't tell *me* that." I point at the captured insurgents. "Tell them that. Get rid of them."

"Okay, Tsegaye, take it easy. This is how it is in war. Those men are soldiers obeying orders from their commanders. The fighting is not their fault. It's bad luck that we're on opposite sides. In a different time, a different place, we would laugh with them like brothers." Wolday is doing his best to calm me down, and I begin to regain a little of my composure.

One of the captives starts yelling at a Red Boot, then

throws the food he was given back at the soldier. Colonel Wolday lets go of me and walks over to the captive.

"What's going on here?" Colonel Wolday asks him.

"You are not the liberators of Eritrea!" says the captive.

"Then who will set you free?" asks Colonel Wolday.

I say, "Tell him he'll have to wait until his Saudi backers send some petrodollars to ransom him."

"Shabia will live for ever, down with the Derg!" yells the captive.

Another captive, an older man, yells over him, "Down with Shabia! This monster does not represent us. He threatened to shoot us if we didn't fight. With him behind us and you in front of us, we were trapped in hell. Glory and thanks to the Almighty God for sparing us. My brothers, we can be free now!" He starts to cry, muttering the names of men I assume are his fallen comrades.

Colonel Wolday orders Captain Gasha to search the aggressive captive. Captain Gasha starts to frisk him but he snatches at Gasha's pistol. Colonel Wolday jumps forward and grabs the captive by the neck.

"You are not going to die," says Colonel Wolday. "Not until we show you this country completely liberated from insurgent bandits. You don't get to die until you've witnessed that." He turns to the other Red Boots and gestures at the aggressive captive. "Take this damn thing away."

The captive looks at Colonel Wolday with disdain, then spits right in his face. Colonel Wolday barely reacts. He calmly wipes the spit from his cheek and eyes the captive. Everyone stands there, no-one moves.

Colonel Wolday reaches out one long arm and puts his left hand on the back of the captive's head. With that hand he pulls the captive towards him until their faces are almost touching. Wolday kisses the captive on the forehead. Then with his right hand he draws his pistol and shoots him exactly on the spot where his lips left a mark. The captive collapses to the ground while the air fills with fragments of brain and skull. The others close their eyes and turn away in fear.

"Search him," Colonel Wolday orders.

In the captive's pockets they find a large bundle of cash and a document indicating he was a top Shabia official. They also find a crumpled piece of paper with scribbled writing that Colonel Wolday reads out loud: "Asmara, Silay Berahi, Paradiso. Code name Oromay."

When I saw Director Betru Tessema at Army Aviation, he had quizzed me about the word "oromay". And here it is in the pocket of a Shabia leader. He might know more about it, but he's lying on the ground with a big hole in his head. Now I understand why he provoked his own death. I curse his corpse, but I'm happy to finally have evidence of Silay Berahi's true loyalties. Silay Berahi, the traitor in our midst – imagine that! But Betru had been suspicious of him from the start. That old fox still has what it takes.

Victory is ours today, though it cost us many of our Red Boot comrades. We lost the Mayor. I watched him fall, saw him bleed, held him as he died, and yet it's hard to believe he's gone. I will never forget Firew, the Mayor, a good man, a true friend I loved. On the other side, the final count is almost nine hundred Shabia soldiers dead on the day. We seized a large collection of their weapons, most still functional.

We plant the Red Boots flag on the summit of Peak 1702. It is a profound moment, a triumph for those who fought hard for victory and survived, and a bitter tribute to our fallen comrades. To honour them, the Red Boots officers fire a series of rifle salutes from the summit and we hold a minute of silent prayer. They sacrificed themselves for Revolutionary Ethiopia. They charged the enemy without hesitation. They leaped into trenches in the face of direct machine-gun fire. They threw themselves on enemy grenades. They all understood the need for sacrifice, they all gave their lives so that their comrades might survive and conquer. No Red Boot died alone, they all took Shabia insurgents with them to the grave. Colonel Wolday gives a final salute to his fallen brothers in arms. Tears roll down his face and disappear into his wild beard.

The exhausted sun sinks down into the horizon to rest. The sky over the Adhoba Valley glows in every shade of red. In the distance, the lights of Rora Tselim wink on as darkness falls. I will always remember these sunsets. They are a reminder that nature still reigns supreme in her glory despite human folly. It invites us to set aside our killing ways and instead enjoy nature's beauty. We survivors humbly accept nature's invitation to enjoy the sunset, then turn to reinforcing our position on the peak, a position we purchased with blood. All we have to do is buttress the existing fortifications, and it doesn't take much work.

Colonel Wolday says the journalists should go back down to Tiksi for the night, it will be safer there in our command centre. I don't care for his suggestion and refuse.

"After all that, you still don't consider me one of you?" I say.

"Fine, have it your way," he says. "You're one of us. Okay?"

"Congratulations on the victory," I say.

"Yes, it was a great victory, but not just for the Red Boots. The analysts came up with a smart battle plan, and there was good coordination with other units. It's a collective victory."

He's right. It was a clever, complicated attack that coordinated artillery, air and infantry forces in a quick strike. It took brains to plan and valour to execute. What a day.

"But there's a problem," says Colonel Wolday. "The only reason the enemy lost Peak 1702 is because our tactics took them by surprise. We're asking for our own surprise if we assume they'll simply give up on it. If we hold this peak, the rest will fall and lead us right into the heart of Nakfa. Their main fortress is just past the next line of mountains. So of course Shabia is going to regroup, and then send every fighter and every weapon they have to recapture this peak. I'm sure of it. So we have a job to do. We have to move fast to consolidate our position here, or we could be in serious trouble."

29

RED THEATRE

Our capture of Peak 1702 has given us the high ground, allowing us to control everything that happens around Nakfa. From here we can launch attacks on the main Shabia stronghold if, as Colonel Wolday Tariku explained, we are ready with additional troops and equipment.

Two days after the Battle of Peak 1702, a joint force led by the 17th battalion attacks Peaks 1521, 1527 and 1590 in one prolonged assault. At exactly 1807 hours we get the good news that they've captured all three. Now it's only a matter of time before Nakfa falls. We spend the evening celebrating, toasting victory with canteen cups of militia gruel.

I'm already thinking and dreaming of Nakfa, which is only about five miles from where we're camped on Peak 1702. I imagine hearing the victory bell ringing out over the airwaves. The Red Boots are busy now, and other units are joining them in a flurry of activity. Yonas and I secure the film we've shot, then clean the cameras and make sure they're in good working order.

The next day I'm sitting in the shadow of a tall rock reviewing my notes when I hear heavy artillery fire. The explosions start slow and then come faster and faster. I stand up and spot Colonel Wolday. He waves me over and I'm excited. This must be the start of the final push to capture Nakfa. Then I notice the expression on Colonel Wolday's face.

"What is it?" I ask.

"We have to abandon Peak 1702." His voice is stern and he's holding a piece of notepaper. "By 1800 hours tonight."

"You're kidding me, right?"

"We've received orders."

Colonel Wolday explains what happened. The enemy has regrouped and is striking back with everything they have. Their anti-tank guns and mortars, supported by artillery and tank fire, have broken through the 19th battalion's defences on nearby Peak 1755. Once that peak is under enemy control, our left flank here on Peak 1702 will be totally exposed to their fire. Reinforcements have not yet arrived, and now it looks like they won't be able to get here in time to strengthen our defences. The enemy is too close for us to use our air-power or artillery, as the risk of hitting our own troops is too great. Worse, the enemy clearly has very good intelligence on our movements, logistical problems, and seemingly even our plans. We have two options: retreat from Peak 1702 and live to fight another day, or stay and be surrounded by the enemy and forced to surrender.

Despite Colonel Wolday's clear explanation, it's beyond my comprehension that all that loss of life was for nothing.

"So that's it?" I say.

"That's it."

Colonel Wolday looks again at his notes from the radio call that gave him the orders. He goes over to Captain Gasha Tena and instructs him to inform the Red Boots to be ready to retreat from their positions by 1800 hours.

The lives lost capturing this key position, the men who sacrificed themselves because they were told that the Ethiopian Revolution required us to control this peak – that was all in vain. As if I'm watching a movie, I again see the Red Boots struggle up the steep slope with their heroic determination to silence the enemy guns even if it also silences them, the Mayor charging forward with his camera. I'm agitated and disgusted.

"How did the army fail to anticipate the problem of holding the peak after capturing it?" I'm almost yelling. "We're only five miles from Nakfa, and now we're giving up? The army has got to be kidding."

"Tsegaye, it's not like that," says Colonel Wolday. "This is the game of war. There are attacks. There are retreats. My superiors understand the importance of this peak. But they also understand that we could be wiped out if we stay here. So they're asking us to leave."

Wolday looks again at his notes on the orders. He stares up at the Red Boots flag still flying on the summit. With a smile, he crumples his notes and puts them in his pocket.

"But I'm not leaving," he says. "This mountain is my mountain. I'll die here before I take down our flag." With that he switches off his radio.

I don't know what to think. The idea of staying is terrifying. I try to work out how this might all go. The return of Captain Gasha brings me back from wherever I was in my thoughts. He salutes the Colonel and reports the response from the Red Boots he ordered to prepare to retreat.

"Sir," says Captain Gasha. "The men are not willing to abandon the peak."

"How many are refusing?" asks Colonel Wolday.

"Sir, all of them, sir. They request permission to stay and fight."

"And are they certain?" asks Colonel Wolday.

"Yes, sir, we are certain, Comrade Colonel."

"Permission granted. Inform them that I'll be staying to fight alongside them."

"Sir, what about our orders?"

"This mountain is my responsibility. I will explain it to them, don't worry."

The two officers discuss whether they have enough kolo. Their concern for a snack confuses me, until one of the Red Boots tells me that kolo is army slang for ammunition. Captain Gasha leaves to spread the news to the men.

Colonel Wolday turns to me and says, "You and Yonas need to leave right now."

"Says who?" I ask.

He smiles. "That's a direct order."

"I'm not a soldier. And why should I follow an order that your own men refused?"

Colonel Wolday puts his arm around me. "Listen, Tsegaye. The order is reasonable. Our superiors want us to survive. But Peak 1702 is too important. Under no circumstances will I give it up. I told you, a battlefield is not always about logic. We've decided to make our stand here. We want to fight and die here, where our friends and comrades have shed their blood. And we will."

"Then I will too."

"No, for two reasons," says Colonel Wolday. "First, if you die here, who will tell our story to the people, record it for history?"

"I don't give a rat's arse about history!"

"Second, I need you to deliver a message for me." He takes an envelope from inside his shirt and hands it to me. "I'm not going to tell you what this says, or even who it's for. If we meet again, give it back to me. If not, open the envelope. You'll see who it's for. Make sure they get it. I will consider it a great favour." He shakes my hand and holds on to it. "The message isn't that important. It's kind of foolish, actually. The important thing is that you and Yonas dying on this peak would not do anyone any good. But what you write, the events you have witnessed, the film and photographs you've taken, the stories you will tell about this special place and these honourable Red Boots – that's what's important. For people today to know, and for future generations to understand."

He continues for a while, trying to convince me that the forks should go. He ends by saying, "In any case, if you refuse to leave, I'll just have you removed by force."

"Okay. But what's the real reason you want us to leave?"

"For history."

I know we have to go. And delivering Wolday's message, if it comes to that, is a serious responsibility.

Yonas and I pack up our gear and by 1800 hours we're ready to depart for Tiksi. I can no longer contain my feelings. I start crying, tears flowing. A week ago we began with bravado, then entered battle and struggled, faced death, gained victory, only to lose it, not by being defeated but by being ordered to retreat. We have experienced every human emotion on this mountain. And now we leave it knowing that more Red Boots will be sacrificed to bad planning.

Wolday gives me one hug after another and kisses my cheeks. He takes his binoculars from around his neck and hands them to me.

"What will I do with these?" I ask.

"What do I need them for? From now on, the enemy is coming to me. Maybe you can watch us from a safe distance.

Or use them to see further. Ciao." With that he flashes a victory sign.

I'm about to leave when I remember something. "Hey, wait, could I have the note we found on the dead Shabia fighter?" I ask.

"What are you going to do with it?"

"I need it, that's all."

Wolday finds it in his satchel and hands it to me along with some other papers for the commanders in Tiksi. With that I give him a victory sign.

"We will meet again in victory," I say.

"Without question, victory will be ours." I give him a final round of hugs, kissing him on the cheek.

Yonas and I start hiking down the mountain accompanied by three Red Boots. I turn around to take one final look at Wolday. He's standing on a rock near the peak, hands on his hips. He looks like an eagle, majestic and ready to soar over the peaks of the Nakfa mountains.

Halfway down the trail our Red Boot escorts hand us over to another group of soldiers and then head back up the hill. We move quickly and there's lots of military activity going on all around. Soldiers pass us carrying several wounded men on stretchers. There's shooting in the distance. One of the wounded gets off his stretcher and starts hobbling back towards the fighting, yelling as he goes.

We join up with a bigger group of soldiers going down the trail. Some are wounded and being carried by comrades who are trying to calm them. One young soldier has had his leg blown off, maybe by a mortar, and he's bleeding heavily, clearly in critical condition.

"You see how badly I'm hit," he says to the men carrying him. "Why didn't you leave me there? Leave me with my rifle to die fighting? Or finish me off yourselves? Please, have mercy. Give me a bullet."

We pass by a few scrubby trees. The legless soldier asks his comrades if they can set him down there to rest a minute. They put him down, but he calls one back over. The soldier listens carefully to him and is just standing up when the wounded man grabs the pistol from the soldier's holster, puts it to his own head and pulls the trigger. With one bullet he purges himself of pain, gone for eternity. I stand there frozen, blank.

The tragedies I've witnessed have scrubbed me of all human feeling. Nothing matters. Anything could happen to me, to those around me, and I would have no emotional reaction. My feelings have stopped, time has stopped and space has stopped – this trail seems to take us nowhere. I am a phantom trapped in a soulless, mechanical world.

We make it to Tiksi at nightfall. The commanding officer there is the young Brigadier General who briefed us in Afabet. I give him the documents Wolday asked me to deliver. The general is clearly angry and frustrated. He pokes the sand violently with his swagger stick, though I'm not sure he's even aware that he's doing it. Earlier he had received the news about Wolday and the Red Boots' decision to hold fast on Peak 1702.

The general starts drawing maps in the sand with his stick. He doesn't speak, but occasionally lets out a fiery exhalation, as if trying to purge his distress. His aides are nervous and watch the general closely. He isn't wearing his usual sidearm and I suspect his aides may want it that way, for fear he might hurt himself. The general turns and starts bombarding me with questions, but there is little I can offer other than what Wolday has told me.

"Why? Why?" he yells.

He stabs his swagger stick into the sand and leaves it there as he strides off.

We spend the night huddled in the radio tent, anxiously following what's happening on Peak 1702. The transmissions are sporadic, the Red Boots engaged in several firefights. Then we hear nothing for an hour.

Finally Wolday's voice comes crackling over the speaker, along with the sound of explosions and loud gunfire: "Surrounded . . . running out of kolo . . . victory will be ours . . . forward!"

We stand there in a circle around the radio for I don't know how long. Time has ended. It doesn't have any meaning when I picture what's happening on Peak 1702.

The radio operator keeps trying to reach the battalion. "Red Boots, come in! Red Boots! This is Dagger command. Do you read me? Red Boots! Red Boots!"

There is no answer, only the silence of the grave. The brave, the heroes, the famed Red Boots – they have been silenced. I have no tears. My soul is as dead and dry as the sand under my feet. No emotion, not even anger. Sleep is impossible. I spend the night awake, dead on the inside, staring up at the dark sky with a blank face.

In the morning I go back to the radio tent to see if there's news from Peak 1702. I have the right to hope. But the only transmissions have been obscene taunts from the Shabia insurgents – they captured a radio from the Red Boots. I go to a hilly spot nearby and use Wolday's binoculars to look up at Peak 1702. I can't make anyone out, and certainly not Wolday. Even so, I can tell that the mountain holds his soul.

The commanders decide it's getting too dangerous to stay in Tiksi, so we start packing things up to move the command centre to someplace outside the range of the enemy's artillery. The retreat is an orderly and coordinated process. It doesn't mean the war is over, or that we're defeated. In fact, the understanding here is that there'll soon be a new offensive. Nakfa might still fall within a few days. Colonel Wolday will not be there with his Red Boots, leading the charge to win victory for Ethiopia. But there will be other heroes like him who will retake Peak 1702 and capture Nakfa. They are Wolday and Wolday is them, they are one and the same.

Knowing that Wolday is gone, I open the envelope he made me promise to deliver. I stop breathing and my heart kicks against my ribs. The envelope contains a photo of Fiammetta Gilay. "We will not meet again, I wish you the best," is scribbled in red ink across her chest. That's it, nothing else, no other message.

I'm furious that Fiammetta lied to me about a man of Wolday's calibre, a towering hero. I failed him.

"How could she do this to me? That bitch, that bitch of bitches!" My anger consumes me and that's all I can think to say. The heavens surely understand my bitter cry.

PART FIVE

30

LEAVING THE FRONT

We drive away from the battlefield and the artillery fire becomes less audible. It seems oddly quiet now without explosions blasting all around. After two weeks of unremitting devastation and hellish noise, you get used to it. You might even miss it. You don't know why you feel that way – it's crazy to miss an inferno. It's one group of humans with clenched teeth determined to eliminate another group of humans, like beasts. It disgusts you, sickens you, and you hate yourself. Why did God make you part of such a vicious species?

The devastation you see on the battlefield disgusts you, sickens you, and you hate yourself. You see a person torn to pieces by a grenade, missing a leg and writhing in agony, and it tortures you to realize that another person did that to him. It disgusts you, sickens you, and you hate yourself. You shared good times with your friends, and suddenly they are gone, dead, their bodies drying in the hot sun. It disgusts you, sickens you, and you hate yourself.

Victory is won, you triumph, but then you realize it is ill-gotten, won with blood. Other men have been sacrificed for you to feel victorious, so your happiness is ruined. It disgusts you, sickens you, and you hate yourself. You are one of the lucky ones who made it off the battlefield alive and in one piece, so of course you feel guilty about why you were spared. It disgusts you, sickens you, and you hate yourself.

You have seen death, many deaths in fact. When you came face-to-face with death, how did it feel? Were you heroic, bravely fighting on, or were you a coward, trying to hide? You gained some knowledge, learned new facts about yourself. What you discovered is that you're not quite the person you thought you were. The image you had of yourself all these years – of your strengths, your softer side, what made you tick – you just found out that it is a myth, a lie. It disgusts you, sickens you, and you hate yourself.

Now you have no real idea who you are. You are depressed, confused, and you want to run away. But where? Wherever you go, the person you are will never leave you alone. The result is confusion, anger, aggravation. Next you start wondering if those who died are better off. Bang! Everything gone in one quick shot. You lose yourself through gradual decay, piece by piece, a death slow and painful. It disgusts you, sickens you, and you hate yourself. The dead are done with the devastation of war, will never hear another explosion, will never witness another human mangled by mortars and bullets, a mass of flesh, blood and bones. They are lucky, at rest beyond the horizon, beyond suffering.

How about the living, we who can still suffer? Will there come a day when life is free of the savagery of war? When we no longer witness its sorrow and misery? We must work in every way we can to shape our existence into something kinder and more humane. To work for peace requires being alive, and being alive requires strength and courage.

Unfortunately, I no longer have the strength to continue my search for the truth of what it means to be alive. My whole body itches and I scratch myself to the point of bleeding. It's been two weeks since I had clean clothes or even fresh socks. It hurts when my dirty clothes rub against my open wounds. I'm constipated. I stink like animal dung. I stink, I itch, I hurt. It disgusts me, sickens me, and I hate myself.

31

AFABET TO ASMARA

We make it back to Afabet and my whole body surrenders. I have no strength left in me. Even sitting down takes more energy than I have. How did I even make it this far? What pushed me to stand, walk, run, breathe? It must be the basic survival instinct, the animal desire to live.

On arriving in Afabet, I'm ordered to fly back to Asmara within the hour. Is this the lot of a journalist? Nobody seems to consider that a reporter, like everyone else, could use a few minutes of rest. A journalist lives by other people's whims, desires and timelines. The news certainly doesn't take my schedule into consideration. But I'm happy to be heading back to Asmara. I'm in a hurry to share what I've learned about Silay Berahi with Director Betru.

The military flight from Afabet to Asmara is waiting on Solomon Betregiorgis, Metshafe Daniel and Yeshitla "Suslov" Masresha. The Afabet hospital was damaged in an insurgent attack and the trio flew here from Asmara this morning to do a quick inspection of the repairs. When they finish, we'll all fly back to Asmara. I'm supposed to meet them at the hospital.

The hospital isn't big enough for all the wounded and many are being treated outside in makeshift tents. It reminds me of the battlefield. There are several hundred wounded soldiers, many of them moaning in pain with ghastly open wounds. New patients arrive constantly. The smell of death is everywhere, in the building and the tents. I feel sorry for the doctors and nurses. They hurry around trying to save lives, operating on the wounded, amputating limbs, letting go of those who aren't going to make it. The doctors and nurses are obviously exhausted. One young doctor walks out of the operating room and mumbles something about another patient not making it. Another badly wounded soldier is immediately carried in to be operated on. The doctor looks dazed with fatigue, standing in the hallway and looking out of the window at the sky. I doubt he even knows what he's thinking about. War stinks.

I don't want to be around the hospital anymore, so I go back to the plane. I'm almost asleep when Solomon, Metshafe and Suslov arrive. As usual, Solomon is in constant motion with no sign of weariness. He comes towards me to give me a hug, but I put out my hands to stop him.

"Leave me alone," I say. My voice is feeble.

"Why? What happened?" asks Solomon.

"I smell rotten, like fresh cowshit."

"He's right," says Metshafe Daniel. "I can smell it from here. Let's get out of this hellhole."

I turn to Metshafe. "How did you manage to survive here for two whole hours?" I ask.

"I had no choice," he says. "So please, let's get this plane in the air."

Metshafe isn't joking – he wants out of here as soon as possible. For such a fastidious man, a disgusting, dirty place like Afabet is unbearable.

351

"Afabet is no place for a civilized human being," says Metshafe.

"Tsegaye, I'm glad you're on our plane," says Solomon. "I was going to leave a message for you. Your fiancée has arrived in Asmara and—"

"When?" I interrupt.

"Three days ago. But seriously, get cleaned up first."

"If I do, will you make me some injera and wot for dinner?" I ask, but Solomon is already off to talk to someone else.

Suslov is talking with the military cadres on the plane. He finishes with them and comes over to my seat.

"How did you find the war?" he asks. His sharp pointy face now looks even sharper and pointier. "I mean, the morale of the troops?"

"It's good," I say.

"It's an army of miracle-makers," he says. "It's growing by the day. It's a Red Army destined to make a great contribution to the proletariat's struggle against the oppressors of the world. You see, Nakfa is insignificant. It's inconsequential, and we need to look beyond Nakfa. There are thousands more Nakfas waiting for us in the future. The propaganda initiatives we carry out should be designed with that in mind."

"Comrade," I say, "one Nakfa is enough for me." I saw what I saw. I'm never going to be a part of war again. This is it for me.

"As long as imperialist powers are opposed to collectivist classless societies, do we have any choice other than to fight them?" he asks. Suslov doesn't get upset over differences of opinion. He respects other people's views and will reason with you, try to persuade you. "The world's progressive elements do not want war. But the way we stamp out war is not by losing hope or pretending it doesn't exist."

Deep down, I know he is basically right. I don't oppose him. But he operates in theory and I have lived the reality. The reality is what I saw in the mountains of Nakfa, a constant deluge of suffering and death. It makes me question the idea that humans are, by nature, good. Of late, I've seen little evidence of it.

Our plane is in the air now, heading to Asmara. The talk inevitably shifts to the war.

Metshafe begins. "We have a massive army and a war machine unmatched in the whole of East Africa. So why can't we capture Nakfa? What's our problem? Who will explain this puzzle to me?" Metshafe likes to provoke people with his questions.

"The eyewitness should speak," says Solomon, nodding at me.

Metshafe's questions launch me into a rant. "Any slug can sit here and criticize," I say. "It's easy to ask, 'How come we can't capture Nakfa?' It's a very very very different thing to go there, to fight, kill or be killed, and actually capture Nakfa. Those who were brave enough to go and fight, most of them are dead or wounded. The reason why we did not capture Nakfa with our first offensive is not because our troops lack courage or training, or because they're lazy. Thousands of our brave warriors fell as heroes, not because they were beaten by the insurgents, but because the natural fortress of Nakfa is almost insurmountable. If anyone wants to complain about why it didn't fall, then they should go to those mountains, fully armed and equipped in 100-degree heat, clamber up the hills, stand at the edge of sheer cliffs, shoot people and be shot at. Only then can someone claim they know what it takes. Overcoming those mountains while being fired on from every angle is not humanly possible. You may as well try to scratch the sky."

The other men stare at me like I've lost my mind, but I keep talking. "So what can we do now? There's only one option. Block the enemy's entrances and exits to Nakfa, one by one, slowly and surely, until they have no escape routes. Encircle them in an iron trap, deliberately and decisively. Then incinerate them from the air, once and for all. That is our only option, but it will take time. Until then our economy will continue to bleed, but what's the alternative? The economy only matters if you have a country. I abhor war, I absolutely despise it. I have seen what it can do. I do not want to see it again. But as long as the insurgents wage war on us, we must punish them, we will punish them. Violence is only ended through violence. The blood of our heroes cries out from the mountains of Nakfa. I can hear them now. They demand we wash their blood off the sand with the blood of our enemies, those insurgents who spilled . . ." It is only the plane landing that stops my lecture.

It's noon and the Asmara air is humid. As we walk towards the hangar, Suslov pulls me aside.

"I want to tell you something," he says.

"What?"

"Do not lose hope for mankind. It's the only hope we have left."

"I wish I could find one thing, one true thing, no matter how small, that might convince me to have hope for humanity. But if such a thing existed, it got blown to bits in Nakfa."

32

LOVE AND WAR

As soon as I get back to my room in Asmara, even before I bathe, I phone Director Betru Tessema. His secretary answers.

"I need to talk to Comrade Director. My name is Tsegaye Hailemaryam. It's an urgent matter."

"He is in Massawa," she says.

My bad luck. Every time I really need him, he's out of town. "When will he be back?"

"Tonight."

"Can you give me the phone number of where he is now?"

"I do not have permission to do that," she says.

"Okay then, could you call him and tell him that Tsegaye Hailemaryam wants to talk to him regarding a very urgent matter. Life and death."

"Certainly, I will try."

I draw a hot bath and submerge myself, eyes closed. I clean my body, getting rid of all the grime of war. Water is a wonderful thing – at least my outer self is clean now. I also manage to wash Fiammetta Gilay off me along with the filth. She lied to me about Wolday. I really do hate her now, from my core. Who can you trust? Suslov is wrong about the inherent decency of human beings. I will go and see Fiammetta one last time, to give her the photo from Wolday. Then it's goodbye. I don't want to see that bitch again.

I'm glad Roman has come to Asmara. I was lucky. In fact, as I think about it, I've had all kinds of good fortune and very little reason to be bitter about life. So far it's treated me pretty well. That my fiancée has arrived in the nick of time proves it. Of course, life has an ugly side, but when it decides to be generous, it's golden.

I realize I don't know where Romi is staying in Asmara. I get out of the bath, get dressed and call my secretary.

"When did you get back?" asks Rezan.

"An hour ago. How's it going at the office?"

"Director Betru often calls to see if you're back from the front."

"Anything else?" I ask.

"Miss Roman often calls."

"Did she say where she was staying?"

"Yes, the Keren Hotel, room 19. Do you want the phone number?"

"I have it, thanks."

I call Fiammetta at her office. She's alarmed when she recognizes my voice and struggles to get her words out.

"What happened?" I ask. "Don't you remember me?"

"I was just about to call you," she says. I can tell she doesn't know what to say.

"How did you know I was back?"

She doesn't answer.

"What happened to you?" I ask.

"Nothing."

"When can I see you?" I ask.

356

She doesn't say anything at first, then asks me, "How was Nakfa?"

"It was okay."

"I hear it didn't go as you all expected . . ."

"It's a matter of time," I say. "It will happen sooner or later."

She gives a sarcastic laugh. "Do you really think so?"

"I'm sure," I say. "Why do you hate us so much? Love always wins, in the end. A person driven by hate and lies, they eventually fall. Even the mountains of Nakfa can't protect them for ever."

She doesn't say anything. I get back to my initial question. "I want to see you," I say. "I have a message for you. When can we meet?"

"How about your fiancée?" she asks.

"So you heard she's here."

"Nothing stays secret in Asmara for long. I've seen her." She laughs. "I swear, she is beautiful. But you're not going to see me again. There's no point now."

I'm furious, my ego wounded. "I have something to show you," I say. I can barely get the words out.

All I want to do is give her the photo and say goodbye, once and for all. I have to punish her for hurting me. I always fight back and I know how to get my points across. People who've witnessed it, they say I'm calm but vicious, a well-mannered devil. For what Fiammetta did, abusing good honest men, well, this bitch has to be taught a lesson she won't forget. Doing it on the phone won't hurt her as much as doing it in person. I'd have a better plan if I wasn't still shaken up from what I went through in Nakfa. Part of me is still there.

I hate what I did to Wolday by being with Fiammetta. What

357

did he want to tell me by giving me her photo? Anything? I can't be sure. And he's dead now, free of pain. I'm the one that's suffering.

"I'll call you again shortly," she says.

"When?"

"In five minutes."

"I don't have time. Why don't you just tell me now?"

"If you're in a hurry to see your fiancée, then go. She's staying at the Keren Hotel."

"Okay, fine," I say. "Five minutes."

I'm not sure what she's up to, but she calls back in five.

"Meet me at the Nyala Hotel at 7 p.m.," she says.

I head to the Keren Hotel to see Roman. On the way I drive by the Paradiso coffeebar, and it's still there. I really need to get hold of Director Betru. He has to know about Silay Berahi and the note we found on the Shabia insurgent.

In the lobby of the Keren Hotel I spot Agent Teklay Zedingl, looking sharp in a black suit.

"Going to a party?" I ask, admiring his suit.

"We may not realize it, but life is always inviting us to a party!"

"What prey are you hunting here?"

"Wa! *Come bella!*" He kisses his fingers. "A very beautiful girl, just arrived from Addis a few days ago, gorgeous as a rose. She's here, room 19. But she stays in her room most of the time. It's a sin."

"Really? How so?"

"Her looks are a divine gift from God meant for all of us to worship! Hiding them away is a mortal sin." Teklay laughs but I don't. "By the way, my boss is looking for you."

"What does Director Betru want?" I ask.

"All I know is that he needs to see you."

Agent Teklay offers to buy me a drink, but I'm in a hurry to see Romi so I decline. I'm about to leave when he pulls me over to a corner and starts whispering to me.

"Look, you need to be very careful, Tsegaye," he says. "We have intelligence that you've been targeted for assassination."

"Why? Why would anybody want to kill me?"

He doesn't want to say more, but I push him and he knows his boss trusts me. Still, Teklay is hesitant. I pepper him with questions and he answers piecemeal. Putting it all together, he says something like, "There's an insurgent terrorist cell called Oromay. Their objectives are to disrupt the Revolutionary Army's invasion of Nakfa and destroy the Red Star Campaign. They've begun to launch sneak attacks on places where military officers or Red Stars congregate, carrying out assassinations, sabotaging our broadcasts and deploying suicide bombers. Their goal is to create chaos, distract our attention from Nakfa, and destroy people's trust in the government. There's a lot we don't yet know, but the intelligence about you being an active target for assassination is solid. You're a top priority for them, so be careful. Don't expose yourself in public, even like being here right now. We're trying to find Oromay and identify their leaders, but it's tough. We get close, and they vanish. We have suspects, but they're killed before we can arrest them, or they kill themselves. Then we have to start all over again. We think Oromay has infiltrated Red Star, so it's very likely that they know what we're up to. Unless we can take down the Oromay cell, all our efforts are compromised, from here to Nakfa."

"Maybe it will get easier to find them," I say.

"How?"

"Oh, maybe a miracle will happen." I don't want to tell him more than that.

359

"A miracle like that would be worth a million dollars," says Teklay. "And it's not just Oromay. There's also an entity called 'The Bureaucrat'. The catch is, we have no idea who that is, where it is, what it is."

"How is Silay?"

"He's around here somewhere, but trailing him is like chasing a phantom."

I'm throwing different things at Teklay, to see how much he and Public Safety know. "How's the Paradiso?" I ask.

"Why do you ask?"

"Maybe I miss good coffee."

"Let me take you there sometime."

"I'd like that. Maybe after you catch the Shabia assassins though. Otherwise, everything else is going well?"

Teklay smiles. "Don't you worry. We have Asmara under control and we'll get them soon. I don't know when, or where, but we will. I can feel it."

I decide to drop my own little bomb. "When Director Betru gets back from Massawa, tell him to get that million dollars ready. I'll be there to claim it. But right now I'm in a hurry – there's this beautiful woman waiting for me in room 19."

He laughs, but he doesn't believe me, either about the money or the woman. I leave him and head upstairs.

Roman is reluctant to unlock the door until she's made absolutely sure it's me. After a long kiss I ask her, "What's up with locking yourself in your room?"

"This city! I have to keep my door locked."

"Really?"

"The men here are annoying, and aggressive. They don't know when to leave a woman alone. I really don't like how they look at me." She looks me over. "You've lost weight, and you're dark."

"You're right, this is no holiday."

"I had to chase you for seven hundred miles. When will the Red Star Campaign be over?"

"Honestly, I don't know."

"Ah, this campaign will ruin me."

I convince her to check out of the hotel and stay at my place. We're at the front desk to settle her bill when I see Agent Teklay again. I bring Roman over to him and introduce them.

"Roman, this is Teklay Zedingl, he's a friend of mine. Teklay, this is Roman, my fiancée."

Roman is none too happy to see him. And as soon as she looks away, Teklay smiles and shakes his finger at me.

Once we're in the car she tells me about him.

"Why do you say he's your friend?" she asks. "He's the main reason I had to stay in my room. Friends don't do that."

"He's not a bad guy." I try to calm her down. "He probably couldn't help himself – you're too beautiful. He's just crazy about life, and especially about women."

We arrive at the house. The grounds of Dr Yohannes' residence are lush with plants and flowers. Romi looks around in admiration.

"Are you sure you're not on holiday?" she says.

We go inside and she's also impressed with the interior.

"If this is where you're living, no wonder you're in no hurry for the campaign to end," she says.

Romi hates a mess, though, and my clothes and belongings are scattered all over the bedroom. Before she even unpacks her own things, she starts tidying my room. I see her pick up a cassette tape. It's one Fiammetta gave me and on it is written "For Tsegaye, from Fiammetta." Typical of my disorganized life, I never bothered to put it away. Now it's too late, there's nothing I can do. Grabbing it from her would only make it worse, so I curse my bad habits. Roman sees the writing on the tape and anger clouds her face. Anything I say or do now won't help. I stand there and wait to see what happens next, like a little boy who has done something bad. Roman takes the tape and calmly puts it in the stereo and presses play. The song is by Kuku Sebsebe. I've listened to it a hundred times and I know the lyrics by heart:

It's my love for you that hurts my heart
It's seeing you that makes me adore you . . .

It's the only song on the tape. After it finishes Roman says, "It's quite a romantic song."

I scratch my head and keep quiet. She is getting angrier. I can tell because her cheeks are turning pink, like a rose in bloom.

"Who is Fiammetta Gilay?" she asks.

I don't know how to answer that question so I stay silent. Roman goes over and picks up her suitcase.

"Where are you going?" I ask and grab her suitcase.

"Hey, leave me alone."

"I'll explain everything if you just give me a chance, please?" I say.

"There's really nothing to explain, so leave me alone, okay?"

"Please, Romi, listen to me—"

"This was exactly what I was afraid would happen, and it happened," she says.

"What were you afraid of?"

"Every place you go, you find someone. You have no idea of how a real relationship works. You just say 'yes' to

362

everyone. Look at what you've done. I'm such a fool."

"Let the past be the past. Listen, the girl is a con artist and I am so sorry. Please, Romi, I'm begging you for forgiveness. Please don't leave."

I'm ready to tell her everything that happened, right here on the spot, but she won't have any of it.

"Listen to me, Tsegaye," she says. "I'm asking you to let me go. You're being a real idiot. Don't make it even worse."

She is beyond persuasion and looks at me as if her eyes are on fire. I don't know what to do, so I stand there holding my head with both hands. I can only beg so much if she won't listen. There's a limit, then pride takes over. I'll go my own way.

"Well, if you have to leave, then leave," I say and step out of her way.

She picks up her suitcase and leaves the room. I punch the wall, then follow her outside. "Alright, leave if you must," I say again when we get to the front steps. "But where are you going?"

"I'm leaving."

"Please, Romi, why are you doing this to me?"

"To *you*?" she says. "I'm not doing anything to you."

She leaves in a taxi. I stand there, a man on fire. I didn't actually believe that this would happen, that Romi would leave me like this. Is there something else I should have said or done? My stubborn pride keeps me from chasing after her. One minute we're kissing, the next we're ending two years of love. So sudden, and so cruel. It's the worst when people lose relationships over small stupid things. We could save so much trouble and grief by talking it over like adults and resolving the conflict.

The conflict between Roman and me is the fault of one

Fiammetta Gilay. I hate her, and I hate myself for letting her fool me. I don't know how to give voice to my rage, whether to howl like an angry beast or cry like a wounded soul. I'm going to explode. I just have to survive, minute by minute, and hope that all this stress doesn't detonate the time bomb that feels like it's ticking away inside me. More than anything, I want to release my wrath on Fiammetta.

It's not yet 7 p.m., so I go back inside and call Betru's office ten times over the next hour. He's the one person with the power and smarts to do the right thing with the information I have. But he's still not back from Massawa. One more frustration to add to the rest that are boiling me towards an explosion.

The day has been a disaster and it's a relief when night finally arrives. I go to the Nyala Hotel, ready to unleash on Fiammetta. It's 7 p.m. and there's no sign of her. She's always on time. Minutes come and minutes go, still no Fiammetta. Yet another frustration – I really might explode. Twenty past seven, no Fiammetta. It's foolish to wait this long for a woman. I give her ten more minutes, but she's a no-show.

Back in my car I start yelling. "This bitch, she stood me up! Maybe she got wind of what was in store for her and ran scared. That's okay, I'll get her tomorrow." I call her every horrible name I know.

Still half out of my mind with anger, I head to the Keren Hotel to look for Roman. I'll try one last time to win her back. One of us needs to set aside our pride to save the love we've built. It's worth it to compromise for love.

This isn't the first time we've had a bad fight. Once, back before we lived together, we even stopped speaking. I was very late picking her up from the hairdresser and she was furious when I got there. She refused to get in my car. "If you won't come with me, then why did you wait for me?" I asked. "How should I know?" she said. Then she jumped into a taxi and left. We didn't talk for a week. Finally she called me. "You arrogant man. If you hadn't answered, I would never have called you again. You're so cruel. And you have such pride, such arrogance. All this because I took a taxi? You know where I live, you have my phone number. You don't understand women and you don't know how to treat us. You are strange and sad."

Now I've made the same mistake again. I shouldn't have allowed her to leave, especially in an unfamiliar city with nobody to help make peace between us.

At the Keren Hotel they tell me Roman hasn't checked back in. I go to the Nyala and Embasoira hotels, but she's not at either of them. I try to remember to keep a low profile after what Agent Teklay told me. But I have to find Romi. I go to a few other hotels, but no luck there either.

I head home to the Dr Yohannes mansion. If I'm lucky, Romi will have gone back there. She hasn't, but one of the guards hands me an envelope. There's no name or address on it, but I'm guessing it's from Roman. I hurry up to my bedroom and open it, but the scent that comes from the paper is not Roman's perfume. Instead, there's a faint aroma of shiro – it's from Fiammetta.

33

FIAMMETTA'S LETTER

Dear Tsegaye,

These are my last words to you. Damn the day we met.

The Red Star Campaign is the source of all my trouble, I swear. If Red Star did not bring you to me, I would not be in this dilemma. Remember when I told you I was on this earth to have fun, and only to have fun? Well, if not for Red Star, and then you as a result, I could have gone out with any man I wanted, had fun and lived happily ever after. But once I met you it wasn't going to happen that way. I am no longer a happy person. I take no pleasure in life. It is unrelenting misery, thanks to you. I swear you are an idiot, and the worst kind at that.

Now that I'm thinking about it, I doubt the years before I met you were happy either. I was searching for someone who would love me, so that I could love him equally in return. Then fate led me to you and I loved you as much as I loved myself. I gave you everything I had and you did the same. But now it seems fate is splitting us apart.

Why did I fall for you? I wanted a man who would respect me, understand me and love me. You were all three, perfectly.

You did not think only of your own selfish desire. You were not like those despicable tourists who say they can't imagine ever leaving their Eritrean lover, only to disappear without a word when the time comes to go back home. But you are not like that, not by a long shot.

When I am with you, my whole body relaxes, like I'm floating in a sea of joy. I give you all my body and soul. If I have it, then it also becomes yours. You are an equal partner in everything that I am. When I'm with you, I forget myself and I do not care what others think about me. I am not ashamed about anything I do with you – that's how much I love you. Your smell has become my fragrance, my body has become your church. To be with the one you love is like being in the promised land, where everything edible is sweet as honey, every plant is colourful and bright, and every sound is delightful music.

On the other hand, to live together under the same roof without love is a waste of time. If you had stayed longer, maybe you would have become like those other men. I swear I'd rather be dead.

The greatest tragedy is to find the person I have been looking for all my life, and then lose him. Yes, I am losing you. Why did I ever meet you? I thought I was created for fun and good times, but now I know better: my purpose in this life is to suffer, thanks to you.

Go and have your fun with your fiancée. She came to Asmara for you, right? I'm happy for you. But tell me the truth – does she love you like I love you? What does she have that I don't? Is it the engagement rings you two exchanged? I guess you didn't realize it, but I was ready to exchange my life for yours. I swear, you are a moron, a total moron. But so am I. What kind of woman is she? Could you please

367

tell me? But I know you can't – you're never going to see me again.

Tsegaye, I have told you everything about myself. I have never opened up to anyone as I opened up to you, and honestly I told you everything. There is only one thing I kept from you. I don't have a good reason for it. I meant to tell you, but it never happened, maybe because I was afraid you wouldn't see me again. Don't blame me for that. Love is blind, and I was blind as a bat. But I will tell you now.

I was with Wolday Tariku on and off for several years. I respected him and he respected me. He has a kind and generous heart, and did a lot of favours for me. But that's not love, not really. If he called me, it was when he wanted something from me. I doubt he thought of me otherwise. I was never in his heart, nor was he in mine.

I don't have a husband or a fiancée. So why should loving you make me a sinner? Don't I have the right to love who I want to love? Am I not part of the human race? I am. Have I committed any crime that should keep me from true love? None at all. I am endowed with the absolute right to be with the one I want to be with, to love the one I want to love.

I didn't think you would be jealous of Wolday, but I knew you would refuse to go out with the woman of a soldier away fighting a war. I love you so much and did not want to lose you for that reason, or for any reason. You might wonder what gave me the idea that you would react that way. Well, I felt it, it's that simple. Please do not judge me, okay? You moron.

Love is what I know. It's easy to get a man to fall in love with you – they're like puppies. Manipulating men used to be my game, and I was very good at it. That's what I was going to do to you, but something felt different. I'm not sure what, exactly.

You're not a fraud, so I didn't want to swindle you. You don't beat me, so I didn't manipulate you into a fight with another man. You are not delusional, promising me right away that we would get married, so I didn't laugh at your stupidity. You don't get drunk and try to break into my house in the middle of the night, so I didn't get you in trouble with the police. You don't come crying to me every time you have a problem with your woman back home, like I'm your sister, so I didn't expose you. You don't lure me with false promises of government favours, so I didn't blackmail you. You don't threaten to have my friends and family thrown in jail, so I didn't find ways to humiliate you in public. I have experienced every one of these things, and worse, with men I've been with. I swear, most men are no better than wild animals. You call women bitches? I swear, there are no worse bitches than you men.

Especially the men from Addis assigned to government posts here. Why is it that good men – intelligent, hard-working, respectable – are never put in charge of anything here? The officials from Addis are the worst: greedy crooks and swindlers, lecherous pigs, arrogant and corrupt. How can the Red Star Campaign not know this? I don't know politics, and I don't want to know. I only know love. Still, wouldn't it be better politics if our leaders had the respect and trust of the people? If a few decent men were assigned to positions of authority here, trust me, the women of Asmara would be relieved. There would be some justice, and we wouldn't have to target Addis men to get things.

Why do you suppose us Asmara women seek out men like you from Addis? Because you have money and influence. Go to the big Debre Zeit air force base just outside Addis and look at the officers' wives. Most are from Asmara. The same with the naval base, we are intermarried there too. Military men, insurgency men, even some of the leaders – they all end up with Asmara women. That's a good sign, I swear. We may have some men here who want Eritrea to secede from Ethiopia, but the women? We are busy cementing the unity of our people.

But you're not like that. Your affection, your company, your gifts – other men used those things just to get what they wanted, but everything you do springs from pure love and decency. You weren't just looking for your own happiness, temporary and shallow. You're a kind soul. Maybe you're another tourist who's just going to leave, but I love you. I broke my own rule and here I am, crazy in love with an Addis man visiting Asmara. A very nice and honest man, but still a tourist. Why am I doing that? What kind of woman am I?

Don't you know that I'm jealous? Or does that surprise you? Even if I don't want to be with a man anymore, I'll still get jealous if I see him with another woman. It makes me sick, sad, and it gives me a heartache. I chase after him again until I get him back. Why do I do that? How can I explain it? I enjoy manipulating men, but it hurts me too. I can't decide. Maybe it's just who I am. Maybe I'm compensating for something. Maybe I'm paying for my sins.

Do you remember that night, not long after we got serious, that I never let us stay in one bar for very long and made you take me around to all the places where Addis men were hanging out? Well, the truth is that I had heard that a man I'd been with before – an important man from Addis, but he's crazy and I was done with him – was out on a date with an Asmara woman that night. So I had to find them, out of jealousy and to defend my reputation. You had no clue what was going on, and you would never have figured it out on your own. See, that's why I call you a moron. I won't tell you what I did after that, what my next step was to get back at him, but I hope you will not judge me too harshly for it. What could I do? What kind of woman am I?

What kind of man are you? You trust people. You do not suffer from jealousy or stubbornness. You try to solve everything by talking. You are a kind soul with a good heart and a clear mind. You do not abuse your power. You are not afraid, but maybe that's because you're a moron. There's something special about you, though, a certain kind of charisma. Maybe that's why I love you. It's not for your money or your good looks, because you don't really have much of either. But I swear, you can talk and you have a beautiful voice. What can we do now though? It's all over.

I have one more thing to tell you. You noticed that something had happened to me, that I was no longer fun-loving and happy-go-lucky. You kept on asking me what was going on. At the time, I couldn't tell you because I was afraid for my life. Also, I couldn't decide what to do. You know I'm bad at decisions. But now I've made up my mind. Why? Well, what kind of a woman am I? Let me tell you.

A month ago a stranger came to my house and told me I had to choose between my life and yours. I asked him what he expected me to do. He wanted me to take you to a certain place at a certain time when given the order. He gave me a phone number to call and left. I was certain that they would kill me if I told you, and so my life became a nightmare. I had to choose between me and you. If I delivered you to them according to their instructions, the man promised that they'd leave me alone, and even smuggle me to Sudan if I wanted. From there I could go anywhere. I did a little detective work on my own and found out that the stranger worked at Army Aviation. His name is Ikuba Arat.

But then you left for the front. I was relieved at first, but then it felt like people were shadowing me wherever I went. I got strange phone calls at home and at work. I thought about disappearing, getting out of town and hiding somewhere. But, no surprise, I couldn't decide. It's been a long time since I had a good night's sleep.

Then I heard that your fiancée had come to Asmara to be with you. So I said to myself, well, if he's not going to be mine, why should I sacrifice my life for this man? I decided to give you up and save my own life. That's why, when you called me an hour ago and asked where we should meet, I said I'd ring you back in five minutes. I called the phone number the man had left me and they told me to bring you to the airport at 7 p.m. tonight. I couldn't decide what to do. What else is new? But when I called you back and heard your voice, well, that's why I told you to meet me at the Nyala Hotel, not the airport like they asked.

After we talked, a strange man, very tall, showed up at my office and sat down in a chair without saying anything. I'm sure he's here to watch what I'm doing. I pretended I was doing my work and started writing this letter. And I have an idea for how to get it to you without him realizing it.

Writing this letter made me realize how much I love you. You moron. But what kind of woman am I? For the first time in my life, I make a real decision, and look what it gets me – probably a death sentence.

I don't think there's anything else I can do with this man watching me, except try to get this letter to you. That way maybe one of us will live. I hope you get it in time. I don't know what you will do with it. I don't know what I will do

next. I'm lost. I don't think we will get to see each other
again. I found you, I loved you, and I lost you. Goodbye,
Tsegaye.

Love,
Fiammetta

34

THE LITTLE FIRE

As I finish reading Fiammetta's letter I grab the phone and call Director Betru Tessema's office. His secretary answers.

"He's back from Massawa," she tells me. "I tried to reach you, but you were not at your home or in your office."

"Connect me now!"

"He'll be at home for a while, then back in the office. He wants to see you very urgently."

"Quick, do you have his home phone number?"

Miraculously, she gives it to me. I call and his maid tells me he's just left.

I don't want to waste any more time so I run to my car and speed towards Mai Temenai. I'll take her to the Public Safety office. They can protect her there.

When I get to her block, the neighbours are all out in the street. Somehow I park the car without hitting anyone and dash to Fiammetta's house. Inside, people are crying and wailing. She's lying on her bed. Her clothes are soaked with blood.

"Fiammetta! Fiammetta! It's me, Tsegaye. Can you hear me? Fiammetta!"

She starts to say something and everyone in the room falls silent.

"Did you get my letter?" she asks in a shaky voice.

"Yes, Fiammetta. Don't worry, you'll be okay now."

I put my hand on her bloody chest and can barely feel her heartbeat.

"Am I dying?" she asks.

"No, no, Fiammetta. You can't die."

"Why should I die? What have I done? Did I do something wrong to God?"

"You shouldn't worry," I say. "Nothing bad will happen to you."

"Will you remember me?"

"Yes, Fiammetta. Of course."

"Always?"

"For ever."

She smiles, then gives a long rattling moan.

"No, no, Fiammetta. We've got to get you to the hospital. Someone, help me lift her!"

"Use what I told you in the letter," she says. "They have no mercy."

"I will, of course."

"I'm a Red Star now too, right? My love for you made me one. You moron."

"Fiammetta! Fiammetta!"

Her beautiful smile remains, but the little fire is no more.

You know who I am.

Tsegaye Hailemaryam can no longer tell his own story. In his grief, he sees nothing, he hears nothing, he feels nothing.

Do I feel grief? They say God created man in His own image, and that He worries about us. I create characters and grieve for their fate. But does anyone worry about God, or worry about the author? I doubt it.

Let us return to Tsegaye.

35

OROMAY

Fiammetta Gilay is dead. Life is a one-way street, so she will not be coming back. And for Tsegaye Hailemaryam, life has become a puzzle that he is no longer able to piece together. Just a few hours ago, he hated Fiammetta because she had made a mockery of his love, or so he thought. As he has just found out, in fact she gave her life to save his. He has his life, for now, but her death torments him. It is tearing something important out of him, but also giving him a chance to change. Fiammetta, who finally made a decision, may in death help him regain his faith in humanity.

Tsegaye calls the office of Director Betru Tessema and, for once, reaches him. He tells Betru what has happened, then drives to the Public Safety office and hands him the note – the one about Silay Berahi, Oromay and the Paradiso that he got from the dead insurgent on Peak 1702. Blaming Betru for his misfortunes, Tsegaye tells him, "If I had reached you in time, none of this would have happened. Fiammetta would still be alive." He doesn't wait for Betru to reply, and instead continues in anger. "I gave you important intelligence about the Paradiso. Why was no action taken? Your negligence cost this woman her life! I don't understand."

Director Betru spends some time studying the note, then gets up from his chair. His face shines in triumph. "Comrade Tsegaye, at no time were we negligent. We have had the Paradiso under strict round-the-clock surveillance. At any point we could have easily broken down the door and entered. But we have to be very careful not to make a move that isn't fully thought through, so we don't tip off the other conspirators. Then they will go to ground and everything we worked for would be lost. When we take action, it has to be a killing blow that eliminates the Shabia spy network once and for all. We think they have many cells that carry out operations, so unless and until we locate and destroy their main headquarters, eliminating one or two cells would only be an annoyance to them. The way they're organized, one cell knows nothing about any other, except for their leadership cell. So if you eliminate the leadership, the main headquarters cell, then the smaller ones will be lost, ineffective. That's why we needed to be one hundred per cent sure before we took any action. I believe that's where we are now, with this new evidence you've given me. Finally we have confirmation about their headquarters, and we have them in our grasp. No need to wait any longer. Paradiso, Silay – that's the main Oromay cell."

The smile on Director Betru's face is getting brighter by the second. Tsegaye flees the office and Betru calls in Agent Teklay. As usual, Teklay is dressed to kill in a fancy suit.

"Are the men ready?" asks Betru.

"Yes, Comrade Director, we are ready. Is there a job for us?"

It's obvious that Teklay is eager for action, hoping to carry out one specific mission that he has long wanted to execute.

"Do you have any additional intelligence regarding the Paradiso?" asks Betru.

"Nothing new at this point," says Teklay.

Now Director Betru gives the order: "Alright. I want the Paradiso surrounded and entered. I do not want any of the employees to escape. Am I clear? In addition, I want Silay alive and kicking. Let's go, we don't have much time."

Teklay is now the happiest man in Asmara, and hurries out of the office with a satisfied smile on his face.

At 10.40 p.m. the Public Safety team enters the Paradiso and arrests the barista as he's closing up. Teklay gives the barista no time to think, no chance to confess, just a powerful kick to the groin. That's enough to get the barista to talk, and he tells Agent Teklay about Gebray Tekeste.

Gebray, thinking all is well, is already asleep at home. Teklay and his men break into the house quietly and find Gebray naked in bed. He's barely awake when a sharp kick between the legs from Teklay subdues him. An unsmiling Gebray survives the blow, but the illusion of their friendship does not.

From there, Teklay's team apprehends Ikuba Arat and two of his friends at a nearby bar. The two friends realize they're out of options and start talking. They confess to planning an attack on several hotels in Asmara and also to shooting Fiammetta Gilay as she returned home just a few hours earlier.

The trio of Shabia agents had spent the day following Fiammetta. Ikuba Arat had told them that she was supposed to meet Tsegaye Hailemaryam at the airport at 7 p.m., where they would kill Tsegaye. But when Fiammetta left the office, they overheard her tell the taxi driver to take her home to

Mai Temenai. They sped to her house in their own car and got there before she arrived, then grabbed her when she showed up.

"What's going on?" she asked them.

"Why didn't you follow orders?"

"I decided not to."

"You're working with the government, then."

"No I'm not."

The men aimed their pistols at her heart and put two bullets in her, then fled.

On hearing this, Agent Teklay can hardly control himself. If not for the other members of his team, he would kill the two men on the spot.

"Berahi is under arrest, right?" Ikuba asks as he wipes the blood off his mouth.

"You mean Silay?" asks Teklay. "I never trusted him, even at the start, that son of a bitch."

Agent Teklay and his team head next to the Ciao Hotel. It's after curfew, but the back door is still open. Silay Berahi is in the bar, relaxing and drinking beer. He's having a good time talking with several Red Star officials. Teklay goes over to his table and calmly pulls up a chair next to him. He orders a beer and almost drains it in one gulp.

It's Silay who speaks first. "So, how's the hunt for the ladies this evening?" he asks.

"You know, I hope God will punish them for what they're doing to me. For some reason all the women are already at home behind locked doors." Teklay finishes the last of his beer. "Did you hear what happened to Fiammetta Gilay?"

"What happened?" asks Silay.

"I think you already know," says Teklay.

"What is it that you want to say?"

"She was killed, you know that, right? What sort of degenerate would kill a beautiful woman like her? But you know who did it. I know who did it. We all know who did it."

"How would I know?" asks Silay.

"Is there anything Oromay doesn't know?"

Silay shows no sign of being alarmed. He looks at Teklay, trying to read anything he can from his face. He glances around the bar and spots several men he knows work for Public Security. Now he understands what Teklay is up to. He reaches into his pocket but Teklay grabs his arm and the other Public Safety men tackle him. In his pocket they find a cyanide capsule.

"Did you already get Gebray?" asks Silay. "He must have been the one who gave me up."

"Let's go," says Teklay.

"Do I have a choice? You got me before I got you."

"For all the good it does me," says Teklay through clenched teeth. He's angry about the revenge he is not allowed to take.

"You should be pleased with yourself," says Silay.

"If I could kill you with my own hands, then I would be pleased with myself," says Teklay. "But I'm not that lucky."

"Where's Tsegaye?"

"Off crying somewhere. Why?"

"It's because of that unlucky idiot and his whore, ricocheting from one mistake to another. Because of them, this is where we are," says Silay.

Teklay is bitter about the vengeance that won't be his and drags Silay roughly out of the bar. The image of his younger brother, murdered on Silay's orders, is invading Teklay's mind. He really wants to shoot Silay, but the double agent is not giving him any excuse to do so. Silay calmly allows himself to be led away to custody without resisting.

Within an hour the secret compound underneath the Paradiso is broken into, with Director Betru there to witness it in person. He looks like a young man after a good night's sleep. He's excited because his suspicions are being proven correct. Part of him admires the organization and audacity of the Shabia spies, but he's none too pleased that all this was being carried out right under his nose. This vexes him and he frowns.

The search of the Paradiso compound yields a list of more than five hundred people in Asmara who are actively engaged in various espionage and terrorist activities on behalf of the Shabia insurgents. There's also a long list of military leaders, government officials and public figures targeted for assassination, mostly members of the Red Star Campaign. Another document contains the names of people who were being paid to carry out the Oromay mission. Among them is Major Koricho Tadesse. Betru is saddened to see that name on the list, and then disgusted. He realizes that tonight's round-up is far from the end of the story. Instead it's the start of an even bigger investigation, and for a minute he wonders where it all might lead. How far up the ladder will this go? Where will it end?

Back at the Public Safety offices, Director Betru is impressed by Silay's composure.

"What's going on, Mr Oromay?" he asks him.

"We are here," says Silay.

"I am expecting you to cooperate with us."

"On what?"

"Who is The Bureaucrat?" asks Betru.

Silay Berahi is out of options and decides to cooperate. He would have accepted a quick death, but he knows they would take their time. He's had enough of suffering, been through enough pain and agony with Jebha and then Shabia. Within the hour it is decided that Agent Teklay will transport Silay on a special flight to Addis Ababa for further debriefing.

At the same time, an operation unprecedented in the history of the Ethiopian intelligence services is being carried out: suspects are being hunted down en masse, arrested wherever they are found, grabbed from bars and rolled out of beds. Director Betru leans back in his comfortable chair, pleased with the initial reports. The recognition he has been waiting twenty-five years for is finally going to come. Still, he is a little uneasy about how far this investigation might take him, where it might go, how high the Shabia infiltration might reach. It could be a Pandora's box. But he's pleased that the money he paid Tsegaye Hailemaryam last month has proven to be such a lucrative investment. He accords himself the congratulations of a job well done, and smiles. Realizing it's almost dawn, he lies down on his office couch to take a short nap and then the phone rings. It's Tsegaye.

"Yes, Tsegaye, where are you now?"

"At Fiammetta's house. There is something you can help me with."

"It would be my pleasure. What can I do?"

"I need a casket."

"I will send over the best casket we can find. She deserves at least that much, a funeral for a heroine. And have some peace, Tsegaye – we've arrested her killers."

At nine in the morning a beautiful wooden casket and four large flower arrangements arrive in a hearse at the funeral home. Fiammetta is dressed in a traditional gown and looks angelic, like a bride. Tsegaye removes the Red Star medal from his jacket and lays it on her chest.

The funeral of Fiammetta Gilay is held that afternoon at four. Betru Tessema, Solomon Betregiorgis and other senior government officials attend her final farewell.

"Take heart," Solomon tells Tsegaye.

"Happiness was our daily bread together" says Tsegaye. "That's all she wanted : . ."

"Take comfort in knowing that she gave up her life to save a loved one. All of us should be inspired by that. The day will come when we may be called upon to sacrifice for the greater good. She is leading by example, showing us the way."

Next to speak to Tsegaye is Director Betru. "Faced with something as devastating as this, you must stay strong. It took courage to do what she did."

"Thank you for the casket," says Tsegaye. "And the flowers."

"You know, she understood something," says Betru. "That her death, while tragic, would give life to many others, and prevent tremendous destruction."

"How's the operation going?" asks Tsegaye.

"Even better than we hoped," says Betru. "We have penetrated and destroyed the insurgency's leadership cell here. We're making good progress with their organization in Addis and should have it all wrapped up in a few days. So far, The Bureaucrat has managed to escape our dragnet, but it's only a matter of time. We think he's hiding out in Dire Dawa, but we'll find him wherever he is. You see, when you have the support of the people, you get great results like this." Betru pauses for a moment. "Of course, it's also very sad. If only Fiammetta had warned us sooner, her life could have been saved."

"She couldn't decide," says Tsegaye. "She was never any good at decisions, always hesitating. And when she finally did make a big decision, to not betray me, she paid for it with her life."

The funeral ends and the guests leave the cemetery. Dust to dust and the living pass on. Tsegaye Hailemaryam stays behind at the grave. There is nothing left for him to do, but his heart won't let him leave Fiammetta Gilay here by herself. She never liked being alone, so he stays with her.

A woman in a black dress stands a little way off. She stayed behind when the rest of the guests left. Most of the women at the funeral had worn white, the Eritrean colour of mourning. She was the only one dressed in black. Tsegaye turns away from the grave and notices her standing there, like a shadow. He looks more closely and recognizes her, then walks over to where Roman Hiletework stands in her long black dress.

"I looked for you last night," he tells her. "What are you going to do?"

Roman ignores his question. "May God heal you," she tells him.

He has nothing to say and stands there, silent.

"Your heart went into the grave with her," she says. "Isn't that true?"

He thinks of Fiammetta's words. *Will you remember me? Always? What kind of woman am I? You're a moron, I swear.* He doesn't have it in him to betray Fiammetta again. He doesn't want to.

"Yes, if you say so," he tells Roman.

"So she will always be in your thoughts, for the rest of your life?"

"Roman, I'm sorry. She sacrificed her life to save me. Of course I will remember her. What else can I do for her? I'm not going to join her in the casket."

"But part of you is in there with her. What good to me is a heart that's half buried, only half here?"

Roman takes off her engagement ring and drops it at his feet.

Gold. Dust. Gold in the dust, life turns to dust.

"Is that it?" he asks.

"That's it," she says. "My bad luck."

"What is?"

"The men I love betray me and I don't know why. I'm cursed to lose them. Goodbye." She turns and goes.

Tsegaye stands there, Roman walking away and Fiammetta's grave behind him. It is the end, he is alone, and his heart begins to sing a song of mourning. We all know the song, but we don't want to listen to it. Why open our hearts to such sorrow? Hope is always better than despair. We need it, for what are we without hope? We keep it in our hearts even when all seems lost.

> *Why, oh why*
> *Is it so hard to cry?*
> *Where are the tears?*
> *The well is dry.*
> *Laughter, laughter then,*
> *Trapped in my mouth, penned.*
> *My poor silent soul*
> *Suffers once again.*

The sun is setting and the horizon is red. Tsegaye kicks at the engagement ring at his feet, but then thinks maybe it was his own life he just booted. In his heart he says goodbye to Fiammetta. The cemetery is quiet. Beyond the silence of the dead, across the high plateau, he hears from

388

the mountains the sounds of a battle raging in Nakfa. Heroes cry out and Tsegaye yearns to join them. He loves all that he finds, and he loses all that he loves. That is life. Oromay.

Born in rural Ethiopia in 1939, BAALU GIRMA graduated from Addis Ababa University and later studied journalism in the United States. He rose to prominence in Ethiopia in the 1960s and 70s as both a journalist and novelist, eventually becoming a top official in the Ministry of Information under the Derg dictatorship. He wrote six popular and critically acclaimed Amharic-language novels: *Beyond the Horizon*, *The Bell of Conscience*, *The Call of the Red Star*, *Haddis*, *The Author* and his final novel, *Oromay*. His candid portrayal of the regime in *Oromay* caused a sensation and the government immediately banned the novel and fired Girma. Six months later, on Valentine's Day 1984, he vanished under suspicious circumstances. No definitive evidence has emerged as to Girma's fate, but the consensus is that he was murdered by the regime in retaliation for *Oromay*, which has since become one of Ethiopia's most famous and best-loved novels. It is partly for his courage in renouncing the hated Derg that Baalu Girma and *Oromay* hold such an honoured place in Ethiopian cultural history.

DAVID DEGUSTA is a writer and translator from California. He is a graduate of the Iowa Writers' Workshop where he received the Henfield Prize in Fiction. Previously, he was a paleoanthropologist in Ethiopia. His work on this translation was supported in part by a MacDowell Fellowship.

MESFIN FELLEKE YIRGU was born and raised in Addis Ababa, Ethiopia, with Amharic as his native language. He has been involved with the Baalu Girma Foundation since its founding and is a long-time friend of the Girma family.